I knew of the 1948 fire in Castries, St Lucia, because I saw the ruins. I grew up in the new, rebuilt capital but the aftermath of the devastating fire provided the inspiration for writing this book.

The characters, while fictitious, could mirror any number of people who lived at that time. The relationships with family and friends; the interactions with the authorities; and the desperate attempts to rebuild lives and homes are played out in colonial St Lucia. The music of the island, however, is ever present.

Throughout the book, I have used the French Creole dialect to authenticate the language used by the story's protagonists.

Gloria Times

RHYTHM PLAYED IN A FIRE

GLORIA TIMES

First published in Great Britain by Hansib Publications in 2018

Hansib Publications Limited
P.O. Box 226, Hertford, SG14 3WY

info@hansibpublications.com
www.hansibpublications.com

ISBN 978-1-910553-83-1

A CIP catalogue record for this book
is available from the British Library

Design & Production by Hansib Publications Ltd

Printed in Great Britain

CHAPTER ONE

Nightfall. The darkness was immense in the cane fields. He used his torchlight to guide him to his bicycle. He was alone. Augustus' eyes roved over the well-known compound near the factory. He heard a noise from afar. It was an animal cry. He arranged his abusack firmly around his shoulders, walked a bit, about fifteen minutes to the front banks of the quiet small river to get to the other side of the cane field, carrying his shoes in one hand and the torch in the other. The water was cool and pleasant, almost a pleasure after the heat of the sugar mill. Through the darkness there was a gleam from the hut of the sole other human that he knew was waiting to see him pass by his workshop, that had to be in service twenty-four hours should the machinery of the mill need a quick fix and he had to hasten over there at top speed. They had given Bob his gum boots, Augustus knew. The water was only ankle deep now, in this dry period; come September, life would be quite a different story. He himself would circumvent the cane field, making the time he got to his bike by the shed half an hour longer.

After he had dried his feet and put on some socks, he crossed the uneven ground where cane had been harvested, walked to the shed, using his torch to look down from time to time. He gazed into the gloom before his torch flared; two bright spots of light pierced the darkness; he was sure they were mongoose eyes. Mongoose, the conqueror of snakes; those ugly animals that made the harvesting of cane much safer for the cane cutters. Now, they loved these animals for being their saviour; those beloved animals had a brand of crepe-sole shoes named after them, comfortable brown mongoose crepe soles that Augustus had seen being sold in the Bata shoe shop.

He got his bicycle, and called "Goodnight, Bob, see you tomorrow." He fixed his mind now for the ride through Morne Fortuna. Leaving the cane fields behind, he had to climb from the plantation valley and up to the ridge, rolling downwards on a straight stretch, engaging his pedals – pushing, rolling and pedalling all the way. It was the thought of running over a cat or a dog that made him concentrate on the unlit road, his own bicycle light a small beam on the way.

The high pitch concerto of crickets came from the trees and bushes that covered the hills; houses were intermittent and many uninhabited land patches lay around him. He hated this shift, which he had started at two and finished at ten. He had no fear of the bolomn nor the devil that people thought existed in the hills. Even Olga, his wife, believed that this devil waited at the Four-Road junction, where two roads met – one, where he was coming from, and the other, where he was heading to. Though he did not believe as she did, the atmosphere was eerie enough to make him pedal furiously, while softly whistling the Christmas carol, 'While shepherds watch their flocks by night'.

The hairpin bends repeated frequently as he approached town.

"Phew," a sigh of relief from him on seeing the town below – a carpet of black velvet dotted here and there with yellow illuminations from the limited streetlights.

He reached Maynard Street, no lights there. It was in total darkness. Augustus slipped into the alleyway between his house and Clifford's tailor shop, parked his bike in the open yard against his mother-in-law's kitchen. He returned to the front to enter through the drawing room door; he turned the key in the lock. He dropped his abusack on the table, raised the lamp wick, glanced at the bookshelf nearby and moved to the bedroom, where Olga sat by the side of their bed, her eyes cast downwards. A mischievous smile played round her lips.

"Waiting for you Gustus."

"I know."

Now it was his will versus her will. He always read for a few minutes before getting into bed. He leaned over her face, nibbled her lips and turned away, picking up a towel. She watched him leave the room, the towel wrapped around his naked self. Out in the yard, he stood in the deep concrete tub under the tall pipe that was between a galvanised fence of the Sampsons' and his house. Water dropped heavy and cool on his skin, he shivered slightly even though the night was warm as he stepped out into the night dew. He quickly returned inside, dressed, saying to Olga, "I won't be long; O.K?"

She heard him, already half asleep, her head on the pillow, the little coiled twists of her hair neatly pinned with hairpins. By the light of the lamp, the beautiful blackness of her round face was broken by her smile; he kissed the spot between her neck and shoulder.

"Won't be long," he said again and moved back to the sitting room. He heard her sigh. As promised, he timed himself; fifteen minutes of a bible section. She was still awake – those geometrical eyes watched him now and drew him to her. He blew out the flame of the lamp and pulled her to him. He let out a long breath as the mattress creaked beneath them.

Era, their daughter, was seven already, but he did not want any more children. She trusted him in this, though if people knew why he did not want any more they would have thought that he was taking things too far. He did not take chances, he told her. Perhaps he was right: she went along with him.

Now, she fitted her body close, her arm over his shoulder. She was happy.

* * *

Olga stopped sewing a customer's dress as the evening approached. She heard the loud pedalling coming from Clifford's sewing machine.

The outside gloom touched her with its grey mood, and she was somehow less affected by that sad turn of the day because of the pineapple yellow of the walls of her parlour. She heard laughter from the shop.

She stood in her doorway, looking to the opposite sidewalk, and she saw her child playing with the neighbour's two little girls underneath the balcony of the beige weatherboard two-storey house she admired for its beautiful white wood fretwork – like lace edging, she thought – along the balcony and gables. Maynard Street had not long been resurfaced and the pitch was luminous black.

"Era come in!" she called.

Era ran across in four jumps and entered the house. Her pale shoulder was exposed, the bodice unbuttoned and her two *jains* hung by her side. Olga frowned at her décolleté dress.

Next to that house was a low dull yellow house with galvanise awning, where people were entering and coming out. It was a grocery shop. She stayed in her doorway gazing at life; in her mind's eye she saw her own three-roomed pale grey house. The tread of hard shoes to her right made her turn her eyes to the Sampson place. A Macaroni man walked by from the sidewalk by the tall brown iron poles that held up the Sampson's balcony. She looked at his feet and the black and white two-toned shoes as he said, "Good evening," passing her.

She answered "Good evening," with a serious face.

He entered Clifford's shop. She heard more laughter from the shop. It was not laughter of musical notes, more like barking, short spurts repeated – rather flat. Clifford sewed for the Macaroni types, Augustus said.

Olga closed her door. She addressed Era, "Look at you, chile, like a common person! How many times I always tell you how you should go out in the street?"

She pulled the two edges of Era's bodice, buttoned it and tied the two *jains* behind her back. She was glad that she had not run out barefooted, at least.

Laughter of a different tone – like someone was being tickled. It was easy to be distracted by that laughter. She opened the jalousies wide. She could see Clifford with his tape measure suspended while he waited for the man before him to straighten up, the man who was laughing now. The Macaroni man sat on a bench near to the sewing machine, talking. Clifford turned to his cutting board which came up to his chest and wrote the man's measurements. She closed the jalousies slightly for her own privacy and turned away, went into the yard and the kitchen, a wry expression on her face.

The houses close to each other shared a large yard, back facing back. All the streets run from north to south and intersected by streets going east to west. Olga's mother's kitchen was in the yard and Clifford had no kitchen, he did not live there; the one-roomed shop that stood at the corner of Maynard Street was closed at night. Only thirty inches separated his and her house. Sometimes she collided with him in the gap but she took pains to avoid this.

One day he had blocked her path. Remembering the distasteful event now, she had scrutinised him, eye to eye, focusing on his cat grey eyes in the reddish-yellow face.

"Gal, you so pretty and t'ing," softly in that put-on Trinidadian street talk, "I wish I was your boyfriend, nuh?"

The idea of the man. She shook with disbelief. He was smiling. She collected her senses to tell him to keep his nonsense to himself in patois, with a parting word, "sot!"

She would not have minded ordinary conversation, just saying hello and exchanging normal pleasantries as people do to one another. She did not even mind a wink: the sweet eye, but at a distance. Her face became hot now thinking of the other time – he had come to her back door. She had heard the swish from a dry banana leaf as he brushed against the tree outside. She had looked into the yard to see him coming; and from her position behind her sewing machine near the door, she waited. She watched him open his teeth, a large smile on his face; the ambiguous grey eyes were serious and intent. When he did not even say a polite good day, but just, "So, wha you say, I come to see you, ler we go inside. Lock da door, ah dying for you."

He was talking as if he was singing a calypso but the man was mad, she thought. She stood up as he had one foot inside the room. She chupsed and pointed her scissors at him.

"Don't come inside dis house. Leave me alone!"

He had seen her often enough cross the road, her steps slow as she lightly moved from one foot to the other with languorous poise like she had all the time in the world. The first time he saw her walk, he whistled softly, "Gee whiz!" Now, he had to back off.

He told her, even as he took in the warm black complexion, fine-grained skin, he could see the rose flush underneath which he found appealing. He stepped outside quickly because her oriental eyes blazed at him and there was water collecting on her nose. That sent a signal he could not ignore, and to belittle her he said slowly, "I don't like black girls anyway. I have enough brown skin woman, huh!"

He left in a huff, sauntering off, pale blue trousers, white long-sleeved shirt inside pale blue waistcoat. The tuft of curly, rope-coloured hair was knotted and thick in tight peppercorns. He had a reputation with women, she had heard, and sometimes there were female visitors in the shop. She had put him in his place. She was glad. And to his disappearing back she had said "*vye' Chaben!*"

They had not met since then.

* * *

The kitchen was a small, unpainted outhouse only big enough for one table and a few shelves for pots and pans. A straw basket of charcoal was beneath the table. The saltfish had already boiled. The coal pot was on the ground outside in front of her kitchen. She dropped the salt fish into a basin of cold water and put water to boil for tea. She saw Era across the yard playing *tiky tok* with stones on the step in front of her parents' bedroom, there was enough light in the dusk, the sky was pale blue and cloudless, the evening star was already twinkling. Through a gap by the kitchen and beyond the neighbour's house at the back Era caught glimpses now and then of people passing in Holymen Street.

Olga watched her a while as she threw one small stone in the air, picked up one at a time from small stones on the step with pincer fingers, and then making a swoop with a fist and picking up the remaining stones. She returned to shredding the saltfish with a pestle in her mortar, stood in front of her table.

"I see Mr Clifford coming, mamma," Era chimed.

"Ay, Ay."

Olga moved to the door, pestle in hand. What did he want? Of course, he would not dare insult her – seeing that her child was present! She arranged her face in her polite everyday smile. He stood in front of the door. With relief, she noticed he had his iron in his hand. She waited for him to speak and she studied his face and whole person deliberately, saw his flush; he looked worried. Good, she thought.

"Evening Olga."

He eyed the pestle, not sure if it were a weapon at this moment. "Could you give a few hot coals for my iron, please? Dis man in one hurry to take his suit. I need to put a crease in his pants; just two pieces to help me out?"

"Of course, I understand. Just now! Let me move my pan off the coal pot."

She was 'one lady', he thought. How she had this smile anytime she walked on the streets, like she was on stage. Could anyone blame him for falling in love with her? His eyes followed her every move. She lifted the pan, turned, entered the kitchen, returned with tongs and bent over the coal pot. He saw the wide neck of the house-dress and the shape of her bosom; she was silent as she deposited the lumps of red coal into his iron. He snapped the lid shut. "Thanks for the favour, I could kiss you, you know?"

She frowned; the man was so fresh – he had to bother her with stupid talk. She looked at Era and back to him. She swore inwardly but her smile remained. "We are neighbours, you can't call me stingy," she replied, and turned away from him.

Thinking of what she had said, they really were not neighbours at all! A neighbour was a friend, someone whose house you entered happily, someone you could call on if you were in need. Not one who could do you harm. She knew some neighbours who resented those close by because they did not know what went on in that house; who kept their distance, became enemies with the people because they never asked to borrow anything not even a match to light a fire to cook. They had the Sampsons as neighbours, who used to employ a housemaid but her mother got on well with them. Ma Sampson talked very well with them. Muriel was one who did not show Olga any malice to anyone, and that was why she still thought that even Clifford, if he was in need, she would help him. But she did not want him anywhere near her; his behaviour had to stop.

The water was now boiling on the coal pot that now stood on the table in the kitchen. She made green tea and began to pour oil into a frying pan to make fish cakes, but before that she peeled some sugar cane and cut them into cubes for Era.

Olga lit the lamp. Darkness and quiet had traded places with the grey evening. Era had been standing against the soft trunk of the banana tree, her eyes trained to the earth below Clifford's shop which was raised four inches with concrete blocks. She said to Olga, "I can see the crabs coming out from their holes under the shop." And Olga came out to her with the cubed bits of cane. And she waited anxiously for Augustus. He'd left before six, and a quiet joy pushed in with the anticipation of his arrival.

Muriel entered the yard, "Bon sw`e" greeting them, and Era received her caress as usual on her arm from her granny's coarse hands. The two entered the parlour. After Muriel lit the lamp, she removed her white apron and the grey uniform, with its shirt collar, that she had worn in her job for twenty-two years. She quickly changed into her loose house-dress and went into the kitchen to see about her L'orangette tea.

The three of them had supper and while Muriel washed the things they had used, Olga decided to spend a few minutes with Era asking her Catechism questions – which she was supposed to study before her First Communion later that year.

That's how Augustus met them as he entered the drawing room. Olga looked at him lingeringly; the handsome face that so wonderfully became hers; full brown eyes beneath a flat brow; his chiselled nose above lips drawn with lines designed for her total enchantment. He touched Olga's cheek, brushing her hair that was loose and came down the sides of her face on to her shoulders in wavy strands.

"I stopped at the gym. So many fellas were there waiting to use the weights, I was detained. If you saw the young boys of fourteen or fifteen, hanging about in there – taking an interest! Body-building is getting more popular."

"You must be hungry," she said, smiling lightly.

"Just a little." He straightened the picture of King George VI that hang askew next to a Shirley Temple picture. Era watched him and that picture of the pale-faced little girl with so many little gold curls and showing pretty white teeth. She was glad that the Catechism questions had come to an end, except her father decided to continue that; so she removed herself.

Olga found a piece of ribbon for a bandeau and made her hair tidy. Evening times there was little or no conversation between Muriel and Augustus. If Muriel spoke patois, he answered in English; sometimes she made the effort to speak differently, he would make no pretence that the native tongue was good practice. Olga wondered how could he live without the warmth of the patois but she respected that his attitude, perhaps, was due to his attending a college for the upper class.

Augustus held Olga's fingers lightly in his, and they walked slowly towards Morne Fortuna. Olga soaked in that old courtship atmosphere as he put his arm around her waist, and she slid hers around his. He stopped for a brief kiss, and held her close as they rounded a corner where an oleander tree stood close to a circular wall. The blossoms filled the air with sweetness, the stars shone. He released her and they retraced their steps; it was one way of seeing the few lights altogether in town from the slight elevation. He surprised her – in fact, he broke her serenity – when he blurted, "I'm only joking if I say I would like to go to America to see the Joe Louis fight." He added lamely, "Possibly."

"How you mean! Gustus my dear?"

"It's only a joke; I wouldn't touch my savings that we need for a better house!"

She interrupted him. There was a frown on her face. "Do you really want to do that?"

But in her heart, she knew if he went she would not fuss: he never squandered money. But she was alarmed. She listened to him.

"Well no, I was wishing," he said lamely, and found her hand again. They walked on quietly, but much was going on in Olga's mind. He saw the moon had just risen and she rode large and white, clouds chasing her.

The room was as she had left it. A half-finished, pale orange dress of a customer lay on the machine; and Era and Olga's clothes for mass in the morning, lay over the backs of chairs. Augustus fingered Olga's dress; it was in pique cloth with an ivory background and decorated with small pink flowers. He liked that particular one on her, the style was a close skirt, puff sleeves and a heart-shaped neckline. Olga felt that everything for Sunday was in order and hers and Era's shoes were whitened and on the mat by the door. She proceeded to get ready for bed.

After a while she came out in her nightdress. He saw her movement, the sparing walk and the see-saw of her waist. She asked, "You not serious about taking your money out of the bank to go and see a fight?"

"I was only thinking."

"Because it's for our own house, uh, I know how you like Joe Louis but I also want to have somewhere and be by ourself soon."

"Don't worry about it, go to bed, be there in a minute."

Next morning at nine o'clock, Augustus walked up to the beach. Once a week he went for a swim in the sea. Almond trees and grape bushes were spread out on the golden sand. They gave privacy and shade at the time of the day when the heat and sunshine was great. It was the perfect place to think in peace with the arc of the sky, the horizon; he could appreciate his own limitations and dream of possibilities, even as he felt the earth move beneath his feet at the water's edge. Although he did not want to emigrate, the thought of another country – he loved St Benedict – sent a rush of blood to his head at the pure meditation. Olga's response to his fanciful idea had surprised him; she had not quarrelled, was just vaguely upset. Was it because he told her that he had not been serious about it? Now he had reassured her and he had to forget about it.

He felt perfectly relaxed after he swam. Sitting under an almond tree he watched the waves hit the shore, a heavy plop and sand being gulped in large amounts in the receding foam.

The problem of Sampson came back to him; he scratched his head. Poor Sampson, so disturbed. They used to meet at Mr Polius' along with some older men who were Union activists. Sampson told them about what happened to him at the Masav men's club. He did not like the colour bar that existed for members; his eyes darted around the room with electrical fury and he poked a finger in the air.

"My friends, I went to the club to get a drink, just to test them, the barman refused me. Those *chabens*! We'll have to make a change, it's time."

The club has its rules, and if Sampson thought that only boldness was needed to change that attitude which had been present more than a hundred years, poor man. Augustus used to respect him before he started to get drunk and behave badly with his wife; the man had served in the West Indian army in the war, he had been to Italy.

He'd been injured, and now walked with a limp. It was his opinion that Sampson should have steered clear of them as he did. That attitude never worried him. What bothered Sampson was as painful to him as what he himself suffered in silence, but he could cope. Fighting was not the answer, as Guy had shown him in his first year at the college. He moved away from the almond tree, ran towards the sea, plunged in, swam for five minutes until he felt it was time to be returning home. He would check on Sampson. He would enjoy it if they managed to talk about boxing.

CHAPTER TWO

Olga had prepared beef browned in caramelised sugar with cabbage and carrots to go with stewed red beans, rice and yam. They both ate; Olga tidied up. Standing in the doorway facing the yard, she felt Augustus nudge her arm and she turned. Augustus stood steadfast, his head down and fists up, and made a little shuffle around her. He punched playfully with closed fists at the air.

"What you doing, uh?" You think you Jolwi?" Olga laughed enquiringly and softly.

Era looked on at this exchange, a round silent O appearing on her lips. Her very black eyes slanting downwards into her yellow face, giggling, she asked, "What Jolwi?"

"Joe Louis is best. I'll be listening to his fight on a radio this week," replied Augustus, grinning at her.

Olga kept smiling at this teasing behaviour as it was a bit out of character.

Augustus tweaked Era's round cheeks. His daughter filled him with a sense of rightness with Olga and his place with them. As if to demonstrate this quiet satisfaction with his family, he suddenly announced that he would go to call on Sampson.

"He drinks a lot. I saw him rocking on his feet outside on da sidewalk, it was Wednesday, I think."

Olga told him, "I know. He really drinks too much."

That morning, Sunday, Olga had awoken feeling good, reassured that there were no secrets between them. After mass, she took Era to visit Boo near St Cecelia Gardens. The house there was a cottage with an enclosed huge back yard. Era ran into the space, stumbling over loose stones that were numerous. There was abundant shade from the breadfruit and paw-paw trees. Era joined the girl on the bench in the shade, the two boys were on a see-saw they had made from a plank on some bricks.

Boo sat with Olga. She said to her friend, "It's so nice to see the children playing."

Boo said casually in her carefree fashion, "I hope this child is my last and I would like you to be God-Mother."

"Oh yes, I will be happy to be *n`en`en*, I hope to have another child but so far nothing doing."

Boo's fingers held the needle as she pushed it into the soft white chemise, making white scallops in a satin stitch around the neck of the baby's dress. A breeze came in through the jalousie flaps from the botanical gardens opposite. Olga smiled as Boo bleated out, "Would not mind trading places with you."

"Uh huh?"

"Yes, I can tell you. All this poverty! No electric, no water in this house, not enough money for shoes for the children and all the rest."

Olga silently reflected. She's short of all these things? Cyril had a car. People would say they were well off. But what was more important was to reveal to Boo, her close friend, why she did not have another child. She wished she could but she was embarrassed to do so. She could not tell anyone; they wouldn't believe her.

* * *

Together, Augustus and two others waited for Cyril on Monday morning to get a lift to work. Cyril came out of his and Boo's gate into the opal morning light. Cocks had not started to crow up in the breadfruit tree as he stood to light a cigarette, saying, "That's better; my head's starting to clear."

Augustus was happy to have this ride to work, saving time either way, even though he felt better for the exercise of his bicycle. They entered the estate before the sun was up at a quarter to six. The cutters had not started to harvest the cane. The sea of green appeared, over the wide expanse as far as the eye could see from the low grassy elevation where they alighted from the car. A mechanic was at work in his shed and as Cyril parked nearby, Augustus walked away from the crisscrossing cane plants. Hidden from view, he clambered over the drains and the built-up mounds of soil on which the cane grew, gaining easy access, the long way, to the factory. Close by, the wagons were stationary on the track. The familiar sounds of the flywheel, the grinding of the cane mill, the heavy water falling and the smell of molasses greeted him.

Inside the factory where the vats boiled the cane syrup, he took his seat on his workbench and took over from the other man and started to test the syrup. He tested for the sucrose content in every boiling batch of juice when the pan-boiler would start to crystallise the syrup. He was going to be busy as there was that other job; he leached ashes for the lime. This was a position that he shared with a handful of others who had been well educated, and they all were glad for this work as shortage of suitable jobs was a major problem. Augustus thought that further education in agriculture overseas was a goal he should be aiming for; others had done it.

His mind, however, entertained personal thoughts. He scratched his head thoughtfully, going over Olga's carping about their house. When his lunch break came, he met Cyril at the fish vendor's pitch whose call was loud.

"Fry fish! Fifty cents." A pause. "Fry breadfruit, twenty cents."

This vendor was elderly and came near enough to the edge of the estate where they found her beneath a tamarind tree on the flat road just before the road dipped into the estate. She came laden with fish she prepared at home and they lay displayed, spicy and crisp inside a once upon a time retailer's huge soda biscuits tin.

Going back and walking quickly, eating as they went, Cyril said, "We have to take cargo down to the bay this afternoon, there's a ship calling from England. I believe she will be given a load of six of the two hundred and fifty pound bags, there will be an extra three bags for the town."

"Uh huh. I'll come down to join you if you're not ready when my shift is over, I could do with the exercise."

The midday sun blazed down. A haze hung in the air as the cane cutters burnt the leaves of the plants after the cane had been cut. Near the factory, the wagons loaded with long canes, their hue of yellow or russet-green, were being unloaded and brought into the mill for the mill crushers.

"Right O," Cyril told him. "I hope you don't mind waiting."

"See you later."

Sitting on his laboratory bench, the syrup before him and the Bunsen burners' flame a steady blue, he began to test for sucrose. His thoughts returned to Olga; where in that town with closely packed houses, straight streets and angled corners would he want to move to with her? Was Darling Hill a possibility, or maybe at the foot of the hill above Spine Road? He liked the cottages of Cyril and Boo's neighbourhood with the fresh breezes from the Gardens, but Olga wanted something with an upstairs balcony. There were houses away from the centre of town, close to the beach, one storey with balcony, and now that people were emigrating there might be places to rent.

He scratched his head. He could see the advantages of getting her away from her mother's old ways. That was something he would enjoy. He liked Muriel, but imagine Olga all to himself for the first time! He would begin asking around for something to rent. That should please her no end when he tells her what he decided.

He put on his gloves and moved to the lower level floor. The monotony of testing syrup over the flame was relieved by the messy job with bags of ash that he had to leached for potash and make a fertiliser for the cane. He thought, 'these ashes – good stuff, it has so many uses: one, it gets the black soot scrubbed from aluminium pots. Two, it's a disinfectant for gum boils. Three, it's a disinfectant on the excreta in toilets.'

After two o'clock, he made his way towards the shore. The gentle gradation of the land at the end of the rail track was a good thing in making access down to the bay a simple journey and he relished the exercise. The Caribbean Sea was in a somnolent mood this mid-afternoon and the heat touched him as pin-pricks on his head and face. Business activities were in full action on the beach; he saw that some women shop owners had come from town in the lighters to buy a 250-pound crocus bag of sugar each. They left for town while the sailors got into their lighters and made for their ship at anchor.

Cyril and a Tallyman finished their business and they ascended to the estate on the mules that had carried the sugar down to the bay at the foot of the low hill. After the mules were left in the paddock, Cyril got his car while Augustus waited and quenched his thirst with water from the mechanic.

Cyril dropped Augustus off on Market Street where he picked up the day's edition of the *Trinidad Guardian* newspaper.

Before he ate, he showered; carbolic soap lather removed the layers of sweat that had formed, dried and reformed during the day. Afterwards, he found the columns in the paper about Joe Louis. He exhaled and stretched his legs in front of him and read. One article praised him as Superman and a do-gooder as a serviceman during the war. Another article described him as the 'Jungleman' and 'Ice-cold fighter'. The photos Augustus gazed at in the newspaper showed his shoulder and chest muscles; thirty-four years old and six foot one.

"Look at this neck! Look at those muscles!" he said to Olga.

But Olga was busy sewing a white dress that someone wanted to wear at a funeral the next day. She got up from the sewing machine and stretched. It was nearly dark outside. Augustus looked at his daughter whose eyes were fixed on him. The heavy lidded crescent eyes, so black and contrasting with the pale yellow of her face, were now focusing on her mother who was silently sweeping the bits of cloth and thread from the floor. He thought of Sampson; he would take the paper over to him later. He asked Era, "What did you learn today?"

She smiled quickly. "Singing and reading." She recollected in her mind what she had sung. How she had swayed against the girls at her sides.

"What did you read?" shattered this reflection.

"I doh know," she lied.

"You have forgotten already?"

She deflected the enquiry by bursting into song: "All things shall perish, long, under the sun. Music alone shall live, music alone shall live, music alone shall live, never shall die."

* * *

Augustus stepped outside and turned right to the Sampsons'. Adora, the oldest daughter, was at the window.

"Hello, is your father in?"

"No."

She seemed anxious, nervous. Just then he saw Guy coming his way. Guy had become friendly with Adora; they met up in places, walked the streets together. Now that he got closer, Augustus saw his outfit – a beige suit, double-breasted jacket, narrow bottom pants. It was not what he wore for liming. Augustus winked at him, shook hands and continued on.

On the sidewalk, he collided with Sampson. Facing each other, he held on to his elbows to steady him, but Sampson's head and shoulders, he noticed, were erect. All Augustus' senses paused to pick up the man's mood, remembering the last time when they had met at Mr Polius' and he had been telling them in angry words his dissatisfaction with the light-skinned people.

"Evening Mr Sampson," Augustus interjected, "I came by twice to see you; I have the paper with a write-up of Joe Louis. I'll just go and get it for you."

He let go of his elbows, realising that he had been holding on a bit longer than was necessary as Sampson was not drunk.

"Oh."

Not the reply that Augustus had expected, so he continued, "You remember his fight will be in the next few days?"

"No, I had not forgotten but I have other important things on my mind. I will be going out again in a minute, so if I'm not in just leave the paper for me."

He moved away quickly with his limp.

"I'll get it now," Augustus insisted, unable to ascertain where Sampson could be going after nine o'clock. And to underscore this questioning, Augustus' speculation heightened leading to his demand that Sampson waited, "Just a minute!"

Augustus returned with the newspaper just as Sampson was inserting his key into his door.

"Thank you very much. Good night."

"Good ... night," Augustus said, elongating his quizzical response.

* * *

Augustus did not have warm feelings for his home village since he adopted the town. Here he was part of the educated people, the intellectual crowd in Masav. He saw the business people, office clerks and well-dressed men and women as his adopted habitat. That made him feel he was somewhere. He felt part of the history of Masav where some of the battles for the colony of St Benedict happened, in Morne Fortuna, high above Masav. He had made it his duty to find out this history because of Mr Polius and relying on the chronicles of an old priest who, now dead, was the local historian.

Colonisation of the area seesawed from the French to the British and back. Seven times French and seven times British till the people became the 'don't know' people: the *M'a sav.*

He could visualise blood colouring the green grass and brown soil that he traverses each day; the vision of his ancestors who had been brought, bought and sold, to do the work for the masters. He cast a knowing eye on the harbour and knows the breath of his ancestors fell in the air as they panted or called to their own parents to save them. He knew also that the last battle was in 1797 when the British stayed in charge till now – 1948. He thinks of that with fascination and some relief that now people are, as he saw them, in changed circumstances.

Each day now, more of the same: days of intoxicating inhalations inside the factory. Days of hissing steam from the generator in his ears and water falling like hands clapping. The flywheels going round for the mill rollers to keep on crushing cane day and night, the heat from the furnace with charcoal boiling the juice in the big drums, the heat in which he could literally melt. That was his lot. At least he was better off now, very different from the men who cut cane and were sometimes injured by cutlasses used carelessly and bearing the scars from the cane leaf abrasions.

He stepped outside for a quick break. Not far away, workers carried canes of equal lengths in bundles to the wagons and by mules to the gate of the factory for unloading. There was nothing sweet in the air, still smoky from the cane leaves being burnt far away, but some air was cooling from the trees up in the nearby hills, the cedars, the manchineel trees. The estate was itself a small village, serving a Methodist chapel, a school not far away, shops up in the hills not too far away.

Another day of sweat and sugar aromas ended. The afternoon was his. Round about five o'clock Augustus went to the Catholic Young Men's Club. After the exertion of lifting weights and a workout on the bench, his senses were alert. Later, in his yard before sunset, the air was lemon, slipping into the room through the open jalousies. He was reading from *The Rose and Cross*. It was his new borrowed book.

He was aware of Olga, busy carrying out her duties; Era was out with Muriel. This book should give him some answers about life that he was questioning. It was heavy, serious stuff and he was engrossed. After supper, he went out for the soft breezes and to make a round of usual pursuits with comfortable Guy.

It was dark by seven. They sat on the platform-steps of Guy's house; enough room to stretch their legs while leaning against the front of the house. It overlooked a long canal that took heavy rainwater to the sea. They usually talked for hours, his pal from college and one of the few people who used the sobriquet attached to Augustus in those days. He was single and enjoyed its freedom while Augustus had got married at twenty-one.

"Ham, have you got a cigarette?"

"No, man, sorry."

"Oh boy, I forgot that I smoked the last one. I need what keeps me sane after spending a day with my class. In that noisy school hall, we speak in verbal collision with each other, all the six other teachers. Ah wonder the children learn anything! Don't you think? How all of us went through primary school in the same confused school rooms, so little space between each class?"

"Like you have to go without!"

A speculative look was exchanged after Augustus added this to the apology.

"No, let's go and find some."

They took a southerly direction. "Will you take part in the 'Body Builders' competition later this year? You should start preparing for that," Guy encouraged him with a laugh.

Augustus laughed in return. "There will be those ready to jump at this chance, parading in public. I won't be one of those."

"We won the Inter-Island cricket tournament, as you know." Guy carried on about sport, and before long they reached the parlour by the waterfront. The sea was a yard width away but it only shone black; a dull glow from a street light in front of the parlour was the only illumination around them. Inside, a kerosene lamp hung on the wall. They stood by the counter and ordered Vat 69 rum, one shot each. The tubby, middle-aged man now got his swizzle and in a large jug poured in water, squeezed lime, poured in Angostura bitters, then rum, sugar and swizzled away.

"No ice, man," he said to the three others in the room, sitting at a table in the dim corner of the parlour. Now that he had served them, Augustus and Guy took their small glass and stood straight up to direct the liquid with a tilt of their head backward.

"Uhm!" they both said.

"Do you happen to have some cigarettes here?" Guy asked.

"Cigarettes a bit short right now," was the answer.

"I'll go over to the High Life Club to buy a packet. I know you won't go in there, but I'll meet up with you in a little while, after I've got some."

"Alright. That's O.K. by me."

They were passing by the cinema and audience participation came out loud into the street outside. "It must be a Roy Rogers cowboy film," Augustus opined as they parted and he walked towards the People's Square.

He sat down on a bench, nearby a group of some other men talking loudly. Guy was so different to himself: he could enter a notorious club that sailors frequented when in port; the women in there did not care about anything. Guy felt respected in his own right and did not care; whereas himself, he had to guard his reputation. A reputation that stands threatened by a deep fear that something out of his control could spoil things for him. He was an educated man but as a Country Bookie he knew his place in the town of groups and societies. His mother-in-law and Olga were as confident as they needed to be observed and noticed but he had yet to reach that place. His fear was almost as big as Sampson's but Sampson's fear had turned to rage. He wondered whether he had inherited that fear, and if he had stayed in Anse Chabon would anything cause him to suffer from shyness and inferiority? He knew also that good family, friends and belonging to certain groups were the things that could remove that fear. That book, *The Rose and Cross*, could help him.

He felt the soft breeze and looked up. There was a full moon on the wane, the sky was violet, thin clouds played with the old moon and diamonds rested on the violet cushions.

"Good night to you." Sergeant Paine stood before him, suddenly, and without warning, as though materialising from air; so quietly did the large tall man appear. He tapped his truncheon lightly against the side of his trousers.

"Night, Sarge." He looked up at the large round face and small head circumference underneath the cap. "Everything quiet?" Augustus asked conversationally.

"All quiet, on the Western Front. I like it like that." He sauntered away, disappearing into the darkness.

Guy was approaching Augustus from amidst the cinema crowd. Guy disengaged himself and came towards the bench, the glow from his cigarette bright in the darkness. His face stood out, his lips sucking in the smoke. They started walking together and talking.

"Sailors were having a good time on leave from their cargo boat that just came in this evening from the Belgian Congo. There was only one woman taking up a sailor's attention, his hat on her head and she all pressed up against him."

Augustus imagined her flaming rouged mouth and glistening smile. Guy continued: "The boat will call at Dominica, Martinique and Guadeloupe. Now you see, if the members of the Masav Men's Club were not creating their Jim Crow tactics, I should have got cigarettes there and also enjoyed the facilities of billiards like the others!"

They walked on in silence. As they were parting at the junction of Market Street and King George V Street, Augustus remarked, "You can survive anything, man, you're a respectable teacher. I, on the other hand, am nothing. I have to be careful; you know the walls have ears."

"You're missing lots of things, you're so careful!"

"Do you know while I sat waiting for you, the sky was a pleasant diversion – the moon, stars and clouds and that was much better than watching a *jamette* making a sailor welcome in the town."

He walked to Maynard Street, arms swinging loosely, footsteps in a straight line.

* * *

It was time for Muriel to settle down for the night; her lids were heavy, her body fatigued. She gazed into the dark yard. Fireflies darted about ablaze – they erupted and faded soon to emerge with amazing speed and dazzled her. But it was time to shut out the yard. The cat near her should be going out. She nudged him but he evaded her and sat beneath the shelf near the door, mewing. This cat was a portent of something, Muriel felt. And those fireflies! She felt something especially more active among them. What was it? She pulled the door shut, shut the window and joined Olga by the table leafing through a catalogue, looking at dress fashions.

Muriel's deep-set eyes were gentle, contrasting with her large square-ish face and straight mouth. Since Harry left and went overseas leaving her pregnant with Olga, she had set her mind to work and keep herself on an egalitarian road. She can look back with some degree of satisfaction now that Olga had elevated her pride by marrying this young man, and her sister, Hazel, despite not having much money, had given unstinting support in the upbringing of Olga.

"*Tan sa! Mamma, Gustus vle alle' - w`e box L'Amerique*," Muriel exclaimed as her breath caught in her throat; even so, all she said in a whisper was, "*Ki sa?*"

Muriel knows Olga's ambitions for herself but she has been satisfied with her own job, cooking for the priests at the presbytery since Olga was four, enabling her to raise her and enjoy the family she had. They were both lost in thought. After a lengthy pause Muriel said to Olga, "This is your house as well as mine. You should not worry if Gustus wants to do something with the money; don't be vex, God is good." She smiled and it was mostly for her own intention of containing all things. "I'll go and rest the old body, I'm tired. Good night." In the comfortable language of the patois, Olga could afford to smile, everything now settled.

"*Bon sw`e.*" She replied.

Muriel lived like a nun and that was all she knew after Olga's birth. She never noticed another man because when she loved Harry it was like being entrapped somewhere; things inside her were under his control. She had only been seventeen after she arrived from the village of Bonne Terre, a small village down the coast, looking for work and to meet her sister who was doing extremely well. Muriel's true joy has been Era, who slept on her bed at night. She had Harry's round face and his colouring, and with this reminder she could not forget him even if she wanted to. He had gone to Panama and it was almost definite they would not see each other again. She felt too old to wish for that and she was quite content. But she lingered on his memory before she slept. She saw him marching in the police band twenty-six years ago, playing his clarinet. Him in her sister's house: there was always music there as Victor, Hazel's lover, had a piano; someone with a violin and Harry's clarinet. Sleep fell mysteriously and covered her.

* * *

Augustus did not mean to stay out that long. Well, he had enjoyed being out. After he had locked the door, he entered their bedroom and noiselessly removed his small grip from beneath their bed. Olga did not stir. The book he had started already intrigued him. He came back to the drawing room with it, sat down, raised the lamp wick. He meant to read first about five pages and then a section from the bible before going to bed. He was awakened by his own voice: "Every dog has its day. That's all I know, Sampson. The meek..."

The bible lay on the floor. He yawned and stretched down to retrieve it.

"Of all the things!" he thought aloud, "I'm dreaming of Sampson now."

His concern over the past months had definitely worried him deeply, but this! He was convinced that this was a hallucination, because he was sure he had not slept. It must be his tiredness. But it was only after ten and so he decided to carry on and read a bit from the bible. He liked St Paul's Epistles and, at random, he picked Chapter 12, Romans: "We who are strong ought to put up with the failings of the weak and not please himself. Each of us must please our neighbour..."

These words were so like the advice his father had given him when he left Anse Chabon for the town. His father warned him not to walk about with any air of self-importance, to greet people and all that sort of thing. People in his village always observed that rule but in Masav, most people didn't do things that way. There was too much of a divide.

He took the lamp into the bedroom, returned the book to the grip. Olga stirred, eyes opened briefly. He said, "I fell asleep in there trying to read." He sucked his teeth. Blew out the lamp and got in beside her. She understood and almost like a hen, she drew his head towards her, her arms like wings around him and went back to sleep snuggling against him.

Listening to her breathing, she was unaware that he lay awake with the thoughts of indecision coursing through his mind. Sleep came but it seemed to be evading him, the deep sleep he craved for. A bit later he got up for some water to cool the heat he felt. In the parlour, he poured from the goblet, and as he started to drink, he was startled and jerked his head to a sound of wood being ripped by something like a cutlass and at the same time like heavy rain drops. The sound came from the direction of Clifford's shop.

Muriel emerged, and so did the cat. She exclaimed loudly, alarmed. "*Ki sa?*" Hearing a bang outside, her hands went to her head. Augustus hastened to unbolt the door and went into the yard. Fear glanced him a blow of another kind, not the weak, subconscious fear he had felt sometimes, but the gut tight cramping sort. His tongue stuck to his palate, ants crawled, it seemed to him, inside his skull – no brain! That seemed to have leaked out. Muriel came behind, pushed past him.

"*J e 'si Mawi!*" she bawled.

The tight band which had held Augustus' throat slackened, he turned. "Get water, quick!"

They collided. "I'll wake Olga and call the neighbours to help us."

He lunged into his bedroom, pulled Olga upwards by her armpits, his bare sweaty chest meeting her warm body, breathing noisily. He pulled her out of the room. She blinked, "What, Gustus?" She stood stupefied.

"Help your mother throw water on the shop. It's on fire. Quick! Quick!"

He tripped over his boots, picked them up and ran into the street through the street door.

"Fire, fire." He banged on the door opposite with the boots repeatedly and calling "Wake up, Fire! Fire! Clifford's shop on fire."

He then turned to the Sampsons' house, banged on the door and shouted at them to wake up. The alleyway between his and the shop was impassable, the clapboard small house was a picture of dragon-tongued shoots of yellow and red, and smoke so thick that everything had taken on a dangerous intensity. He stopped in his instinct to save Era, take her to safety, but he had to join Muriel and Olga with water in buckets and bowls and throw on the shop from the back yard. The roof blew out and flames were in the air.

"*Dife', dife'! Pote' dglo!*" Muriel called out to Olga.

"*Ayde' nu! Dife'! Dife'!*" came back from her. Olga came on to the sidewalk and looked across to the balcony of the house she admired. Someone was on the balcony there.

Augustus saw the hopelessness of their efforts after he had thrown two buckets of water from the street side of the house to little effect. He decided to get Era ready and take her to safety. He ordered the women, "Olga put your shoes on. Gather some clothes Mammie and get the fire police."

He sat Era on a chair while he got his grip and books. "Era," he said to her urgently, "Come. We are going to Aunt Hazel."

He picked her up and ran calling as he went, "FIRE, FIRE, WAKE UP."

He heard Pierre from across the street, he had appeared at his door. He sighed with relief and ran quickly, his hard shoes beating tambu on the sidewalks. The air was still, windless. He thought, would Muriel have any luck getting the police to move quickly enough? The town he loved, what was its fate?

Sergeant Paine looked up out of his window from his rented house on the hillock adjoining the Anglican Church. It overlooked St Cecelia's Gardens; the high palmiste trees were sentinels in the dark, their fronds as shadows in the night. They shook gently. The misshapen yellow moon shone, softening the night. He heard a shout. He first thought, some drunk; may even be a fight on the streets.

Then with the repetition of shouts, his ears tuned always to noises meaning some affray – someone may be getting murdered.

What with the small police force! He knew he should go out of his way to investigate. The rise of the land outside his house gave him the view of a pink haze in the air. "Fire" he said aloud. He had not undressed from his day clothes, and moved in the direction of Market Street. Lights shone dimly around the police station; somewhere around Maynard Street was on fire. He barked an order as he approached, ambling, not able to move quickly.

The two constables inside the station saw his large body. Their agitation was visible, pulling out hoses. They said they were waiting for the pull cart to transport the equipment. Philosophe knew what to expect: they were not prepared. One of them told him, "Sarge, a woman came and told us about the fire a moment ago. We sent Frank for the cart."

Philosophe felt his worried perspiration drip down his back. Frank arrived, short khaki pants and shirt, soft shoes. The others were in rubber boots, wearing helmets. Now they were off running with the cart down King George V Street. Frank rang a hand bell loudly.

Olga could not see through the smoke, her eyes stung. Mr Pierre touched her, "Give me some buckets."

"In our yard by the pipe," she advised.

She led the way into their house while Mr Pierre went into the yard. Her mind had stopped working. She prayed silently: 'Have Mercy God'. She sat as if paralysed on her bed, her arms immobile – unable to retrieve the large grip to pack the clothes, unable to open the doors of the press to empty all the clothes. She just left them.

This fire was an intruder in the pleasant night she had been having, a thief to steal her life from her. And she prayed for God's intervention to save her house. But outside, she saw the huge flames on her house, Clifford's nearly flat. Augustus returned, entered his home as she came outside, he pulled her sewing machine out to the sidewalk, his grip, chairs. She was afraid. Where was her mother?

A sudden wind blew from nowhere; danger became nearer. The police whistles were blown in sharp trills as they came running toward the hydrant a few streets away from Maynard. Olga ran a little way and collided with her mother. Mr Pierre's sons threw water on their house with Muriel. People gathered on the street, they had come out at last.

As the firemen delayed, it was impossible to move in the vicinity of his house. Augustus found the help of the Pierres heartening as the sons handed buckets and basins from their own yard to him, the father, and Olga and Muriel throwing the contents on their house. But Augustus knew, in his heart, that failure to save it was becoming a reality. Just then, he saw the police arrive with two hoses as the wind had turned direction again, becoming even more menacing. A piece of blazing timber flew and landed opposite as Augustus dodged the flying ember and stood behind a fireman, mise-en scene, holding on to the hose that was trained on his home.

On the sidewalks and the street, it was an impasse with furniture dragged from the houses on the street, hampering the firemen's movements. A dog wailed a saxophone-like lament.

Muriel started to pray, rolling her beads, "Hail Mary…"

The north-east trade winds had made up their minds to come to the fire. Olga's heart lurched; she felt cold in spite of the heat. She watched Augustus movements as he now turned away and disappeared to come back with a cart. He heaved the sewing machine and the chairs and his grip of books on it and moved away from the crowd. He stopped in front of the Sampsons' home; they were just coming out carrying bundles. It was Ma Sampson followed by her two daughters. They were having an argument, words loudly spoken in anger.

He called, "Where is your husband?"

No answer. He entered the door which was open, saying, "I'll give you a hand to save your furniture."

The irate woman followed him, talking in French, the distress of this disaster weighing heavily on her shoulders. She started to empty her chinaware waggonette so Augustus could move it out for her. Augustus assumed that Mr Sampson was sorting things upstairs. He gathered some furniture and rushed with chairs outside. She put her wares in a large cloth. The daughters came in, and they pulled that large load, together, heaving.

Augustus managed to get the waggonette outside as flames made a long red line from top to bottom on the house. He just had to move his cart towards Aunt Hazel. Thick smoke and heat around, he did not see his family. He wondered whether they quarrelled because Mr Sampson had been too drunk to be roused!

"Bitch; leaving the blasted man to die upstairs!"

He ran up the stairs with no anxiety or concern for his own safety.

Wind-slapping flames ran wild and started to ignite the grocery shop opposite the Sampsons'. The kerosene in there would make the flames stronger, more dangerous for the whole place, even as Olga dashed across the street, Muriel pulling her.

"Let's go to the Square, people are now going there with their things."

"Where's Gustus?" Olga's high voice was shrill as she screamed and moved towards the Sampsons' house where she saw Augustus enter. She feared for his safety.

"Leave the house!" she cried out imploringly. She repeated her cry and started to sob. She was dragged away by Muriel as the Fire Police sprayed water at the Sampsons' house, getting doused in the process. Muriel moaned; she had no shoes on, wishing she had at least taken them out of their house.

A red ball of fire rolled down King George Street as Augustus emerged without the man he had gone to rescue.

His mood, as black as the shell of his own house, propelled him to return to the street, now more impassable. He fixated on the library; books should not be allowed to burn. Others were in there with the same idea. A truck was in front of the wooden one-storey house with its galvanise awning. He ran inside, taking books down from the shelves to drop into a large crocus bag where others had started to collect them.

The library always made him feel a glow of comfort in the knowledge that he, because of his education, fitted inside those walls and was then equal to all men. But the town people – owners, domestics, clerks, teachers – all back-to-back on the People's Square gawking at the fire. After the books had all been secured and put on the truck, he moved on to the Square to take stock.

That image of an admiring crowd content to just witness the destruction of the library was etched in his memory. How the mighty had been reduced!

Noise like thunder! Explosions from Market Street! What were those he wondered? Someone said, "Rum barrels exploding in the customs buildings."

There were lots of people running with him and they collided with some white sailors pulling fire hoses with them coming from the direction of the wharf. 'Thank God' Augustus thought.

Sergeant Paine's large body moved among the crowd on the Square. He called from the loudhailer: "I phoned the police station at Anse Du Fort for assistance. Their Fire engines are now on the way to help us."

The fire was coming towards the Catholic church in the centre of town not far from the People's Square. He located Olga and Muriel, and now the priests had left the presbytery and called for prayers, they started to pray loudly to God with the Credo, the Hail Marys, the Pater Noster. Voices rose and fell. He stood there for a while, silent, not understanding why the fire had started. He bowed his head as the prayers were said. Half way through the Rosary he moved away, too restless to stand still, too concerned to ensure that every target of the fire was being tackled.

The sailors from their ship in the harbour used sea water in their hoses and fortunately saved the presbytery and the boys' school by persistently pouring water in their direction. Other fires were reported all over the town. If the fire engines were coming from the south of the Island, that was twenty-six miles away across hills and bad roads. When would they arrive to help? That was no comfort to anyone that night.

And to add to the many challenges facing each seat of the fire, the water in the reservoir was not enough to cover all the fires.

Augustus heard this news as he retraced his steps southwards in the calm part of town, people on the streets waiting and watching.

"A hell of a night," he thought. "If only we had known what was happening next door to us? Had I spent more time reading I might have smelt or heard something in time. What had Clifford done in that shop to ignite this fire? Could he have left his lamp alight, had there been fire in his iron and a paper pattern started to burn and some cloth started? Could it have been something from outside the shop? Olga had carped on about their house. Had that been tempting fate?"

A dark thought entered his mind. Could Sampson have anything to do with the fire as he considered that he had not seen him anywhere.

Ashes fell on to the streets. He returned to Maynard Street, saw its ugly face with rotted teeth, large hillocks of black wood, metal, twisted galvanise. In that moment, a rage swelled in his head. He imagined fighting, fighting a bloody fight. He was in a boxing ring: he moved menacingly, fists up, eyes trained on someone from the Town Board. With a left hook, he hit him. The official went down at his feet. Next opponent, the police chief: he was in charge of the Fire Fighters. He threw a volley of punches there – a right to the head and a hook to his jaw, the man toppled over in the ring and he was removed. Now he was facing the administrator, he who represented the Colonial Government. Ha, Ha! He thought, eyeballing the man, he should have made sure that there were fire engines in the town. He heard, "Come on Ham, come on Ham." A roar of excitement from the crowd. He circled him feeling confident, and next thing, he came out of the trance completely disorientated.

"What in the name of Mike's happening to me?"

Tambu beats accompanied him towards the square once more. The fire was mostly raging in the west, devouring homes and businesses.

The three policemen knew that they had to be quick; they wanted to get through doing something before too late. Close to the waterfront they stood close to the Crown Agents office, a drug store and the 'People's Bank. They saw that the flames were heading that way, they had to be quick, they moved to the side door of the bank. O.K. Pal was leaving and he said to the policemen: "Mano in dey; he sleeping."

Challo, Felix and Oceancy had a plan.

"Go home, O.K. Pal. This is no place for you," Oceancy said.

They were inside and upstairs.

"Challo, keep watch at the window!"

Felix and Challo, young constables, were obeying their senior sergeant who moved to Mano, asleep and he smelt of alcohol. Oceancy took hold of Mano, shook him, slapped his face. No response from the watchman. He kicked his legs and got a slow response.

"Er, er, wait..."

"Mano, give me de keys to the money. Keys! Keys! *U tan mw`e? U konpwann? vite!vite!*"

"You understand?" He tried English.

Felix worried: "We don't have much time."

He saw Mano move towards the safe. "You is de police awright."

He had no idea but he had to obey the police, automatically obeyed and went back to sleep. Well, Oceancy thought, at least he did not have to worry about testimony from this watchman.

Felix was excited: "Time is running out!" in a high, frightened voice.

Oceancy was having difficulty opening the safe. Having finally succeeded, he began to collect notes. Challo blew his whistle. Oceancy dropped the keys on Mano and, followed by the others, exited through the door. Moving closer to the wall, Challo noticed the bank manager and Town Board men approaching the bank through the smoke haze.

Miss Hazel stood on her upstairs balcony that faced west. Spine Road outside was having a nervous fit: doors open, people rushing past carrying goods. From her height, she knew the situation when tall buildings fell like sick people in a faint. Two men from opposite the street talked loudly of what was taking place, and she heard that the water had run out even before the help from Anse Du Fort had arrived. She waited for her sister and family and whoever wanted shelter.

It was sometime later when Augustus came with Olga. She rushed down to meet them. "Ay, Ay, you come now! Come si'down; Oh Bon Diey! *Sa move', wi, dife` a!*"

She saw a stunned Muriel flop down, her eyes shut. Augustus grasped his throat.

"I need a big drink of water please Miss Hazel."

Olga spoke in a faraway voice, "Gustus, you did not even come in the church to pray with us."

Moving up to him, she put her hands on his arm, he winced. "Ah burn on your arm?"

"It's nothing." He knew there were a few blisters on his hands, his chest, his arms; he felt like he had been bitten. "I must change this pyjama, anything in the grip?"

But before Olga could answer, Muriel came to life and told her sister in a toneless voice, "I see da bank, burn down flat. Flat."

She repeated, "Burn down, wi!"

"Aunt Hazel might have some old pants upstairs," Olga said, bringing the conversation back to the enquiry from Augustus. "She only had a few vests and drawers in the grip."

Miss Hazel went upstairs to search in her trunk. Augustus made a quick change and went back into the streets. It was three o'clock.

On Market Street, fetid odours of all the foods in the grocery shops, burnt leather, burnt everything made him put his hands over his nose. He left the darkness of the smoke-covered streets and stood on the Masav Bridge over the dry riverbed with people watching all the events. He felt an arm round his shoulders and heard, "Man, I've been searching all over for you. Where you going to stay?"

They heard the clanging of bells, red fire engines racing down from Morne Fortuna. He said to himself he would not go back to the house till the fire was out. They talked. They who had been out enjoying the night in the night looked on everything so horridly changed.

* * *

The scene in Miss Hazel's parlour was like a moonlight picnic. The women who sat there in their zombie state heard Augustus' return. Olga, the top of her nightdress off her shoulders and unbuttoned showing the swell of her breasts, sat motionless, her eyes in a distant stare. And who were those two elderly women? Their plaid headscarves rested on a chair. They sat with their legs planted wide apart.

Augustus scratched his head. 'What next?' he asked himself.

"You must want to sleep." Miss Hazel organised sleeping arrangements even as the new day had started and it was a day of darkness. Augustus was surprised that Olga chose to accompany her mother, even as his eyes held hers, longing for her. Yet, he slept deeply on the small bed. As he awoke, memory returned. His anger and disbelief made him want to kick something; vault and swerve. He paced up and down in the limited space of the little room that just had a single bed, and resisted the urge to stamp his feet to a beat in his head – to what was louder than he could bear. Visions of the night returned, spinning the thoughts in there and feeling new emotions – he thought, "Now I understand how men at war could kill the enemy."

Olga came into his room, his eyes brightened at the sight of her in her maroon kimono. He asked, "Did you sleep?"

"Just a little." She went to lean against him, needing his strength. He put his arms around her, becoming calm.

She heard her mother calling her. She said to him, "We might be able to have some coffee. Come."

Muriel sat on the side of Aunt Hazel's bed with Era on her knees. They all went downstairs, looking for Miss Hazel. The door to her kitchen was open, but she was not around. It was dark and tomb like. Augustus opened the door to the street and shut the door against the smog. He remembered the smell from their house, the nose irritation as the pitch pine wood burnt.

Half an hour later, there was activity after Miss Hazel got back with some charcoal. The old ladies were in the kitchen adding their saved pots and pans to their cousins' lot on a shelf. She cut some breadfruit wedges and left the cousins to attend to breakfast. Muriel went into the enclosed yard with water after it had warmed a bit on the coal pot to wash her face and limbs.

Era's serious face looked firmly at her parents; she could not understand how she had got to be awake in her Aunt Hazel's house and her parents looking sick. Her grandmother, with uncombed hair in that mess! And her bare feet!

"*Pov peti,*" Aunt Hazel said to Era, appraising the child who looked so much like her grandfather, Harry, except that she did not have the sleek hair but a soft fuzzy mass around her pale, yellow face.

Olga took the child's hand and followed Aunt Hazel into the shop at the front of the house, partitioned off from the parlour. Bolts of cloth were on the shelves. The glass counter had buttons, thread, fasteners, buckram and needles. She said to Olga "Let me find something so you make a *dan-dan* for Era."

They heard Augustus say to them as he passed in the long corridor by the shop door, "I'll be at Guy's house, be back later." He went out through a door facing the shop door into the lane on the right side of the house and into the Spine Road it joined.

In the afternoon, Guy brought them a few dresses belonging to his sisters. Olga was happy for that giving her some opportunity to go and clear her head. "I feel like a walk in the Gardens."

After she had changed into the large dress she swam in, her slippers flapping on the floorboards, she went out the way Augustus had to the lane and to Spine Road and to the St Cecelia Gardens. All life was happening there on the east side. The others she met carried possessions passing through from the centre of town to find a place to put their possessions.

The big trees bearing star apple, jugger plums, little coco and gooseberries were full of the edible food, but it was the air she appreciated, the peace she felt. She breathed in and out underneath the star apple tree, and did so again and again, slowly at first until she felt the sensation of life returning to all her parts, from head to toe. She moved to a green bench beneath tall bamboo trees by a small ravine, breathing in harmony with the wind rustling inside the small thin bamboo leaves, breath with breath until peace came to her.

Having to occupy the little space with Aunt Hazel, squeezing in with cousins, brought with it its own challenges and problems. She knew these cousins but they had kept themselves to themselves in the past. She did not know their ways though it might even be good having them and getting acquainted. Aunt Hazel was domineering, imposing in appearance, but her bark was worse than her bite. She had been kind to her when she was a little girl. Her mother's back was very straight, having few words to say, quite different from her aunt.

And Augustus? He was stubborn; not speaking patois. Deliberately. His stubbornness the very part of his people in the north, who were thought of by the town people as having their own hard ways, not slow to pre-empt a custom and making sure their ways were water-tight; they, the first to come running to show what they could do. Sometimes Olga knew how he responded to this concept that they up there at Anse Chabon were crass and problematic. They could not be genteel and that made them the butt of jokes.

Much later she made her way back to her aunt. Muriel had gone to church. She said, "Aunt Hazel, I feel much better now. I'll see to Era, get her tidy. Come!" she said smiling to her daughter. "Let's comb you."

There was the town out there, impassable. There was sadness too. Augustus came back from scouting and took a seat on the hard wooden varnished chair, one of Aunt Hazel's. Miss Hazel and Muriel sat on straight backed cane chairs facing each other by her dining table, studying each other's faces. Era sat quietly on a chair of the same, her legs dangling to the floor. Olga ran her hand up and down her neck, massaging it. The two old ladies hovered – all hope shone from their faces and that attracted Augustus. Who were they? He studied his daughter; he wanted her to smile today. She hung her head. He stood up now; she looked up, her eyes so black. He saw the stare, the rapid movement across the whites, startled she appeared to be. The small pink lips slightly surprised, moving to show her teeth. Usually he tweaked her round cheeks and she would smile shyly. He spoke to her quietly, they all looked at him. "You see, you cannot go out today. The fire was very big. We have to live here now. You see?" She nodded.

Aunt Hazel called, "Cousine, come make acquaintance with Augustus – husband of Muriel's daughter." She said in patois.

The two gave furtive looks towards Miss Hazel and approached tentatively. Augustus was puzzled again. Muriel got up saying, "Sid-down, sid-down there, we are we!" to her cousins and turned away to fill a cup with water from the kitchen tap, drinking thirstily.

She did not notice that Aunt Hazel blinked strongly with a stern face before she introduced them to him, and their look so full of something troublesome. He felt a frisson. The first to approach him was Ma George and Ma Boy followed, as opposite as two people could be. Their heads tied in Madras bright coloured yellow, red and orange cloths knotted at the forehead; older than their cousins; their complexions – one coffee black, the other Carib brown.

Olga also felt the frisson. She knew what Muriel had told her, that Hazel had displeased them immensely when they were young with her blasé behaviour. Hazel left a poor husband behind in Bonne Terrre and became the white man's *Jabal*. Hazel knew how to shrug her shoulders in those days and laugh with the saying, 'that's their business', to anyone who became disagreeable towards her, including her cousins.

She now said, to break the silence that Olga had endured, that she was going to cook supper. Augustus said to Olga, "I've not seen the Sampsons today; they may have got shelter somewhere."

"Say something", he thought, as she remained silent for what seemed like an eternity.

Olga observed that nothing had changed with him – his absolute attachment to the English words although she knew his very soul had been affected by the disaster, even though the cousins would have preferred the comfort of the old tongue. Muriel changed the topic and said, with her hand on her heart, that God had punished the town because the officials had failed to provide them with a fire engine. The officials had not cared after the fire of 1918 destroyed the fire station. She concluded, "Why? I don't know."

The cousins talked in whispers to one another. Era gazed with wonder at their lips. The child's expression was like her father's. But what did Era find amazing? But she failed to arrive at a conclusion as Augustus announced, "I think I'll go to see Cyril to tell him where we are."

Just then Aunt Hazel uncovered her pot of salted mackerel braff. The aroma attacked Augustus mercilessly; he changed his mind. Muriel went into the kitchen and returned with a plate of food for Augustus and one for Era. The cousins went into the kitchen, followed by Olga.

CHAPTER THREE

Dressed in his borrowed clothes, a bright blue shirt more like Guy than his own sober colours, Augustus stood against the shut door and open jalousies. He felt the old visitation of the complex – he was a country boy and his hold on the town was not iron-cast. He entered their door coming from the dirt sidewalk.

"Mr James, Mrs James. Good afternoon, how are you all?"

He wished he could remove this feeling as he stood like he had never been in their house before. He took a grip of himself and tried to speak normally. They asked him where he was staying and about his family.

"Er, ah, you realise-ah, I scarcely could manage to save things from our home in time; everything was tha-a-t fa-a-st!"

"But of course," Cyril agreed, "The speed of the fire, ay, ay!"

Augustus had heard his own voice and now recomposed himself. His Ham speech at the college had sent some boys into bouts of giggling and they mocked him. At first it had angered him that he had been called Ham. Guy had been his one ally; he had mastered his English to be as good as the English masters in the school.

He explained now: "I, er, could not have anticipated at the start of the blaze that, errr, this disaster would ensue."

He noticed a light of wonder and admiration on the faces of those others in the room who usually spoke slap-dash English with patois words thrown in; now they had no words for him.

Cyril studied Augustus in his soft grey twill loaned trousers, which belonged to Guy, who was taller. They were turned up twice round his ankles. He shook his head sympathetically. "In these hard times, man, I so sorry for you."

He was silent and then said, "I won't walk all that way to work; I'm staying right here till the roads get cleared of rubbish, by hook or crook it must be done. I want to see what they gonna do. *Me'sye'*! *Ki sa?*"

The silence was broken.

Augustus listened to conversation in patois and English as those in the room talked on, their salvaged goods scattered in the large yard. When he left he moved quickly, not thinking. Automatic footsteps went along the road and up the hill that led to the north. He was leaving the town behind. At the top, even as he had been oblivious to who had been walking up or down, he braced himself for the long walk to Anse Chabon, his village. He had a new feeling. Did Cyril see him in a different light? Did he think that because he had seen the fire first, he could have put out the flames? This thought pulled him up short. His footsteps dragged, he was aware of the painful blisters on his arm and hands. He retraced his steps towards the town. Olga's face, her Carmen Miranda walk, urged him back to Aunt Hazel's.

As he put one foot in Aunt Hazel's doorway, he listened intently before putting the other into the room. He walked slowly in, on his face a vestige of one of his sudden smiles – soon to disappear when he sat down with the women. They waited for him to start. He did not know what to say though he knew that Muriel and Olga were looking for a lead. But they had been talking before he'd got inside. He had heard them, in their patois. Olga asked, "So, how much news you heard?"

He said, "It will be a week or so before I could get through the town over so much debris. Cyril said he was going to wait for the streets to be clear. I'll give a hand doing this tomorrow if I can."

Miss Hazel said, "The water pressure low in my pipe."

He looked at Olga sewing by hand on a small dress. Outside, the sun had not shone all day after the death of the town. Era fidgeted in her new home, prised away from Maynard Street the night before, running with her father. Her fear still clung to her, like how she felt fear of the traditional characters of the masquerade, wanting to hide from their entreaties, their demands – pay the devil!

She missed the caress that Muriel had given her every morning when she woke her up at seven. It was the first face she saw every day, but this morning she had awoken beside Aunt Hazel. She had cried and even though she listened to gentle words from her, she had shied away from the hands which had reached out to her. She did not want Aunt Hazel to hug her and when she heard her mother's and father's voices she had run out to find them.

She had waited for the return of her father, Augustus, after he had been out for ages; then he came back. 'I wonder where he went,' she thought, scrutinising his face. It looked the same as the previous day but against this new background she was not sure it was the same face she knew.

"These old ladies whisper, I don't know what they say. I'm in my nightie all day, Mamma is making me a dress. The fire burnt everything. Upstairs on the balcony it's nice and bright. I counted thirty houses around the other streets, looking out at them. I came downstairs; I wanted something to eat. Where can I get some sweets or cake? They not giving me any more things to eat and I don't know what anybody is talking about.

"At last I have bread and a cup of tea. I have to sit here on the bottom stair. I cannot keep my eyes open so my mother come and take my hand and I get on a bed with her where I sleep after a while. In my mind I wonder: I never sleep with Mamma, only Granny. I am never with Mamma and Pap at night. It feels strange.

"Next morning, to my surprise, Daddy is sleeping by me. Mamma where are you? I sat up, she was standing by the open jalousies. I blinked my eyes and folded my arms and waited. Will I be taken out later to go somewhere? They will tell me what I have to do. I do what Mamma want me to do every day; she used to be busy all the time, sewing, washing, cleaning, cooking, ironing and talking with Daddy or Granny in the house on Maynard Street.

"I spy on Pap as he sits by the side of the bed and talking with Mamma. He just woke up but I want Granny, I don't feel right.

"They look sad! I hear fire, always fire all the time. Mamma took me to be on the balcony. Aunt Hazel was leaning out, then Granny came to meet us in her nightie, a comb in her hand. Mamma left us, Granny took my hand and caressed my face and arms as she used to do every morning. She combed my hair while talking to Aunt Hazel.

"Soon I was left on my own and I stood by the balcony high above the streets feeling as big as this big house, while seeing a very grey sky with a shine, but it was not blue as before, it was very close."

* * *

At the crack of dawn Aunt Hazel had found her old cousins whispering in the kitchen.

There were other homes along Spine Road, all jostling for space with small shops in the same fashion like hers – selling odds and ends.

"*Alo*, we will eat; *tout moun*," she said to them.

When all was said and done, Aunt Hazel felt collected and ready for this position she was in. Her solid house reflected her – no ornaments, dark wood panels in all the rooms, mahogany tables and waggonette. She had running water but no electricity. She opened her shop, waiting for someone to buy something, maybe some buttons, thread, elastic, safety pins. She was hopeful.

She heard some footsteps and Olga and Era joined her in the shop.

"Can I beg for some elastic and some cloth to make some panties. I won't be able to go out without wearing that!"

She gave a wry smile, and her Aunt's rejoinder was funny too: "Oh yes! You have to cover your backside." In patois.

Era made to follow Olga after she received some white fabric, thanking her aunt, "*m`esi, tant tant.*"

But the command came loud and clear, "Stay here!"

Olga sat by her sewing machine and the pedal bounced back and forth. A small light came into the drawing room with its dark panels. The kitchen, so close to the yard door, prevented light entering, and to increase the gloom, the shop partitioned off at the front facing the street took the rest.

"Bondye!" she said quietly. She would have to ask Augustus to place the machine nearer to the door. She had done enough on the machine and decided to move to the balcony to do the hand work.

Some while later, Miss Hazel was surprised when Olga called to her on her way out towards the door with Era. "Aunty, I'm going out with Era, won't be long-g-g-g," the word trailed as she suddenly realised she could not take Era barefooted, and added "Oh bother!"

She released the child's hand. "You know Aunty, it's like a dream; I cannot believe what happened. Stay with Aunt Hazel, Era, Mamma is going to make a message."

Aunt Hazel and Era watched as Olga walked away, her slippers flapping against her feet, but her airs of, 'I'm a lady', was back, that smile of gentility and the weaving, swaying gait. She passed outside on the sidewalk and disappeared.

She looked out for Augustus and her mother. Her thoughts dwelt on the streets full of black heaps, bricks piled high, stone walls eaten up. She made up her mind to pass near the streets, through rubble, towards the site of the big stores. She would go to the People's Square first to check the situation. People were still standing or sitting on their salvaged chairs. There were beds and dressers and bundles; men, women and children. She heard hawking and spitting and crying. It was so crowded! She thought some people had nowhere to take their things, having to stop right there in this open space; why couldn't they go by someplace? So they had to stay where they were. The heavy smoke that filled the air remained. What misery!

She wanted to get away urgently. The slippers prevented her from running. She hoped against hope to avoid the observation of the police officers she had seen walking in the Square. She wanted some shoes for Era and herself.

Oblivious to the dirt, the dross, the wood sticking out, she successfully got to a blackened coral wall where she hoped to make a find from the spoils of the fire before others beat her to it. The man nicknamed Uncle Sam bent over an iron trunk. She watched him open it; ladies dresses and hats inside. He looked at her. "What you want here? It's not safe, the police just left here, chased people like us but I came back."

"I want shoes for my little girl." But she then heard footsteps. She stopped in her tracks and quickly moved towards the sound. Someone had dropped something as they ran. She surmised it had been to escape the police. She moved toward the jute bag on the ground. She rushed before Uncle Sam got to it, opened the bag and whispered, "Praise the Lord," for this moment of serendipity. An assortment of shoes, white crepe soles, different sizes, sandals. If only they could fit – Era must have something. Then she saw small yellow canvas shoes with side buttons and a cross over strap. She stuffed them inside her bodice with a pair of white crepe soles for herself and left the rest to the man, hoping not to meet any police and have him show her the rough treatment. She was not the type, and she would give them a piece of her mind if they bothered her.

She arranged her dress and for a moment her mind had gone blank. And as she stood there dumbfounded, waiting for something to happen, a childhood game came into her mind – 'twenty men soldiers, what's your trade? All sorts. Work one out!' As a little girl she played this game, miming a trade for the others to 'work out', to guess. What came into her mind now was: 'Thief'. I'm a thief.

The other trade that then surfaced in the forefront of her mind was, 'Magician'. Yes, I'm a magician, she concluded, and dispelled any thoughts of being the thief.

This thought brought her back to reality as she stumbled along, her slippers no help on the slippery surfaces, until, not looking right or left, she reached Maynard Street. She walked away from the blackened town, not rushing into the darkened interior of her Aunt's home with any more joy than she had at the sights she had seen. Everything in this world had changed.

Aunt Hazel was absent from the shop and she had left Era in charge for now.

The child came towards her in the corridor outside the shop but she shook her head at her. "Just a minute," she cautioned. The child's eyes looked at her mother's larger bosom, her filthy dress and feet with horror. "Stay till Aunt Hazel come back. OK?" she added.

* * *

Upstairs in that room which had become hers and her family's, Augustus sat by the closed window and read a book by the faint light from the open jalousies. He looked up as she came in questioningly; she dipped inside her bodice, dangled the shoes at him with a smile.

"You skylarking, girl! What have you been doing?"

There was an unwelcome look on his face but she hurriedly said that she had not stolen the shoes, just looking for an opportunity. She realised how shameful it was that she had secreted them as no lady would have done what she did but she looked at him defiantly. Wait, she wanted to say, wait till Era saw the little shoes that she could wear.

"No more of that kind of thing, it could be dangerous for you." Augustus rubbed his neck. "I had not expected you to go out."

"I just had to."

Forgetting everything but themselves, they kissed and embraced each other. She felt better but soon disengaged herself. He looked into her oriental eyes beneath his, was dragged into something he saw there, as if they carried all the secrets and mysteries of the Island. They had always held an allure for him but never as strong as now.

In the morning, cramped and sweating, they looked at each other. The thick stubble and his hair had the appearance of peppercorns. She sat cradled in his arms as Era slept. They discussed a plan for everyday business; she listened as he did most of the talking. He sounded confident about the situation. His book was probably the reason for this assurance, she mused. He said he would go to the beach within the next half hour and suggested that she rest a bit longer.

After he'd gone, the house was quiet but she wanted to be prepared in her mind for the new day. It would not be long before the others started to move about. She stood on the balcony watching the quiet empty street, the galvanised roofs, the dry gutters on Spine Road. She wished that someone else would open a window or a door to show some life. It seemed ages when she heard Aunt Hazel and her mother talking.

She joined them in the kitchen after a while.

Aunt Hazel positioned her coal pot on the upside down wooden box inside her kitchen, close to the door. Her hand was steady, movements assured as, like the Harbour Master, she navigated her vessel, filled with fire-rescued people, away from the treacherous rocks and tempestuous sea to calmer waters.

Olga felt both superfluous and reassured as she stood and watched Aunt Hazel.

The old cousins came down at last. Olga looked from one to the other while they talked in a desultory way with Aunt Hazel. They were trying and having some difficulty just then to bridge the gap of the years. Olga left them in the kitchen, took a bucket of water upstairs to freshen herself. She checked on her mother. How could she be going to work without her own clothes? Muriel had always been no nonsense, so stoic. She was half dressed, a bodice and a skirt. She was trying to squeeze herself into it, and needed Olga to use a safety pin and close a gap where the bodice edges did not meet. Luckily the skirt was elasticised.

"I'll be sewing some clothes today. Poor Aunt Hazel, giving us everything! I'm not expecting that. Just because we are family, it should not be take, take. But I need some cloth."

Muriel took her up on this quickly – "I'll pay her rent, thank God I..."

She did not finish as Olga said emphatically, "Gustus said he will pay the rent money for all of us, so let him, Mamma."

Muriel's serious face looked resigned but there was a glimmer of a smile; she pushed her feet into her sister's borrowed shoes and shrugged her shoulders. She stood in the centre of the room and was pensive, not ready to leave.

"The rosary! The rosary! Where did I put my rosary?"

She turned around in disbelief at herself for having misplaced it. Last night she had not even had the comfort she got from feeling the beads before she slept, but she was sure that she would find it now.

"I looked under this bed and lifted the mattress already, and you can see it's not on the dresser."

She moved away to the door saying that perhaps she might get another one from the priest later. She and Olga parted in the corridor while Muriel went downstairs. Olga decided to wash clothes after she had made Era's dress. She felt obliged to keep the few clothes that she had been given, make alterations and make do, and try to keep Augustus in the way he was accustomed.

She had the first sighting of the sun late in the morning, through a hazy sky. At twelve mid-day, the Anglican Church musical bells rang. They always rang with their tune that fitted to the words of a song jokingly about goats, sheep, rams, funeral hearse. It made no sense to her.

She was not hungry. Some food was being cooked by the cousins but all she wanted was water. The heat after the fire still stuck to the air, she had never felt as hot anytime she could recall. She thought of Augustus soaking in the sea. She let her mind rest on the idea of her body immersed in water. She closed her eyes to drink it, letting water from the cup go down slowly. "Um!" she sighed.

Before she started to sew she sat in the shop with her Aunt. Augustus had not returned. Lethargy settled in her limbs. She looked at her daughter, indulged by Aunt Hazel who tied a bit of pink fabric round the child's head with a knot at the front, just like the madras head tie style. "*Ti madanm.*" The compliment made Era smile. She said to Olga, "I have to do something to pass the time."

She pulled out three small card boxes from the shelf under her glass counter, and she tipped the cards of buttons and put all in one box, handing Era the two empty boxes. The simple sleeveless petticoat dress she had quickly run up for the child the day before was better than her being in the night dress, but now she would go to make something for the child to wear out and the yellow shoes had been nearly the right size, just a bit big but that was fine.

* * *

Augustus and Guy faced the mountains of broken concrete and black timber on the road, as a pale and eerie sunlight engulfed the blackened houses left standing – open doorways without faces or voices. But to Mr Polius' pink house they approached, entering through the door which had been left open. No one saw them coming in. The small parlour was bursting at its seams. Dujon, who was leader of the General Workers' Union, was the closest to Mr Polius. They sat on his Roman-style sofa; it held four men. They were talking loudly, and other groups of threes and two talked with each other. Augustus squeezed up near the sofa. He felt for the first time as one with the rest, a citizen feeling a loss. Dujon was totally focused – concentration on his face, his hand gesticulating in front of him. He shifted his tightly squeezed hip and settled it again.

"A new Town Board election will have to be brought about this year, we have to demand this," Dujon said.

"Agreed," a loud voice responded.

Augustus was back to back with someone. He heard a high-pitched voice, and another one deep and heavy, with the answer, "It's high time." Augustus wanted to ask what was going to happen if the streets were not going to get cleared soon. Suddenly the noise lessened and Augustus heard Dujon continue. He would send a cable to the Union leader in Jamaica to get help in whatever they could offer, money or food. He digressed, "I will know how to steer clear if I'm in the middle of a fracas, you know from my experience in the States."

Mr Polius got up. "You've seen the world; now it's time I went out to see what's happening in town."

They all left together. Mr Polius started off down through the cleaner streets and they arrived at one untouched bastion of strength – a drug store. It was made of concrete and stone, with cast iron rails upstairs. The residents upstairs had received a visit from their friends who now welcomed Mr Polius (Sir). These men, a newspaper owner, a lawyer and a doctor, were having a meeting of their own – in politics.

It was quieter in here than at the place they came from. Augustus heard mention of the words struggle, power, election, work and money, and each man carried their communication with the other as if oblivious to those who had arrived. After a few minutes of being spectators, Guy whispered into Augustus' ear.

"It's going to take a lot of talking and more talking among those upper-class people. Let's go."

Earlier, Augustus had caught sight of Popo, the Town Clerk and also Manager of the 'People's Bank' called the Co-operative Bank. As usual, he carried his rolled-up black umbrella pointed at the ground as a walking cane, lifting it up away from his body stylishly as he walked quickly, light on his feet. He walked alone. Where was he coming from and where was he heading? Augustus felt an urge to go to talk to him; this man should have some important business to attend to, why had he not been at the drugstore at that meeting? In the past he used to visit Mr Polius' house with others, knowledgeable, clever with words. But Guy was talking now about his apprehensions about the town.

"This is where the Co-operative grocery store was." There was now dross, thick black, slimy, bits of tin and shards of glass. This is the mess that had to be cleared. The store, opened the previous year, sold liquor and food commodities, the grand idea of the Co-operative Union. Guy continued, "We were starting to make progress in town. Our Co-operative Union had plans to exact a new lease of life for the unemployed. Look at it!"

Augustus retorted, "But what have the Seamen and Waterfront Workers Union, or the General Workers Union done? Are they expecting the town's hard-up people to listen to their voice, to just accept that there had been no fire engines to protect them?"

"I'll tell you what they had done," Guy hissed. "The Co-operative Union recently negotiated with some employers to secure a promise to give holiday pay, and Dujon had the support of the factory workers on your estate, but no! You! You are not a member, are you?"

"I don't have time for this Union business."

Guy listened to his friend and chupsed, then said sternly, "Don't you think it was time you came off from your fence? All you want is knowledge about this and the other."

"I find that knowledge in itself is satisfying."

As the exchange of words seemed to be changing to polemic proportions, Augustus walked away. He could not take this argument right any further. "I am not in the mood for this Guy, I'm telling you. I am only interested in helping with the clearing of the streets if Dujon and others have a plan to do so. See you later man."

Augustus landed back at Miss Hazel's. In the corridor outside her shop, he was accosted by her. He made no response to her but looked intensely at this middle-aged woman with a smile that played at the corner of her mouth, and sat with her on the vacant stool behind her counter, facing Spine Road. He then told her he had been with men from the Union, and they were getting some plan organised but had not got far in regards to the direction they would take. She asked him whether he would take a position on a committee of a Union. She saw his frown and silence.

CHAPTER FOUR

Augustus and Olga awoke to the hard stare from the morning. Augustus dressed, moving around softly, but Olga said in an anxious voice, "I expect you going to get a sea bath. I wish I could come and have one as well."

"I will be walking too fast for you; on my own, I can get to the beach in half an hour. I want to be back by seven."

Her slow two-step-dance-walk, which made her appear almost not moving at all, was a delight to his eyes, but she would keep him back since he had to return to help clean up the town. He had never thrown himself into the activities of the town and it was a first experience for him. He had the image of the town as being full of intelligent and well-dressed people; in a conceited fashion – just like himself.

He stood on the sand bank beneath russet and green trees, their breezes blowing over him, lost in thought, watching the waves time themselves in regular rhythm and making ribbons of white foam on the blue water. The sea hissed, calling to him, but he was distracted by, "*Bon jou.*"

It was Sergeant Paine, or Philosophe as he was known. "You were living in the house next to the tailor shop where the fire started?"

"Can't talk now Sarge." Philosophe, in his swimming trunks, his big frame and somehow benevolent in appearance, made it easy to be dismissive of him. "I'm only here for a quick swim."

"Best time of the day for it. Enjoy it Sonny."

Augustus nodded. He then joined some early morning bathers and for a while he basked in the pure pleasure of the warm water, but experiencing it as a new joy as if he were a novice to the sea bath. There were some boats far off on the horizon somewhere between St Benedict and Martinique. Then reality took hold again. The town he loved had been destroyed.

He got to his feet feeling the moving earth underneath him. He heard the sound of squelching sand as the sea pulled the sand back to its depths, almost as a game. As repeatedly, the water settled for a brief moment, so he moved his feet avoiding the suction of the sand's power to pull him back into the water. On firm dry sand once more, he walked towards the almond trees. More people had arrived for a bath. There was no sign of Philosophe.

He looked for shells in the dry sand to take to Era. The larger corrugated ones were plentiful together with tiny conch, pretty coral pink and cream. He placed a few in his pocket, pulled on his shirt and started his walk back to town, with short quick steps as people from his village usually walked, hurrying.

At the top of the hill facing Masav, he stopped for a second. It was a steep walk down, the land spread out on either side. He was forced to lengthen his stride as he was propelled downwards with a casual swing, then he regained his normal tight walk. Cyril lived at the bottom of the long road. He stopped by the house. Cyril's wife, Boo, had gone to the hospital to give birth to their fifth child.

He headed for Dujon's house, a two-storey building with the downstairs used for selling cakes in a small cake shop, in close proximity to the Catholic Boys' school. His house stood unscathed. The small-framed Dujon opened the door to his knock. He could hear talking coming from a room in the back, could hear talking and movement from upstairs. Dujon spoke directly to Augustus, "The sugar cane harvest will soon be over. Do you, um, like it up there?

We can say it's a blessing that some people still have their work up there in the factories."

"Yes, I agree."

"Long live sugar cane," Dujon said.

His small face looked haggard, dry grey lips in the brown chocolate concerned face. His soft eyes held pain. Augustus took in the sad face of a man who promised to improve work conditions and make all the people think for themselves. He said that they would go to the Public Works Department as soon as they opened.

The owners of the voices from the back room and from upstairs came to join them. Those who had never dirtied their clothes doing any kind of manual work were in the room. They now forgot what had kept them separate from labourers. Even so, not every man present went along to the Public Works Department. They got buckets, shovels, pick axes and wheelbarrows. Augustus picked up his shovel and listened to directions from the employees of the Government. They gave the go ahead to start to get the debris off the streets and sidewalks.

Augustus bent over his shovel and felt good doing this. In tireless movements, he shovelled the dross that he put into a bucket and carried over to a truck parked on the periphery. The work gang hacked at solid debris, ash-coloured and blackened objects lifted away from the streets, slowly and steadily. In conversation, Augustus heard of other efforts; a boat was at the wharf, arrived from Anse Du Fort, the American town, with relief goods, and people from the wartime A.T.S. were supporting the crowd on the People's Square.

After many hours, Augustus, tired and hot, stopped and headed home to remove his filthy clothes. Though he was soiled and mangy, Miss Hazel and Olga saw that he stood with a confident look on his face, telling them he was to go to see about the relief food he could well receive from a boat by the wharf.

Era appraised him with her bright curious smile, well-known to him, her eyes glinting. Olga said, "You so dirty! My God! You know you don't have any clothes these days. There's a clean shirt you can have but no pants."

Then she wished that she had not spoken. She saw a change in his expression. He washed his arms and face, drank some water and left. He was at the wharf in no time but left for the People's Square to get to the two servicemen's jeeps, the focus of the food donation. Augustus was pleased that he had not wasted any time, as the lines of people waiting were long. His new dependency was manifest when he got into the line, waiting.

Fear and anger alternated, his sweat trickled down his back. People pushed and shoved each other in desperation. He glimpsed Ma Sampson at some point. When his turn came he was given custard powder, corn meal, corned beef, condensed milk and rice. With the soft packs resting against his chest, he held the tins in both hands.

With determination to put his anger aside, going back home, he thought instead of what work he had done and what work he would resume to clean the streets. Coming towards Miss Hazel's house, he saw Era hanging out of the balcony. He smiled up at her and she returned hers from her round banana yellow face. Olga and Aunt Hazel were in the drawing room. He handed the things to them. Olga thought, trust him for that, he always took his duty of bringing in food very seriously.

"Thank you," Aunt Hazel said in patois. Then, "It's very hot today, maybe I will make ice-cream tomorrow?"

Olga picked a clean pair of pants from the line and gave it to Augustus. She went into the kitchen. Ma George's hands worked on a grater, wrist flicking up and down, diminishing the piece of coconut. It was part of the same coconuts given to Miss Hazel the week before. There was still a half left in the shell.

"Ma George, I want to make some *p`e mi* with that piece of coconut. I have some corn meal, I'll get some pumpkin tomorrow, if possible."

"*Kouman! Pwan'y souple'.*" She said shortly in patois.

The kitchen was not big enough for all the women. Ma George and Ma Boy were so willing, doing anything in the line of shopping and cooking! Olga had noticed and they always stood whispering to each other. It was disheartening to her that she was ignored by them in their total absorption of a task and their whispers.

That moment, away from the kitchen, Era stood by Aunt Hazel's counter. She observed Era eying the red plums for sale across the street. They were displayed in front of the window on a shelf outside the house. The child obviously wanted some and she said to her: "Go and buy six plums."

She stood in her doorway with Era, gave her some money and told her: "The road is clear, quick, I'm watching."

The woman sat by her window, saw Era coming, dispatched the wine coloured squat plums with their tiny round heads, took the money and craned her neck out of her window, surveying for the bicycle or odd vehicle and said to the child. "Run quick, cross over."

Aunt Hazel waited for her customers to buy cloth or ribbon, maybe buttons or buckram – anything! The bolts of material cost too much in the present climate but she wished all the same for more customers. She had relayed her wishes aloud to Olga, who reminded her: "Like you forget the man that bought some domestic, and the other one bought something to make a suit because he was going to America and the lady who bought khaki for the school pants for her son?"

Aunt Hazel examined the plums for blemishes and they did look delicious. "Go and wash them and bring them back here, I well feel like tasting a plum to pass in my mouth. It's so hot."

When Era came back, she was given four, one was reserved for Olga later and Aunt Hazel popped one into her mouth.

CHAPTER FIVE

hear they have a tent on the square and a Government man sits inside to talk to all those who need a house to stay. The Red Cross people doing their job too on the Square."

This titbit of information from Aunt Hazel prompted Olga to action.

"Well, it's time I went out, I'll go and take Era with me."

She hated to look where her home used to be. Now some trucks from the Public Works Department were still being driven to pick up fire rubbish. She was able to stand not far from her old home, looking in disbelief – the coils of bed springs, the old concrete wash tub in the yard, bits of wares. She also imagined the pineapple-yellow walls that were the interior of the house that she had to flee. She gazed at the Era's face, upturned to hers. Neither spoke as they walked towards the People's Square.

She took in all her surroundings – treeless streets, blackened wood stacked in piles. The white stone Catholic church was like one good tooth in a cavernous tooth-decayed mouth. She crossed over from the church to the gravel of the People's Square, losing her balance temporarily but regaining her composure in a few seconds, smiling, determined. The well-known appearance of a place, with croton hedges and wire enclosing the perfect grass-covered areas or the flowerbeds, and outside the dirt square for constant use where the homeless people gathered these days. The loud talking hit her ears and she walked on.

Suddenly she came to a halt. "Ay! Ay! Mr Sampson?"

Her words dropped and her mouth remained open. She stood before him. He held a piece of rope around an iron post and there was white canvas dangling about his feet. He paid no attention to her. She saw his blank stare; startled further, she touched him. He pushed her hand away, and if looks could kill, she would have fallen at his feet. Pulling back in alarm, still smiling, he acted as if he did not recognise her and was determined to get on with erecting the tent which was lying in a heap on the ground, but why was no one helping him?

"How's your wife and daughters?" she ventured. He ignored her.

"Well, well, well!" she said to herself, "What's the matter with him?"

She left him, walking slowly, uneasily, looking for familiar faces. It was painful, each one she met. She was not homeless, but she registered inside the official tent that she had lost her home and had temporary housing. She then moved away from the Square towards the Riverside clean road, making her way to Spine Road and back to Aunt Hazel's.

A line of people waited for water from a standpipe at a street corner. Even underneath Aunt Hazel's balcony there was a group of people talking, and Aunt Hazel, behind her counter, joined in the conversation. She entered by the side door not to interrupt them.

The cousins were in the kitchen, whispering while cooking a meal. She left Era by the living room door looking at them and she climbed the steps to her room. She intended to iron some clothes that afternoon, do some of her Aunt's ironing for her. Now, she reflected back to her childhood when she lived here with her mother before Muriel had her own house, and here she was again with her Aunt trying to cheer them up. Her mother was finding it very hard and the cousins were finding it hard too. They looked so ill at ease.

Upstairs, the light from the balcony reduced the stuffiness of the house, the darkness dissolved. She called to Era. She sat her next to her on the balcony. "I'm going to hem some skirts, I'll show you again and you can try to hem your new dress, uh?"

Olga broke off a length of thread from the small soft ball of base thread. Era obediently took a needle from her mother, threaded it and started as directed, pushing her needle in and out again, slowly without talking. She glanced at Olga for encouragement, her round pale yellow face gazing as intent as her hands.

"Be careful not to prick your finger."

That they should have things to wear the coming Sunday was imperative to Olga. She was going to make a beret for each of them to match the dress they would wear. She hummed "Skylark", one of her favourite songs. The words played the images in her mind. As they sat on the balcony, her mood improved. There were sounds of people passing by, even jocular words. Half an hour later Era said, "I finish."

Olga told her, "I'll finish it later. Just put it on the bed."

She observed her daughter 'hanging out' of the balcony, leaning over the edge looking out on to the street. Just behaving like a child, not unhappy as she herself was. Tears suddenly welled up as she pictured Augustus' unshaven face, his dirty clothes. She put the clothes away and decided to go downstairs; it should be lunchtime.

"Come on Era. Let's go down."

Era rushed ahead of her, skipping down the stairs. Olga met Ma Boy and Ma George in the kitchen. She stood with them. They both looked her over, not quite sure what they should do or what she would say to them. There were questions in their eyes, not unfriendly but guarded.

Ma Boy uncovered one aluminium pot, showing the small Jack fishes in a golden sauce. She pointed to the grey dasheen in the earthen Canari pot. "The food is ready; Cousin Hazel will come and share it out. I'll call her."

Olga gazed at Ma George who remained silent, her hands at her sides.

After her Aunt had done the sharing, leaving some for Augustus, they all ate quickly.

* * *

When Augustus arrived early in the afternoon, he found Olga on the balcony in the bright light, doing hand sewing. She had picked up a piece of dull striped cloth that she had cut into a shirt for work for him.

"I've got some clothes for us; they've started to give out relief clothes."

His thick growth of beard was a strange feature, but as well as this, Olga did not like his look – his reddened eyes and a face full of anger – he looked disfigured, and she saw that his mouth looked crooked and his face swollen.

"I know how you must feel."

He looked at her. "I'm alright."

It was two days since she had touched him and she wanted him to hold her, and she stood up to reach and put her arms around his waist. What a hard block of concrete he felt against her body! She dropped her arms. No way in there for her. When was he going to cave in for her, for him to look at her with the old invitation?

"Aren't you even combing your hair?"

She went and came back into the room with a comb and handed it to him. He made a few flicks on his hair and handed it back. He passed his hand reflectively over his face and he asked whether there was a small mirror he could borrow. Anyway, he had no blades to shave.

"I hope to return to work next week. Now that the road is cleared, Cyril can use the car."

His unshaven face looked back at him from the small mirror.

"Heck, I don't recognise myself."

He handed the comb back to her.

"If I can get some blades tomorrow, I'll be pleased you know."

A moment passed. Then, "I'm so glad I saved your machine, I see you have been busy."

Era had been watching from her position on the small bed, and she now lay on her stomach and looked at her face in the mirror. Augustus said, "I'll be doing some reading now."

Olga had thrown down her almost finished dress on to her chair and was loathe to resume her sewing. A feeling of loneliness descended, all bubbles fizzed out and certainties becoming uncertainties, while Augustus settled himself close by and began to read, what she did not know. She hummed "Skylark"; that song seemed to want her to sing, a song of wishful thoughts.

Sunlight fell on the floor around them. She could not disturb him and she knew she should carry on doing something – the right thing at the right time, as now all she could do was wait for this or that. She thought about the nature of deceit. She believed all that she had been told while growing up and she hoped she would not have to deceive Augustus or Era ever. And take Aunt Hazel's situation: Muriel had told her how Hazel had fooled everyone. That deceit had travelled and returned to the place where it had originated, on her Aunt's face. She lived with it right then. Deceit was empty. The guile that Aunt Hazel had used to tell the untruth about herself and the man she had been carrying on with while her husband, still in the home village, thought that she had a job, a good job she had written to tell him. Even when Muriel joined her unwittingly, Hazel had found her a living in job as a housemaid. Her cousins found out eventually, and it got back to her ears that they were ashamed to be related to her and how the feud between them and her had lasted till now. They knew that they had been her enemy then, but Aunt Hazel, now a mature middle-aged woman and with Victor dead, has to accept that she had shocked them and her family. She had not arrived at the method to remove the barrier between the old cousins and herself as yet, and their ways made Olga uncomfortable too as she hoped that soon they would all be out of their current sidestepping.

It was now time to light the lamp for the evening. Downstairs, the cousins had lit a coal fire. She entered the kitchen and to her chagrin, they were, as usual, not saying anything to her as she stood by the kitchen door, looking at what was happening. She needed to be busy too. She was quite unfamiliar with them and not getting to know them at all just yet but she respected them. A light drizzle touched her skin; she looked up.

"A little rain," she said to them. "Weather seem to be changing."

Ma George, the cousin whose face was most open, answered her in the same patois, "The sky looks very tied up, some rain will fall."

"Could I heat an iron? I have one shirt to iron for Augustus, must make use of the little fire, you know."

They smiled briefly. The two windows were on either side of the kitchen. It was a decent size for two adults but it was now crowded with Olga in there. A big concrete fire hearth for cooking also took a large space, as well as a small wooden table and a few shelves.

The fire had been lit in the fire hearth and Olga fetched the iron that lay on a shelf. She went to get the shirt and returned.

There was something else about these women that Olga did not know; they had been employed in domestic service and knew how to become invisible. It was no use expecting conversation. They sat in the yard on upside down boxes and waited till she had finished to carry on doing what they had planned to do in the kitchen. She did not want to keep them back and called after a short while, *"mw`e fini."*

She noticed the drizzle had stopped and as she went into the sitting room, going upstairs, Aunt Hazel was coming downstairs. They smiled at each other. The lyrics of 'Skylark' came to her, words that were in Olga's head trying to get out, words that she could not hold in. Such a lovely melody. *"My heart is riding on your wings, over the shadows in the rain, will you lead me there, to a blossom-covered lane, have you heard the music in the night; Skylark…"*

She sang the words in a low voice, almost a hum, totally lost in the words. She carried the shirt to Augustus. "See, all nice and spruce."

"So I see," he answered. "Thank you."

"I'm thinking about Aunt Hazel's tin bath," she spoke very quietly, "I don't fancy sitting in that, I wish I could come for a sea bath with you."

"Apart from the walk, you do not like going to the beach. I know you may not wish to go to the public shower which Cyril and the people in the houses over there use. It was put there for the cottage dwellers, but seeing people need to bathe, maybe others are using these two showers."

She was quiet. It was something to think about. He said, "I have to go out and hear the latest news, I won't be late back."

Olga, close to Era on the small bed, was restless. She heard children singing, outside in the direction of the lane. It could be about eight o'clock, she guessed. She peeped through the jalousies. She heard familiar children's songs, she had sung them herself and it cheered her immensely to know that there was good life outside created by others in the same old ways. Satisfying her curiosity, she crept downstairs with her candle, left it on the table and went out of the gate. She moved to view the dark lane and heard the singing, "Jane and Louisa... please come home..." then "Blue bird passing through my window... Oh Johnny I am tired..."

She made out the silhouettes of six or seven youngsters in a circle. "Ah!" She sighed, returned into the house, retrieved the candle from the table and returned to the bedroom, and lay flat on her back next to Era. It was the start of the night when she would sleep fitfully as she had done for the past few nights since they had come here. They had lived, Augustus and herself, as passengers in a boat at her mother's house, and it worried her that they had boarded Aunt Hazel's boat and were now out to sea.

She remained awake, going over small things and big things. After Era had been born her mother had said to her, "Your child come out the picture of the man that is your father." Another thing, the way she had been courted by Augustus, against her mother's wishes at first and that later she had changed her mind, saying that Augustus was a decent sort. But it was Muriel who had given her smooth passage to life, she had to be grateful. It was Muriel who had asked her to let Era sleep with her from the age of two. She doted on the child; Era sat on her knees every morning receiving cuddles, and so Era was closer to Muriel than herself and Augustus.

What would become of all of them? The candle was almost out. She waited till it burnt out, then she closed her eyes and waited for Augustus. In the dark night he was somewhere talking to somebody, and he was going to come back through the black streets. She felt herself slipping reluctantly into sleep, then Augustus came in. He was next to her in the small space. Era was usually between them and they scarcely moved from the spot in which they had lain down. Now, she moved a hand and felt him close, she felt his hard bristles against her face, with surprise she picked up a melody at the edge of the small bed. His arms enveloped her, they rolled out of the bed on to the floor. They sat up with shock and looked at each other. Her eyes held his.

"What's a matter, Gus?"

"Sorry, my darling."

He put his cheek against hers. She could feel his pounding heart. He was distressed; she could feel it coming out of his skin, his naked chest.

"You not feeling well?"

As the day before, he had not needed her to hold him. She said, embarrassed for their situation, unexpected words. She heard her voice, "This is bad, this small bed and this small room."

She changed her position and moved to kneel behind him against his hunched back, and rested her head on the hard muscles with her arms around his chest.

"I feel so lonely; it's like some bad dream until tonight. Now it really hit me that I am stuck in something totally awful, something where I cannot see my future at all. And not that alone – what about us, living as man and wife, Era sleeping next to us! I can't think of this part of ourselves, to be together, it's only my discipline makes me behave now."

The words poured out of her. Her immediate relief of having a roof over her head, there had been no thought of her married life and her behaviour with Augustus. It was too soon and all the adjusting that she had to do. She thought of Boo who had just given birth to her baby son. Lucky Boo. She adjusted her mind to think of her own child, happy to have her. He said to her, "Let's go and sit on the balcony just for a little while, this might let us relax and come back for a shut eye."

"Oh no, I will get back in bed, I'm so tired."

She moved away from him. "I know you love me, I'm happy about that at least."

She wondered whether they disturbed her mother and Aunt Hazel.

CHAPTER SIX

er right foot met his left foot. Content with playing footsies with him, they lay in bed with the sleeping child, their faces towards the ceiling in the dark.

"I'm missing the conversations and the big arguments I heard at Mr Polius.'"

"Uh, huh."

Her quiet husband had his depths. She knew his stubborn ways. She made an effort for conversation.

"Did I tell you I saw Mr Sampson on the Square and he looked at me like he never saw me before?"

"Yes, you did, and I saw his wife when I got the relief food."

Waiting for sleep, Augustus recalled that he had felt some peculiar sensation on the beach, walking away from the sea, his shadow huge and elongated behind him on the sand. It felt like his shadow meant something. In this room now, the shadows of the night against the wall thrown by the candle were huge. He got up to blow it out and settled again on his side next to Olga who squeezed against Era.

"I am in shadow of time and when time moves how will I be? Time is dragging its heels. People on the square are waiting in a shadow. How can I step out of this shadow?"

People's music strings were playing tango rhythms, those people on the Square as they were gathered, necks stretched, rigid backs, chests outthrust, a raised foot, bent thigh, a grimace showing strain. Mr Sampson heard his own music and had been oblivious to Olga that day. It was not time for gentle quadrille. Augustus would have to be ready to move his heels and make his own tango.

The book that Augustus had been reading, *The Rose and Cross*, was borrowed, recommended as a good book in the sense that it gave one certain philosophies. It explained the Rosicrucian way. It was inside his small grip in a corner of the room. He had read some pages and felt like rejecting it, the difficult subject, but he knew he would see this task completed; one of his goals was to get hold of the ideas in there. He had been advised to read it carefully and not confuse it with religion. They told him that some people in the Island lived by those higher levels of consciousness about human endeavours. It was in the book. He only meant to read it for information. The Rosicrucian Order was banned by the laws of the Catholic Church and so his reading of this recommended book should be secret. He had even heard that some of the philosophies could pose a mental strain on a reader, one with a fragile nature.

At four thirty the following day he returned to Miss Hazel's. She sat at the corner of the shop counter where she liked to watch for people coming from the town end of Spine Road. Olga and Era looked at Augustus as he entered. He noted the child's anxious face; he knew he was filthy and he rubbed his hand against his stubble.

Olga said, "You only just missed Philosophe. He was nobody's idiot today. You still expect an old joke from him, but not today. He was not in his police uniform."

Miss Hazel, her face like a squashy fat poke, square with a sheen of sweat on her brown face, dimples deepened, said, "Police! They useless!"

Philosophe arrived at the shop and spoke to her about the thefts of dress material from the stores during the fire and, though he had not accused her directly, she had been affronted and asked him why he was telling her, why was he nosing about in her shop?

He had been given some addresses to investigate.

"Voila," she said. "Philosophe thinks he could outsmart thieves and he said he was going to try all how."

She turned up her lips in scorn.

"Oh good!" He said.

He abhorred thieves and started to move upstairs. Back again he moved into the yard. Era stood near to him, fascinated as he washed the sand that still covered the shells and now glimmered wetly – pinks, yellows, white and grey.

"I got you those."

Her two open palms were not big enough as she opened them to receive the wet gift.

"Put them on that large stone over there to dry out."

A few minutes later, he was putting on a clean shirt and pair of pants given to him by Olga.

"I should visit my tailor tomorrow and see what he can do for me."

Her day had been spent scrubbing their bedroom floor. She had also visited her old school friend who taught at Era's school.

"Agnes said Era will have another week at home."

"In two days, all the streets will be cleared so that trucks and cars could pass on their business. Me and work, I have to manage without the bike."

This was one of their losses which meant hardship for Augustus, she thought, and an inward prayer went up to God. Every day a burden. He had told her he would apply to get some money from the Beneficial Crisis Fund as he could not get money from work till he went back.

"How's Guy? How come I've not seen him since four days ago?"

That was something else he had to do, make peace with his friend. This was not the right time. He still was in a mood to be disagreeable, his first anger about the fire, weaker but ready to glow with the wrong words about anything he disagreed with.

There were rows of wooden benches on the large concrete open space of the presbytery court where Muriel handed cakes and tea to people from the People's Square, her frilled white cotton apron tied behind her back over the soft grey uniform she wore. She had made large cakes, on the priests' orders, for the people on the Square. A second cook who was the second usual cook made the priests' meals. Olga cut slices of cake and served the waiting people.

The sun was low, lemon light on the streets. Augustus headed for Mr Francois the tailor's shop. He stood in the doorway of the bottom floor in the white wooden two-storey house. It was a wide airy room. Mr Francois had his tape measure round his neck. He stood, scissors gripped firmly as he cut some cloth. Four men were in the vast room. They acknowledged his arrival, and Mr Francois stopped working after Augustus had made polite greeting and said what he came for.

"Well, Sir, I have a lot of cloth. See all these beneath my cutting board, I can make pants for three shillings and sixpence. What's happening? I've got arrangements to make different size clothes and share the earnings with those who saved material from their stores, you see?"

The man surprised Augustus in this manner. He had one sewing machine. The three others were busy, sewing by hand or pedalling away. He would have brought his own cloth, got from Miss Hazel, but this was Mr Francois' method of business. He had to think about that.

"I'm looking to borrow another machine so I can get through this sewing. Choose which cloth you like and you could have something the day after tomorrow."

There were always young men interested in the trade. Of course Clifford sewed for the Macaroni sort and he, Mr Francois, for the quietly dressed, no fuss type. Augustus had used him for years, he trusted him, he knew of his honesty and now, what was going on. He had to believe what the man just told him, so he chose a bit of material for two pants.

"Very well, I'll be back in two days. Good evening."

My goodness! He thought Mr Francois was not going to do much for him if he had this plan of agreement with others to deliver this sewing service, unless he got more sewing machines. His own ideas to help a person in a weaker position than he was made him think of Olga's sewing machine. Would she be able to spare it?

Too early now to return to the house, he thought of Guy who he expected was busy with the Union Men, planning their own actions. What he had pulled himself out from. But his atavistic way, staying away from the main hub of life, would not crack; he was sure where he should stay. However, he decided to pass around and look for Guy at his house. He was out. He went back to his house reluctantly.

He smiled, surprised to see Guy sitting in the living room at the house with Muriel, Hazel and Olga. The cousins were standing in the yard in the fading light of evening. His smile faded at Olga's face. She looked spiritless, her serious sad face looking at Muriel who was talking.

"What happened?" he asked, coming to the group.

They stopped, interrupted. After two beats in time, Guy said, "Two people were murdered on the Square today. My sister who was with the Red Cross there, nearby, said that the killings happened quickly, unforeseen. It seems that three people – a woman, her husband and ex-boyfriend – were getting on well one second. My sister said the woman sat on the knee of her ex-boyfriend. She looked drunk and sang a song that infuriated her husband."

"Did they quarrel?"

"No, apparently not. She said they may have been all drinking, acting happy. She was not far and had got the words of 'The man I love.' You see, she even said it was a favourite song of hers, one of Gershwin's. Never mind all that, it's a tragedy."

"My mother came and told me, before Guy came."

Muriel looked extremely tired, the grey uniform with dustings of flour on the three-quarter sleeves.

"Do you want to go out?" Guy asked Augustus. They went to the parlour where they gave their patronage. Guy paid for their small tipple of good rum, sweet sugar flavour, a tawny colour.

"Dujon found out that the Barbados civil servants will arrive soon, for the British Government to investigate our situation."

"We don't have a chance of receiving money from the cold country; since the war ended they have their own misery, of course."

Augustus expected that Dujon and the others knew what was happening in England as much as he did, but the island was a colony after all.

"It's not the best time to have our problem."

Guy agreed. "I feel like a stranger in my own home. You don't know how crowded we are, it won't be too soon when our guests will get another place to move to. There's even a baby among the families. They are sleeping downstairs and upstairs."

"Since the trouble on the square, this murder, it should be urgent to remove everyone from the Square, I say."

As they walked away in silence, Augustus' mind was on his work. The sugar sales would drop; loss of money for the sugar business. His mood was morose when he got back to the house.

CHAPTER SEVEN

Shac Shac and bongos played in Olga's head since she had taken up the book where Augustus had hurriedly left it, on top of his grip. After she'd sent Era to say goodnight to Muriel in the next room, she stood by the side of the bed looking down at his supine form, and with arched eyebrows, she asked him, "You looking for wisdom?"

"Uh?" He studied her, surprised by the question.

It was her duty. She felt that she had to show her disfavour in this business of his. The fright it had given her, leafing through the pages! A tightness had pressed on her brain. It was the magic of the book she had felt; she had not been untouched even just by looking at its diagrams.

"I think so. Isn't dat why you reading dis strange book?"

She had talked about the book with her mother for clarification. She took a deep breath. "The church says it's a sin to be in a secret society; do you want dat?"

"What?" He sat up. "I'm a free man. I won't be controlled. I can think."

He knocked his head with his palm flat, pressing on his forehead.

"I will keep a clear head."

The atmosphere was heavy around them. He demanded, "What sin? What is sin anyway?"

She was not one for arguments. She sat near to him and spoke quietly. He did not need this at this moment. "You know what is sin. You a Caflik, too!"

"I'm not a baby anymore, it's time to think seriously where I'm going in this Island. There are ways and means of becoming a person who is something in life by understanding some ideas, you know, principles."

He watched her face.

"Well, I don't know!"

She flounced off the bed and headed to the doorway, throwing over her shoulder as she left the room. "People become stupid and *deck-deck* when dey become involved with the Rosicrucians."

Her abrupt exit brought him back to his small room, and as he spoke it was as though there were others in an audience that he was trying to impress.

"Olga, some things are strange only when we don't understand. Right now, this town is a strange place. Is it any wonder that I do something that disturbs you? You married me!"

He did not want this to become a mountain standing between them. His earnest answers surprised her and he knew that she was going to keep on about it. She came back with Era and with a chupse said, "Fings are hard as it is already and will get worse. Do you want a curse fall on you?"

He lay down carefully, not taking too much space, wishing that the night was over.

"Era was saying the Rosary with her Granny and Aunt Hazel."

"Uh huh."

His path seemed clear to him – his responsibility as husband and father, to seek all provisions to aid him and to be accountable in every sense.

* * *

The Sunday clothes lay on the bed. Era's new dress lay with the red satin sash next to it.

Olga got hot water from the kitchen for the ablutions – Era's sponging and her own wash. Silently she mixed the water in the large basin in the yard on an upturned crate. She sent Era upstairs while she attended to herself. Then they hurried to get ready for mass. The minutes flew after that, and though the dress she had made for herself with a matching beret got her a compliment from Augustus from where he stood on the balcony, looking on to Spine Road with some interest, she was conscious that her arms felt heavy and clumsy. She felt all wrong.

As she left the yard into Spine Road, she saw the group of people that Augustus had been observing. They were assembled under a large breadfruit tree not far from Aunt Hazel's. It was obvious that they had formed for a purpose. Three men of different height and build, all young, stood beneath the tree. Children stood bunched close by and there were no women. The men held bibles and were all dressed severely as though this was a portent for everyone. Olga only gave them a quick dismissive glance and walked away to her church. There was sorrow in her heart because of Augustus and what he had said to her, but her smile and lazy carefree walk belied this.

Now that the cousins had almost been dragged into Miss Hazel's forceful well-behaving ways, the women usually sat on the balcony during quiet moments. Muriel sat with them, a company of women. Ma Boy talked about *Lizin* with stories of the stolen children. In the valleys of the cane plantation, children sometimes disappeared, taken for mysterious purposes, and *Lizin* was to be feared. Ma Boy did not talk in a whisper any more.

Aunt Hazel considered her crew – all aboard except Augustus. She was the ship's captain. She did most of the talking. She said she had heard that the Union men would be having a public meeting, open air.

Olga was silent. It was all very well for her Aunt, she had her cooks. Olga experienced unwanted feelings; her unconscious emotions in this time of changes were fed by the mess and destruction around her. The hostility she felt towards her Aunt just then surprised her. That also included Ma George and Ma Boy. She had mentioned to her mother that the cousins monopolised the kitchen, and Muriel, the self-contained person that she was, looked at her saying, "Things will work out; we manage. Customs are hard to break."

Aunt Hazel was still talking about the Union. "I will go to the meeting wherever they keep it. Dujon wants to be elected to the Town Board."

"Who would believe that this town could change as much as that to see Dujon, so brave, to take on these *chabens*!"

Muriel's patois was sharp and acid. She looked at Olga, who looked disengaged looking out on the balcony. The sunset left a bright orange and purple spreading in the western sky, more vivid in colour it seemed to her since the fire.

"Dance Marie, dance!"

* * *

Combing her hair, Olga felt wet. The red spot on the bed where she had sat told her that her little suspicion had no substance. She was disappointed. She sighed. What had happened the night of the Joe Louis fight resulted from the high that Augustus felt because Joe had won. He had been different. It wouldn't do to dwell on it.

In the grip with the few clothes she had saved, she had both old and new diapers. She kept the new ones in readiness as a good luck talisman, for a new baby when the time was right. She had enough for her sanitary use. At least on this count, she was in order.

The night of the fight, his mood was elated and talkative. He had sat her on his thighs and made love to her with ardour – his strict avoidance of intimacy during her fertile periods forgotten.

"I adore you Olga."

She remembered his voice now. He had squeezed next to her on the bed and told her about the fight. His dissipation still lingered, still feeling what he had felt when Joe Louis hit Walcott hard in the eighth round, a knock-out, the men listening with him laughing and jumping in the house where they had come to hear the fight on a radio. "A magnificent effort," Augustus had said to her.

She smiled wryly, contemplating the unease she would have when those towels hang on her Aunt's clothes line. Her state exposed, her intimate life for all to see, and each time Suzi arrived it would be the same thing. Aunt Hazel had surprised her niece, after observing her tense face with, "*Ou pa ans`ent?*"

"*Non! Mw`e pa ansent. Tant tant.*"

Was Aunt Hazel sympathetic? Olga gave her a level look. After taking a long breath, Aunt Hazel comforted her with, "Keep doing your sewing, keep busy; you have to overcome all this."

Did her Aunt know how much she wanted a baby? That Aunt Hazel!

* * *

"Help me to unpick this dress."

Olga had taken a donated dress, a soft fabric of marl with small white dots, and armed with one of Augustus' razor blades, she invited Aunt Hazel to begin the unpicking. They found the stitching, Aunt Hazel pulled the bodice towards her while Olga pulled the skirt end and she snipped the stitches. In a few minutes she had separated the garment and now thought how she would remodel to suit her taste.

The morning was still young.

She moved into the living room with ideas of her dress – a frill in the bodice would be attractive. Or a fat frill in the same cloth down from the neck.

"Bonjou."

The greeting came from the shop and there was talking, voices of women.

"Ay! Ay!" Aunt Hazel exclaimed, "Bondu! What a surprise!"

To Olga their appearance was like water in a desert, in the aftermath of this fire. They were muscular women in pale blue or pink simple dresses, with broad brimmed straw hats on their heads. Augustus' mother and female relations stood in front of the counter where they had rested their two round baskets. In them Olga saw *topi tambu,* manioc farine, plantain, Okro, limes and cassava cakes.

She smiled.

"Augustus is out. I don't know where he went."

They had walked the seven miles from Anse Chabon; she looked in amazement at her mother-in-law. It was some years now since she had stopped walking to town to sell food at the market but today she had done it. Aunt Hazel closed her shop.

"We are grateful," She said in patois. "Oh my, I must see to the lunch with my cousins, Olga come."

The women sat themselves down politely, hats off, shoes off, as they drank cool water from the carafe.

They ate at one thirty and left for the market to meet others who had brought food for hopeful sales. They said they would return before going back to the village.

"I wish Augustus had been there to greet his mother! I'll go to see if I can meet him, I must find him. I don't know where to start."

But she headed for Mr Polius' house. First call. She was relieved her decision was the right one. He was the only visitor at his ex-teacher's house. She apologised and then told him the news.

When they moved toward the market, he asked, "How did she look? She has some heart palpitations, she should not have come."

"She was tired but she not looking sick," she said truthfully.

Mrs James saw her son appear in the market, she got up from the wooden bench to greet him. The spaciousness and cleanliness with long rows of concrete slabs for the vendors' food for sale was an appreciative sight in contrast to the streets of town.

"I must take you all back to the house, I know you are ready. I'm so happy to see all of you," he said in English.

As they walked to Aunt Hazel's house, he explained how the fire had begun. They heard the emotion of sadness in his voice, in their view the empty eye sockets of buildings stared blindly at them as he identified the people no longer in those houses.

They stayed till five o'clock, rested. They made their goodbyes, Mrs James saying she was happy that they were alright. She shook

Aunt Hazel's hand, kissed Olga and Era and shook her son's hand. The group made their way up the road, their large brim hats shading their eyes on the long walk. The cousins joined in and stayed watching till their pink and blue dresses were no longer visible on the long Spine Road.

With the departure of the country people, the house settled down. The dullness returned in the sitting room where they sat. Just the women. Ma George talked, her voice just above the whisper; Ma Boy tipped her face towards her. Olga thought back to her childhood when she and her mother lived in the house with Aunt Hazel. She thought of the men. Now their faces became dim to Olga. Victor, Aunt Hazel's lover, and Mr Bonnet playing piano music were hazy. Mr Bonnet, his face elusive except for his bronze colour: a Chaben man, his hair the colour of coconut fibre which matched his complexion that was a few shades lighter. Very straight-backed, his tall spare body wearing trousers with patches. He played the piano, beautiful music. She remembered Victor asking him to play 'Moonlight Sonata', and that was the evening she remembered.

The feeling of delight she had experienced came over her again. She arose and moved upstairs to find Augustus. He saw the smile transform her face, the hand toward him. He shook himself awake, not quite sure what had happened to her to cause that bright expression. She told him about that night from all these years back and suddenly he saw another aspect of his wife. Her round flat face, the long sloping eyes and bow-shaped lips. He loved this woman beyond his ideas of what "the wife" meant. It was she, nothing to do with being married. How could he tell her? But he said nothing, just held the hand she offered him. She leaned against his side while looking out on to the street, the darkness deepening.

He spoke. "It will be months like this. No shower, no proper place to sleep."

She was silent.

Augustus broke the silence. "I went to see Mr Francois about him making me some pants. If you saw the amount of extra cloth in his shop that he was given after the fire. He needs another machine."

"I need mine. I have to make clothes for Era, my mother and myself, and shirts for you."

More silence. Then Augustus: "I'll be going up to the estate tomorrow to talk to my boss. I have to explain that I have to change this two to ten shift. I cannot do it right now. Cyril will be going up there too."

CHAPTER EIGHT

The baking hot sun stung her arms and legs. It was mid-July. She had been in Aunt Hazel's all enclosed yard, washing her Aunt's and her own family things, pleased now that she had hung them on the two wire lines at the back of the kitchen.

Time seemed to drag. She could hear Ma George's voice. Since the old women had stopped being nervous and found their own voices she had felt amused by this two-toned voice interplay – a low contralto suddenly changing to high trembling quavers. It made Olga want to listen to them if only as a distraction.

At the moment, her urge to do more work to expend all that spurt of energy she felt was new in these series of despairing thoughts that had seized her more often than not.

Ma George had gone out and returned with Dorado. It was almost a miracle that every day there was food cooked and deliciously flavoured by her hand and Ma Boy's, but Ma George was the forceful one. The cousins talked to Olga politely with some deference and she wished that they did not. There was no need for almost bowing before her but this was preferable to their old hush-hush behaviour.

"I am going to scrub inside the house," she told them.

She used to scrub her wooden floor in her house. Aunt Hazel's floor had been polished but she felt it looked dirty. To her dismay her Aunt did not want the floor scrubbed.

"Alright Aunty, I'll scrub the stairs."

That energy she felt bursting out of her would not be denied and so she started bringing into the day the sound of the brush bristles on the wood. She bent with determination, back and forth with the rag drying up, and was satisfied to see the gleam of the pale brown wood afterwards. She was exhausted but was not done. As she considered other business, she changed her dress and arranged her hair – parted in the centre, and her two plaits made a tiara as she pinned them up. Augustus' account of Mr Francois' shop had made her curious. She would go to see for herself and ask him how soon Augustus' trousers would be ready.

Aunt Hazel heard Olga saying that she would be back shortly. It was eleven.

The tailor's house was within fifteen minutes' walk, but she was thwarted in her aim because as she approached the tailor's house, a white two-storey building, she saw that in the green-framed doorway there was an obstruction. She had been walking along a wide road which led to the reservoir and verdant lands. She stood opposite the house. A small canal stood between them and she would have to go round a corner. The obstruction wore a black cap with a shiny black peak on the large head, and the large uniformed frame took up the whole doorway.

Philosophe had got there before her. There was no point now to continue with the visit; he would be in there for some time.

When he had visited her Aunt's shop, Sergeant Paine had spent quite a while with his insinuations and innuendos, annoying her Aunt. She turned around thoughtfully, and made up her mind to visit the school hall where relief goods were handed out. Many people were there. She took a seat, observed the Red Cross women giving out items. This had not been her plan and for this reason her head ached. She imagined a waterfall from high up tumbling from a rock, bathing and comforting her. She decided to leave and return the next day, better to return to eat something at their shelter.

To her it felt that she had awoken from a long sleep. Perhaps she might be allowed to do the cooking next day and feel some connection to a life as it should be lived, even in these hard times.

Her lunch was kept. She ate it quietly, sitting in the yard and in the company of Era who hang about. Olga glanced towards her daughter, observing that she too showed signs of restlessness. She went towards the gate and back and forth, then she opened the gate and stood in its entrance staring at the lane. Olga called to her that she would take her to the Gardens.

"Do you want to go and play in the Gardens?"

"When?"

"Now. Let's change your dress."

Emerald green trimmed grass covered one side of the well-kept garden. The children's merry-go-round, the swing and the slide stood out in a far corner below a ridge of brown earth. Olga sat in the round, pink summer house which itself resembled a merry-go-round. She watched Era go towards the group of unattended children. The child threw herself about and tackled the six-foot slide unreservedly.

Now she thought that her daughter would be growing up in a different world with new things, and it looked like big changes if the Union men had any say in matters. Now the Impresario of the Times had thrown a dice in the town to make people go different ways. She pondered, "Would Augustus decide to move to his village now?" She preferred the town and so did he. Era was running towards her.

"Oh, look at you! Your dress so dirty! We are going home now."

They passed beneath the large tree with overhanging swathes of tiny leaves and yellow pokes, walked on towards reclaimed open land close to the sea, saw canoes on the pebbled beach near the harbour. Walking past the burnt streets, she saw patches of new grass; nature threw up this surprise, and she gazed at it in wonder. Then she saw that old Mr Rawlins, who had lost his business, his goldsmith shop, had set up a table on a sidewalk on the western side of the 'People's Square'. He grinned at her as she passed. Rawlins and Sons had made a start so people could pawn their jewellery for cash. This sight pulled at one of the strings of pain. She had lost her own chain, bracelets, Era's earrings, her mother's chain. She said chupse and tried to dismiss the despair trying to engulf her again.

Dance Marie, dance!

* * *

"Ay, Ay *tant tant,* how come dese clothes are on my bed, where did they come from?"

Olga caught her breath in surprise at the sight of dresses left on her small bed. With eyebrows raised, she enquired of Aunt Hazel.

"From Gustus and Guy. Dey gone for a sea bath now."

Olga smiled, saying softly, "Well, well, well!"

She had to think what to do with the clothes, trying two that she liked. Era looked on, eyes unblinking and she stood very still. She wondered where were the small dresses?

After Olga folded the dresses she said, "Come, let's go and see Aunt Hazel."

Guy and Augustus walked on the long tarmac road in the dry warm air along the beach front. On their left a long wire fence enclosed the airport, and on the right the sea lapped on the sand away from the line of almond trees. A Pan American plane had just come in. They moved close to the wire fence to watch. Unexpectedly, Mr Popo descended the steps in the company of the servicemen as if he was part of a set-up there. Augustus said with some puzzlement in his voice, "I wonder whether he went to beg for relief food on behalf of the Town Board?"

They waited.

"There's a jeep over there by the almond trees, did you see it?" Guy pointed behind them.

"Either the G.I. men will be going to Anse Du Fort to their air base or they will be helping us in the town."

Mr Popo now came out of the gate, carrying a briefcase. He wore the usual small brim black hat and carrying also the rolled up long black umbrella, using it as a walking cane in the most stylish manner. Moving nearer to the jeep, Augustus felt that he could make eye contact with Mr Popo as he passed to let him know that he had been observed. He, the ex-manager of the People's Bank, had some answers to give the people of the town. And when it was not clear at all, up to the present time, if the money had been saved. Even though it was safe, Augustus felt that as a good citizen, it meant using restraint and being selfless, even though it was as comfortable to him as eating cold porridge to be facing poverty; it would not be right to go and demand his savings.

"Did the Union men know that he had gone to America? Had you heard about it?"

Augustus broke the silence.

"Yeah."

Dujon was aware of that and he quarrelled against the movement of business at the Town Board.

"I suppose now he's back, we must learn what's happening."

"I'll keep my ears open. I'm as surprised by what I just saw."

The men in khaki drove off in the jeep with Mr Popo. Augustus and Guy moved toward the almond and the pink Fat Poke trees to strip off and plunge into the tepid water. The sun was low on the horizon. Lots of pale golden light touched on the shore. The white of the foam took on a hue of gold.

Augustus could not let the picture of Popo go. Him getting off from the plane and holding this leather business bag! This held huge significance of a plot.

All the way down to town he wondered about that trip to America. Guy and Augustus parted company at the junction of Market Street and Spine Road. Augustus continued southwards.

At Aunt Hazel's, Olga moved away from the sewing machine where she had stood, not quite in the sewing mood. Muriel eyed her daughter; saw the restlessness. Olga moved into the yard and entered the kitchen. Conversation came from that quarter. Muriel caught the pitch of one voice, Olga's, in short phrases, who then returned to sit by the table with Muriel. She said to her mother, "You must be tired. I see Ma Boy making bakes."

After a pause she continued, "Gustus went for his sea bath."

Muriel nodded and Olga, short of conversation, said, "I just put water to boil for tea."

Earlier Muriel had tried on a pair of the shoes given to them by the Red Cross; she had grimaced as she worked her feet in with a 'Voop' sound. She stood in the laced-up black leather, rounded tip shoes, raised at the heel half an inch from the floor. Now Olga said to her, "At least you have a pair of shoes that fit."

"Even if dey fit me, I cannot move about in dem. All da standin I do, O prefer the sandal that Hazel gave me. It O.K. Even for church. Now, Olga, you know somefing, da new cook is a teef. I saw her, I gave her one eye! She know I saw her."

"What she take uh?"

"I see she put crème of wheat and flour from da store chest in her basket."

"You see her?"

"So, she put dem back; all shame and smilin'. If she steal when I don't see and if da priests find out, dey might even fink it's me. Time's strange now. Nobody finks in the old way."

"You worried?"

"Yes. Very worried. And also I don't know about my savings dat was in da bank."

* * *

Augustus left after seven in the morning for Anse Chabon. Olga awoke early too and lay on the small bed, waiting for the action mood to fall upon her. Era slept on. The words and tune of the song "Skylark" came back to her while blue shadows installed themselves behind her shut eyelids. She held her palms flat against them to shut out the daylight seeping in, slightly bright, from under the closed door. Finally, she arose and opened the jalousies. It was Sunday morning, after all. She shook Era awake. They would have to hurry to make it to the eight o'clock mass. Half hour was all they needed to pull on their clothes and be gone.

Era's arms and neck would not be adorned with her bracelets and chain. This hurt she felt anew was the result of the goldsmith whom she had seen at his table by the Square looking for business, offering money in exchange for jewellery. She would not have parted with hers no matter what, but having the fire snatch them from her, *Ah ya yi!* she thought. She may now have to wait for years to have her earrings, chains and bracelets replaced.

After she had quickly uncoiled the small rounds of her twisted hair and combed all the hair back into one coil which she secured with some hairpins, she attended to Era's hair, holding her between her knees by the bedside. She opened her plaits and now made them fresh, one towards her forehead and two at the back. They barely reached the nape of her daughter's neck. They should swap hair and so be a true one thing not half one thing and another – Era fair with wiry hair, and herself black with silken hair.

Olga flew downstairs and up again, carrying water in a basin and the dresses they would wear. Her mother came out of the bedroom as she was rushing down the stairs, saying she had slept longer than she had intended and would go to the eleven o'clock mass.

Very shortly, Olga led Era out of the house, walking very briskly to arrive before the Gospel.

Augustus' journey would take him on a long flat road north of Masav. After he climbed the Darling Hill, he was able to reset his steps and walk in his usual short, quick busy fashion. He covered the first two miles in half an hour. Then, he could see the sea on his left where there were no houses. It glittered silver beyond the grass and trees. The sun was to his right, rising quickly over the houses and vegetation on the sloping land.

As he navigated through these vistas, some invisible finger kept prodding him as he tried to make sense of these scenes of past experiences, to make these past portals the openings to find his secret self. His true self.

The awareness of the importance of his attachment to Mr Polius as his surrogate father was reinforced by the experiences of his school days as a boarder – not feeling quite at home with the family he was placed with. But when his problems started both Guy and Mr Polius had helped him stay afloat.

When months moved into years football made him some friends, but he had never stopped being grateful to his English Literature master and the way he had absorbed many of the man's expressions and words and made them his own.

The sun was pleasant very far overhead, very warm only, not yet reaching him with the punishing mid-day strokes. After two hours he found the trail between the grassy verges on his left that led to the beach. Later on as he walked it would be quite difficult to find the beach through all the trees that would line the road all the way.

He stood on white fine sand. Close by, the vacated American Base still remained with the empty pitch pine building. He undressed and ran into the water in his drawers. Close by, a small group of boys ran a race on the beach. He swam quickly, floating on his back, not forgetting his mission. He had a cold thought. This morning – this visit to the country – was he escaping from the life he worried over? He was due back at work tomorrow for the six a.m. shift. How could he do that? He had no idea. There was no transport to take people to town. Usually when he visited anytime, he would rent a canoe and row up the coast and now he did not even have the bicycle. He indulged in the sharp coldness of the sea and finally set himself back on the road, shoes and pants in his hands and allowing the wet drawers to dry on him as he walked.

He was greeted and he greeted other men about their business. In the countryside, barefoot was the norm and so he felt at home, no different from those he met. Sometimes, a man would leave the road, carrying his cutlass, to disappear into the land among the many trees or others, accompanied by a dog, moving along, coming out from one path and going into a different path. Augustus suspected that they were hunting animals to get meat; a manicou was what some people put in their cooking pot.

All the land was green with coconut trees, left and right of the road. There were mango trees, and in their midst were African tulip trees, very large trees with big red, glove-like flowers. In the distance, other big red flame trees mingled with the greenness.

He was approaching Anse Chabon and he could see the sea again, he could smell it. Everything was peaceful. His village was a sleepy place, except in August when the La Rose festival brought music, drama and dancing. The Rose Society meant so much to his own mother who had a love for the concerts they performed in August, which were about situations that gave laughter, scenes involving judicial cases, Kings and queens and making speeches. His mother had her turn of playing Queen of La Rose, he remembers.

It was the words of his Mother that he suddenly remembered as he approached the village, words of wisdom given to him when he left for his education in Masav: "We are not like the town people. We have our own brains. We know the tricks of the aristocrats who do not live among us: thank God."

It was starting to feel very hot and he was glad he was going to sit and rest. He put on his pants and his shoes as he got to the un-pitched entrance into the village, houses on either side, pale blue and pale green, small two roomed or one roomed homes. The hibiscus and zenia flowers were surrounded by white lime-wash stones in front of the houses – yellow, orange, pink and red flowers were in front of some houses. A bird with chunky yellow scoops of a beak lay into a pawpaw in the tree, scooping out the flame-colour flesh. The humming birds hovered, sucking from the hibiscus flowers, their vivid green tiny bodies still while the wings whirred around. He stepped confidently on the sand-coloured ground.

"*Bonjou!*" he heard.

An old man sat on the doorstep of the one room, shingle house. Augustus nodded and waved to him. "Good day." People were at church, which accounted for the lack of movement but there were small children's voices coming to him. Someone was playing on a harmonica. He turned right. Someone collected water from the standpipe, another leaned out of her window; he nodded his head politely. His relatives lived close to his parents away from the three roads and he walked quickly to get there in the shade of trees.

He arrived within the family compound the same time as his father, the older man soberly dressed in a black suit, coming from the eleven o' clock mass in the chapel. He stopped abruptly facing Augustus.

"I had you in mind, you wouldn't believe it."

They shook hands and continued the next few steps to the house, a two-roomed shingle house in pale blue.

"Mam!" Augustus greeted his mother.

She bent over a griddle on a stone and charcoal fire cooking cassava biscuits.

"*Ish mwe.*"

She came towards him and embraced him. The surprise to see him, the look of him, showed her delight. She had to ask how he came; did he take a canoe? Hearing his answer she shook her head, not that she felt he should not have walked but knowing about the loss of the bicycle.

He entered the house, sat down heavily, remaining silent while having a drink of water he'd poured himself from a jug on the table. There was always water in a jug, this way he remembered. His father's face showed concern as he sat facing him.

"Papa what will I do? It's hopeless for me."

"You went to work yet?"

"I should go back tomorrow."

The bemused look on Augustus' face said it all. He heard, "It looks like all our beliefs will make you stronger, even though you have to change your course of action."

"What action do you mean? I will have to jostle with everyone constantly! I was not like this!"

"Yes, your ways were quiet, part of the nature you adopted when you went to live in town."

Augustus stretched his legs. He said, "I need to lie down for a while."

He stood up and walked to the door, smiling at his mother.

"I told your sister you come," she said in patois. He nodded.

"I'll have a few minutes' rest. I'll get up in a little while."

His father and mother exchanged a few words; they spoke quietly. It was not unusual for him to visit unexpectedly in different circumstances.

The one big bed in the one bedroom house served the purpose. He closed his eyes. A reason he came today was to take a little food back to town for Aunt Hazel. He did not relish the walk back.

At the four houses nearby at his mother's relations the people heard that he had come. He heard sounds from the open window, he lay down there – his limbs felt like elasticised parts, stretching, recoiling and stretching – thinking what was he to do! He thought that he should return to town that night with what food he could collect from the food gardens. His mother called from the doorway. "Carmen is cooking the food for us; she'll call when it's ready." He heard children's voices in the next room. They sounded like his sister's boys. Carmen was his elder sister. He waited for the return of his legs determined, controlled tonality; until then he kept lying down, hearing the life sounds outside.

Later his father came into the room. "We will go to Carmen to eat now. You ready?"

"Yes I'm coming; I was thinking, I should return tonight. My rest has been fine."

Between the houses bush grew tall, some were for medicines but guavas and lime trees were also prized crops. The round green guavas were ready for picking. White light made him squint. Marcel, a tiny dark, wiry man arrived; he'd been mending his fishing nets, ready to go out later in the boat for an evening catch.

"So, Carmen," Augustus asked "When's this baby due?"

"I'm five months now"

The business in hand had to be dealt with and when his father took him round to the distant relatives after they had eaten, on the route, boys, including Carmen's, whipped their bicycle tyre rims with long sticks and ran down the path behind them.

The older man had exchanged his town life for the country style. The people were not always jocund but were able to become that way much more readily than town people. That was how it was and the old man behaved that way as he entered the house of the cousins on his wife's side. Augustus had left all that behind so long ago that he could not even be that way for a short while and appeared as a foreigner among them.

They were laden with vegetables and sweet potatoes, which Augustus was grateful for. There was still the food he meant to collect from his parents' garden and some charcoal his father would give to him.

"I wonder if, I was only thinking, Menal is a man with a horse and cart. He takes flour some mornings to a baker in the town; I'll go and look for him. If he's going down tomorrow, I'll ask him to take you."

"Do I know him?"

"No. He used to be in Venezuela and returned three years ago, he used to bring coals to town and other things for small shops."

"Flour? Where does he get it to sell to the baker?"

"He gets it somewhere. Now since the fire he seems to be trying to supply more little bits to people in Masav."

"So I'll come with you. I have to be in town for five in time for the six o'clock shift."

Suddenly his churning emotions turned into a gulping sob. His shoulders shook. He stopped, his sack of food hanging down; tears ran down his face. He made an effort to control himself.

"What shall I do? I thought I was getting where I wanted to get to in life this year."

"Keep your head my boy." A strong hand gripped his son's shoulder. "If Menal is not going down tomorrow what will you do?"

Augustus was silent. He felt such apathy about the whole thing but he thought he would return in the night if he had to.

Away from the women, now able to show this wounded self, he swallowed the lump in his throat and his hand went up to dry his face. They stood on bare earth close to a cluster of banana trees and were on the way to a clearing towards their house.

* * *

This morning on the square, the Sampson family, among the throng on the People's Square, were the centre of attention. The wife watched warily as he came. He ignored her but that was not unusual. He appeared to have lost his speech since the fire. He had been absent during the days, hanging about, silent. He had not been able to say where he had been the night of the fire. He was in a bilious mood. He said loudly that he had come to take Betty to the new church under the breadfruit tree. He only spoke to Betty, the youngest daughter.

She said, "Your daughter is Catholic."

"I want her to become a Christian."

He ground his teeth. Betty looked indifferent so he took her arm.

"You are coming with me to the Church of God. You hear? Adora did not even tell her father she was going to Barbados." He pointed to his wife and said, "You are the cause of it. You told her to get a passage and go away. I know it!"

She threw herself at him; this stirred the placid Sunday morning air. People gathered near, anxious for the small scrunched up woman after the last tragedy on the Square.

"Vous parlez betise. Vous etes sot! Comprennez?"

"You can go back to Cayenne."

She insisted that if he wanted to be a Christian that he should go but leave them alone. She questioned him about where he had been the night of the fire. Another woman, most likely! Defiant, she was standing, fists tight, neck elongated and eyes cutting him down. Her anger was getting the better of her, her restrained anger from the night of the fire when he had not been around finally surfacing. He had not cared one bit about the disaster, she announced. And this morning, at last, even though he started to talk again he was talking pure stupidness.

Still holding on to Betty, Mr Sampson was equally determined.

"Come Betty."

She went because she knew, as of old, when her father is determined, nothing stops him.

Maryse Sampson felt the blood drumming in her ears, felt someone's arm around her, calming her.

As she began to settle down into a more comfortable and calming demeanour, she thought of the people who stood by the side of the road and called themselves a church. Since the fire, some men had come around and invited whoever wanted to join them. What she could not understand was that there was a perfectly good church there! She pointed her finger across the street to the white squat building where she would be going to the eleven o'clock high mass and put candles before the Sacred Heart.

Her husband joined the group of well-dressed men with their bibles. They handed him one; each would take turns to read a section chosen by the leader of that new gathering. Their children stood quietly under the large leaf tree in a clearing by the roadside. There was no singing.

Olga could not believe her eyes. She saw them and felt a pang of pity for Betty who it seemed was embarrassed to be standing there among them. She wondered why there were no women in the gathering. She would have to tell Augustus about that.

With half her mind here in the house and the other half occupied by Augustus' absence she let the hours pass, doing first this thing and then that. It had been refreshing to go to the gardens with Boo and her children mostly for Era's benefit. Now the evening stretched. While she sewed, pedalling with her back arched over the machine, Era sat next to her. She decided to be entertaining for the child's sake and she told her the story that she had liked as a child.

"Do you know dat people are changed by magic? Long ago these things happened. Dis little girl had a way of talking to a special big fish in da river near her home. She went to da river sometimes and sang her special magic song: 'A la voila voye Giwa mute veni, a la voila voye Giwa mute vini'.

"Her fish appeared and she fed it. It played about on da surface and then disappeared. It was a big river down da coast. One day the girl's step sister said to the mother, 'My sister have a big feesh, we could catch eet to eat, we so hungry.'

"The mother was going to make her daughter sing the song and so, they went one day. They caught and killed the fish, took it home and cooked it. You know what happened? Da girl went to feed her fish the next day; she sang and she sang; she spent hours waiting. No fish come up to her. When she went home, crying, she would not eat.

"Her wicked step sister told her that the mother had killed the fish for their food. So, da little girl went to the pasture where cows were tied. She stood in front a cow with one horn and sang 'Bef an kon, u sa mange mwe, u sa sa la la mwe.'

"But da cow sent her to da cow with two horns. Again she sang, 'Bef de kon, u sa mange mwe, u sa la la mwe.'

"She was crying, she asked the cow to butt her, she did not care what happened to her, she was so sad."

Olga stopped and looked at Era, whose mouth made a silent O, her slanting eyes squished almost to two slits in her banana-yellow face. Olga pedalled on, keeping her eye on the cloth, and she continued the story.

"The cow sent her to another cow, the one with three horns. She sang in front of it, "Bef twa kon, u sa mange, e-e-e-e ..." She never finished her song because it picked her up on the three horns and tossed her in the air. She fell back down to the ground as a lot of flour, white flour and that is why we have flour today."

Olga finished her story. She cut the thread from the dress and looked again at Era, she was smiling and waited to see Era smile too. It came. The child did not think that this was the whole story, she waited expectantly, but that was it.

Olga rose from her chair. Era ran upstairs. She wanted to get the mirror which had been left on the bed, it was shaped like the brush her mother used – a long handle on the square body. She did not want to be disturbed and, as no one was on the balcony, she lay down. She put her face at an angle so all she saw in the glass was a space far below and she was falling, falling into that space, just like falling into Aunt Hazel's bed the night her father carried her through the streets, half asleep, and then she was dropped hurriedly into softness, engulfed by warmth and oblivion.

Just then, she heard footsteps coming from the corridor to the balcony. She stood up and saw her mother, Aunt Hazel and her grandmother come through and they glanced over into the street.

"It's getting really late, he should have returned by now. He said he would be back around this time."

Olga dropped the words into the air. She'd had every confidence in his promise, though he had not walked up to the village in years, but he used to do so three times a week while he courted her, before he got his bicycle. And he liked exercise. What she worried about was that he said he would bring some food back, walking; so how was he getting on? She asked that question of the women.

"It is still early," Muriel answered. "Nothing you can do, don't worry."

Era marched up and down. Olga suddenly became aware of her. "Put dat mirror back before you cause it to break, you hear!"

She turned back to the street and craned her neck in the direction of the Gardens in the distance and she chupsed. "What's da time Aunt Hazel?"

Her Aunt left to check the time in her room, and Olga said quietly to Muriel, "I knew dat since he started reading dat Rosicrucian book anything could happen with him!"

His face rose before her eyes. The face of a hard firm line, tobacco brown, thin moustache, long nose bridge and flattened nostrils. His prominent eyes, always either dreamy or thoughtful when he looked her way, which told her that there was lots going on in there that she knew nothing of.

"It's half past six," she said in patois. "I'm going to lie down," she heard Aunt Hazel say.

"I'm going for a walk along the road, I might meet him coming," Olga said, and to Era, "Stay with Granny."

Muriel went downstairs. She lit the lamp, kissed Era and went into the kitchen to light a fire and to boil some water. The child moved into the yard where the darkness had descended, but she felt her way on the smooth stones, walking in a circle, her arms extended. Looking in the gloom, she heard the sounds of the grandmother's activity.

"What you doing chile?" Muriel brought her back to reality.

She remembered her father and she sighed as Olga returned with a deep frown and a pout, her hair still in the style she had worn for church in the morning, the curls of her ponytail still held.

She suggested that Olga should do some hand sewing to make her waiting less tedious.

"If it's nine o'clock and he don't come yet, I expect him to come in the morning," she said in patois.

Olga moved into the house while Muriel opened tins of sardines for supper.

Ma Boy, Ma George and Aunt Hazel joined her in the drawing room. Olga's mind was occupied and she did not join in their conversation after she had finished sewing and after eating the supper. She got Era ready for bed, left a candle lit and moved to the balcony. With the darkness now a profound dark blanket that covered everything, if he was coming down Spine Road he would be invisible till he got under her direct vision.

She felt Era come close to her. The child moved from one foot to the other, the anxiety of the child was like sticks hitting a drum, one beat followed by another in slow tempo.

"Be still!" she said to her. "O.K. I'll come and lie down with you. Come on."

Eventually, she left Era and returned downstairs to meet the others who were staying up later than usual to wait for Augustus' return, until at ten o'clock they all said goodnight to Olga and she made her way to the bedroom with Era. Her eyes did not close for long periods. Era spoke in her sleep, and Olga felt guilty. It was surprising to hear Era's dream that seemed to trouble her.

"Suppose Papa change to flour. Da cows might butt him, cows dangerous," she whimpered.

She shook the child and moved closer to her on the narrow bed, rubbing her back.

With the hint of dawn as she peeped through the jalousie, she went on to the balcony, unprepared for the sight of horse and cart on the street. She quickly went through the side door and into the lane by Spine Road as Augustus swung his legs over the side of the cart, saying his thanks to the man holding the horse reins, not a very common experience in that town for years now. Her mouth was open. She folded her arms across her chest and managed a smile in reply to his.

"Here I am. Now, I have to meet Cyril in a few minutes."

Of course, he had to get off to work. She saw the two jute bags bulging with provisions.

Back at work, the noise on the estate had cut through him viciously after only the few weeks' absence, but he had welcomed being busy and resuming everything. Now, he wanted to back Olga against the small bed and embrace her, but Era was asleep already. She watched him, sensing his mood, a playful mood. He smelt of sweat and she left him, then she returned with the large enamel jug and a basin. They settled on the rough red blanket on the floor. She clung to him. A refrain of a song with the day's closing notes made an arpeggio and ended as they wished it to. She had given him the news of Sampson, the image of him with these other sorts of people standing by the side of the road reading the bible, and accompanied by his daughter! What would become of that family?

Everything seemed to have been different in Sampson's view when he had not been accepted in the Masav Men's Club. He had wanted to change the world. And the song he was heard singing from his own home sometimes: "Come down I tell you, come down! With your boots and stockings – come down!" Now Augustus remembered it, but lost it again as Olga kept on talking. She surprised him, saying that she was considering lending Mr Francois her sewing machine, taking up his idea that he would get on with his clothes – making items much faster. It would be only for a short period. She would make some arrangement with him, she told Augustus.

It surprised him. Although he had thought of it, he did not know how it happened that she had considered the affair of Mr Francois as quickly as that. Now they were in one mind about that and she was giving the future serious thoughts, he hoped that it would be the right thing to do.

And in the morning, she started the new day with new ideas.

CHAPTER NINE

Sergeant Paine – Philosophe – knew what they, people in town, called him. A man who had no grievance with Benedictians, even their patois; learning to speak it and to make a bridge over that wide chasm. But still, they referred to him as Philosophe with a smirk, as he fell short and off the mark even as his confidence was ever on show. He made out as if everything and every situation was under his control. He patrolled the streets with the aid of his wide, deep memory for events and people.

He was tired since the fire. He smelt something new in the police barracks. His Colonel cracked the whip at the corporals as if he had a new mission. The force was small and now they were waiting for the arrival of some police from Trinidad and Dominica. The Barbadians were not willing to come to an Island with so much French patois. It was a preference that the local men had to join the police band.

The five local men were close to the Colonel, Philosophe knew what their plan was.

He had to visit a large number of addresses this week to check on stories about misdemeanours. He sat down at the desk, going through the addresses even as he caught the frisson. Two to stay in the building and three to go on the beat. Was it because more police were due to arrive that the man called Colonel thought he was an Inspector and the most senior in the force with no superintendent?

Their plan was to set up a Lodge just for policemen as there were for the Odd Fellows, the Pegasus, The Star of the Sea lodges for other people in the island. He, a Guyanese, had no wish to be included. With his fifteen years on the island, he felt strong enough in his own skills even though there was some justification for wanting to set up such a lodge – to improve their efficiency in solving crimes and bringing people to justice.

He left the station. Sergeant Paine decided to walk along the north wharf and talk with the old man who rented out canoes and who was always in the mood for gossip. Then these words, displeasing to his ears, interrupted this conversation: "All police are dogs." He turned and saw the speaker of those words.

"No respect," he muttered.

Those sort of boys had no decent parents and roamed the streets. They did not even go to school. They mostly lived about the wharf looking for what they could beg or steal from the sailors. He forgot them almost immediately.

Four brightly coloured canoes were beached on the very dark sand. Lots of boats in the sea. What was going on, he wondered? Two schooners! One warship! He stood in front of the board advertising 'Denbows' Canoe Rental'. He had seen Philosophe cross from the road towards him.

"Morning Sarge"

Philosophe was witty. He listened to the line of conversation of the man as he engaged him in the conversation concerning the happenings on the wharf. What was happening with the boats?

"Well, the warship arrived last night and today the two boats came in. I don't know yet what's happening or if they brought goods!"

He shrugged his shoulders.

"I have not had the information about this warship. It's all very quiet. In a short while I'm sure I will know about these schooners."

Sergeant fixed his eyes on the vessels; no movement from over there. He said, "I'll be off, I have to see to other business. Bonjou."

All around the large semi-circle of Masav in the little yards like his own, people wrested an elemental life from meagre amenities. He had visited all of them over the years. Off Spine Road there was more space around the homes near Miss Hazel's, with the long lane to one side, but behind her fenced yard were other enclosures for privacy. He mopped his face as he entered Miss Hazel's shop.

"How are you, Miss Hazel?"

"Well, thank you."

"Is Augustus here? Poor boy, I have not yet had time to talk to him."

They spoke in patois. Augustus had not long got in. He overheard Philosophe and joined them standing behind the glass counter. The policeman regarded him with respect. A man of all weathers like himself. He'd seen him cycle in rain and sun going up the Morne. Could do with somebody like him in the force: stamina was what they needed.

"How friendly were you with Clifford?" he asked. "Do you know where he is at present? We are sure there are people who wanted a fire in Masav."

He had his notebook in readiness for any information he would receive.

"I'm just as wise as you are in all this."

"So, you saw the fire, and woke everyone – all the neighbours?"

"I had not seen Clifford that day and not since the fire either."

Augustus knew Clifford's style and social habits but the family did not belong to Masav. He watched Philosophe chew on those words, and feeling mischievous he continued, "I don't know whether Clifford's crab traps were the cause of the fire."

Philosophe laughed heartily. "Ay, Ay! What next!"

"Come, come Sergeant. I'm telling you all I know. I'm mystified about the source of this fire."

Then, as the man looked lost in his own thoughts, Augustus moved away, lost also in his own thoughts.

Miss Hazel eyed him suspiciously. She asked him, "Was there a reason why anyone should start a fire? A fire could start so easily from inside a house. The man could have been careless. The tailor, he did not sleep in the shop. I heard that it was his iron."

"You will have to ask Clifford, I think."

He felt comfortable standing there, smiling at her. She could be a distant relative. She resembled some of his people in Guyana and he never passed the shop without stopping for a chat for a short while, and today was no different. He would have to move on. She stood up, her great tall body almost as tall as his own, and she smiled pleasantly, saying she would close the shop for lunch.

He had much to do back at the station. The rat that he smelt included the 'Colonel' that wanted that Lodge. He was not satisfied with the status of the police force or that people had made derogatory comments about it. Sergeant Paine had put his foot in it a few days previously by saying that he himself would make a better job of the training of the men that came into the force. That was to the annoyance of the 'Colonel' who had heard him having his say.

'Dance Marie, dance!'

He was now on his way to talk with the night watchman of the People's Bank. If thieves had to be rounded up, what had he seen that night? Things were slippery there. He tapped lightly on the shuttered blue house. A woman with a goitre opened the door just a little. "Who d`e?"

He said he wanted a word with her husband. She opened the door very wide then. He asked, "Where's your husband?"

He turned sharply around on hearing, "Something on the captain's head, nobody knows, nobody sees." A multi-coloured parrot was perched on a chair, looking at the startled policeman who moved to the opposite side of the room.

"My husband lying down wi, sid down; I'll call him, boss", the woman said nervously.

She came back followed by Mano, a very serious-looking man.

The wife opened her palms wide. "Every day, he say da same words and he don't say nuffing else."

As far as Philosophe was concerned, he could see that something had frightened the man. He pressed him with, "What did you see during the fire, Mr Fred?"

Silence. Even though he opened his mouth, no words were uttered, to the policeman's disbelief. It was truly one of the occasions that he felt that he was at a loss. He said goodbye to the wife, a frown on his large face. To his departing back the wife muttered, "Goats give a dance – sheep get drunk."

He felt the piping hot sun, and it felt like he himself was being punished for what he did not know. He wondered about Fred; had he made a deal with someone about the money in the bank? Who was in collaboration with him, what had happened to the money? Next, he made his way to Mr Francois' tailor shop. Much was going on there. All the windows of the white building had been flung wide open. Four men were in the large room. Trousers and jackets were displayed on the walls. He took on an attacking pose like a flying cockroach.

"I have no grounds for suspecting you personally, Francois."

George laughed, "Ha, ha. That's what's bothering you; I think you might have to travel the length of the island then. So, you won't buy anything, Sarge?"

"When I get a salary rise, maybe."

Mr Francois oozed charm, but Philosophe added, "Is that all the cloth you have in the shop?" He pointed to the stack beneath the cutting board.

"Of course. You finish nosing around? I hear you looking to arrest thieves, you don' come this way accusing me man!"

"I'm doing my duty."

He walked out of the shop and did not hear George say, "Earlier this year, it was the police that were frightened of people stoning them, now they waving butus, arresting people."

"The real thieves, too clever to get caught," Carl said.

He walked away, his butu in his hand, every now and then whacking it against his leg. Well, Clifford's shop was out of business and Francois was the tailor in town. He walked away, along the old streets on the east side in a sauntering gait and a beatific smile on his face.

CHAPTER TEN

On the sugar estate, the new instruction from the bosses was for lower sugar production. Augustus could not imagine there never being sugar factories; the cane grew as naturally as the hair on his head and so his work must be assured, even if his position was changed and he had to stand in front of the furnace and vats of boiling juice.

The employees doing work in the laboratories were other ex-college men like himself in the three factories. Likewise, they could be made to man vats.

He now sat with Olga. She smiled, warming up in his presence.

"The sugar could not be sold in town! Who has shops now? Just two."

"Yes, that's true," she replied.

"We have to boil off the syrup more now. My work is less. I may have to work on a machine alongside the boilermen to check steam pressure. There will be more molasses for the rum."

She listened to him and turned towards the passage on hearing the voice of her mother.

"Olga, Hazel will come with me to talk to O.K. Pal to find out the bank money business, right now," she said in patois.

Aunt Hazel stood near. She saw how all her 'People Cargo' could remain in fine condition: as long as everyone occupied themselves and the lids firm on their lives. However, Augustus could well need more vertical placement; he should be a pillar in her house and in society, she thought. She would talk to Electra about him.

After they left, Olga said "O.K. Pal, my god-father, is the messenger who used to work in the People's Bank."

Olga moved away, went downstairs into the yard and collected clothes from the line. She acknowledged the old cousins by the table in the sitting room; too early for supper preparation. Augustus and Era met her on the stairs on their way down, carrying a large sheet of paper and the painting set. The child skipped down. Now Olga felt a pang of anxiety because Augustus had spoken about change, her mother was anxious about money, and yesterday Muriel had said in a low voice, "Big shots try as usual to close the door in poor peoples' faces. Augustus should try to find about his savings."

It had been a mistake when she had got out of the noisy La Rose Society and joined the sedate and refined Marguerite Society with aspirations to be like the middle classes, like teachers and clerks. She said to Olga that she wished now that she had had the sense to put money into the Good Shepherd Society like poor people who could not afford to save. That money did not get put into banks but looked after by trusted people.

She carefully considered her sewing. Would she lend her sewing machine to the tailors at Mr Francois? What about her clothes she made for the family? Next week Augustus starts the two to ten night shift. He said he would spend the whole week on the estate, he would live with the foreign cane cutters in the building on the estate. It was big enough, he said to her. Would he be taking his small grip with his books? She noticed the Rosicrucian book, what he called his knowledge book, was still in his possession. This house got on her nerves so much and when she offered to help the cousins in the kitchen, what she heard from them was they liked helping Aunt Hazel, and also she had enough to do for her family. She protested in vain.

She would make another attempt tomorrow to help with the cooking; she would give the sewing a rest.

The areas uphill from Spine Road were heavily populated with cocoa trees. Miss Hazel and Muriel set out with the hope of getting comforting news about the money. The man sat on his door sill smoking his pipe, looking out into the twilight. He watched them approaching, he scratched his head and stood up.

"Ay, Ay, Gens mw`e?" He said to Muriel.

"*Sa u fe?*" she asked.

He answered that he was well and led them into the small room of the shack. They were almost touching one another in the small space. "Long time I haven't seen you, come let me hold your hand girl." This he meant for his godchild's mother.

Muriel was surprised at the words. He was jovial but she did not beat about the bush, he was in the hot seat listening to her. Her question? "Do you know if the money in the bank was saved?"

He was not going to dance in their Paso Doble. Earlier on, he had got to the bank anxious about his friend, the watchman, who spent the night inside the bank. He had seen the door was open and he went in to see Mano drunk and sleeping, and on his tail were three policemen. He heard the policeman's excited commands to his friend. They took no notice of him; they wanted the keys to the safe with the money.

He wouldn't tell Muriel that. Instead, he answered Muriel with, "All I know is that the money never got burn."

"Dat's all we wanted to know," Muriel responded.

He had stayed around the bank, hoping to save Mano. He did not trust the police in there. Not long afterwards, he saw Town Board constables and the manager coming their way and what he had seen was the policemen running from the bank. What had been the reason for their visit? He had kept away from the town; he had not even visited Mano.

They talked for a bit while he rose and lit the kerosene lamp. They listened to the opening chorus of the crickets. Muriel was content with his information and told him, while moving to the door,

"What I had is all gone. I'm thinking of going to Aruba to find work, I'm still young."

"I think I will move back to St Vincent pretty soon; you could come wit me?" he teased Muriel.

"Leave me alone Mister," she told him in patois.

The few lights that came on sometimes were not working just then and Miss Hazel spoke her thoughts aloud, "If the earth could talk, we would have stayed in tonight, O.K. Pal, but we will be back home soon, thank you."

"What to do?" he answered and said his goodnight.

And Muriel's vision of going to Aruba was more firmly rooted now. Her plan was to find a way to ask for her savings.

CHAPTER ELEVEN

Olga had visited Mr Francois, and what impelled her to offer the loan of her machine was the airiness of the large room, the white paint on the building. She was tired of darkness, Aunt Hazel, dark wood walls, the lack of light in the drawing room. This shop burst with sunlight coming in from the open windows and doors. And she said to Augustus as they lay on the red blanket, "I wouldn't mind going to Aruba too, what do you think about that?"

"Why? I am not leaving the island to work overseas; not now things are changing. There's so much talk going around. You know they put up a temporary Town Hall in the empty space behind the houses by Cyril and Boo? You know the large space coming towards the wharf! They took the empty pitch pine building on the American Base close to Anse Chabon and brought it to town."

She felt that if her mother got herself over there, they should all go and be together as before, but if Muriel went alone, her own place will be with Augustus for the first time. She was quiet. He held her very close with extreme care not to crush her. It made her think of soft caressing long grass. She thought back to their courtship days, sitting on the soft grass in St Cecelia Gardens, shoes off, the green grass soft and cool.

Two weeks in a row, he was away in the night. She had already started to spend some time at the tailor's shop since he had collected her machine. She did not bother to tell him a man had come to Francois' shop and, seeing her, asked: "Who is that craff you showing off here, Francois?"

"Yes, she's a nice chile," Francois answered.

On the one hand she had felt flattered, and on the other hand she had wished that nothing had been said and she had kept a straight face. Mr Henderson, sitting by the machine, portly, respectable and a bit slow, stated that the young lady was married and they did not want any slack behaviour towards her. But sometimes Francois pretended to be a Casanova, calling her things like Mona Lisa or Angel. He never called her by her name and he made bowing or saluting gestures. She had had to smile as Augustus had told her that he was a good decent man.

When Era surprised her, she told her that Ma Boy had made her a doll; she showed it to her with a happy smile one day.

"She gave it to you today?"

"Yes. I saw her making it. She sewed it with her hands, she pushed some cotton in da body and arms and legs, she put a piece of wood in its neck, and she made black thread for da hair."

"You happy? I'm glad you have something nice to play with. I can't make dolls."

Now that she left her a few times a week, it was good to have Ma Boy who liked children. The cousins were usually attentive to Era, she had seen them give her sweets when she hung around them in the kitchen.

"I call her Peg."

The child went up on the bed at night and she placed Peg next to her. She was no trouble at all, she thought, and she played her own games. When school resumed, it would be a relief. But sometimes she found her staring at her, more intently than she had months ago. As she sat on the chair twisting her hair into coils, and the child's slanting eyes met her own slanting black ones, she wondered whether she wanted something and was not asking. In the first two years of

Era's life, her regard of her yellow daughter had given her some discomfiture: so unlike herself and Augustus, not even like Muriel, how could she have been hers and Augustus' daughter? She had got used to the fact that she was different.

Now the only tiny concern she had about Era was that she had started to utter sentences in patois, which Augustus did not like, but that came from Ma George who would address her and say things to her in patois. Ma Boy was the better behaved of the two, of course; she used to be housemaid and Da to white children, whereas Ma George used to wash clothes for families. Well she would tell Augustus that beggars could not be choosers, in their case it was doing Era no harm to learn what patois meant.

She was busier in this new period, doing so many things when she left Era in the house. She stood in the queue by the relief building erected by Dujon and the Union men. It was true there was a shortage of sugar in town, you had to know where the small home shops were to get some, but fortunately Olga thought she was luckier in that respect. No worry there. She still felt unhappy collecting relief food, her smile fixed to meet the Union workers as they continued to become an important force in the town, and she showed gratitude for the soda biscuits, oleo butter and sardines.

Sometimes, she spent a little while idling in Aunt Hazel's shop as she waited for customers. One afternoon her Aunt wore a large dress of small brown check, long sleeves, dress down to her ankles, the bright foulard on her shoulder she tucked into the waist. Her Aunt seemed dressed to go out; her hair was combed back in a small knot. She served a customer measuring some ticking. Olga thought "Well, O.K., things looking up a bit." After the man left she sat keeping her company.

It was with surprise that Olga watched the entry of a large fair-skinned woman, a committee air about her, with a dapper, yellow-skinned young man with straight black hair, his eyes in his face, small and sharp and angled at the outer edges. Aunt Hazel asked Olga to excuse them while she took them into the living room.

The frisky way in which Miss Hazel led the way out of the shop put a quizzical smile on Olga's face. Then she thought of the young man, who was he? Except for Era's tight hair, he could be her father. Same face. She felt something like a frisson. She could hear the speed of the woman's speech when she stood in the corridor outside the shop, wasn't her Aunt getting earache? She herself could not stand the reedy sound of it. At the same time she kept an eye on the road if perchance someone was to come in from the street to buy maybe lace, bias-binding or rickrack. She played her hands on the lengths of silver sequins. They spent about an hour and they left by the side door to the lane. Her Aunt joined her and all she said was, "This lady's son just come from America. Same age with you."

She was quiet and added, "How old you now?"

"Twenty-six."

"That's right... I remember..." She did not say anymore.

Olga thought she would ask Era what she heard because she had seen her in the room even though her Aunt and visitors had been behind the partition. But one thing she had heard as the woman went through the door to the lane in her loud voice, "You'll come tomorrow? Things moving fast."

She felt that her Aunt had had a very cosy chat with her visitors; sometimes they had only spoken in muted voices coming to her through the partition into the shop. Aunt Hazel told Olga they should shut the shop. It had been a long day. She was going to have a rest. Sometimes, her Aunt looked like a ruler of people – her eyes commanded the respect or instead demanded it. Olga did not wish to converse with her. She seemed to be in one of those poses.

Era hung around as usual, doing little hops. She almost tripped on Olga's feet as she walked to the sitting room. They sat by the table; she looked at Era with a smile, then picked up the doll that she had put there when Miss Hazel had come with the guests. Olga wondered what her daughter had picked up from the conversation in there.

What was the business about, and that young man, who was he? Something about him! The child played in the strands of the dolls hair, she made a few plaits with the black thread, totally absorbed, and looked up suddenly as her mother asked her, "Did da lady speak to you?"

"No, mamma."

"What about da man?"

"He said hello."

"What did dey talk about?"

The child wondered why her mother was persistent. She shrugged her shoulders and smiled and was silent. Then she answered, "I dunno."

Olga was disappointed, she wished she had picked up something. She moved to the kitchen. Ma George's small hand held a fat six inch length of black pudding, the other hand held a knife going to cut it. Next to her, a pan of oil on the fire hearth. She sliced the moist seasoned pudding into thin rings, put them on the oil for a second. She did not look at Olga, so intent she was on her job. She turned them over and removed them to the enamel plate from where she had taken them. Olga looked on.

She thought of her own kitchen on Maynard Street, herself preparing sprats in batter for Augustus, herself and Era. These cousins were surprising – Ma George getting some meals for them all, she had some suppliers, lifetime of know-how.

Now, as it seemed again and again to Olga, she has been displaced. A dependent; they were the adults – Aunt Hazel and her cousins. They controlled the domestic operations. She stood listlessly near the kitchen door and let Ma Boy help her cousin prepare the rest of the evening nourishment.

"*Bon swe.*"

Muriel came from work and went into the living room, raising one hand in greeting towards the kitchen to Olga and the cousins. Era went to her grandmother and sat at the table with her.

There was water boiling in a pan, green tea leaves waiting to be drawn for tea and the supper. Muriel loved the softer taste of L'orangette and Olga found the leaves that her mother kept just for this, put one leaf in a cup and waited to make this for Muriel.

The air in the yard was torpid and warm. There was calmness in the cousins' movements and when they took the black pudding to the table in the house with the sharp ended small loaves, Olga stayed in the kitchen to make her mother's tea.

As they sat down, without Aunt Hazel, Olga wondered whether her Aunt was asleep. They had eaten in silence and the cousins removed the dirty used things to the kitchen, leaving Aunt Hazel's covered over and the green tea in the jug.

Olga watched Muriel sip her bush tea. Then she stretched, arms in the air, and yawned. Era stood near to her. For a moment Olga felt the feeling she had in Maynard street when Era had leaned against Muriel in the evening, her mother stroking the child's arms and they would go to bed in Muriel's room. They were silent but she could hear the voice of the woman buzzing in her ears, the speed of her words, one on top of the other, some gramophone machine she was.

"I can still hear da voice of a lady who came here today, it was like *fiong, fiong, fiong*, of violin playing bad music. She came to see Aunt Hazel."

"What she like?" she asked Olga in patois.

"Oh, light skin, fat. Her son who just come from America was here wif her. He and Era could be related," she answered in patois.

Muriel took her eyes away from Olga's face and looked away. Olga waited. Muriel would not meet her eyes even as she kept looking at her. She waited, her own heart fluttered in the tight silence. Muriel was usually a peace-loving person, the waters around her never left a ripple as far as her daughter knew, remembered. Now, Muriel swiftly left and almost ran up the stairs.

"Se'se!" Her voice was pained. Olga heard her say loudly, "La La was here today? W-h-a-t was that woman doing here, with her son?" in patois.

She entered the bedroom where Hazel lay on the large bed. She was surprised by this angry entry of her sister. Wasn't she the captain of this ship? She couldn't have any spillage. She said calmly, "*Chonje? Egal?*"

Muriel relived sad emotions. Her face was set.

"Glisse!" Hazel sat up, got out of the bed. Her Virgin light danced in the oil on her dresser, this was the only light in the dark room. Muriel sat tiredly on the bed now.

"Don't be upset, we were all friends when we were young, you fell out with her, alright – that was natural. You blamed her for Harry going away but it's a long time ago."

They never argued. Muriel knew Hazel's redoubtable reputation but there was never that between them, but Muriel's excited voice, her displeased expression, was not wasted on Miss Hazel.

"La La's son just come from America so she was making her rounds, taking him everywhere. She did not think about you because she did not stop to consider meeting you here. Just as well you were not."

"*Vye'vache la,*" she hissed and stormed downstairs, Hazel after her.

"*Vap la pwan'y,*" Ma George whispered to Ma Boy, looking at Muriel's face.

"Careful! Careful!" Ma Boy said in English, aware some rocking was going on between the sisters. Ma George's words showed the break in Muriel's usual calmness. They were worried.

Olga noticed that her Aunt was still dressed in the same dress she had worn when the visitors came, usually she changed to a house dress if she had dressed in one of these special old fashioned ones. The dissonance fell on ears attuned to the music of moods, which was always a natural attitude among St Benedict people. Era was no exception. She moved from foot to foot and gave a little hop of nervousness.

Glisse! Dance Marie, Dance!

Muriel saw that the tide was out around her, and not much could she do to cover the old buried creature of her younger self which her daughter had never seen. She willed the tide to come in before Olga found all the patterns of her passion and ignitable debris, and Aruba beckoned again.

"Unity is strength. You know that," Aunt Hazel said to Muriel, to steady things as she saw her sister take Era's hands and they went into the yard into the opalescent light of the evening. Just who had subdued who, Olga was not sure, but a balance was being attempted. Miss Hazel lit the lamp in the drawing room and poured her tea which was cold. Olga stood looking out into the yard, her lithe body erect on her bare arched, narrow feet, her arms folded. The gate of the yard clanged open, someone without water came in to ask Miss Hazel for a bucket-full.

The sisters argued late into the night. Olga heard their voices, what was going on between them? It was all about the fat woman and her son, she knew. Why wasn't she put in the picture? Her mother's old attitude with her would prevent her from questioning her but she was uneasy about this thing.

"Don't be vex, sister. I did not mean to upset you but now you must not forget Olga and Era. They should know their other relations."

"That woman is my enemy; she's the worst of all the nations of women. That happened twenty-six years ago. If she did not come in and play about with Harry, I am sure he would have stayed with me. She made him ran away to Panama."

Muriel, who had contained her emotions and disappointment for years, was shouting at Hazel. The situation had become volatile, and with aplomb she soothed Muriel. "You were the more decent one. He was scared of her, he had to run."

She had to patch this hole in the bottom of this ship that she was trying to steer away from rocks, she put herself firmly at the wheel.

Muriel said in an aggrieved voice, "You telling me all that; next thing you will say I should tell Olga that La La's son is her brother, and also who Harry's people are!" she chupsed.

"It's time."

"I can' see why. We never talk about it."

"If this opportunity pass you by, that her brother is in St Benedict! My conscience is troubling me, I want to have a clear conscience about all this."

"My conscience is clear. I have brought up Olga properly. See that! Augustus made her a good husband. Voila, my heart's content." She liked her sister quite well and if it were not for that she would be telling her what she really thought of her past behaviour with Victor, and that she was a little like La La, pushy, getting their claws into someone.

The flame in the lamp burnt from yellow to orange while the reason for the argument became stale. A new day began and the words went back and forth.

"I'll wait. When Olga asks the question I'll tell her everything, you must not do it for me."

"What you think about Harry coming back to the island?"

Muriel clapped her hands in false merriment.

"That's his business. My daughter is big woman now." Because Hazel has been rattling on about Harry's family, about Olga and Era, the younger sister knows that she will re-examine her feelings about the whole thing. Hazel and her ideas! The older sister had been quiet for about long enough, she was quietly breathing. Muriel blew out the lamp with the soot collecting on its chimney. It had not been her idea to stay talking into the night as their voices echoed against the varnished wood of the partition towards Olga's ears.

The night was nearly over when Muriel fell asleep. Soon a cock from somewhere crowed the new day alive. Olga's observation of her mother, day by day, inured by her stoic ways, meant she did not expect she would find out what had happened between the women. She did not see Muriel before her mother left for the presbytery. Augustus woke her; she had overslept. He picked up a wrist, encircled it and then kissed her forearm, upwards, something that always made her chuckle. He felt that her wrist bone was prominent against his palm. She did not wake with a smile even but jumped up startled.

"You were in dreamland, you must have been tired."

"Have you seen Aunt Hazel?"

"It's pretty quiet downstairs."

Olga settled down on the bed, she shook Era awake. "Wake up, papa want to lie down to sleep."

"Anything wrong?"

"Something new was going on here last night, there was a lot of talk between mamma and Aunt Hazel but I don't know what about. Not exactly a quarrel but something."

He looked at her with raised eyebrows but said nothing. Then, "Are you going to Mr Francois today?"

"I will."

"Alright, I'll get a shut eye."

"Perhaps it's nothing. You get your rest." She took Era's hand and whispered, "Let's go downstairs."

Era followed her into the yard and into the kitchen. She watched her while she made the fire to boil water, she was going to heat some sardines and make cocoa. While she was busy she said, "Go and get the comb for me to comb your hair after breakfast."

She wondered how Aunt Hazel would carry herself in this new day. She could not help the new anxiety but she wished she could brush it to one side because she did not know what it was, so she concentrated on grating the stick of cocoa, then mixing it into the water. After she had mixed the powdered milk, she added it to the drink and sugared it. She took the enamel jug to the drawing room and arranged the other bits, some bread from the night before. She was going to call Aunt Hazel, her door was open, Era was with her. "Good morning, Aunty, I've made breakfast."

"Good morning. I'm coming now." She picked the covered enamel white pail to take with her.

"You have the comb, Era?" The cousins were quiet, were they keeping to themselves this morning? They would come down when they were ready. They usually knew what to do for the day. They probably did not hear the talking going on next to their room in the night, Olga thought. She was looking forward to make herself active at Mr Francois' with the tailoring going on around her.

Aunt Hazel kept her tin bath close to the fence at the back of the kitchen. There was a space between the kitchen and the fence by the spinach bush, the only thing that grew in the big yard. The latrine was far back behind a pile of big stones, the little house with a seat and a bucket which someone who earned some money doing that came and removed weekly, brought it back empty.

Olga got water for Era's bath as the morning progressed and was satisfied that her Aunt seemed her normal self. There was nothing else to do, she left Era playing with her doll in her Aunt's shop. She would go out at about one. There was ironing of clothes to get on with, but she longed to lay next to Augustus; another night without him. If she left the shop after three, she would have some time to spend with him before he left for work. Then there was, she felt, the importance of trying for some flour, milk, oil, tinned food and fire relief goods from the Union shop.

"I'm going to town," she called to her Aunt, as she passed into the shop's front and on to Spine Road.

In that night, something that was going on was only a taste of what was in store for Muriel. Miss Hazel was sure. As La La said, Harry was going to make a journey to see his family, being concerned for them since the fire and the problems around the town.

She looked at Olga as she passed in front of her shop on her way out, and Era sat with her; Harry's grandchild. The child was as much her responsibility as Olga was. She felt a responsibility for their welfare, their sustenance. They were family.

That very afternoon it was a good idea to visit the Chapit to get a reading from her and be prepared in these uncertain times. She would close the shop after two and get ready to walk to Electra's house. It would be a bit tiring going uphill, but life, she thought, was all about playing a part and she was so used to doing that. She had to play her part with some style. Era had moved away with the agility that Aunt Hazel noticed she had, she expected that she had gone to find the cousins.

A couple was walking with linked arms and came towards the shop, a couple around the same age as Hazel. She had known them for years, they lived on the Darling Hill and he kept a few animals. He wore a dark suit, a black hat deep on his head. The woman wore a bright check dress but knee high, and she wore a small straw hat. Mr and Mrs Henri came to her sidewalk; she saw the small straw basket he carried.

They spent some time with her, a soft spoken man, almost effeminate, his face wreathed in a warm smile, and his wife a firm bodied woman of pale brown complexion next to his very leathery black person. They always walked with hooked arms, the only couple she knew who did this. Before he left her he kissed her on the cheek, and left some salt pork which was wrapped in banana leaf.

She moved into her corridor towards the drawing room, calling loudly for one of the cousins to hand them the salt pork. Olga came just then and she passed it to her to take to the kitchen. "I don't know if my cousins are in the yard or upstairs." She looked at Olga's laden hands. "Tell them I have something for them to cook today, thank God," she said in patois.

Olga had not forgotten the night's behaviour of her Aunt and her mother, and she looked at Miss Hazel with a questioning look before turning away towards the kitchen to relieve herself of the few tins she had been given at the shop.

The cousins worked together, washing some clothes. She delivered her Aunt's message; did they need her to help prepare the food? A slow smile played Ma George's small face; she shook her head. Was there a new, sly smile on the old woman's face? Her bare feet were planted on the small stones of the yard as she bent over the large basin, rinsing clothes. She asked Ma Boy, who was hanging them out, "*u vle' Olga e'de'u, uh?*" The refusal of help came:

"*Pa jodi-a*"

So it was and was to remain. Olga was sure of it. She planned to go to the shop around two but she was better off going now. She told Era to go to Aunt Hazel and find something to do for her in the shop and said goodbye.

CHAPTER TWELVE

The heat of Augustus' kiss was still on Olga's mouth as they walked downstairs and into the yard, where Muriel sat on a wooden crate eating supper. She smiled as they joined her. She knows she has sheltered Olga, who had never had domestic difficulties or even marital strife. She knew that now, in this period, Olga was to encounter the realities of life. She had even taken herself off to the tailor shop; that had surprised her. In her mother's heart she feels the tugging of care, even though Augustus was the type who would look after Olga.

Golden yellow sunlight pooled around them, even the cousins sat on the bench brought out of the kitchen into the yard. Era watched the scene perched on one of the brown boulders nearby.

"Hazel should be back by now," Muriel said, and exclaimed, "Well, well, well! I just called your name *Sese*..."

Muriel's jaw dropped as Hazel came through the gate of the yard. Aunt Hazel's indigo and rust check long dress of glazed cotton made her look taller, Era thought. The long sleeves tapered, the tip of the skirt on the right side was brought up and tucked somewhere at her waist and the white lace of her petticoat was visible. On her head she wore a head tie of indigo and rust. Era had never seen her grandmother wear a *booboom fly* dress like that one.

"How's everyone?" Aunt Hazel enquired, then she went into the kitchen.

Muriel followed her in there. She moved upstairs saying she was going to get changed. While her sister went to her room, Muriel rejoined the others. A sense of unreality descended on Augustus, sitting there with his supper before going to work, but Olga was basking in the warmth of her family as this was one of the few days that everyone wanted to be close. She wondered whether it was because of the delicious salt pork meal that the cousins had given them. Aunt Hazel returned and sat with them eating.

Era stood behind Augustus, leaning on his back.

Gaiety could sometimes take hold of people in spite of themselves as they relax, making tangled masses of raw angst turn into ripples of laughter and raw talk; Ma Boy's slow easy patois broke the silence.

"The person or people who started the fire at Clifford's shop will pay the price soon; if this happens after my death, the ants will bring the news to me."

The others let her words drop but Augustus nodded in agreement. Olga looked searchingly at Aunt Hazel as she chewed her food meditatively. Ma Boy spoke some more on the subject of the fire.

Muriel said to her sister, "Mr Henri must have been pleased to see you, Hazel, the time has passed since he stopped running after you."

"He still gives me a good piece of pork."

Olga's wistful expression caught her Aunt's eye even as Aunt Hazel observed that Muriel, unusual for her taciturn self, joked in a capricious manner. Augustus stood up, easing Era gently from off his back.

"Time for work," he said.

After he left and they had gone to sit on the balcony, Olga felt cold and deserted. She folded her arms, goose pimples suddenly appearing; she hugged herself. She sat pensively; something of her need played in her mind – a baby, a baby. She felt Era pinch her arm.

"What child!" She knew that the child missed playing with other children. It was still light, might be a good idea to take her round by Boo's house to play with her children.

One – two – three; one – two, the *Son* music call deep in Muriel's veins was being felt by her in the evening pre-sunset and as if clave sticks were making rhythms beat on her brain, the whispering *shac-shacs* and marimba brought her out of her reverie.

"No sign of Sampson my neighbour! It's strange; don't even talk of Clifford, he too ran away since the fire," she said.

"Remember that bird looked as if it was leading the fire. It really frightened me." Ma Boy spoke in her low voice. "That frightened me."

"A mystery!" Aunt Hazel said slowly, her mind on Electra, who she had visited earlier for her protection.

The glow of sunset disappeared and violet colour stained the sky. Muriel said, "I must find Mr Popo and have a talk with him about my savings."

"I'll come with you," her sister told her, nodding her head in agreement.

The change of subject back to the Sampsons, from Muriel, "Ma Sampson is on my mind every day. The older daughter left and went to Barbados and the man is acting oddly. I heard he took himself to stand under the breadfruit tree church with some people. He is not even talking with his wife; he just causes a lot of trouble for her. Hazel, do you think she could come for lunch on a Sunday?"

"Yes, of course, she can come anytime, if she is your friend."

"She is very proud. Anyway, I'll ask her."

Olga and Era came from the east side of Spine Road from the direction of St Cecelia Gardens. Soon, they heard the child bolting up the stairs.

"The speed of that fire, its rage and the lack of water to fight it. The other one in 1927 happened when I arrived from Bonne Terre, before Olga was born, you remember?"

Aunt Hazel looked at her sister and Muriel began talking about the Sampsons' life. While he was away during the war she had been a frequent visitor to the wife, but since he returned she rarely went inside their home. She liked Maryse Sampson because she was a decent woman like herself, even though they sometimes had a maid in their home.

"But something happened to Sampson about a year ago."

Olga joined them as her mother said this and she was forced to join the gossip from what Augustus had told her. "Because he went inside the upper-class men's club one day and the barman did not welcome him because only the light skinned men were members. That burnt him, made him so miserable, because that's how he started to behave. He started to beat the woman..."

"Yes, she stopped hiring the maid..." Muriel said. "Poor woman! *Bad boy* did not help her when she had to take things out of her house, Augustus was the one who pulled out her waggonette and went to call for him to come out in case he was in bed sleeping strong because of the rum he had in his body."

"And you know when I met Sampson one day on the Square, he looked at me as if he never saw me before; but I don't see him now."

As Olga said that, Era had a picture of her old home as they talked, she remembered something. She said, "Mamma, I see Mr Sampson in the night stoop down by Mr Clifford shop." She used to stand on a chair sometimes and peep through the jalousies towards the Sampsons' house and there was the time she had seen Mr Sampson and Mr Clifford have a quarrel in the gap by the tailor shop.

"Time to go to bed Era, come on."

"Dis fire is *miste*." Muriel stood up and kissed Era. "Go and sleep, say your prayers, good chile."

The final darkness of night made itself felt with the suddenness of the daily pattern. There were the usual routine things: Miss Hazel went to her room; Muriel went with the cousins downstairs.

CHAPTER THIRTEEN

Era awoke to the sound that made her feel more of the new feeling that came over her these days, because she was with Mamma and Pap as she called Augustus. She was a big girl knowing so much more about the life of adults.

The room was dark. Mamma's body felt warm against hers, she opened her eyes, saw her father where he sat on the side of their small bed. Her mother was talking softly in patois; she did not understand most of it and what did it matter? She did not care what they spoke about, but then her father said slowly, "Man know thyself and to thyself be true..."

Era sat up and rubbed her eyes which felt heavy from sleep. He was talking about not telling lies – was talking about something, he said, "Be true." Be true meant don't tell lies. What was he talking about? She wondered.

She felt them look at her, together. "Morning Era," Olga said.

"Morning Era," Augustus added.

"Morning Mamma, morning Pap." She answered.

"Go on downstairs, see if Ma Boy is there. She'll give you something."

"Yes Mamma."

The irregular time her father kept since they were living on Spine Road made Era's life get into the Rubato fire rhythm; that she saw her father behave in a humane, reachable way as the days went by – he was like a new person as well as her Pap.

Her view of her world was as though everything was a reflection of the solid, the tangible printed in the air, or like looking at a picture in water inverted and winking. The transient town and transient people were on shifting sand. She could, these last few weeks, feel her own impressions changing, bending. Some brightening, others fading, even as she perceived her mother's changed habits. She kept her eyes trained on Olga and her movements in case she took her presence for what it was not. In case what she should take for granted might vanish.

Era used to play at play-time in school as children do, when with her friends they said "*the rain falling – the sun shining – the devil marrying his daughter behind the door.*" She had looked behind the back door in the house on Maynard Street when the sun shone and rain drizzled at the same time, white clouds in the far away blue sky. Then the sun dimmed, the yard became a bit dark. Then, the sun shone bright again. She had looked for the devil and his daughter and found nothing – not the devil, but she had imagined something there.

Even when her classmates played in the *cachot* under the school building in the dim brown earth-covered area, when whispers became private and games took her imagination to secret places, doing what '*O'grady*' said. Then her eyes would shine with her secret joy in the limitless space.

The drawing room door was open, Aunt Hazel moved about. Era sat at the foot of the stairs and watched quietly. White light outside was in the quiet morning, silence profound. She thought she could play this or that if only! Not quite sure what to do she went back upstairs and stood on the balcony to watch the houses far away, the tree tops, the belfry of the Anglican church on the hill, till she heard her name being called. She skipped downstairs once more. Ma Boy, Ma George looked at her, both smiled at her. They sat by the table sipping breakfast drink with Aunt Hazel who gave her a piece of cut cake and weak black coffee, urging her, " Siddown by da table."

She moved from the table into the yard as soon as she finished, picked up some small stones, dropped them through the gaps in her fingers. Things were going on around her, the hum beginning to pick up force as the women moved about. She waited for the sound of Olga's voice and she came talking to her. She collected water from the small pipe close to the kitchen. "Sponge yourself, Era, take off the night gown."

She did those things and then had her hair combed. At last her grandmother came out of the bedroom, she talked with Olga while she wrapped her hair with her *muchoir* of pink, white and brown large check, and she was dressed in the grey as she did for work. She put her warm hand on Era's face in a caress and moved towards the stairs, Era saw her on the street and she disappeared out of sight.

The morning was still new, Miss Hazel went to open the shop. Era put on her shoes without a definite plan. After Olga left for the shop and she stood by the door watching the women, Ma George and Ma Boy, talking more like a repetition of sighs, turned to her. "*Pov ti bet!*" Ma George said.

"*Bel ti ich wi!*" she heard Ma Boy say. She knew what bel meant, it meant nice; if only she understood the rest. Ma Boy was pointing a needle into a piece of black shiny cloth. She pulled something out – a shiny thread with nimble fingers. Era went into the shop. "Can I have some water to drink, Aunt Hazel?"

"Go and ask Ma George and come back here."

She quenched her thirst in a few gulps and quietly slipped into the yard and out of the gate as Ma George was busy stirring something. She ran.

"I have not been to the Gardens on my own before; I don't think Aunt Hazel saw me pass in front of the shop, somebody was talking to her. I ran down Spine Road. Children in the Garden, wi! I see dem pelting stones at the jugger plum tree. I go de and dey say to me doh come near so I stand back. When dey finish I see dem pick up da Jugger plums from the ground. Some of da boys and girls older dan me. I ask for a plum. I have one in my hand, it look red like wine in the sun, its skin smooth and nice; it not very big, it long and round at da same time. It so juicy and sweet, I close my eyes and suck it. I follow dem. We pass close to the lines of red hibiscus trees and go to da canal. Da deep dry concrete canal. I stood in it and watch da children pull the branches of glu glu seeds from the palm trees.

"Miss Boo's children come in the Gardens too and I went on da merry-go-round, swing and slide wif dem. I stayed a long time in da Garden. When Miss Boo's children went home I ran very fast between da bamboos up to Spine Road. My heart beating fast as I see the foreman who used a belt on children when dey misbehave in his Garden.

"Aunt Hazel and cousins were on da sidewalk. I was frightened. I give a little smile and look at dey feet so I didn't see Aunt Hazel's hand come towards me. It is a strong burning feeling on my arm; I jump. She make me sit in her shop wif her till Mamma get back she tell me."

"What will your mudda say? I won't even tell her. Don't do it again!"

Augustus had slept enough and went downstairs dressed in his drawers, making this quick move before he went out in this house of so many women. He had heard talking in Aunt Hazel's room. Her shop was shut. Olga was absent. Every time he entered the yard for exercise or to slosh water on his body as he had not been able to go to the sea for a while, he hoped not to meet the cousins or Aunt Hazel, not yet used to them and aware of his over developed muscles. He now sluiced his body, soaped with carbolic and threw a couple buckets of water over his head and down. Feeling refreshed he moved away from the back of the yard, crossed the yard and returned upstairs, dressed and left to search hopefully for Sampson on the People's Square.

He only saw people sitting on the green benches. The Square being less noisy, some people sat under the tents, some beds remained and blocked the paths. Ma Sampson sat on a camp bed next to her waggonette and her bundles, her face woebegone, head bent, oblivious to what was happening around her. His feeling of helplessness in the face of what he now saw came back.

Carefully, he made a path to her side and called her name.

"Eh!" she became aware that her name was called.

"Where's your husband?"

"I don't know." She answered with a sad look and her arms pointing to the sky.

She added that Sampson had two brothers who now lived in Curacao. There used to be a sister but she died; he may have gone by her family, maybe. He was puzzled that they did not find a place to shelter in some house. He asked whether he might have gone to some friend's place and whether she had a vague idea at all as he was anxious to talk with her husband. She answered in her Cayenne French. She said that she did not see him for lengthy periods, he appeared and disappeared, he was untidy and he did not seem to want what clothes she had with her. Augustus was more dumbfounded by this impasse. He shook her hand and moved away quite briskly towards the church, walked behind it where houses had been left intact.

He still respected Sampson; the man was a war veteran; he had had good ideals, and he still, in Augustus' estimation, had good ideals, which was why he had become disaffected during the last year. Puzzled and disappointed he moved back to his lodging; his agenda did not allow him that much extra time to go on a wild goose chase.

At that moment, a restless, aimless man walked with a limp. He dragged one foot behind the other. His shirt was wide open and flapping with his mahogany brown chest confronting the world. His mind was in Italy with the servicemen carrying armoury. Men, killing men. That was a shadow for some people but not for those who had served, like him, and then resumed an old, everyday job! He had resumed his clerical job; people soon forgot he had been in the war.

Augustus missed seeing him. He might have seen him – it was a possibility that Sampson had seen Augustus and evaded him to be by his wife, so soon after his neighbour had left the Square.

CHAPTER FOURTEEN

Olga checked their room for Augustus when she got back from Francois' shop. When she set out earlier she had felt uneasy, ready for some unstable new thing on the verge of happening, after the scene she had witnessed between her mother and Aunt. Now she sat by the drawing room table before she resumed doing some kind of work, either dusting or scrubbing. The shop was shut and at this time of day it was not customary for her Aunt to be in her room. The table where she sat was square and large enough for everyone in the house to squeeze around it. She held the dress she had sewn for Era in her hands, the green material with small red dots that she had refashioned from a bigger dress received as fire relief.

The bright sunlight of the yard where she faced invaded the skin against her eyeballs; red, then blue then red, like the night of the fire was behind her lids. She sat like this and remembered the night it had happened.

The line in time, firmly drawn by the fire, has put her in the space over that line. She had frog-jumped to this new place. She has seen people behaving like orderly ants; not like the mad ants, blindly scampering in all and any direction and away from each other. She had settled down comfortably in Mr Francois' shop. On her second day she had asked for bits of the garments of men's clothing, and had done hemming and buttonholes. She watched the men's technique in waxing the long thread before starting on the buttonholes, and Mr Francois saw that she was genuinely interested as he got to do blocking on the jackets.

She opened her eyes now, thinking of Carl, the religious preacher who said he came to learn to sew but spent more time quoting scripture to the rest of them. He had fixed his eyes on Olga while talking but she only gave him half an ear, his voice adenoidal, and had to look his way as he addressed her. He stood tall and lean, with curly black shiny hair, about the same age as herself. "Mrs James, in my church, our Brethren would welcome your husband." She wondered did he know Augustus.

"His church," Mr Francois said, "is the church under breadfruit."

Olga kept a straight face and watched him, inwardly amused. He stood with one hand on his bony hip that tilted forward while his index finger of the other hand wagged at the air. He preached at them with this adenoidal voice. She was more fascinated by the voice than what he said. "Proverbs fifteen verses three to six says: 'The eyes of the Lord are everywhere, keeping watch on the wicked and the good. The tongue that brings healing is a tree of life but a deceitful tongue crushes the spirit. The house of the righteous contains great treasure but the income of the wicked brings them trouble.'"

She had wondered what kind of thing she had let herself in for. She wished he did not distract her from her purpose. Mr Francois carried on with aplomb, dressed strangely in short khaki pants and a shirt. His tie was part of his daily preparation in showing his respectability, along with brown shoes and brown socks. Heavy veins grouped on his calves. What Olga liked about him was his way of encouraging anyone who had a topic, and so Carl was lucky there, she thought. She concentrated on hemming the bottoms of a leg of a grey tweed pants. She was jolted into the present. "Olga where are you?"

She faced Augustus as he came by the table giving off the scent of carbolic soap.

"I went about – I hoped to find Sampson but I only spoke to his wife. I surely do not know what happened between them; he has deserted her on the Square. It appears he has someplace where he goes."

"I don't know." She was mystified as much as he was. As he appraised her he thought her face was pinched, less round, and said, "Your face looks small!"

She perked up. "You surprise, uh?"

"Small, but just as charming, you know."

He put an arm round her shoulder and she said, "Did you see Aunt Hazel and Era go out? I only reach back here a little while."

She spoke in patois connecting her heart with the words she spoke to him.

"No but I heard voices in her bedroom before I went out. I thought Era was with her."

"I did not think of that." She left him. "I'll check." After she knocked and entered she was taken by surprise that her Aunt lay on her bed with Era.

"Oh, I was getting up now." She told Olga. "I was feeling a bit tired." Actually she could tell Olga that because Era had misbehaved badly she had used this as a punishment – having her stay in the bed with her for a few hours, mid-afternoon.

Era had brought her doll and Aunt Hazel herself had forty winks. The child looked anxiously at her mother and waited for Aunt Hazel to sit up and stand before she got down from the tall four poster bed with a small jump. She let her mother and great Aunt do some talking while she slipped out through the door, looking towards the balcony. Augustus sat away from the balcony edge but resting back in the chair against the wall of the house. Era moved quietly to the balcony rail away from him. The balcony runs on two sides. The smaller end looks towards the hills and faces the road; the other side faces the whole spine Road.

He sees the low hills. Bordering Morne Balancer, all types of trees intermingle with the houses, lots of people up there in small houses. They were the lucky ones with homes, Miss Hazel among them. The backbone, the long Spine Road that curved twice, remained as the flesh of the broken Masav; the road connected the head to the foot of the town, he mused. He looked over his shoulder at Olga and Era, who stood overlooking the street. He heard, "Granny coming." Era moved away.

He moved toward Olga. "Time's approaching; my duty calls. What is there to eat?"

They went down together. Not much food in the house from what they had all brought in but Ma Boy and Ma George brought some fishcakes from the kitchen for them. So little time before Augustus would leave for his night shift, Olga felt the need to draw his spirit towards her and she spoke in English to him while they ate together. She told him about Carl and Mr Francois' tailors, especially Mr Henderson who had explained about all the branches of the different societies and Lodges in Masav. "Mr Henderson used big words, like you, and they all spoke English." She looked at his face keenly and continued in a careful tone, "You would find the place interesting, I enjoy going there. They did not mention the Rosicrucian society though."

"I know it was my idea that you should lend Mr Francois your machine to help him but I hope you will only continue for a few weeks."

They had finished the small meal, and as he stood up he added, "I hope he pays you something for helping."

She was silent, having not considered herself as an employee. It was not really a job, she felt, but they needed money. She answered, "I know money makes the mare fly!"

He collected the things for his journey and said goodbye.

The sad twilight presented itself to the yard and the streets. Sounds were muted and the few phrases that the women communicated passed easily among them which dropped in the grey pool of the evening. Muriel said she did not get Ma Sampson to accept their invitation. More phrases dropped, exclamations and muttering between Muriel and Miss Hazel. Olga thought of taking herself off to bed, but stopped to listen to Ma Boy in a sudden garrulous mood, in her soulful patois.

"I worked for a long time as cook and Da to look after Mrs Prospere's family. She was fussy about her tea. She used to say to me, 'cook, don't draw the tea so… not all the water at once.' So, I just wet the leaves with enough hot water, give it time to soak and after a few minutes I used to add all the rest of boiling water. 'Give it time,' she used to say."

Ma George sipped something, holding the tumbler close. Ma Boy continued, "I liked it up there on the hill, not too far from town for me to walk every day. I carried Edison to his christening. I was his Da. Nice people; Mrs Prospere was a nice white lady."

Ma George smiled at her cousin. Her brusque patois was much in contrast, and there was her voice which rose, faded and started up an octave constantly. "You were inside, I was outside. You think I even got a smile from that Mrs La. Pat?" She shook her head from side to side "Never, all these years, three days a week I washed her clothes, put blue in her white clothes and starch up shirts, press everything perfect, but she and her French, always speaking so fast, whether I could understand she could not care at all, not that she said much to me. It was mostly when I got my money she would say things to me."

Her two-toned voice that amused Olga carried on with the high Doh reaching Doh in descending scale and up again. Her face showed the displeasure she felt for the woman. "Her children went abroad, her husband dead some years now. I don't know what happened to her."

Era's head dropped forward. Olga nudged her. "I think you want your bed. Let's go, goodnight," she said to the women.

Something that Augustus implied when she spoke to him about the shop was one of two things she considered. He had not said what he really thought, she knew that. In Mr Francois' shop she had the chance to make up her own - Era's and her mother's dresses, that was the arrangement. And the other was Aunt Hazel and his need to give her financial help.

CHAPTER FIFTEEN

ugustus had a secret prayer. He asked forgiveness if God was listening, self-blame that he had not been aware of the fire next door to stop it spreading. Other people made frequent visits to the Catholic church – there was vespers as he passed by on his way to work. Then he argued: God would know he had done his best, called the neighbours, helped save the library books, put his hand on the fire hose with a policeman who levelled it high up towards the Sampsons' house.

He was hating this walk up the hill. He would have to try to get another bicycle, second-hand, any kind as long as it did the job. He used his flash-light as it got darker. He got into the cane field, then crossed the sodden stream bed, glad he had got the gum boots from among the fire-relief goods. Frogs called to him, mules brayed. The air was still this August night. He was perspiring, even as his mind was cool and sharp.

The work at night took on a sinister air, the danger more evident, the rushing water, steam, gurgling hot vats, the revolving drums in the factory.

Now, the fields were empty of workers; only the creatures of the night were present. Before he entered the factory he made a path to the workmen's house. Most of the itinerant cane-cutters had left and fewer men were about. He enjoyed the atmosphere with the other workers, not feeling the least bit ill at ease. They talked cane-talk and land-talk, mostly. He sat comfortably in a cane armchair. Mosquitoes hummed around his ears; they were going to be more troublesome when the rain started. He would walk across with the two pan-boilers, Jain and Tomas, whose bawdy conversation amused them more than it amused him; the love of the word 'Salop' never far from their mouths. Pan-boilers were not like the other workers; they put a little of their magic in making the sugar just right, without lumps. There was the joke Augustus heard that they talked to the syrup; they had had special training in sugar making. Augustus knew how tricky this sugar making was. There could be spoilt syrup if the steam got out of the control of the men. Things went wrong when the ball bearings got too hot and the engineer had to come and attend. He was not far away, within calling distance in his residence.

The night usually passed quickly and it was always pleasant in the morning. It was a crisp dawn air up there and he enjoyed his return journey down at six o'clock. He was glad that the harvest was over, and now the air was smokeless, he could see a skyline. No swish of cane leaves as he walked on ash coloured ground, his shoes knocked on the stubs of cane plants. Far away was the engineer's house on the hill close to the dam, he could see the dome shape on top. On close inspection, it was a white two-storey house of wood with triangular corners. The engineer could use a telescope to get a view of things from a distance, but not these days, only in days when there was trouble on the field. Well, Augustus thought, the observance of those unfortunate people had no limit.

He wondered about the money situation of the estate with so many employees to be paid. The mechanics, the office staff, the managers, the loaders, the other laboratory workers like him. One of the laboratory men, an ex-teacher who left teaching because of low pay, had talked of emigrating because here his pay was still small. This man had suggested to Augustus that he should borrow books from the estate library and learn about soil conditions best for successful cane, and that he should do a correspondence course in agriculture from an American college. Then he might get a promotion.

His stomach rumbled and his lips felt dry. He moistened them and quickened his steps down into town, past the small hamlets of the small houses, making all the hairpin bends, and reached town two hours later.

Now, Dujon has at last begun to think of politics. He might have a chance to be a member on the Town Board. Guy had given Augustus the latest developments days before but he had not been able to attend meetings.

They had arranged to meet on Sunday evening for companionship to walk and to talk and argue, and so when they started their stroll, Augustus whistled a tuneless tune. Guy said, "My sister complains that the administrator keeps her very busy; she cannot type fast enough. I have no idea what government business will do in these times, her lips are sealed, secrecies rule prevents her from telling me anything."

"What of the future, do we have government? The Employers' Federation have power and the sugar bosses."

"True, two steps forward, two steps backward is our story. Seven times British, seven times French. Maybe now is the moment and it should be used properly by the Union."

"I know all what you are saying about me, not getting involved."

Earth crunched beneath their feet. They were descending to Denbow's side of the hill to the waterfront. "You should hear Dujon, he's looking for somebody like you with your perfect English and memory of our history to be an Executive member of the Union."

"Me!" Augustus stopped.

"They want to ask you. I'm only preparing you for that time so you won't be surprised when one of the Union boys approach you."

"I cannot do it." Abruptness told his friend not to prod. Augustus tried to wriggle out of it in this way: "Man, I might be taking a correspondence course in Agriculture from a college in America."

"When did you decide this?" Guy had thought wrongly that Augustus would be wasting his life by not trying to get further.

Augustus knocked on Mr Denbow's door, few pleasantries passed between them. They left soon. He told Guy, "I need to get a canoe to get up to Anse Chabon next weekend for some food. Will you come with me?"

"Yes. Sure. I know your ability Ham and trust you, for that I'll come as I know I will not end my days at the bottom of the sea." Guy laughed.

They climbed up, made a circle towards town and Augustus said, "You remember this Thomas Hardy poem we learnt in form four? He wrote about the 'Primeval rocks'..."

"Yes. I remember... what they record in colour and cast is – that we two passed..."

CHAPTER SIXTEEN

Olga had not gone to Mr Francois. She said to Aunt Hazel that she felt feverish. In spite of that, in the afternoon she took Era to visit Boo and was surprised when Augustus entered the yard with Cyril after work. He must have passed to collect something, she thought. He said that they had seen a lot of activity at the police station. Olga picked up on that; usually, she was not garrulous – being brought up by taciturn Muriel – but the change in their lives he had seen her loosening up, speaking with less reserve. He saw her gesticulate with her arms and shake her head with positive agreement to what Boo had said. She talked and laughed loudly with Boo in her kitchen where the men had seen them. She seemed a trifle too animated in his opinion.

Later at home when she told him that she felt feverish he told her she needed more rest.

Muriel told her, "*Ish mwe,* we have to keep strong."

He noticed that her arms were thin and today her face looked dull. Panic got him; was there something wrong with her? He studied her seriously, but he could only think that she could not be pregnant, he knew that she could not be, and whatever it was would be helped if she spent a couple days resting.

But in reality it came down to generations. She did not have some of the philosophical humour of her Aunt or of the cousins. Even her mother, if pushed, found some of the ironical jokes to ease pain. Olga saw a surface layer of life; her syncretic views did not reflect the oldest memories of Masav. She was beginning to feel that.

Later, when she went into the kitchen, Ma George, bare footed, turned her rumpled ochre face to Olga with a questioning look. She offered to make a tisane for her. Olga was grateful; the older woman said a few more words to her before she moved from the kitchen to sit with Miss Hazel. Ma George had said to her "I do it like dat, I does make every day for me, to do my business. If dat day fink it bigger dan me, I look it in de eye and nuffin stop me. My eyes always open wide to see."

Olga thought of these words and also those about Ma George's husband, who had drowned while fishing, and her only child had died young.

Olga's pride was her mainstay because she had been given it by Muriel and Augustus; she was proud of Era and more so, because Augustus was strong and spoke such good English. She waited for the tisane. She was tempted to ask her Aunt to give her the whole story about Harry. It would have been easier with her Aunt rather than her mother, whose past life had been a closed book, who lived without much conversation, never chatted. How could she bring up this subject of her past boyfriend? She had repeated her mother's silence.

She had a strong need now to speak to her mother as a daughter – with respect – but pry all the same. She just had to find the right moment.

Ma George brought her the drink, warm and pungent.

Aunt Hazel said, "I smell *shapantey* and *shado bene*."

Ma George had her neck to one side and a faint smile. She told Olga she should also take *twa tas* to relieve the inflammation.

Lying down as Augustus recommended now seemed enticing, and she did so. She entered the dark room and slept soundly till the next morning. The sunlight forced itself through the jalousie and she jumped out of bed. Augustus had left for his early start.

Aunt Hazel knocked on her door.

"When you change your clothes, come in the shop, I want to tell you some things," she said in patois.

That surprised her but her Aunt wanted the best for them, was generous with cloth. She imagined her Aunt was up to something, was she feeling some kind of pressure because things were not going according to her liking? She dressed quickly, combed Era's hair, sent her down to sponge herself.

Obediently she placed herself in her Aunt's shop. Aunt Hazel appraised Olga, her elegant form, the hair like tiara on her head, the half-moon black eyes. She did not tell her that Muriel went about copying her all through their young days had followed her to Masav, no surprise to her. Then she fell in love with a yellow man as she herself had a Creole man. What she said was, "Your mother really made up her mind to go to Aruba. What about you, do you want to go over there too?"

Olga only wanted to unburden her mind. She responded, indirectly, "My mother was living only to give me a decent life. When Augustus came to the door the first time she told him not to darken her door if he had no good intention towards me."

Miss Hazel was deep in thought. "I promised to go with your mother when she goes to see about her savings."

Olga changed tack. "Harry was my fadder?"

Her Aunt's very round black irises gave her a serious look – just as serious as her own hooded one.

"I liked Harry."

Olga remembered her Aunt's white boyfriend. Atavism had not happened in her own case. She had not chosen like them.

She said to her Aunt, "My mother never talked about him with me and I did not miss having a fadder."

"He played good clarinet. Everybody liked Harry."

She thought that her Aunt would now give her chapter and verse about him. She looked at her enquiringly; there should be some more to come. But she studied her niece as she usually weighed up situations, and told her, "Your mother should have stayed away from him." As an afterthought, "She loved you and she loves Era but I too know her ways – buried the past before you were born."

Miss Hazel stood up. "I know perhaps it takes patience to untie the knot. Patience! Patience!"

They could hear talk from the kitchen, Ma George's two-tone voice: Doh in the ascending and then the descent, "*I pa sav, I pa sav no.*"

Olga wondered who did not know what, and who was going to inform who about whatever. Ma Boy looked serious at what she had heard. Olga noticed she had a Canari in her hands, holding it over the coal pot where she would place it over the hot coals. They were in the yard. It was not often they cooked in the open. Her daughter was in attendance.

Aunt Hazel wondered how these women and the man in her house would maintain a good nature – the 'cargo' of her ship. She did not want any spillage. She now stood on the bridge and played her role as she tackled the dasheen and green bananas. She started peeling them. She felt a new surge in the waters. The waves and eddies were getting to be more and more of a pattern.

"*Danse' mawi danse'*!" Ma George made her pronouncement. Marie's music was unmistakable, awesome. Some old people marked the time this music was heard. All sorts were the things that people saw and heard in St Benedict.

CHAPTER SEVENTEEN

The air was warm and thick. An important man from town had just left Electra's house. He wanted a Chapit reading and her guidance to keep harm away. She swept the room after he left just as she had swept it the day Miss Hazel had come to see her recently. With all the hardships in town she had got quite a few people calling on her. She came out to rest against the side of the house.

"The wind is springing up." Fredericka, her daughter, nodded assent.

The mystic continued, "This fire was not as big a mischief as that which was caused by the powers of evil. Two hundred years ago, the French were settled well in St Benedict. The English and French made war and the British won, so the French put a big fire before they gave up. The Africans ran away, the Caribs ran off to Marie Galante. The French people went to Martinique." She rambled on in the old French language.

This island! Electra the Chapit knew all the past events of the times. The fact that she was wise and gifted was never disputed – outliving a normal life span. Her daughter was over eighty years old. Both were masculine looking with low cut hair. Electra's sex was disputed. It was difficult to tell by her mode of dress and her voice. "After the next war the English was pushed out; white men came from Belgium, the D'Auvergne and Corsica. Greeks came. The white men brought Africans from Dahomey, Senegal, Congo and Cayenne. Ships took our coal, there were rich people in this land, you know these things already. Creoles from Martinique, Barbados, Grenada as well as Mulattoes and Douglas came to live. It was a lively place, lots of music and dancing, big stores. Later, Indians came from Bihar and Uttar Pradesh bringing Madras cloth; Madras ways." Her eyes were closed and she rubbed the smooth stone caressingly, inside her palm. "Duck Island is where the Caribs come to bury their dead in the cave; their spirits so powerful, I hear them talking. It's an angel that put the fire in town to bring back egality and fraternity in the town." Then, "Come close, I'll give you the secret words I use before my readings."

The sibilant tone changed to something harsh. Frederica trembled. "Be warned! Do nothing to harm anyone. I only work to help those who come to me."

The two-roomed clapboard house stood on a low mound of earth close to Cocoa and mango trees. A slow, narrow river ran over glistening white rocks, they could see the whiteness of that from where they sat. A little way off was an asphalt road where a few cars passed now and then. Electra said that she was going to lie down. The wind fanned the leaves and Frederica saw her mother slip but did not fall. She seemed to have shrivelled before her eyes. She followed her inside.

They passed through the first room, where every wall had a mirror and there were oils in bottles and seeds in jars. Her windows and door stood open during the day except when a client called. Neighbours treated her with deference and brought her food sometimes. Electra waved her daughter away.

Later she resumed her determined repetitions of the things she knew. Her grey kaftan billowed around her. The daughter, unlike her mother, was bare of beads and bangles. They wore the same clothes, a Kalson on their lower half. She had regained the seat against the side of the house. The evening collected the glow of the low sun; the sky began to purple. She stood up. "The Chinese came from Canton with bright silk cloth, more Greeks from Corinth. Leprechauns came too! So much mischief! They tied up the minds of all businessmen, made money for themselves and took off. That was when people lost their minds and there was a malediction as if they had glass eyes, eyes being plucked out of their heads. That blindness spread on everybody because of the tragedy of their ancestors.

"People took to the seas, went away and came back, go and come, go and come. Never ending. I see the misery that greed for money brought on people's heads, malediction – envie! So many people…" she spoke slower and slower now.

"Now after this fire, things will change and those who went will be able to come back to a better place."

She stood up and like a dervish whirled around and round, reciting some verses. Frederica thought that she might have to catch her if she started to fall but she stopped suddenly and was in the present, saying, "No more slaves, no more white people, only the people of the Island – just Benedictians."

The sun set on the horizon over the harbour. The bright orange tinged the blue orb and radiated pink and violet in the sky over the sea, and over Electra's head it was an empty pale blue of twilight. "People that feel the squeeze after this fire now want big room to pass through the present time, to practice politesse, bon coeur, *bon volonte'* et courage."

Frederica was used to the sudden movements of her mother when her extra sensory moods affected her and was not surprised when Electra started walking off towards the river and disappeared, the clothes flapping around her emaciated frame. It was not long before she reached the police station in town. She disturbed the air by her aged appearance. Her eyes glowed as she asked to speak to Sergeant Paine. As she waited by the counter, the corporals felt their neck stiffen. They worried. She muttered.

"Good evening Electra." He knew of her, had seen her before in the town. "You wanted to see me?"

He preferred being on the beat and welcomed this interruption.

"I have news for you," she told him in the sibilant, singular voice she had.

He had enough understanding of things in the island to ask her into the private room even as she unnerved him. She named three policemen who had gone into the Peoples Bank and taken money. She spoke in French and he did not understand much, but seeing some patois was similar he got the gist pretty much. That was serious news. He believed her. He asked her to write the statement.

"Mais bien si"

Her bangles jangled as she reached her hand for the pen, dipped the nib in ink, signed when she finished. She stood up, looked down into his upturned face like she was reading his mind and he, with the back of his hand, wiped away the beads from his forehead. He felt hot. He let her make her exit as she wished him goodnight and he answered the same.

After she left, his thought was 'more trouble for the police'. The report would find itself before the administrator because that was what he expected the Colonel to do, naturally. After she left he told the two in the station that he was going out.

She was out there in the dark moonless night. He saw her ahead of him, then she was lost in the dark. He stood before the small side door of the Catholic church and made the sign of the cross, knowing of the sudden demise of people through sorcery – what was locally spoken of as 'somebody doing you something'. He had heard cases of some black magic when he attended court cases, murders because of *zeb,* and he continued in the direction of the chief's house.

The long road taking him there was usually thickly populated at all times. He walked quickly, unlike his usual way, but it was unusually quiet, houses closed, lamplight from half-opened jalousies. He knew some people saw him pass by and may have used the epithet that was used largely, taking liberty with their tongues.

He saw a girl looking out of the Colonel's window. He stood in front of the house, he spoke to her and she said quietly, "Papa, someone to see you outside."

He joined her at the window, "Come in Paine, the door is open."

"How come you here?" he asked, screwing up his eyes with a twitch of his nose.

"Well, sir, I have some information. It cannot wait till tomorrow."

He made a motion to his daughter to go. Then he told him what Electra said. "Statement was written, what you going to do? Felix and Challo now down the coast, you sent them to new postings!"

"I cannot believe it!" the Inspector told the Sergeant. "I'll deal with them."

Their views were different. The inspector was a man with a rough edge, and his favoured men, Oceancy, Felix and Challo, behaved with bullying ways in the course of duty. It was 'them and us', society and them, and having the lodge was their ambition.

Glisse!

The spinning vortex was in motion and Philosophe was wary. The Colonel, an arbitrary title fixed on him by his own men, was the most senior officer. There was no superintendent. They were waiting one. He was drill inspector and person in charge. His usual way was to evade questions asked by his Sergeant.

"I would like to be present when you speak to Oceancy."

"I think it will be better to get Challo first, much quicker than with Oceancy."

The West India Regiment had been stationed in St Benedict to maintain law and order but when they left, the police had a difficult job. The Sergeant had arrived from Guyana to work on the island. The Colonel spoke of that period with pride. He was a very frustrated man and Philosophe knew that. He left the man's house.

Dance Marie, dance.

He saw young men in groups, young women strolling in the dark, typical of this sometimes-volatile area of town. He caught a few invectives thrown in his direction but he was not worried; water off a duck's back.

Electra walked; her body took on the lightness of air but she kept her feet moving, hurrying. A full moon was shining bright. She knew there was to be an eclipse that night. A time when the sun and the moon were in confrontation, the earth making its shadow a kind of warning, fire in the sky!

She had not eaten for the day. She should hurry and have a meal. The power of earthly spirits would make a small shift, something being destroyed and being born again in the nature of things.

She watched the eclipse; the moon appeared to die for a long while; a death of fire. The blackness on the sky! Then, the redness of the moon happened as if it was being cooked, so Electra said prayers for protection, to protect her life. Her mind travelled inwards and backwards.

Next morning her restless body delivered her message by the roadside. She stood on a small hillock a mile away from her house. She came back to her house and returned to the spot, talking to passers-by in a high loud voice. Her neighbours saw her pass frequently, right through the morning, and they found out what it was about. Carl passed about nine o'clock on his way to Francois' shop.

Electra said, "Please listen! Chicane is what I have to talk about. Go to town and find out about your money that was in the old bank that got burnt. During the fire some people stole money. This is no *pala pata*. I am telling you, go and ask the police!"

The loud voice sounded mad and she looked disturbed. Frederica was worried. Something was happening to her mother. Just before noon she stopped and returned to the house.

Her daughter did not want a surge of people coming to see her mother that day. She made a decision. She sent a message to a young man who owned a horse and cart – she would pay him a fair price to dismantle that clapboard house and take it to the place she told him. She waited through the afternoon and was relieved they had peace about their house. The white of the small river was visible through the trees the same way.

Electra took this decision of her daughter calmly, and the man came and laid clapboard upon clapboard in the cart. Electra moaned and whimpered loudly as she watched. Her daughter none the less was anxious but she thought it was best. They were busy together, taking care not to break the jars of ointments, the oil in bottles. The dry herbs were gathered, put together safely.

In the evening, as the sun appeared to increase its size going down, she said, "I'll sit by the river till it's time to leave."

Frederica approached the shady spot where she could see her mother's large kaftan between cocoa trees and she came to her from the back. Her mother sat erect. Something that the daughter could feel, unease, made her heart race. Electra turned to her; she gave a start.

"*Oye*! Mamma!"

"Don't jump Frederica, it's me. I'm passing through something. It just suddenly happened and surprised me just as you are shocked."

The sibilant French more pronounced than ever. Electra had changed; she had the face of a young woman.

"We must go now. Both of us."

Frederica was beguiled and confused. Their things were on the cart. They climbed up.

"I'll come back for the little that you see I left behind."

CHAPTER EIGHTEEN

Tantara sounds, quick quadruple notes, were everywhere in Masav. Philosophe was surprised when Popo entered the station; he flew past with the Colonel. All he could do was speculate as to this meeting.

Bright and early, before the heat descended, Philosophe had been writing some reports on his interviews of suspicious people in town. He had used his own brand of working on people. Some mysteries had been solved because of his hunches; when every path seemed a dead end, with a boldness of his own peculiarity, tinged with bravado, he had made progress. He had made a few arrests even as he was mocked. Mr Popo always hurried in a black suit and a rolled black umbrella. He used it as a cane and as a protection from the hot sun in the middle of the day as one might have observed him. He had style.

He spent some time with the chief, and after he left, Philosophe was summoned into his room. He heard that Mr Popo had handed in his report of the affairs of the bank and he said that the papers were there for inspection. The chief seemed pleased. In the other's mind he thinks that the chief is happy, things going his way. Earlier with the start of the day he had kept a drill session in the yard, he had shouted his orders: right turn, left turn, right about turn! And he had them marching up and down.

This morning, clumps of people stood on sidewalks. Miss Hazel and Muriel reached the rusty bare earth where the Town Board now stood – what had been the American servicemen quarters, brought down from the base and now standing close to the sea of the wharf. The sisters saw that others had the same idea as themselves.

Mr Popo had already made a deal with the bank, De Monde, in New Orleans; this idea had the consent of the Town Board members, so he felt righteous and unafraid. He envisaged a good return for the people of the town in two years because the stock market in America was in a profitable phase. He sat in the Town Board, heard some voices from the exterior but not aware that people were coming to ask for their money.

Muriel had put on a dress restyled for her by Olga, one of her sister's clothes. It fitted her loosely. The pale apricot crepe dress. On her feet were the usual priest-like black sandals, her head was covered with a dusky pink small straw hat. She carried a small black purse. She planned to humble herself before Popo because she wanted her savings.

Two council constables stood by the entrance. Miss Hazel pushed to the front before them.

"We want to see Mr Popo."

To their surprise they both shrugged, and as if they caught the mood of the people just waved them inside the building, but said, "You all can't all see Mr Popo uh!"

While one went from the position, came back about an hour later, people were standing on the sidewalk waiting.

"Some of you have to come back tomorrow. Only twenty people can be seen today," he told them in the vernacular.

"This is a *mamaguy* job," a man said loudly from outside.

Muriel felt humble sitting in silence, waiting. When she went in with her sister into the large waiting room, she looked at the man with the sloping backward forehead above the sweating cocoa-like face. He mopped his brow. He only smiled when he put his hands together, finger tips touching before him. Muriel could see his caracole eye movements.

She was poised, and took her small bank book that she had kept in Augustus grip for safe-keeping along with his valuables.

"So, you have savings?"

"I've been stripped by the fire. It's only dogs left waiting to come and attack me, I want my savings." In patois.

He had spoken in English, but she did not mind; she would speak how she felt was right. He was silent. Then he said in a stern voice, "I have the money in a bank in America and I can give you bonds for your money. In a year or two, you can use that to get your money and there will be more than what you had saved." He smiled.

Miss Hazel's nostrils flared, she made a movement with her hands to draw his eyes her way. And she said slowly in patois, "I am member of Pegasus Lodge, so, I tell you to give her her savings."

Somehow, she said to herself, he knew what to do if he was forced. Popo was thoughtful. The room was silent. They could almost feel the intensity of his thinking. Miss Hazel always said that he had lots of brains. He took a pen and paper, wrote a few lines, folded it and gave it to Muriel. "You know Mr Lord. He is a lawyer. Take this to him and he will advise you."

Muriel smiled, satisfied, but no inkling that it might not be as it seemed – cut and dried. Miss Hazel's mouth opened wide to ask more questions, then closed again. Muriel stepped out in a good mood.

"Why did you not read the note in front of him?" She felt the anger in her shoulders and neck. Now, Muriel's mood adjusted to yesterday's feelings when she stopped and looked at the note with Miss Hazel.

Olga, hanging out some clothes, saw her mother's serious face. She heard conga drum beats. Why couldn't she bend down, wiggle her hips, move her feet to the sound of the anxious beats? But her mother was calm and remote as habitual style. The whole business was in God's hands, she thought, and this was what she said when Olga asked her what happened. Oh yes! Olga thought, it was like this all the time; that's why the rhyme went:

Teddy bear, teddy bear turn around
Teddy bear, teddy bear, touch the ground
Teddy bear, teddy bear, shoot out your foot
Teddy, bear, Teddy bear, bow to your master.'

She saw Muriel scratch her left hand and smile a wry smile; right hand itch – you received money, left hand itch – you spent money. Even the sky looked wounded she thought, looking up. Clouds hastened speedily; this was an indication of a storm ahead, it was mid-August after all. The large drops of rain plummeted down in an instant and were over. "Only a blessing," she said. Thunder rolled softly far away after the rain stopped. Muriel stayed in the yard after she had helped Olga gather the clothes from the rain and she was soaked, but did not seem worried. Miss Hazel watched her, concerned by her slowness to get in out of the rain.

Later, Olga went to vespers with her mother; she took Era along. Muriel said, "Olga, since the fire, first time water fell down on me, the rain felt so good!" She had sat squeezed a few times into her sister's tin bath and Olga got her meaning.

While they were out, Augustus pressed to finish the *Rose and Cross* book so he could return it to Mr Polius and then start on the book about soil and cane cultivation. He sat by the open window in the small room. The part of the book dealing with occult things made a type of impression, as though it was a nervous reaction – his head felt full and heavy. He read on about members being adept and practiced. He was alerted by one proposition that followers finding the light with training, found the good path when they could cure ills of mind and body. This was way above him, he thought. Anyway, one of the things he understood was the sacred nature of work, members excel in this creed and the members practiced humility and lived for justice. Well, if that was the case, why did not this society have more members who come out and say, 'I believe in Rosicrucian things'? He wanted to return the book to Mr Polius that day whether he finished all of it or not. He had found out enough. He saw no reason to change his lifestyle. He would not copy anyone. If someone told him that he was false, a false person, he would say no. He was sure in his bones that he could not be anything but what he was.

He entered the familiar little pink house. The ex-school master was having discourse with Mr Richardson. He listened. "The spark of the Divine is in all things…"

To Augustus he said, "The body carries the spirit; be good to the spirit inside. The body upsets the spiritual by stupid deeds. The spiritual is fragile."

Richardson could not resist: "Dancing vigorously strengthens your spirit. Don't you agree?"

"Will power is the thing to make all things possible with faith, I believe many things and I doubt nothing." Mr Polius was his usual self.

"Sir, I finished *The Rose and Cross*, it held a fascination for me. It is a strong book, I felt."

Mr Polius answered, thoughtfully, "Life is easy with shut-up eyes. Sometimes, the reality is…"

"I agree sir."

He wanted to get back home, since it was only with his ex-teacher that he wanted to discuss the book. He allowed the conversation to go on between the men.

"Trade Unions are now stronger because of support from England Trade Unionists and The Jamaica Trade Unionists."

"Mr Popo is a very powerful man. Since the fire it surfaced that he had lots of connections in money things. He has a tight grip on St Benedict."

"Do you know America wants to lease our island from England?"

"Of course not! But we have lots of Yankees around, especially in Anse Du Fort."

Augustus got up to leave. He looked at Mr Polius with a mischievous, slightly arrogant smile, his teeth glinting below his moustache and chiselled bow-shaped lips. He was a reflection of the two, their discussions nothing new to him.

"You must be wise, be strong." Their look said: You know how it is.

"I'm strong." That stayed in his mind, moving along in the early night of his home town, so suddenly changed.

Olga sat twisting her hair, and pinned them before lying down. She sensed his moodiness when he came back. He opened their room's window, which faced the lane and looked outside. Their candle burnt with a long flame. When she cut into his thoughts with words that dwelt on the business in town, he brought his eyes towards her. The room now seemed bright and she stood in front of him. "You must be wise now, after finishing your book!"

"Me! Wise! You joking?" He took her seriously. "Knowledge is like soap. Soap can do lots of things, like bubbles – but in order to make bubbles you have to agitate soapy water; see how quickly these bubbles disappear. Everything is flat again."

She touched his shoulder lightly. "You know what Mr Popo did, he gave my mother a note to take to a lawyer. She could get a loan it said."

He had heard about the American bonds.

"I'm thinking of going to see Mr Popo myself. These times are different times for us all."

This ball game was getting faster every day. He was watching that ball.

"That's a good idea," she said.

She was happy to stand with him by the window for a bit while Era lay on the bed with her doll. The stars were out above the thick black of the night. In Augustus' mind was the word 'light' and the meaning of that which was something so opaque to him, and if he mentioned to her that one thing the book advised was that people found the 'light' she would talk about the ways of becoming *deck-deck*.

He shut the window, took the large red blanket and opened it a little on the floor. She said, "Mammie's got a headache. I'm so worried about her. She got a soaking in the rain and did not change her clothes; stayed in them for a while."

Muriel's soft voice in reply to Olga's words assured her that the headache was because of the heat and that was all, though she held a bay rum soaked cloth to her forehead.

"Goodnight, sleep well," she told her.

Back in her own quarters, she found him asleep. She got up on the bed next to Era. The things worth talking about had not been said yet. He really had not told her much, and what kind of talk about bubbles? What kind of parable was that? Did he expect her to understand talk like that? And not a word of patois, have a little patois humour? He had not said a thing about the Rosicrucian book and the way things might be turning out, some of the chicanes and scheming that people were getting into. People had to know where to put a foot.

The first words she heard on waking next morning from out in the street, "Your *mudda* head!"

Someone was cursing somebody's mother. The sun was up and Augustus had left. She rushed into Aunt Hazel's room. Muriel was alone, still holding a cloth to her head with eyes closed. She said she was not going to work. Olga's anxieties were doubled. "You must take some medicine. But what else you feeling? Apart from your headache?"

"That's all and I have a little fever."

"Aunt Hazel have mustard, uh?"

"She already rub some under my feet."

They were silent. Her aunt came back with something hot in a cup.

"The coals got wet, took so long to light. Anyway here is some arrowroot pap to give you strength. I'll go out to look for some *kokom coolie* bush."

"I'll find it; I saw some growing by Mr Francois'. I'll go by the presbytery to tell them you are sick."

That day had begun with somebody out there annoyed, letting out insulting words to a person, but now all was quiet. Olga made her steps a little quicker, tripping over her feet with the unaccustomed pace. In the large cobbled yard of the presbytery, beneath its covered yard, a car stood taking up much of the room. She squeezed past, saw the face of on older woman who had been at work for years in the kitchen. A young priest entered from the street with a group of people. He stopped, thinking Olga was someone asking for help with their facilities as well. His brows went up after she introduced herself, and he told her in accented English that she could find the Vicar General up the broad concrete steps, over a balcony, and she should enter the parlour.

But he was coming towards the door and she came face to face with him.

"Morning Father."

He'd been there for many years; they were not strangers. He was fully dressed, black hat on. She had never seen a priest with a bare head, except when saying mass. She told him about her mother. He was sympathetic, patted her shoulder and spent a few moments telling her how stoic her mother was, and so good. Olga was touched and he told her that Muriel should take a week off to rest.

She brought the news back, knowing that it was good news but her mother had not been ill in bed ever, not liking to be idle. But her mother, facing the disappointment about the money and now this, waiting around while life slowed down, accepted Olga's news and said, "I will get up later."

Earlier Olga had seen her mother physically gather the day to herself when she sat by the side of the bed to drink the pap. She felt her forehead and was surprised how hot it felt. She asked for the lime squash that was on the table across from her.

"Ma George said she want to go back to Bonne Terre." Muriel told Olga.

CHAPTER NINETEEN

Routine's way just slipped back. On Thursday afternoon, Olga sat on the balcony with Muriel. She looked better, and surprisingly, Olga realised that she was not itching to return to work. They spoke about the Aruba idea and her mother could not ignore this possibility to make a better situation for herself. But how could she do so? That Ma George was also making plans for herself was big news to Olga, that old woman who said that she would look at life boldly and it was not bigger than her.

"Hazel did her best for me about the money business, what will I do?"

"Augustus told me he will go to Mr Popo's house today to tackle him. He knows him well, you see, from the past."

That evening as Augustus rode past the police station, he was sure there were more comings and goings than usual. He could not help thinking about the missing money. He was doubtful whether the police had investigated it. He speculated that Mr Popo had his clique to organise something strange – a new idea – for Masav. These bonds! He had to visit him with more questions. He did not want to get into any argument with him but his rein on himself seemed not as tight.

When he returned to the house he was glad to see that Muriel looked better.

"I rubbed down with coconut oil and camphor," she told him.

"Later on, I will go to see Mr Popo," he informed them.

He turned on his heel, entered the bedroom, and came back and said, "Olga I am going to Cyril, there's something we have to talk about."

He took a stroll about town. September was looming with the rain; what will these people on the Square do? He felt strongly that they should be moved, as he headed for the bad luck town people still living there. It was fortunate, he said to himself, that he had put off going to Cyril, and now he saw Sampson sitting on the camp bed. The air was heavy. Clothes were spread on the croton hedges behind the wire fencing.

Augustus was speechless facing him. Sampson was looking at his feet, a scowling, fierce stare as if they annoyed him. He did not see Augustus until he heard, "Where have you been, Mr Sampson? I've been looking for you."

He stood up from where he sat and made a movement with his head for Augustus to follow him. They walked out to the dirt walkway to the far corner of the Square, close to the street. They stood amidst the chatter going on from different groups and Sampson said, "I was arrested earlier and released."

All of Sampson's old angry outbursts were the things before his eyes. "I made a bad mistake," he said.

"What's that?"

"Things went wrong."

Augustus was waiting for something like sense to come out, then he heard, "My fate is sealed."

Sampson walked away with his limp. Augustus stretched his arm to grab him but he moved among the people in a hurry. Ma Sampson was not far, she saw him rush past. When Augustus came to her, she said, "Good thing he did not break his neck climbing the church roof early this afternoon in the hot sun. He is insane, that's what."

She had given the police assurances that he would behave after they released him but she did not have any hope of that.

"Come to have some food at Miss Hazel on Sunday. I believe my mother-in-law asked her for you to come and stay with us. She said you are welcome. I think you should bring Betty and you can stay."

"O.K."

There was no sign of Sampson. It had taken great effort to get him down from the church roof where he had climbed, first on to the side wing and then higher up. He reached to the bell tower when people who had been watching got a ladder from the presbytery, while some got Philosophe from the station. In spite of his gammy leg, he had been agile.

The night before the fire, he paid another visit to the Gentlemen's club, again to test the attitude. Clifford was there having a drink. He sat with a mulatto Bertie and when Sampson came in, Clifford came to him and harassed him in sly statements, annoying and embarrassing him.

Augustus stood on the dirt ground facing Ma Sampson, stressing that she should take her possessions. He would help her, if the next day was alright.

"Where does he get to?"

"Family somewhere, I do not know them."

He thought how could that happen, Sampson not taking charge of his family? He also wanted to continue on his intended journey to visit Mr Popo but he would have to leave out the visit to Cyril. He shook her hand. Mr Popo was such a busy body but because it was now late, he would expect to find him in.

Mr Popo's house, two-storey, up a narrow path, close to its edge and the tallest in the south, was in the thickly populated part of the town. His wife sat in the corner of the balcony, rocking steadily in her chair. Out of the corner of her eye, she saw her husband come and look over the balcony. He had heard her answer Augustus' question from the street. Popo let him in downstairs and he led him upstairs to find the wife no longer on the balcony. He shook Augustus' hand effusively. In the back of Augustus mind were Guy's words, "I want Popo to lose his seat on the Town Board, this election coming in December."

He looked at the man's large Adam's apple bobbing up and down. He felt that he knew the man and answered to, "How you doing Gustus? I have not seen you anywhere but I've been thinking of you. I offer you my sympathy. It was hard. It used to be a good town. People got on alright uh?"

Augustus was taken off guard because he agreed that the town had been a good town. He had liked it. He nodded his head in agreement but that was not what he had to talk about. He talked with a respectful tone.

"I'm afraid I'm disappointed. You have been missed since you have been absent from Mr Polius' and not even at Dujon's house the times I've been there."

"Other more pressing matters, you must realise, as my position entails. I cannot meet anyone on the same level again. What can I do for you?"

"I've heard about the American bonds. My mother needs money. She does not want a bond."

"I read in the Trinidad Guardian very encouraging details which helped me with my decision and with other information that it seemed wise that I invested in a bank in New Orleans. It's a good time for American money. I know the score; all the money will be safe."

He remembers Augustus at gatherings in the past of course, he knows the attitude of his respect and the older men's eyes meeting his as if he was sounding board when they spoke and he remained silent.

"I want the advice which will help my mother-in-law."

"The business people will get together. I know what I am about. Barclay's Bank can assist someone like her with an urgent need."

Could he trust this man when the Union men had hopes for a better life for everyone? Did they agree with Popo? He did not think they did. He had acted so quickly and done this.

"That night of the fire, all the fear and confusion, the safety of my child – all that which I took for granted, I was so full of rage, I was unable to save our house."

"Couldn't you and the family put out the fire in the shop?"

"Of course we could not, by the time we woke up, it was too late."

Everything changed in an instant. Talking to Popo he saw that he took Era off in a panic before tackling the flames himself. He stood up feeling unsettled.

His feeling of anger had returned because of the man's insensitivity. The idea! Anyway, he did not come for that.

"I am not asking for my own savings but if my mother-in-law will definitely be able to get hold of the money she had saved, this I think you should be considering. Goodnight Mr Popo."

From his side of town, he did not see Sampson being escorted again into the police station, a small crowd behind in the street outside.

I know he looked at me as though I was a stupid Anse Chabon man, he mused on his return to the house. It was late and he went into their room. Augustus looked at Olga, her face outlined by the lamplight, the black hair like a soft black cloud, full and all over the place. She plucked some chords in his heart, her sharp angled eyes cast their spell as she smiled, putting down the dress she had been hand sewing. Her receptive face welcomed him.

"Guess who I saw."

"I cannot think of anybody."

"Well, Sampson, and he was arrested today."

"He was arrested?"

"I'm telling you!"

First, Olga thought, what is wrong with men? Then, poor devil, more charitably. She changed the subject.

"You saw Mr Popo?"

"Yes, I spent a long time with him. All the money of the bank is truly resting in New Orleans. He said it will be worth more and the town will be better off."

"Oh!"

"Let's get to sleep. I'll tell you more tomorrow."

Isaac Popo was a man of mystery to Augustus. Driving home next afternoon in Cyril's car, he reflected on it. Who would have thought, if not told, that senior Mr Popo had cut cane? Cyril's cigarette hung from his lips while he steered down the hill. His knowledge that he gathered from people who were related to older estate workers used to mention the mystery of the Popo men. It was said the older man had not been part of and did not have the normal mentality of those labourers. He used to laugh more, he used to talk of his old country, he talked of the Limpopo river. His son, we now know as Isaac Popo, followed him cutting cane. What other work could they do in the time of 1887?

Isaac took a correspondence course in accountancy after cane harvest. "So he qualified as an accountant, without going to a college. The boy had good brains, no wonder," he had told Cyril.

People said he had gone to Venezuela to work and spent many years, then he came back. The only black man to be a member on the Town Board, now as a senior man is the manager of the People's Bank. Cyril added, "He was first an ordinary employee in the bank."

"He's one smart man. But he had to go away first, if not he could not even get a job in the bank with his colour." Olga had to say so.

"They say he works magic! There is talk, did you ever hear about that one?"

"No. I never."

"Why I know, is because I know a family in the lands up in the hills. They told me confidentially. That's why I'm telling you. He is one of them. They work a magic with spirits you and I never heard of."

Morning time, he met Guy to get moving on to the canoe rental. They walked to the edge of the town. Brilliance shone on leaves of trees on the small hill above Mr Denbow's canoe rental place as the rising sun hit the dew to sparkle there. They saw diamonds. The men trampled on the pebbles and knocked on the man's door. He came out, and not long after saw them on their way at the waterfront. Augustus thought of hurricane; right now hurricane weather was absent. St Benedict had no hurricane for years now, only heavy rain and rough seas, but he kept it in mind this August day. He sat on his straight bar facing Guy, his oars in his firm grasp. They hit the water that was silvery blue and flat in the land-locked harbour. Guy watched

Augustus' mischievous smile. He was slightly nervous; he was not best in such pursuits, aware that Augustus enjoyed being in control in his familiar hobby.

Augustus has a dream to be a man without a shadow, being inferior even to his friend Guy, feeling apart due to his origins in the village of fishermen and coal makers at Anse Chabon. He likes to row boats, just because he knows how to, and he muses he may have been a fisherman now, like his brother-in-law. From now on, he thinks, his shadow he always sees will annoy him less.

They were silent for the first hour. They passed Duck Islet and then Rat Islet, out in the open sea, the water now green. He lifted the canoe and dropped it again. He persuaded Guy to row for a short while; they had both been sea cadets.

CHAPTER TWENTY

The sand from the beach encroached on to the wide lane leading into the village. To Guy, it looked like a desert outpost. Augustus had not come empty-handed. He carried the thick cane syrup, a quart of white rum and two pounds of brown sugar in an empty milk powder tin.

His parents' home was deserted and he set out into the village. His mother approached, walking quickly from another direction, and she stopped short as they came up to her. A priest revved up a large motorbike; he was going to move on somewhere. A group of young boys ran behind him. "What's going on?" he asked her.

She took time to get over seeing him. She was silent, and he could see women coming from the direction in which she had come.

"They've come from Felix's mother's house. Felix died."

The air was white, everything stood in this light. Augustus wanted shelter and something cold.

"This is my friend. You know about Guy, mam?" he said to her. "It is a visit I thought to make. I don't need much but I was hoping to collect what I could to take to town."

They changed direction, moving the way of the family house.

"Your father went early with the cow. He should be selling the beef to customers now."

The day took on a sober atmosphere as they returned to the house and spoke about Felix, who was their cousin, four times removed. It was sudden death. Preparation of the dead and the funeral preparation make everything else take second place. She needed some coconut leaf stems to give them to finish the wreaths. Carmen's husband went to collect those for her now, and she had to return to the women and invite them to return with her.

"A! A!" she said in a troubled tone, "Felix only came back this way three weeks ago. They sent him to St Ange police station, to be in charge."

"I did not know where he was. I missed seeing him about."

"He died last night. He ate pawpaw when his body was hot."

They entered the compound of this place of bereavement. Augustus entered the small room. The coffin with Felix lay on three chairs. He looked at Corporal Felix and clamped his lips, shook his head in disbelief. It was strange to see him there. He turned away. Men in white shirts and dark pants sat around in the compound on whatever there was to sit on or lean upon – five men, dressed for the funeral. Some women, including Ma James, pulled at swathes of white and purple crepe paper, and curled them to make flowers to attach to coconut stem hoops with fine wire.

Guy stood patiently by the men. One of them spoke quietly. "Felix brain confused before he died; *Gason!* He thought he was in the fire in town. Ha ha! And was looking for money. If he was not so sick then at death's door, I would think he stole money from the bank."

Augustus left with Guy. He said he had to return to town and would miss the four o'clock funeral. Senior Mr James was at home. He made a shout of surprise seeing his son. "You come at the right time. Some beef here for you."

"You know Guy, Papa?" The old man said he was happy to know him, having heard much about him.

"You heard how Felix die? What a big man like him doing something so foolish! This sudden death business, perfectly healthy and getting buried! It's a joke. Remember your mother's sister she died when she ate *z'abrico* when she just finished pressing clothes?"

"How's Carmen? I will quickly go and see her. Is she in the house?"

"She is and must be getting ready for the funeral."

His sister was of enormous size last time he saw her and would be doing things slowly, whatever she could be doing in her home.

"Gustus," she screeched, and took hold of one of his biceps, squeezing it. She stared unbelieving. Life was so hard for him. "You must have some farine from me. We have enough. Pick some limes out there."

"I will leave before the funeral."

He smiled at her, at the size of her. She got busy preparing her offering as she wrapped the farine in cloth and tied it tight. Augustus stood in her doorway.

"I will go and get some mangoes, I see you have pumpkin? I'll be back in half hour. Let's go Guy to get some coconuts and what we can get."

He got a willing boy about twelve years – eager to show off – to go with him and to climb two coconut trees. He knew the boy, had seen him enough times before.

The dry coconuts he was happy for, to take to town while they refreshed themselves at the house with a green coconut. Augustus busied himself, dug up a pumpkin from Carmen's garden and got the limes she offered. His father said, "I'll wrap this beef well in lots of banana leaf."

Half an hour later, with the beef well stacked and put in additional paper, Augustus said, "I have to go now Papa, must get it home now otherwise we won't be able to enjoy it. Thank you, say goodbye to mam for me."

He took some money out of his pocket. "Here's a little something papa; now, there's something I need, a bicycle. Second hand will be all right; I cannot get one in town. Can you see for me?"

The journey back was laborious. Guy talked a lot of Union talk and school talk, the reopening of school, the difficulties he met at the school. He then said, after he had had his turn at rowing and now Augustus had the oars, "Man, you did not hear what somebody said about Felix, you were inside looking at him. The man said, Felix's mind wandered last night – the thing about the fire – he talked about the money in the bank; he must have had some dealing in that situation, I believe it worried him and that was why he rambled about it."

"That was what we will not know. It leaves a question mark."

They pulled up at the water's edge in Masav. Each took an end of the crocus bag; they left the canoe on the pebbles. Mr Denbow had been looking out for him, they waved to him and left quickly. Guy said, "It was a nice break from the dark broken town to be watching the sea in all its colours, turquoise, indigo, pale blue, green."

He had met Augustus' parents for the first time. The difference between him and his people was huge; his lisping sister lacked resemblance of him and it was like a secret side of Augustus had been newly revealed, but he was fond of his family, Guy realised.

"*Shite!* This bag is heavy man!" Guy adjusted his grasp on his end and stood still. A mass of sword ferns brushed against their pants on the shortcut through the vacant burnt house lots, near walls and concrete steps.

At the house, Augustus was greeted with Ma Boy's faded smile. The men dropped the bag on the kitchen floor. Augustus picked up the parcel of beef and opened it up; she rose from the small bench and ventured, "Put it in the sink. Quick, boss."

He asked for a knife and started to make divisions, gave Guy his share, other shares for Cyril and Mr Polius. He had to deliver those soon. Guy left. Aunt Hazel came into the kitchen to hear what was happening. She called Olga. Muriel followed with Era. Augustus put the beef to be delivered in a large pan and left.

"See that good piece of beef we have for tomorrow. Thank God for Augustus."

Aunt Hazel faced the others. "I will *woosi* ours tonight. If those people don't have coals to light fire they will only have to salt theirs. I have coals so I'm pleased."

Olga went for the lamp.

"*Meci.*"

Suddenly, what had been fixed and ended that day needed another effort. Muriel had spent the afternoon resting, she would have liked so much to go to confession but it had been out of the question in this leave from work phase. The very priest that employed her did not expect to see her there, she stated wearily. Now she looked on, not participating.

"*Fe dife' a pu mwe, cooze, souple!*"

Ma Boy responded to Miss Hazel's request and removed the coal pot from the kitchen, placed it on the back step of the house, lit the coals and stood fanning the flame alive. Aunt Hazel got salt and vinegar and some of their dry herbs and spices to mix in the beef.

Olga took the lamp off the living room wall, carefully shone the chimney, adjusted the wick, struck the match, replaced the chimney and returned to the kitchen with it. Aunt Hazel nodded. She held large portions of red meat in her hands; green and brown herbs were on the table. She left them to it.

"Come Era go and sponge," she urged her daughter.

Next morning Olga woke with the unspoken conversations she had planned and still not yet able to have with Augustus, about Philosophe and the tailor shop, what she had seen there and about the money situation which troubled her mother. But he got ready to leave for a Union meeting down the coast which Guy had urged him to attend.

The Anglican bells had not yet rung the mid-day mellifluous sounds calling to the rams, sheep and goats; the tune of the words sang by children when the bells rang. Ma Sampson with Betty arrived at Miss Hazel's for Sunday lunch. The daughter sulked.

"Bon jour Miss Hazel." She explained that she came early because that young lady was disagreeable. Olga asked how the husband was. She said he was sick in hospital now with a bleeding ulcer. The others, Cyril and his older children, arrived.

Miss Hazel took Olga upstairs to get the plates from the black iron trunk beneath her bed. There were bed sheets put away with wares. Damask white tablecloth wrapped the white plates with large pink roses. Into that dark space beneath the bed, the bright yellow dress with small bright red and bright blue shapes caused Olga's eyes to open twice their size with delight. This was a dress worn years ago, by her Aunt when people wore brighter colours.

They took the wares, closed the trunk, got up from their knees, straightened with the plates in their hands and went down to the kitchen where Ma Boy said everything was ready. Muriel put in her appearance in the yard, went to Ma Sampson in the golden midday sun, kissed her cheeks. Her lips moulded to the moist warm face and slowly she unstuck them. They spoke and Muriel made consoling sounds.

Miss Hazel and Olga carried the tureens of beef, the dasheen, yam and green plantain in a bowl and Era's eyes widened in surprise, never having seen so many plates of food. Olga noticed Ma Sampson's admonishing look at Betty, who scowled. She wondered what had newly happened to cause this bad humour. Ma Boy brought a jar of tamarind jam, Ma George some Rum Punch.

When Cyril and the children, Ma Sampson and Betty left through the side door next to the shop, it clicked after Betty. Olga sat unable to move, she then made a Herculean effort to collect Augustus' share of the meal for the night when he came back. She thought about the ephemeral food that had taken so much of their time to prepare – where was it now? No sign of the work that had gone before. The primal need to eat had been satisfied.

"*Mi chale!*" Muriel said, moving toward the stairs. Era, who had been leaning her head on the table, got up and followed her grandmother upstairs. Olga said, "I'll wash the wares later when it's cooler. I'll go and lie down now."

They left Aunt Hazel sitting by her table in this disorder but she was pleased that her food had been enjoyed and had left people satisfied.

Olga wondered how long Augustus was going to be, she scarcely spent time with him. She waited, the jalousies were open and the August heat close. Why had Aunt Hazel never installed a long pipe so people could bathe properly? Era fell asleep. Olga's restlessness took on an edge like an old hand strumming double bass. She loosened her plaits, she had the urge to look different for when he got back – so the maroon kimono in the large grip. She usually kept it there, in case of a special occasion, but now she lifted the heavy cold silk gown and put it on. The neck line left her neck and upper chest bare, it fell at her ankles. She tied the thin sash and sat by the window, peering through the slats. The light in the room was a wick floating in oil in a small bowl. When it seemed pointless sitting, looking out into the dark night, she lay down on the red blanket, every nerve tuned to the sound of his footsteps.

"Have you had your food?"

He nodded and she said, "My God, you're so late!" Her knees were drawn up to her chest, her eyes full on him, the geometrical eyes baleful.

"What's the matter?" he asked, worried.

"I just want to touch you, I am alone so much," she said.

"You have changed!"

"I don't know."

He looked anxious. She asked in return, "What's wrong?"

"The state of things."

He sat on the blanket and she lay her head between his neck and shoulder, then put a soft kiss on his neck. She said, "It's as though I've just met you, that's how I feel tonight."

"Why?" he asked.

"Don't know."

She felt that she had to familiarise herself to keep what she had been sure of, her hands touched his face and hair and found his hairy chest. He knows how to suppress most of his desires about everything by habit, he feels that their past lives and present life are in collision. He told her about some things of the day – Oceancy, the police down at Anse Du Fort had been a menace. She did not want to talk. They just made love.

Olga slept fitfully and was awake hours later, fore day morning, aware that he sat with the small grip on his knees, writing by candle light.

"What's that now? A! A!" he heard her say, so he put up a hand to shush her and wrote quickly; she chupsed and settled down again.

"Hear that, I dreamt of my voice saying these words, I have to write them."

"*Mwe mem!*" Now. She sat up. "Let me see!"

"Look!" She squinted sleepily and attempted to read where his finger pointed: BURNT OUT - EVERY LINE - WHICH MARKED MY HOME.

"I can't read anymore," she grumbled.

"Go back to sleep, sorry I woke you."

He was gripped by the excitement, and happy, asking himself, why he had dreamt those words now, not when his mind had been full of anger in the days following the fire? The verses laid his soul bare. He stared at them.

WATER!
NIGHT TIME DARK.
THROAT DRY, BITTER
ROSE FROM BED; DREAMS AWAIT.
DRANK A DRAUGHT
CAN'T RETURN TO MY SLUMBER.
SOUND-PICKED AIR WAVES:
BANG! CRASH! IN GROANING SWAY
HISSED AT ME FROM A BLACK NIGHT.
I REMEMBER THE STARS;
NIGHT IS A FRIEND – HOLD ON! I SAY-
RED WITH ITS OWN VENGEANCE
BURNT OUT EVERY LINE
THERE, WHICH MARKED MY HOME.
YELLOW OF LIFE'S BLOOD SEPARATE,
INVADE
STREET BY STREET IGNITE.
SO MUCH, SO FAST, THE FINEST PLACE.
FIRE! FIRE! I CALLED WITH PANIC
A QUIET SLEEPING HOUR –STATIC.
MY RIFF PLAYED OUT WITH PASSION;

MY SHOUTS UNHEEDED – FIRE WAGON,
DUTY POLICE?
THEN, THE FUGE –
I HEARD BEDLAM, PEOPLE ARGUE.
FUGE, WIDE-SPREAD. FIRE! FIRE! FIRE!
WAKE UP! TRULY MUSIC WAS SAVIOUR
IN THE FINAL HOUR.

He replaced this in the grip and blew out the candle, lay next to Olga and held her. When the day lightened enough he would go for a sea bath. His thoughts ran in threads and knotted in his brain – the Union, work, daughter, wife! Money! It was the future waiting for his attention. As the light seeped into the room, he moved quietly, found his clothes.

Olga sat up. If they had to continue like this, she was sure this life would snuff out her very breath. His movements! Going, forever going. Tears fell slowly; she let them fall. He was unaware that what he had shown her 'burnt out – my home…' had recreated the fire scene she had tried to blot out. She gagged, trying to stop the tears, both hands cupped her mouth, eyes closed. She pulled herself together and followed him downstairs.

He unbolted the door and stood looking out at the yard, but she looked inward. If her mother could get to Aruba for a new start, what about her? Could this be an option, had he considered a voyage abroad for them as soon as some money became available?

He broke into her thoughts. "Did Ma Sampson come to lunch yesterday?"

The picture of the woman came before her eyes: gold earrings – two curled leaves from her ears; a gold chain of leaf design came down to her chest; both arms bore her gold bracelets. Her daughter wore her chain, bracelets and earrings. They wore good clothes, this had amazed her, but their faces had been tight, the looks they had thrown at each other!

"Yes, they came. Betty and Ma Sampson made cut eyes at each other, if you saw it, but Ma Sampson spoke to my *mudda*. I suppose it's all to do with her husband. They did not eat a lot."

Olga told him how the lunch went, his face towards her from across the table held a thoughtful look. "You know I invited her to bring her things her and stay here, because Aunt Hazel doesn't mind? But she said no, no hesitation at all. She wants to stay on the Square."

"O.K. I'm off now, the sun is up."

She wanted to tell him about Aunt Hazel's visitors, about the young man who had interested her. She felt there was something about him that she would find important to the family, and because he had come with La La who was her mother's enemy, it would have been something about her mother's past. Things about her mother were happening quickly all of a sudden. She watched him go into the yard, heard him unlatching the gate.

Rough waves pounded the shore of the beach. That was not a welcome sight. He scanned the shore for a calm section of the sea but all over, the high waves hit the shore far on to the sand. No wind but the froth was extensive, the height of the waves alarming. He hesitated before diving in a short distance from the shore and then swam for ten minutes and was out. He did some on the spot runs to warm up. Underneath the almond tree where he had left his pants and shirt, an old woman was bent picking up fallen almonds; they exchanged good morning. She had a small straw basket full of dry beige ones and olive green ones. He let her continue her search and put his clothes on. He stepped on the reddish leaves among sparse grass and walked on to the pitch of the long stretch of road parallel to the sea to get back to town. After twenty minutes, he reached Darling Hill and directly opposite there was the white administrator's dwelling on Morne Fortuna with the shape of King George VI's crown above it, clearly visible among the trees on the hill. The man was answerable to the King of the United Kingdom; was he involved in the peoples' dance?

Augustus thought about the administrator in the government house. He saw him at Remembrance Day parades on the same Square where homeless people stayed now. He stood in his white drill suit and white cork hat to take a salute from police, scouts, guides, cadets, ex-servicemen, including Sampson who marched to the music of the police band in November. The administrator was only a showpiece, he now believed. Even though Guy had told him that he composed letters, gave his sister to type and dispatch somewhere, Augustus had not heard that His Honour had been in town since the fire. Dujon and the Union men had never mentioned him in the times politics had been argued over. Who was making the decisions about the town?

He came back to the house. Olga was alone in the kitchen with a large enamel cup in her hand, a spoon stirred something in it, a bag of powdered milk stood at her elbow on the small table. She was aware of his return when he reached close by to the tap close to the kitchen window, for a drink from his cupped hands.

Augustus nodded at her and went upstairs, opened the window wide and woke Era up. He lay on the bed and closed his eyes thinking of the day before; the trip to Anse Du Fort and why he had not eaten lunch with the others. The truck with the Union men took them from Masav, they had left just before nine o'clock – Dujon, Guy, Gordon, Michael and Earl. On the highest ridge of the mountain at Anse Du Fort, they had looked down on an abyss, mist hang thickly on the trees and the bush and more likely snakes, he had thought. The town was not far away. It was a flat town, hot and dry. Guy had twisted his arm for this and he said to him, "I'll come and feel out the strengths or weaknesses and hear a bit more how Dujon will advance in his hope to do things for people of the town."

To him, the Union acted as if he was already a committee member. When he had arrived at Dujon's home earlier he was enthusiastically brought inside and he heard, "Good of you to come. I know you could help us."

He had felt his heart swing to his left and then to the right in a lurch, felt it thud. A warm flush spread through him, to be accepted in this respectful way. The men were: a jeweller; a newspaper owner; a clerk; Guy; the teacher, Dujon, a clerk; and himself.

They arrived at Anse Du Fort and headed for the market hall. They waited in the hall close to the police station and waited for the Seamen and Waterfront Union men. The arrival of Corporal Oceancy in the hall, an unexpected and troubling addition, had been an event in itself. The policeman seemed very unwell and he was dressed in ordinary clothes. He sat close to the door on one of the benches that lined the hall. The fact that he came unofficially could be significant, he was not there because he was fond of the Union. His personality as a policeman had been one of hostility to people. His mind went back over the meeting in the hall.

The Seamen and Waterfront official had said, "The sugar cane owners do not want union involved in their workers' life, but the oil factory workers need the Union for the trouble caused by their time keeper."

Michael had said, "Yeh, yeh."

The official continued, "When bosses sack you, many are waiting for your job and your bosses will be as unfair as they like, so please support a Union that the men from Masav will talk to you about."

Oceancy appeared to be leaning heavily with one hand against the wall; there seemed to be an air of pain about him and when the meeting was over, he disappeared in the groups walking out, He himself followed his own set, who seemed at ease and on familiar ground. They passed the police station, and walked along the wide, sunny streets with sparsely scattered buildings, some with the familiar tall balcony on long poles, but mostly two-roomed, wooden, unpainted houses. A brown town was the impression.

He had entered a drinks parlour.

After they sat round the only small square table and Dujon went to the bar, Michael flattered him. As he listened, the man tried hard to press him to be an official Union man because Guy had spoken in high terms about him. He had never met Michael socially before and as he listened to the acclaim that he had an impressive and charming way with his words, he shook his head with a wry smile. Michael, the owner of a newspaper, was himself a master with words, wasn't he? Augustus, so flattered, did not want to let anyone down.

Dujon returned with some delicacies from Singerman, the bar tender – sea eggs padded into its own fragile spiky shell, tasting like fish roe with a faint sweetness. At this point a party of American men in khaki, shirt sleeves rolled up, entered. They all talked at once;

the tension went up; Augustus felt it in the air. The bar tender grinned widely. Gordon moved quickly over to the bar, like metal to a magnet. They greeted him enthusiastically; Augustus nodded in silent acknowledgement. The Americans beckoned him to join them in their social drink. "Have a drink with us, partner."

"Thanks, partner."

He had taken the coke offered and drank from the bottle with a few friendly opening words. Augustus listened to them while also listening to Michael talk politics; the Americans were going to build a hospital there when they had finished the current domestic housing project. He looked into Michael's hazel eyes – which were two colours really, brown and grey – and said, "The poorly paid, ill-treated domestics and shop workers must have us behind them to get fair play, don't you think?"

"I know. We'll see how things get after your municipal elections in December. You know this atavism thing! We'll see."

All the way down the mountain to Masav, he turned the idea over in his mind. The mugginess of the late afternoon suddenly changed with dollops of rain hitting the bus. They had lost lots of altitude but the hairpin bends were dangerous and rain came in through the open bus. Puddles gathered in the mud; the driver grinned, battling with the slippery surface. It was another hour while the men talked very little before they saw Masav.

CHAPTER TWENTY-ONE

Olga and Muriel had not spoken any words in the morning. There was something other than her mother's usual demure nature, though. Even as she helped her get her few things together for the trip to Bonne Terre, her mother mostly made hand signs and head movements. She used lots of *non* and *wi* when she asked her a question. For the most part, they were occupied in busying themselves in silence. Muriel did not want to talk. For Olga time was passing, and it was not the time to be passive and silent as before, although all her impressions of the town had come from the matrix here.

Olga walked into her Aunt's shop meaning to ask her about the woman with the loud voice with her son, but there was an interruption. Her Aunt was about to answer her but her jaw dropped, her eyes moved to the darkened doorway, she gave the man a beaming smile. "What would you like to buy?"

"Oh, nothing at the moment." Then, "On second thoughts, I need some domestic. Give me two yards."

Mr Francois touched his right ear and she touched her right ear. Olga was sure she had copied him. She measured the cloth. He said a pleasant good morning to Olga, stopping his interaction with her

Aunt. She replied to his greeting and was surprised when he asked her Aunt to sell some of the trousers he had made in her shop.

"That would be a favour, Miss Hazel."

"Alright," she obliged.

After he paid her, they shook hands elaborately in a way which made Olga think that they were closer than she had known before. She was getting to acknowledge that she knew very little about everything.

After he left, her Aunt said, "I hope I can sell them; everything so slow!"

They looked outside and saw Philosophe pass on the street with a wave of his hand.

"I must talk to mammie."

She left her Aunt, found her mother and Era together on the balcony. She observed Olga in silence.

"That day, the day you were so vex about that lady who came here with her son. What about them?"

It was a big move she had made, and Olga took a breath before asking, "Is he something to Era?"

She felt shaky, light-headed.

Muriel looked at her and at her granddaughter, she wanted to kiss both of them, show her love for them. She said "*Silans!*" She did not want any conversation. Olga respected that and moved away. It was not her plan to go to the shop till Thursday. She collected some unfinished items for hand sewing and got busy with that downstairs, thinking of ways to have this conversation with her mother in the course of the day. Her thoughts went to Augustus, who was out and who should be coming in to eat and leave for the Morne and she would not be seeing him till the next morning.

Olga put a double stitch at the armhole to finish the pale yellow crepe dress for her mother. She stood up, shook the dress and examined it. Nothing left to be done in it. She took it upstairs and handed it to her mother. Muriel just smiled and nodded in appreciation, but remained sitting, her face towards the opposite house with its mangoes for sale on the usual tray outside a window. She had been thinking of what to tell Olga about Harry. She got her thoughts together. She had not gone back home all these years; Ma George caused her to make that decision.

In Aunt Hazel's room, Olga had taken the large grip to put the new dress in for her to carry with her; she would need it. She heard Muriel say in the doorway, "The day is getting hotter. I'm going to wash my hair and bathe. Thank you, Olga."

She looked at the grip on the floor. Olga nodded. Maybe, in the afternoon, after Augustus goes to work, they would be able to find an opportunity, in peace, in quiet to talk.

"Poor Augustus," she said to her mother, "he had to walk up to work, climbing the Morne in this mid-day sun."

And as though her words summoned him, Augustus appeared on his way to their room carrying the small grip.

"A! A! Gustus, I was only just thinking of you. It's about time for you to go?"

As they exchanged looks he nodded in their direction, and she thought of preparing some food for him.

In the kitchen, the cousins gave her their deferential look.

"Food ready for your husband, Miss Olga," Ma Boy said in a quiet voice.

"Thank you, cousin."

Olga examined the salt beef bouillon in the pot, and then returned to the bedroom. Her anxiety was transmitted to Augustus. She came in and gathered the sheet from the bed to wash later. He took both her hands and held them against his chest. Her fists were clenched. He loosened them and kissed her fingers. She relaxed a bit with a tentative smile, and settled against his chest. They stayed like this for a moment until she turned away announcing, "Food is ready."

She went ahead downstairs. By the time Augustus came to sit down, she had a plate of lunch to give to him. She sat with him. "Yesterday I saw the rain in the hills, but so far the town is dry. September is round the corner, we'll have the rain for sure."

He nodded.

"The sea was rough when I had my sea bath. I hope your mother will be safe going down the coast tomorrow. I have already told her about the rough sea."

"Humph! Ma George planned to return to the village, she's such a determined, strong-back person. I think she can make the sea behave." Olga smiled.

"Well, I must go now, my dear." He stood up. "I hope to get another bicycle in a few weeks. Don't worry about me."

After he left, Muriel and Olga ate and tidied the kitchen together. It was Muriel who said that they should take a stroll in the Gardens.

"Take Era," she said.

This had not been Olga's idea for a personal talk but she would still use this time to say things she had not ever spoken of before. The sunshine was gentle; best time to be in the Gardens, after four o' clock. Muriel felt Harry's presence here more than ever.

Olga said quietly to her mother, "Since I was a child, every All Souls Day, I prayed for my father. I thought he died." After a pause, "He must be a saint already, huh?"

Muriel's eyes were drawn in a frown, Olga saw the two vertical lines above the square nose and one hand went to her breast as if she waited for instruction from her heart. Then she made some quick movements from a closed hand, then the index finger jabbed the air when she started to reply to Olga's words.

"I wish I never have to see his face again, but he's still alive in Panama."

"Alive!"

"But yes, he definitely got to hear about you. Oh yes. When he played in the police band they called him Silky; he played clarinet to caress."

"It's not like I want to meet him either but I'm thinking of Era. Suppose Harry returns here; we see him. Era gets to see a family person looking like her..."

She remembered her Aunt's visitor.

"That woman. She came to Aunt Hazel. She made you vex; you knew her well?"

"She – La La? She liked Harry so bad, she ran after him. It was she that made him run because she wanted him to marry her. Harry did not know that she was pregnant when he left but he knew I was, he knew about you, but it was like that song, Brown skin girl, go home and mind baby. I'm going away in a fishing boat and if I don't come back, throw 'way the damn baby. I expected him to send some money for you, so I started to forget him. Better so."

Far away beyond the hibiscus hedges they saw Era slithering on the summer house circular benches. Many children ran about in the playground. They walked slowly in that direction.

Olga's idea of fathers was that many children she had known were like her. She did not know who their fathers were. If anyone had asked her in her childhood where was her father, she'd be puzzled. She had not missed a father and felt as if he was dead.

They called to Era, turned around to get to Spine Road. Muriel was to go to vespers.

"I'll come as well, with Era."

"I want to talk to Ma Sampson, I'm anxious for her."

The large airy church welcomed them. The hymns and Rosary with the Litany of the Saints gave them the usual sense of place; it put a small reality in the life they now led.

Maryse Sampson was higher up the aisle from where they were, praying. After it was over, they waited by the church door. As she came up to them, surprised to see them, her hands were spread out, palms up, she stood still.

"Mamselle St Juste, Bon soir!"

Ma Sampson, usually voluble, kissed Muriel and Olga on both sides of their face. She was never without jewellery, the gold bracelets slid down her wrists that held on to Muriel's shoulder. Her gold rings gleamed on her hand in the dusky light. Betty stood silently waiting for her mother.

Ma Sampson whispered into Muriel's ear.

Olga felt Era's fingers clasp her hand, she looked down at her, they started walking slowly on the long sidewalk. When Muriel caught up with them she said, "Living in this world, if you don't get licks today, you surely get them tomorrow. You see Ma Sampson, she thinks her husband is mad, but she only told me in secrecy and she is so worried. Still for that, she said she will stay on the Square till the government gets a proper place to put her and those with her."

It was all the talk between Olga and Muriel later about Sampson. Era said, "One day, Mr Sampson was quarrelling with Mr Clifford in the yard, Mr Sampson was vex, so vex."

"I never saw that." Olga doubted that Era had seen the men talk, ever.

"But suppose Sampson was indeed a bit mad, how did anyone know about what he did or did not do that night?"

The adults let her words drop and Muriel went to bed early. They shut the house for the night. Aunt Hazel took the lamp up to her room, said goodnight to them. Era's eyes were very bright in her yellow face.

It was a bustle in the house next morning. They all went by the wharf to see Muriel and Ma George get on the boat. It was a good size and had an engine with a cabin for the passengers.

Philosophe was on street duty. He passed by the wharf later; along the north side, business was brisk, boats discharging goods like buckets, basins, shoes and oddments to people on the wharf side. A big ship along the wharf was unloading to another ship. This was a new order of which he knew nothing. The angled wharf could take four boats along the north side and there was the western shallower side. He just looked on.

He pretended that he had not seen them nor heard the mocking comments of the wharf rats, and strolled to the west side hoping to chat with Mr Denbow. The man came towards him from his place by his three brightly coloured canoes. He told him the warship had left in the night. He answered questions that Philosophe wanted answers to, he was full of gossip. The sergeant got an earful to satisfy him of things happening on the water. He moved off to Mr Francois' shop.

The floor of the shop was littered with thread ends. The large white airy room contained the team busy at work.

"I see you still busy."

He stood in the doorway, keeping watch on the street. Mr Francois answered him.

"I'm trying to please customers as money is scarce. The clothes going cheap."

Philosophe rested his eyes on a roll of check in strong horizontal bands of brown and grey. The speed with which Mr Francois used his tape measure and turned a fold and started to tack with his long thread in his needle fascinated him, and he was at the same time talking to the other men. They forgot that he was there. Finally, he heard a strange question from one of the tailors. Henderson was his name – the policeman knew all their names.

"What can you see will happen in town? I know some people want to go to Curacao or Aruba a soon as they can get some money."

"They put a ban on us police from going anywhere. In my opinion, it will be a long time before we have town again and it's going to be the bravest who will get in front... I can see more drunks, more insanity, but I won't say any more."

After he left he patrolled the lower end of Spine Road, watching the life on the street. All was quiet and he reported back at the station. Not long after, he headed for Aunt Hazel's shop. The trousers hanging up were something new, and he saw that she now sold some rock cakes in the counter where she previously kept buttons and buckles and things like that. She sat behind the counter.

"Yes Sarge?"

She eyed him with interest. He looked sure of himself and rested one hand on the counter, the other by his side. He stood erect; his cap's peak was low over his eyes. He spoke.

"Morning, Miss Hazel. I was hoping to talk to cook's son-in-law. I want to ask him some questions about the night of the fire."

"He's not in."

He smiled warmly at her. He thought her a fine specimen of a woman. He liked her rough tongue and her humour. He spoke in patois to her. It was quite good, she thought, for a Guyanese man; if only she could prise a morsel of fresh news from him. She eyed him with interest, he stood further back now and rested his back against the door post and relaxed.

"What time is he going to be back?"

"Impossible to say, his wife is there, if you want to talk with her."

"No, I won't trouble the lady."

"You catch any thieves yet? What does it matter if Augustus talks to you about the fire, you need Clifford the tailor, you know where he is? Nobody seen him since."

Philosophe enumerated on his fingers the reasons why he did not know where Clifford was; maybe fear, secrecy, peoples' accusation, recompense, vendetta, all kinds of reasons. But the police were looking for him. His air of knowing it all, that he could get to the trouble spots and put things to order, made him flare at his nostrils now and curl up his lip.

"I have someone searching for him, you can count on that."

"If he does not have guilt on his conscience he would have been in town, crying about his bad luck. Eh, Sarge?"

She frowned with the certainty of it. She never mentioned that she had heard that Sampson had been seen at night hanging around, and he did not get on with Clifford. She wanted some news about the police force.

"We want a superintendent," he said briefly

"I suppose a new fire engine will be in the station grounds eh!"

"Oh ho! You ask me that? It's all to do with money. Where is the money coming from to buy fire engine?"

Miss Hazel chupsed. She said that Augustus may be back from work soon.

"I'll come back. Right?"

"*Daco!*"

She watched his very big body move away from her sidewalk.

After Olga had seen the boat carrying Muriel head toward the promontory on the west – the reason why the harbour was usually calm – she walked away with her Aunt and Era, along the other side to the basin of calm water along the western wharf. They had walked towards the burnt-out People's Bank, walked at the back of it towards the end of Church Road. The important shipping office had not been touched by the fire. It was of white stone, three-storey, open for business. Some people did have a job. Augustus was not the only one. For the first time in her life she thought about what might be going on in there. She had parted from her Aunt to join the line outside the Union Relief shop in the hope of getting some essential things like a bed sheet, pillows, toothbrushes, a hair brush and possibly bath towels. She had none of these. She waited, and while there was desultory conversation among the women, nothing interesting was said; nothing new. She wanted those items desperately. If only she had some money, she had seen some kind of sale on the wharf. They must have been people with knowledge, those in touch with the people, 'in the know' and who could afford the money she did not have. So she waited, an hour she believed, before she got inside.

She made her way back to her Aunt laden with some of what she needed. She was pleased.

It was about half an hour later that Philosophe started a slow walk towards Aunt Hazel's. He patrolled the Spine Road, keeping an eye for Augustus. His thoughts drifted to the customs of St Benedict. The people liked to talk about law. This law, that law, the judge in court, adjudication. There was also the matter of the money that people had been questioning. They had gone to see the Chairman of the Town Board. He had seen the man come into the station to see his senior. The money business that Electra had given a report on.

Electra wrote something down in French. He had not understood the written report, the report he had shown the Colonel. In speaking, Electra had been careful to do so in the patois so he understood. She had put in words about the law, the court and such things. She had stressed on the law. He suspected that the Colonel had not done anything official about the report regarding Oceancy, Chalo or Felix. The last time he made a bold attempt to bring this to the surface, it was like playing a game.

His senior knew that Philosophe was trying to trip him up, that he was ignoring the theft because it suited him to ignore what the other policemen had done that night. He said that he was dealing with the matter. He had faith in Challo. All the three had been reposted and not even on the streets of Masav. The new men did not know anything about the Colonel and his slyness.

He now saw Augustus go into the side way of Aunt Hazel's house; he waited fifteen minutes and made his way back to keep the meeting with him. He was hot, perspiration poured down the side of his face. Miss Hazel acknowledged his arrival, standing with her arms folded on the counter before her. Era sat on the chair, practicing stitching on Olga's instructions. On the far end of the counter, Mr Francois' pants for sale lay loosely. He stood away from the counter.

"Has the young man come in?"

"He just came back from work."

To Era she said, "Tell papa, Inspector Paine wants to talk to him."

Philosophe made people want to smile when they saw him, it was his large body, the cap never quite sitting properly on his head. Now on his face he had what could be described as a baby's smile, full of innocence and kindness. Augustus looked at him and smiled. "Come in Sergeant."

They moved to the drawing room.

"I know that I already spoke to you about the fire. That's gone on the record. Can you remember what side the fire started on the shop?"

"From the back – near the yard. When I got outside, it had spread toward the front."

"We have so many directions to follow, it's going to be sometime before the arson investigation has proper light shed on it. So whatever you can add to it I would be happy to hear."

"I know nothing else."

Olga and Era listened from a proper distance, remaining quiet. Olga wondered whether she should say that if he asked Sampson he might have more facts to look at. Also she thought that the fire may well be the result of black magic on Clifford's part, but the whole town had to pay for that.

Philosophe's next question surprised him.

"When last were you at Anse Chabon? Did you hear about the death of Felix?"

Augustus was obliging and related what he had heard being said about Felix – the cause of his death, his ranting about the fire. Philosophe for some reason was quite attentive now, more than minutes before, looking at him more directly.

"Is that all, Sergeant? I'm going to rest now. Excuse me."

It was Denbow who had told him that Augustus had hired a canoe and rowed to the village, he also told him about Felix's death. Augustus felt outrage. How come that his business was part of Philosophe's concern? Who was the man kidding? Acting as if he knew all that was going on. The important things that concerned the town should occupy him in a way to make people respect the police more than they do now.

The bile rose in Sampson's throat. Bending towards the crab trap underneath Clifford's shop, he lit a kerosene soaked rag inside the trap and walked away. The lid fell and the flame was extinguished.

His wish found an accomplice. He moved away, saw the first flames on Clifford's house. He nodded with satisfaction and walked away. He limped off into the dark night toward a vacant rise of land where some Flamboyant trees were in red bloom. He stepped on a long black pod and it cracked open to release the sweet aroma. He could see the smoke and the pink haze starting to appear above the shop.

After the melee started in the town, he returned in the vicinity. He did not want to be seen on Maynard Street, to be part of the scene. Later, he was gripped by fear. The sacrifice of his home for a cause – he had only wanted to punish the *Chaben* man. That was all. He thought that the fire would have been fortuitously extinguished, but no! He had not wished all those houses to be burnt and even his own home.

When it was all over, he had seen his family. What was it his wife had called him? An unfeeling vagabond? He! Unfeeling! It had been too much feeling which had given him resentment for the town, for Clifford and for his type of person.

In the following days, his burden of shame and guilt created a chasm between himself and everyone. What propelled him into action was the tarpaulin for the tents on the Square; as if a magnet pulled him to assist in erecting the poles in the ground, something in him from the past took hold and he could focus on something. As night came, that night, he dropped down to sleep beneath a tent.

Today, Betty made a discovery. He lay down on the sidewalk on Maynard Street in front of his burnt-out house, she told her mother. The girl listened to the tirade made against him as her mother seemed unmoved. People came to her later, begged her to see to her husband, eventually she moved toward Maynard Street, her scrunched body ready for abuse from him.

He seemed prostrate, not looking well.

"Get up Joe from the ground. Eh, you hear me!"

He was unresponsive to her urgent tone.

"Well, bon!"

Knowing herself to be helpless, she went quickly to the police station and made the police take notice. She said she had washed her hands of him. They could do what they wanted with him.

In the morning, she returned to the station and they told her they had thought it best to take him to the mental asylum. Philosophe came in on the morning shift. He smiled. Another case closed. He pondered over the Sampson story.

Saturday morning, Augustus was met with sights that stopped his normal arrival in the house from the quiet sameness. There was Ma James, well settled, and he was overjoyed. Aunt Hazel said with a friendly smile to soften her words, "Your mother bring trouble for us."

Ma James held this bare neck fowl under her arm while Aunt Hazel looked for a cardboard box so it could sit on the eggs that had been brought as well in a round wicker basket.

"I'll build a coop for it and it's not too much trouble, bit of watergrass and coconut."

"No rice these days! I cannot feed this hen!" Aunt Hazel continued.

Augustus took a seat by the table. His mother's visit added a certain climate to this house: her loud voice above all the others, and there was the hen's disturbing noises. Ma Boy eyed it with scepticism; Olga wondered how they could keep the hen from escaping from their yard. She thanked her mother-in-law for her thoughts of them because they would be having some chickens later on.

To Era, her granny's absence had been sudden. She had cried every day, and this morning the arrival of her grandmother was something to take her mind away from Muriel. She took in the sight of Ma James, who in her judgment looked poor but not common – the exposed knees, her hair combed in short fat plaits on top of her head when she removed the Madras cloth from her head. She thought the hen was ugly; its neck had no feathers and its eyes looked bad, really bad, as if it would peck somebody if it got the chance. She was scared of it. She would never touch it.

She listened to all the talking in patois except when her father spoke. He spoke to his mother about money, he was smiling happy at something she told him. Ma James told Augustus quietly that his bicycle was waiting for collection at home, his father had been able to see about it.

"In just a week! That's good luck, I can see."

Era felt that her new grandmother kept looking her way each time there was a pause in the conversation and she felt as if she was being examined. The moment Ma James handed the hen to Aunt Hazel, it jumped on a chair with cricket-like screeches and flew through the doorway into the yard. "Ki-keet! Ki-keet!" Ma James went after it. They were all in the yard trying to corner her without success.

"She wants food."

She scattered the grains on the ground, they dropped among the stones. The hen began to peck at the grains while Ma James pounced again on her and handed her to Aunt Hazel. Eggs at the bottom were waiting for her. Aunt Hazel left some grains of corn on the floor, pressed the hen down to sit on the eggs and shut the door.

"*Tonnerre!*"

She had to attend to the business of the day. Ma James went off to the market to meet others like herself. Olga followed Augustus upstairs, followed by Era.

Olga thought that now her mother was away, Era sleeping with Aunt Hazel, it was the wrong time for Augustus to be on the shift. He had to sleep on the estate; their bed was only for her own self. All he could do was agree, and then he added, "I was thinking of renting some rooms up in the hills near the sugar estate for us. Era could go to school up there in the clean air and when things improve we could build a home of our own."

Olga flared her nostrils but said nothing; after the silence, he added,

"I would prefer this than what we have now."

She made a caracole towards him, smiled brightly. "Maybe!"

After a beat in time, "If my mother gets the money maybe you could get yours and we could try to go to Aruba also."

"There's life for me in St Benedict."

"Really!"

There was doubt in her voice. Her laugh was quiet as she thought of his Rosicrucian book that he said would give him a new way of doing everything. She looked at him; his eyes were closed. She got up to let him rest.

She heard Carl's voice as she came down again on her way to the kitchen. She made a detour; he stood by her Aunt's counter. He looked the same in ill-fitting clothes. Since he became one of the Brethren, as he called himself, he had given his best clothes to the Red Cross for fire relief – a man without vanity. His wavy jet-black hair was brushed back. He turned his face towards Olga as she came inside the shop.

"How are you?"

"Well, thank you."

"I came to buy some buttons. I want a dozen brown bone buttons, if you have them, Miss Hazel."

"But of course, I have bone buttons. I'm glad for this sale."

He looked at Olga. "I'm going to get my picture taken to get a passport."

"You going somewhere?"

"I might."

"That's good," she said, but found hard to believe that he would go anywhere. She could imagine him getting completely lost in a foreign place.

"I'll come to the shop on Monday."

There was so much of her work for the machine and she had to be prepared to make Augustus' suit. She was going to take his measurements, perhaps on Sunday. She would see little of him the next day. Even after his mother left for home, he would be going up to work. "Here you are."

Aunt Hazel handed the buttons, she put them in his hand in a small pile.

"I have no bags for them; put them in your pocket for me."

He looked at Olga, bowed ceremoniously as he turned to leave with affirmation. "I should get my passport just in case I should make a move to see another place."

"Aunt Hazel, I'm going in the kitchen."

On the domestic front, it was less interesting without Ma George; Ma Boy had no one to whisper to. However, now she was composed, getting on with her routine – knife in hand cutting up the big dasheen, peeling it gingerly and putting the segments in a pan of water to boil on the fire hearth. Amazingly the hen was quiet, and Ma Boy, as usual, insisted that she could carry on with the meal. It looked like she would put some spinach in the pork bouillon.

A surge of energy came over Olga. She decided to scrub the floor of the drawing room, found the brush, a bar of blue soap and took the bucket of water in. The wet floor was the only thing that mattered, wiping the wet with the big cloth that she wrung of its dirty water. She flung the water outside, replenished the bucket. Her feet were bare and her skirt collected in a knot at the side of her upper thigh. She knelt down on the floor, moving on the dry space till she completed all of it. It should be dry in half an hour. She thought about her mother. She felt hopeful in how everything seemed to be progressing. It should do her mother good to be away from work and the burnt town. She looked forward to the coming week when Augustus would be on days once more. There was her mother-in-law who added something valuable in the present situation, how she gave support to them.

September was approaching and something good was bound to come about. School should be reopening for Era; it should anyway. She placed her feet back in her slippers, washed her hands at the tap by the kitchen window. She smiled at Ma Boy as she moved to go upstairs to find the child. As she not downstairs she expected that she was looking out from the balcony. She rushed to her, she was crying. She held a pillow. A piece of ribbon was tied across the centre; it pinched the pillow to resemble a body with a chest and a belly. Olga wiped her eyes.

"You crying for granny, I know dat. First time she left us. Why you didn't come downstairs, just staying by yourself?"

Back downstairs, "You best keep out of the kitchen, but you stay in the yard. Food should be ready soon, your grandmother still here; you'll see her in a little while."

Ma Boy came out from the kitchen and handed Era a little roasted top-shaped dumpling. Era moved near to the kitchen door and from her position she kept her eyes on the business in there.

La La's high pitch voice came through from the shop. Olga was surprised. The last time she came, there had been unhappiness in this house. Olga expected she had some news to pass on to her Aunt, so it would be a private matter and she was not going in there.

La La joined Miss Hazel behind her counter; Aunt Hazel offered her friend the chair she had sat on.

"Woy! Ma fi, things moving on. They told me Harry coming soon and will stay for six months."

She blinked repeatedly even though she smiled. Her nerves on edge, Miss Hazel thought.

"So Harry coming back to St Benedict. His daughter will meet him at last. I so happy about that."

Olga waited until she heard the visitor say good-day and left, then she went into the shop.

"La La Etienne's boy is also Harry's son; you should know."

Her Aunt did not beat about the bush.

"Harry will be here, coming to see his family."

Shock waves passed over her body; her head felt light. She could only feel as she walked upstairs, side by side, apprehension and expectation fought with resolution about the new event when it came. Inside their room, Augustus' eyes found hers. She had interrupted his train of thought about the day when he had spent time at Anse Du Fort, their difficulties had been far away but the present lay as a burden on his back. He looked at the doorway expecting to see Era tailing her, then at her round face, the arc of her eyes. She read no message in his own, he was inscrutable; however, she sat next to him. She could not tell from a signal or a movement how to respond, but then she thought he almost never acted on impulse, and he ignored the flutter in his loins because it was not the right time.

"I'm going to make you a suit next week with the cloth you got from Aunt Hazel."

He swung his legs out of the bed, kissed her cheek. Her pensive expression made him say, "What happened?"

"My father is coming from Panama soon and I have a brother."

"Who told you?"

"Aunt Hazel, because the boy's mother just left the shop. She gave the message about my father."

"I'm glad for you. I am very happy indeed. His space will be filled now. It is a good thing."

"My mother will not like this news. She wants him to stay in Panama. It's not long since she said that to me."

"Is my mother downstairs?"

"I dunno, maybe."

"I'll just do some press-ups and then I'll be down."

She met Guy coming up the stairs; she greeted him and turned round ahead of him to let Augustus know.

The cramped look of the house, its dark panelled rooms, once more made her compare this house and their old home. Aunt Hazel's one room downstairs, divided from the shop at the front. Upstairs the rooms were very small, the balcony seemed the roomiest area, going on two sides of the house. Now, Guy took a seat there and in a short while Augustus joined him. He explained the reason for his call was that the crowded situation at his home was getting unbearable.

"I wish something could be done right now to get some houses for all those without a home in this town."

"Your visit is a break for me likewise. So what is the Union doing now, what's the latest?"

"I cannot tell you much but Dujon talks a lot about the Trade Union in England, he had communication from them. It's only a guess but I think some official from there will be here soon."

"Wait for me while I get something to eat and then we can walk together. I have to leave for work."

His mother had not returned. If by the time he left she was not with them, it would be next morning when they would meet again. Meanwhile he received a plate of food from Olga, cooked by Ma Boy. He was grateful to the old woman, the way she quietly did so much for their comfort as though it was her destiny to do for others and not expect thanks. He walked to her, her lean coffee brown face was calm and she nodded in acknowledging his gratitude. He tweaked Era's cheek as he passed her by the table, Olga sat with him.

"I'll wait for your mother to eat my lunch."

The house settled after Augustus left. She sent Era to sit with her Aunt and she prepared water to bathe herself.

That night she dreamt a dream she'd had before, just close to the dawn because she woke up soon after, her eyes wide and incredulous. She felt as though she had been watched – her secret was known. She woke up with this feeling, ashamed and excited.

Augustus walked with Guy but the silence was lengthy. Augustus' mind was weighed down as it had been before. As with close friends, Augustus was simply happy for the company on this mid-day walk to the estate. They had had many outings in their teens with the sea scouts, then, the Cadets of the College. They walked with long strides going up the Morne, went round many bends. They had got up quite high, not many people on the road. A man passed with a crocus bag of charcoal on his head, going down to town, looking neither right nor left and he passed them.

"The amount of trees we have burnt over time to make the coal and make us a big depot for ships, it's a wonder so many trees are everywhere that we pass," Guy spoke at last.

Augustus heard him; his own thoughts were far from such mundane things. He gave his friend a glance. His own were about how to bring up the subject about the excommunication of people from the Catholic Church, that what people thought about spiritual ideas embracing self-discipline could be at odds with what people must think because of being brought up in a way that everyone had to believe the same thing. There was much that they shared but he had not talked about the Rosicrucian book with Guy, who taught in a Catholic school and went to mass on Sundays.

"My father makes his fair share of coals too."

Then he brought Guy into the latest news in his life.

"I got my father looking to buy a bicycle for me and my mother came down to town today, told me he got me one so now I have to go and collect it."

"That was lucky man."

"I don't know where he got it but I need it badly."

The subject changed to the men of the Co-operative Union.

"We're counting on you," Guy reminded him, but the heavy ball thrown at him by Michael at Anse Du Fort had set up a motion in his heart after it had hit him hard. It still worried him how he should co-operate with them.

"Please Guy, don't start. Since we went down south I have thought about it a lot but I'm not that willing to serve on the committee."

"It's a shame." Guy frowned.

They were approaching the Four Road junction. In the daylight, the junction had the air of events having happened there, crowds must have gathered in the spot in the hill. To the right and the left wide brown paths were going into the vegetation, intersected by the road they were on. Augustus quickened his steps.

"Hold on!" Guy said.

Augustus pulled on Guy's sleeve. He had stopped.

"Never stand in the middle of this junction in case something bad befalls you; it's a knowledge held by people in those hills."

They walked on a bit more and stood on the edge of the road in the shade of trees.

Guy said, "I've heard talk about Moloch worshippers very, very long ago. They killed children for this God they worshipped who would bring them prosperity, and those people were involved with cane planting. So, the *Boloms* came out at night in vengeful errands."

"I never heard this one; anyway, some people are very afraid of this spot."

"I'll head back to town. See you tomorrow."

"Thanks for your company."

CHAPTER TWENTY-TWO

Half an hour later he stood on a ridge above the cane valley. He pulled the brim of his brown felt hat over his forehead against the glare of the hot sun. The skyline was in the distance over the sea at the bay below. He walked down the gentle gradient, passed the vendor of fish and green bananas, passed the mechanic's shop. He called out to him. Now he avoided the murky stream and traversed instead through the stumps of cane on mounds of earth, made for drains to keep cane roots from too much hydration when the rains started any time now. His gum boots sank into the soft carefully kept drains.

The workers in the field moved around with shovels. He wondered where Cyril could be but the Cedars by the bridge had hidden part of the land.

He entered the factory, relieved to have a few minutes to rest before he commenced his shift. The vats of cane juice bubbled, the usual aroma of cane syrup, not unpleasant. He felt some stomach cramp and held his tummy. After some word exchanges with the men around he settled down on his bench. His manager came to see him with what tasks he should do when the syrup did not need testing by him. This new change at the factory he knew about and did what he had to do.

At ten o'clock he walked out into the dark night with a Guyanese pan-boiler, both shone their torch lights and it took twenty minutes to get to their lodging. A dull headache with a sour taste in his mouth made him taciturn. He entered the estate house and dropped heavily into a comfortable canvas chair, sighed deeply.

"Bilhari," an overseas worker asked him, "How's wok?"

"Hi man, I'm glad to see you. Work? Huh! Now that we cut out the amount of sugar, as you know, it was less hectic for me but we had overheating of the bearings. When the whistle blew, the engineer came out of his bed. Yu know the fuss he can make at times like that, to have to leave his bed."

He got up abruptly, took his torch to find the pit outside, a short distance away. He was sick, his guts felt wrung out.

"I feel a bit shivery," he said to Bihari. "I can't understand it."

"I hope it ain't bilharzia. I can fix you wit some of dis misture; I make it myself."

He disappeared while Augustus could have just gone to bed. Lots of room in the house since the seasonal overseas labourers had returned to other islands. The house was noiseless with the absence of the kind of music they played some nights to make the atmosphere cheerful. Bilhari came back, gave him a cup of something with a hint of rum, he thought. Augustus drank it quickly, thanked him and found his bed.

Waking up, he felt enclosed in darkness. Alone. He had dreamt of red cockscomb flowers, red fallen African tulips. He now felt his old sensitive nature, knowing his weakness. He recalled the sea of red things around him as he stood panting, and the New Year's devil with his pitch fork calling, taunting.

"I'm not afraid," he shouted in his sleep, as the devil tried to get to him. The devil masquerade, who scared children every New Year on Masav streets, appeared in his dream; something was afoot, waiting to get him.

He found the powdered milk, farine and sugar to make breakfast. Biharri must have gone out to the factory, no sign of him. He felt less tired, though the nausea remained. He heated the water on a kerosene stove, mixed the milk powder, added the farine and sugar, sat down in the common room. He was alone. He ate slowly, comparing this dream to another he had weeks ago, when he and Olga crossed the bridge over Masav river and then Guy came calling them back after they had already moved away from the bridge. He was coming to meet them. Augustus had seen himself walk with strides in an almost careless manner, shoulders back. It was like Guy had had some news for him and wanted to bring him back to town.

He belched, felt he might bring up what he had eaten. His stomach settled with his concentration on keeping it down, the churning stopped slowly. He stepped on to the wooden veranda to breathe in the cold morning air. The fellas approached across the field, returning from work.

The eerie canefields, razed with the harvest, now all brown and flat, used to be the contrasting scenery when he left town; to be in the green valley. Now it almost resembled the dark town. The fellas and he made small talk as they passed. Time to get going, he thought, to return to collect his belongings, his hat and his bag. He put the shoes in the bag, gum boots on. He called, "I'm on my way."

He could walk unhindered and moved quickly. He climbed up from the valley, the trees on the wayside were still, everything was still. He stood and contemplated the walk down the hill.

No caracole in his mind, determined to avoid this old sensitive nature of his. He walked on the People's Square to find Ma Sampson. He needed news of her husband. The people moved about. Elderly men who were widowers or old bachelors, old forsaken women, middle-aged ladies with daughters but no little children around which was a good thing, he thought. The white canvas camp beds beneath the tent covers were being sat on or laid on, and Ma Sampson sat on hers. Nearby, her large bundles were on top of her waggonette. Betty lay on the cot next to her. They watched him come to them. His crocus bag was hanging from his hand with his boots jiggling inside.

"Morning, Ma Sampson."

He was going to speak English, could not be bothered doing French so early in the morning. He expected that she would elicit

Betty's help to translate what she said to him as she spoke rapidly about her husband.

Betty translated that he was at the hospital, not saying why but Ma Sampson had used words for drunken, blood and vomit. Augustus said that he was sorry. He watched her heave her shoulders, the gold earrings glistened and her gold chain rested on the simple brown dress. She said in French, "He's better off in hospital."

"O.K. Well, good day, I'll tell Muriel the news."

Era sat up in bed, retched. She flung a leg over Olga to get out of bed and her sick mess dropped on Olga's clothes. She jumped out, looked at the child with annoyance.

"Get the *po*, quick!"

The child sat on the floor. Olga took the *po* from under the bed. She pulled off her old dress and changed to another, then opened the jalousies. The bed had no vomit in it; she was pleased. She touched Era's forehead, it was cool to touch and she wondered what had upset the child's stomach.

"Is your belly hurting?"

"No."

"Alright."

She would not return to lie down, the morning was too new. The house kept everyone confined for a few more hours, she sat on the chair.

"You still feel sick?"

"A little bit, mamma."

She sat with the *po* next to her for about half an hour, and it was safe for her to get back on the bed. Olga sat on the chair, not able to get back to bed. A while later she listened outside her aunt's door. She heard talking.

In the next room, Ma Boy was possibly turning in the little bed, spreading out without Ma George. Olga sat on the balcony thinking of Era. School was due to start in the next week. September was here.

It could not be what they had eaten the day before. But if so, was it the milk brought by Ma James? It had not turned when boiled and

Era had that with farine. What else had she eaten? Ma Boy gave her sweets and bits to keep her happy. Later she would ask her to tell her what she had had to eat.

She heard movement and there were the women leaving the bedroom.

"*Bonjou.*"

"*Bonjou.*"

She got up and went downstairs in tow. The day began, one thing to the next. Aunt Hazel usually made the shop her first task but she got some coals out to light a fire. Olga said to her mother-in-law that Era vomited once. She returned upstairs, Era was sick in the *po*. She went back to the kitchen and returned with some water in a cup to give to her. Maybe, she thought, Era needed worm medicine or some senna, but she had none of these things. She worried.

"Is your belly hurting?"

"No."

"Lie down. I'll make a tea for you."

The women were talking together. Aunt Hazel asked, "How's the child?"

"Still vomiting."

"*Simme contwa* is what you should boil if you could find the leaf."

She decided first to make L'orangette tea, always lime leaves in the place, and then would go and search for the *simme contwa*.

Olga wondered if unhappiness was what caused Era's vomiting. The child had been crying, she had looked miserable. She made the L'orangette tea, gave it to her and she stood in her doorway to catch sight of Ma Boy when she appeared. If anyone knew about the leaves for bush tea, she would.

Olga knew through Muriel that the Good Shepherd Society appealed to many of the older, humble people. For now, she talked quietly to Era, rubbed her stomach with her bare hands to rub some heat into it. The pale face close to hers was like the pale fruit of the banana; much lighter than the usual yellow skin.

She wondered how long before Augustus returned this morning. He'd be wanting to lie down for part of the day before he went again that afternoon for the late shift.

She decided to wash clothes that morning and expected Era to be better later on. Era drank what she had been given; she followed Olga on to the balcony where the sun was warm. Ma James joined them and was silent as she observed them, to take the memory back with her to Anse Chabon. She said a few words, almost like a soliloquy; she expected no reply. It sounded like a blessing on Augustus, herself and Era; she used the word God so many times in the few words she had said. So Olga answered,

"*Wi, mesi byen,*" and was pleased that Ma James smiled, saying that she would be going soon and that she may not see Augustus before she left. Olga nodded regretfully. She moved away and went down the stairs as Augustus came on to the street below. She sighed, relieved. "Stay here, Era."

The child anticipated something happening again, newness. So far it was things coming, going, disappearing. She constantly felt like she was falling around in a feeling of hopeful waiting, and so much space to fall into, the space only for her alone. She found the rag doll in a corner in the room and started twisting the silken strands of thread into a style. She felt a new attachment to Olga now – a smell like cornmeal and pumpkin and coconut pie which was delicious and made her happy when she ate it.

Augustus entered the yard. He felt that if he had no work today, he would go to the hospital to visit Sampson. As it was with his nausea, all he wished for was a cool rum punch with lots of lime and bitters. The first person he saw in the yard was his mother. She came inside the house and sat by the table. He sat with her, they spoke briefly, and then she got up and said goodbye to get the mail boat that was going to Anse Chabon at 10 o'clock. That was what he would do also when he would go to collect the bike; he wanted his father to be told that he would be coming next Saturday on the mail boat to get it.

Olga emerged from behind the kitchen, went to the tap for water. She felt the morning like one of these days, moving like butterfly wings.

He had observed Olga going to the back of the yard, disappearing at the back. He wondered whether she was going to have a quick bath. She emerged with the *po* to come inside the house. As she passed him she said, "Era was sick last night. Twice."

He did not say he also felt nausea. He was determined to finish his quota of the two till ten shift. He hoped to have a small nap, undisturbed. He came upstairs after her, saw Era looking pale on her chair. No little smile. He stood beside her, tweaked her round cheek, got a weak smile. "How are you?" he asked her.

"My belly hurt."

"You'll be better soon. Later today."

"I'm going to lie down till eleven, Olga."

"I'm going to make a bush tea for her. Ma Boy went looking for *simme contwa* for me."

"Olga, Ma Sampson told me this morning, her husband was taken to hospital last night, vomiting blood."

He saw her startled eyes become larger, quite semi-circular; her hand went to her bosom. "*Bondous!* What's all dis vomiting everybody have! After da fire, maybe we will all get sick. The air was so bad on the streets."

He slept, was up. He lay on the bed a while, deciding what he should eat, still feeling nauseous but he would say nothing of that to Olga. It was so sudden that people had started to vomit; it could mean so many things, the weather was not even as hot as two weeks previously. He dressed, kind of dressed, his face had too much beard but he would see to it next day.

He went to Olga in the yard, concerned about Era, who stooped in the doorway watching them.

"At least she stopped vomiting this morning. I'll give her some more bush tea later."

"I'll have to leave for work soon. I am not that hungry."

"Breadfruit and fish broth is ready. So, I'll get you some in a while."

He considered his obligations, one of them to give aunt Hazel some allowance for them. As Olga gave him the plate he handed her money.

"Give that to Aunt Hazel."

She came and sat with him as he ate. He gave her two dollars. She received it and nodded, "Good thing you have a job, eh! I'll get some groceries dis afternoon."

She looked at the American dollars.

"You want some razor blades, I'll see if I can get some. I suppose the Union shop could have them."

She did not like to see him looking bad.

"You yourself don't look well to me!"

"I'm alright. Is there coals in the coal pot? Can you make me a cup of what you gave Era, I just feel like a cup of a bush tea and then I'll go."

Half an hour later, Olga packed two rock cakes for him that she got from Aunt Hazel and corn beef in a small loaf. He left quickly.

Every Saturday, the way it went was that no new cane juice went to the vats for boiling and so the night staff spent the time cleaning the machinery, left them clean for Monday when cane crushing started again.

Knock-knee Sabu did most of Augustus' work, He was sick a couple times, the fact that both times was small vomits and nausea meant Augustus was not bothered. He told Sabu that he did not feel tired, when his friend said, "What's going on? I hope you did not ketch bilharzia!"

It was the longest eight hours in his experience. He drank small sips of his rum punch that he had made during his breaks.

At ten o'clock, he shook hands with Sabu as he went off to his family in one of the estate housing sites not far away. He walked across with the pan boiler, went straight to bed. He hoped to sleep for many hours undisturbed.

Feeling so relieved that he had had a good night sleep, after he had a shower and coffee he went with the men of the house to the eight o'clock service in the chapel.

There he saw the engineer, a manager, about fifteen men altogether. He heard the prayers and hymns for one hour. He remained silent, the hymns not known to him, and he heard the sincerity in their collective voices. He remained meditative and respectful, head bowed. The preacher read St Paul's letter to the Corinthians about good neighbourliness.

After the service he walked on, whistling a fragmented tune softly when he entered Miss Hazel's yard and entered the living room. The place was empty, where was everyone? The house was so dark as Olga always said, especially if the shop at the front was closed. The light coming in was from the door where he stood, coming into the room. Even no Ma Boy! She may be resting in her bed, but on Sunday morning, ten thirty! He thought not. He sat by the table, there was an acrid taste in his mouth.

First Olga and Era came.

"Aunt Hazel went to visit some people. Ma Boy went to Good Shepherd meeting and I went to see Boo after mass. A! A! You know, Cyril was vomiting this morning."

He looked at Era with concern, but she seemed well, her pallor had gone.

"The *simme contwa* I gave her stopped the vomiting you know. I still have some leaves. I made her drink the tea three times."

He had to tell her now that he has a bit of stomach upset too and asked her to make him the same tea as he intended to go to the hospital in the afternoon to look for Sampson.

"You don't look well with all dis beard."

He scratched his head and looked at his lovely woman. She was attractive this morning. He touched her arm, felt a thrill along his arm, he felt heat coming off her; all he wanted was to pull her close and squeeze her so they could melt together in her heat. But then, she pulled her arm away and went to the kitchen. He had forgotten Era, who stood in the yard looking upwards.

He went upstairs to change his shirt. Olga, he remembered, promised to make him a suit at Francois' shop; he had only bought two pants from him so far. He'd seen those in Aunt Hazel's shop but either they were too small or too big. That was a hare-brained idea Mr Francois had, not measuring people for individual clothes. If what he made fit, you wore it; if not, you could have some alterations to make before it suited. He lay down. It was Sampson he thought of.

The man had a beautiful voice – he used to sing some years ago, especially the song 'Ramona'. He had sung it so often that he knew some of the words: When evening comes I hear your call, we'll meet beside the waterfall... I'll always remember the rambling rose you wore in your hair. The tune was a lovely tune, and that voice, tenor, it trilled and resonated across the fence to their own house. But the man had stopped singing. He drank and became drunk instead, and was a problem to his wife. Why? No wonder hearing this news he felt some grief and he had to go and look for him.

Guy came to meet him about one o'clock to attend a meeting for Red Cross workers, A.T.S., the Union men and some business people. Augustus saw that Aunt Hazel sat in the room as well. He heard of the plan for a new building in the town, a refuge house for the old people without homes or family. Because that was urgent, the speaker said no time should be wasted now, there was a vacant spot on Spine Road and that a moderate shelter should not take long. There was clapping and talking among the listeners.

"That should be a start," Guy said to him.

Everyone had the bad weather in mind with September two days away, and when the meeting broke up, that was the only proposal put forward that Augustus heard about. This building was owned by the Red Cross; the Red Cross mark was reassuring; they could be relied on.

The room had held a good crowd of concerned people, the town people who he used to feel uncomfortable around socially. Today he did not even give that a thought. He left Guy, who did not have his own family and always socialised across a large group of town people. He shook hands with his friend, to return to the house.

When the sun changed its position to a more oblique angle to the streets, more people came out. Augustus passed them on his way to the hospital. He could not afford to be sick himself, he would knock it out of his path. Cyril was in bed and he would not be going to work tomorrow, he said. He decided to visit a doctor at the health centre for medicine as he had been nauseous since Friday. No wonder he had not spied him at work once. Augustus was sure his own mind would control this sickness and he would stay well.

It was the custom of people to visit strangers in the hospital on Sunday afternoons. They also went to the asylum some distance away, where people stood outside the grille window to stare at inmates. He met some town people on their way up the hospital hill; they came to the gate of the hospital alongside him. They would just stroll through the wards, most of them, if they had no one specifically in mind. The nurses were used to these socially minded people – to visit the sick was a Christian duty.

He hoped that a short stay in hospital could bring the man back to himself. He looked at the men in the three men's wards and did not see him. One of the ward sisters said that if he was admitted and not in the hospital, he may be in the asylum. The place was half an hours' walk away; did he have to try that? With a wry twist of his mouth, he moved out of the ward and set his mind to do this walk. The path ran through rocky terrain. The noisy sea bashed against the rocks below. He could see it.

A stone rolled underneath his boot, it pierced his foot. He stopped for a while. There was a hole in the sole of the shoe. The rocks were of shades of mustard and grey. Then he saw the dark stone asylum against trees bearing small white flowers. An air of desertion came from this hospital. He walked to the grille window, the spectators stood nearby. At the entrance door, he rang the brass bell. He would have turned away for the length of time that he waited before the door swung open. A male grey-haired orderly asked what he wanted.

"I'm looking for Joe Sampson, is he here?"

"Yes."

Silence! It was no point asking whether he could enter; no sane person went inside that hospital, and when men or women went in they were there for an extremely long time. The orderly smiled a worried smile at Augustus.

"He is dangerous!"

After he shut the door, Augustus stood there. He was lied to by Ma Sampson and that hurt. Standing in front of the lunatic asylum he felt alone with words in his head, because they were in patois, and in the silence, they did something to help the sadness he felt.

There's something that lingers for people of the island, the words of the older generation to protect them in times like this. When unease comes, a vague memory of something on the edge of unhappiness, they whisper immediately in patois – something like 'when your friend's beard on fire, you sprinkle yours' or the other one, 'when bad luck comes, it comes mercilessly'. Who is sure of anything? he asked himself.

As he walked off he looked once more toward the grille window. Arms were outstretched through the gaps. He stared at the faces but Sampson was not in sight. How can he pass this news to Olga and Muriel when they come back!

Ma Sampson was as much in need of a strong hand on her shoulder as her husband. But he had just collided with life, it touched him and held him close. This patois, how could he continue to ignore its importance after this? Consolation was what he had rejected before.

Not having any gymnasium – gone in the fire, the weights, the bench – where, at this moment, he would have been heading that way to spend an hour on the bench, he made his way to the drinks parlour he visited sometimes with Guy. He would meet pleasant company there who talked about sports.

"How you keeping, my friend?" the bartender offered a handshake.

"Finding it hard, like everyone. You know how it is. Just a shot of Vat 69 and some water please."

It was late Sunday afternoon and soon there would be a few more men drinking than were presently enjoying a quiet conversation. Augustus leaned against the wall next to the three men in the room and listened to football talk. They were all looking forward to the day when the game would recommence, so many teams in the island. The men were of a similar age to himself. He had stopped playing football three years previously. He had different things on his mind and he left with one more stop.

He had not been to visit Mr Polius for a few weeks. It was quiet on the shady street and pleasant away from the burnt town. He entered the small pink house. His ex-teacher sat reading. He entered, took the extended hand and took a seat.

"What are your plans Augustus?"

He could always talk honestly with the older man.

"Nothing new – almost – but I've discovered the importance of our patois language. It's become like an itch. It's a new certainty; I believe now that speaking both English and patois could be a good thing."

He then lectured Augustus, quoting W.E.B. Du Bois, a man new to Augustus; a man who wrote papers and books for encouraging ambitious black people. Augustus listened to the scintillating verbiage with rapt attention as usual. As he was leaving, Mr Polius said quietly, "Think about that which I said before. When I step down from President of the Historical Society, why don't you take this on?"

He looked at his *doogla* ex-school master with his unpleasant thoughts rising again to the fore, thinking, I can't rise above my station and not feel unpleasant consequences.

He said, "I don't think I am right for that. I would not get support. I'm sure."

"Listen, this fire was a frog…"

"What's that?"

"I mean Augustus, now, people will join in, fill gaps previously present in our society."

"Oh, I see. Goodbye, Sir."

He had not eaten a meal, and in spite of that he did not feel hungry. He expected that something from what they cooked earlier would have been put aside for him. In these difficult times, they had managed to eat every day. He entered the darkness of the house, which felt part of the ground it stood on. It was all enveloping too in its repose this evening. Surprisingly, all the women sat sewing a bit of garment with Olga in the living room.

"Era's school starting again on Tuesday, I'm so glad," Olga said.

"I know that all the schools are reopening. The college on Wednesday, followed by the convent. Slowly, much more will get started I expect. Just wait and see. But without money people cannot get the best. Aunt Hazel isn't so?"

"There some smart people in town, people who know how to take a sixpence and make two pounds, like Ma Lodamise. Things will work alright, I have confidence."

Olga got up first to go to the kitchen and returned with a plate of his meal.

"I must take your measurements for the suit I will start tomorrow at Mr Francois'," a smile of hope flickered on her lips.

He nodded. "When I go upstairs."

"Uh huh."

Upstairs they were alone. Olga saw Augustus examine the sole of his shoe, a frown on his face.

"It's got a hole; boy oh boy!"

She sat near to him with her arm around his shoulder. She wanted to get closer still but it was not the right time of the month. She jerked away from him, shocked by his words.

"Sampson is in the mental Asylum, I found out today."

She stood up, her lips compressed, unable to reply. Then she broke the tight silence.

"My goodness, how come?"

He could not tell her, he said, but he knew because the wife told him that Sampson had been taken to the ordinary hospital. He had gone there today and it was not that hospital but the mental hospital.

"Dat lady! She is so strange but she is my mudda's friend."

They lay down on the bed, spent half an hour comforting one another and came back to the present when Era entered the room. What did she want, Olga asked herself? She arose and went on to the balcony with her. Her happiness marred by this thought – poor Era, it's not your fault child but I could have had another baby by now, but your father is scared that it won't be as light as you. Of course, she thinks he is right, no cause for jealousy later in life if Era gets a better deal in life than a darker sister or brother.

He had his own thoughts, that in their cramped condition he could not allow her to go and get herself pregnant, but he wanted them to have another child as much as she did.

CHAPTER TWENTY-THREE

Olga dreamt of eyes on the walls of the room, each way she turned the eyes stared at her. She was strong and playful, demanding love from Augustus. She lay atop of him rather than below in a new way. He smiled up at her. It was a vivid dream. She did not really wake up from it when the morning came, and she opened her eyes in dismay and looked around her at the same scene. He had gone to work without disturbing her.

He reached the estate. The programmes for the day were underway in the fields, bundles of cane trundled on the tracks in the iron containers to the cane crusher. It was usually forty tons of cane to be crushed every hour. The flywheels moved, water came in and washed the cane. The usual strong aroma of cane syrup made him feel like heaving when he got the first breath of it, but that settled. It certainly was a new experience to him, that unfamiliar sick feeling. Right now, he felt a little rain to freshen the air would be welcome but so far it remained dry; but the workers maintaining the drains were marking the fifteen-foot-wide beds on the banked earth ready to prevent soggy earth when the rain started.

The morning wore on, engine sounds, steam hissing, heat and more heat on his body. He gave some thought to the possibility in doing the correspondence course in agriculture. Later that week he would go to the library and search for a book on cane cultivation but today he was in a hurry to get to town.

He collected his bag, put on his rubber boots, and with his hat on his head headed across the field, in and out of used paths. The river waited for the rain, trees on the hillsides far across stood motionless, horses and mules did their work, men carried bundles of cane from far, loaded the mules.

He walked down the hill, kept his mind on the walk. Half way down, when he had just passed the government administrator's house, the white building with a copy of the crown of King George on the top which was visible from town, a car horn made him stop. The black car, not a usual occurrence since the fire, came alongside. Augustus heard his name called. Guy's sister asked him to get in. A policeman drove, he had acted as she asked him. She was on her way home having done the hours of work she had to do that day.

The young man was nicknamed Carafe, his dull reddish-brown face smiled at Aunt Hazel. He was in the final year at S.M. College. She knew him, one of the youngsters down her lane. She asked where he had been since the fire. He was a garrulous bright young man.

"And what you going to do when you leave school?" she asked him.

Augustus came in by the door of the lane, saw him by the counter; he knew that he went to his old college and smiled warmly at him.

"How are you?"

The boy admired Augustus because he knew that he worked at the laboratory on the sugar estate. He also had the wish to do so the following year when he finished school. He perked up.

"Mr James, any chance for me to get work in the laboratory on the estate next year when I leave school?"

"You can apply for a job in the factory, you might be lucky."

Aunt Hazel cut the cloth, Augustus continued on through to the back of the house. The boy told Miss Hazel, "I wanted an office job but after this fire I cannot hope for that at all."

He spent a little time because Aunt Hazel asked him some inquisitive questions, as was her way. He chatted on.

"People talking about getting rich next year when they use their bonds…"

"Who tell you so?"

"I heard people say that, I don't know anything about it."

"It's nice to see you, say howdy to your mamma."

She gave him the cloth and watched him go. His mother worked in the tuck shop of the S.M. College. He left her in a bright mood as though he had painted he shop with the colours of the rainbow. She hummed a quiet tune. She closed the shop early and hoped the next day would bring her more sales. She heard Augustus in conversation with Ma Boy and Olga.

He had a pre-occupied face, Olga thought. He'd asked Ma Boy, did she like to talk English? He knew that she had many English words to explain herself when she chose. She said that it was when she had worked as a maid in the house of the white English people that she had learnt some words. She never went to school. Augustus thought that she would not have been taught French, and Miss Hazel knows that there is importance in patois, how it thrives in its environment. The habituation of English had not touched that many people. They were riveted on Augustus' words.

"Yesterday, for the first time in years I saw the importance of patois: I felt the words in my heart."

He had thought patois, felt it working on him and occupying his rational mind.

What a change, Aunt Hazel thought, that he was engaging with Ma Boy. She picked up his words, adding hers, "No flavour! No salt in English!"

Olga felt Augustus make a new rhythm among the family like old music, the beat of sticks knocking, 1-2-3, 1-2. She felt the relief of tension, and sucked in air and let that out quickly. She said, "I never fot I would hear you wanting to like anyfing in patois!"

It was like they were really acting like a family for the first time – one relating to the other.

She was happy for that, watching him now put one leg over the other as he sat back. He began to tell them about his parents. His eyes met Ma Boy's, the old lined face gleamed in its old softness, gave an old smile with her knowledge of the treasure of her patois. He spoke in English, not quite ready to fall into what his heart had to feel before the urge would come on him.

He praised the type of man who was his father, whom he knew as a mature man because it was after he had worked as a farm labourer in French Guyana and returned to the island, he got married. He was a town man but married a countrywoman and went to settle in Anse Chabon. He and Carmen were the only children. And his father always said that going away had made him smart. He preferred to work on the land; he said he worked hard, not for a boss but for himself.

"I on the other hand prefer living in town."

That was the limit of his opening up. He still felt unaccustomed to the older women who looked at him, and was surprised by Aunt Hazel's warm approving look as he moved upstairs.

"Your husband is a bright young man; he went to college, passed all these exams."

The idea came to Olga that tomorrow she would do something different so the night would be special. She looked surreptitiously at the women with a straight face as they talked about girl days at Bonne Terre. Olga paid attention too; if it had not been for the fire these two would still not be speaking to one another. They say every disappointment is a blessing – some better behaviour came today from Augustus.

She left Era at the school gate for her first day back. It was good to see the fresh-faced children trooping into the solid, massive wooden building. On the streets were older young women of the convent and young men of the college; all very close to the Catholic church.

There was much to do this morning, mambo strings strung alongside her steps on the street.

The hibiscus leaves she had used before to wash her hair, but today, the luxury of sitting in Aunt Hazel's zinc bath immersed in perfumed water was what she needed. Boo and Cyril had a big sour sop tree in their back yard and it was easy to say to Boo.

"Please let me have some leaves from your tree. I'm going to soak myself in the leaf water."

"I've had a few myself – what with giving birth, it's the best way to clean my blood."

It is not blood cleaning I want, she thought, all I want is the smell of it on me for Augustus to inhale when he holds me tonight. Cyril sat on a bench made for one. She had never been to their house and seen him like this, bare chest, legs out of the khaki shorts that were thick in the calf, his belly heavy over the waist of the pants. His curly black hair lay in the centre of his chest. He was a stranger to her in his domesticity.

He said, "I'm taking a sun bath before the day get too hot."

To her question about his health, he said that he was feeling much better. Boo relieved herself of the baby she held, passed her to Olga.

"The doctor say Cyril got asthma, he must stop smoking."

"People does get asthma sometimes from working in the cane fields, Boo, that's what it does."

He got up, went to the tree in the corner and pulled a branch with a dozen leaves. Olga sat on the stool he had just vacated and examined the baby. Boo's body had not yet returned to her old slimness. She studied the baby's sleeping face and smiled at it, not without wishing that she was holding her own child. Cyril came back with the leaves wrapped in paper.

"Tell Augustus I'll go back to work Thursday and give him a ride. I can't understand the way I was vomiting, I was the oney person in the house with it."

"Augustus was feeling sick too but it was not bad, he said, two days he had it."

"Thanks for the leaves, I must go now. Bye, bye."

When she returned to Aunt Hazel, after the water in the tub stood getting warm in the sun for one hour, she locked the gate of the yard, shut the living room door. Ma Boy excused herself and Aunt Hazel was in the shop. She squeezed the twelve leaves in the water, took off her dress and sat in the water, anointed her body with its perfume. She felt like a baby.

Augustus reached the house about four o'clock. The other day she had made him feel this shock up his arm when he put his hand on her arm. Now, as he passed her in the yard, his hand touched hers and he felt the same shock. He is aware of a new effect that she had on him, to make him forget the troubles of the fire, the Sampsons and the expectations of the Union men. As he moved to a chair by the table and bent to examine a shoe, he saw the hole that was a new problem. He pursed his lips. How could he get another pair when there was no Bata shop? They had made good shoes, the only shop that sold the brown canvas mongoose shoes that people liked. He removed a book from the bag he had dropped on the floor. Olga noticed and started to read it.

He read for a bit, marked the page and went upstairs. He stretched himself on the bed, then stopped his mind from returning to the estate or what he had read. After he rested, and shaved with the long-awaited blades Olga had got for him, he thought about going to have a chat with Mr Denbow to find out how he managed in the slow canoe business. That was why he thought again that if he tried to get work in Anse Du Fort, get some Yankee dollars, make a better life in a town where business was O.K., it would be better than waiting for this town to begin rearranging its affairs. *By sloth a man perishes,* came to his mind. He sat up quickly as other words.... *The heights of great men reached and kept,* followed. He would go out now. He returned downstairs; Olga swept the floor.

"I'm going by the wharf, I'll be back soon."

Mr Denbow walked on the pebbled shore line below his house, saw the sun had arrived at a position where it would stay for a couple hours before going down for the day. Two boats had come by the big wharf in the day with some relief goods. They had gone. One of them had picked up some local cargo too. His canoes had not been used by retailers, who had previously used them to get to the bay for their sugar straight from the estate. No shops and no business for him except the occasional rentals now.

"Think of the devil and see its shadow," he spoke to himself.

Augustus came into his view. He watched the young man remove his shoes. That surprised him; Augustus did not usually do such a thing. He nimbly walked on the pebbles and came to talk. They both raised a hand in greeting. He heard the complaint from Augustus.

"I need a new pair of shoes or boots; this one has a hole in the bottom."

"I see a Martinique boat come to the wharf sometimes with shoes to sell. People buy from them."

Augustus asked him about his business.

"Two fishermen got to return soon with their catch. They went out quite a while, I hope they get a good catch. They're the only customers I have apart from you."

Augustus heard that Uncle Sam was an extremely tall, well-built man. Nothing escaped his notice and because he had money he used his influence everywhere. His boat, Lady Joy, was the only locally owned vessel that went inter-island and also went down the coast of the island.

"He might have shoes to sell, find out."

He would ask the women of the house to find out when they went to buy his bread at the bakery.

"Thanks for the tip. I'll wait to see how much fish the fishermen will bring."

They sat down to wait, eyes fixed on the headland, the low hill dotted with some big homes and at the lower slopes trees rose from the rocky earth. Pink and mauve touched the sky, the warm rays of golden sunlight warmed the pebbles beneath their feet. They were in companionable silence until the older man spoke.

"I see them, they're coming in now."

"I did not expect to be around with the possibility of taking fish home tonight, I hope I will be lucky."

They had caught both red fish and flying fish. It was because people had been watching from the hilltop that they descended now to buy their own portion.

A lot of loud talking was going on around the fishermen. Mr Denbow had been quick to get his and Augustus' share before the selling got slightly complex. He put all in a basin. He had been prepared. Augustus followed him into his house to borrow a container for his red fish, they had sold six fish for two shillings. People took both dollars and shillings and pence, and he had paid one dollar and fifty cents for them.

He hurried back home through the quickest route – a right angled walk along the streets where the houses had stood, through deserted broken walls, concrete steps and broken houses. Augustus hated to walk but it was the quickest way and he had hoped to have some fish for supper.

He surprised Olga and the women. The fire had already been lit to boil water. Ma Boy, usually quick off the mark, got a knife, and her fingers and wrists gutted and scaled in a flurry. Olga got green onions, garlic and thyme, and watched Ma Boy put the seasoning on. Aunt Hazel looked around. She thought she had a lime, and she remembered she had used it in the morning. She went out through the gate to return a short while later, in time to put it in the braff in the pot already on the coal pot.

"*Voila, bon vwezinaj!*"

She lit the lamp in the kitchen. There was the sound of the hen, making them aware of her presence beneath the table, keeping her eggs warm. She had not been any trouble, she did not leave the eggs for long periods and as Olga had thought, she had not disappeared. So they waited for the chicks to hatch. Fish broth kept Ma Boy near, she never disappeared when she had a pot on fire. She stood over the pot and was totally absorbed as usual.

Aunt Hazel looked at the fine end loaves in her bread tin, counted them. She said she would go to Uncle Sam's bakery to see if there was bread on sale. It was not every day she could get some even though he was her good friend. Sometimes, very rarely, he had been there when she went to his bakery but he was not there today. The bread had all gone. She returned to the house.

Aunt Hazel and Ma Boy went to bed early. Olga had difficulty in making Era go into her great aunt's room for the night. She allowed her to fall asleep on their bed and take her by the hand, not knowing what was happening because she was such a sound sleeper. She returned. Augustus' book, 'Cane Farming in the Tropics', was on the chair where he had left it. She thought that on this matter he was serious in wanting to know more about it.

Augustus stood at the back door, his anxieties pulling him this way and that. In the yard, fireflies moved in the darkness of the night, sharp, white and suspended in a black curtain; they died and returned brighter yet. He thought, 'GOD WILL PROVIDE!' We are going to have His help. Now, Olga stood at his side.

"My *mudda* may be back later dis week. Dey oney gave her a week sick leave."

She twisted an arm around his arm by his side and leaned against him. He shut the door, blew out the candle, they went upstairs. Undressed and in bed at last, she lay close to him. They faced each other sideways, he laid his cheek against hers, she touched his smooth face, at last he had shaved. She heard his whisper,

"You're beautiful!"

She wriggled closer. "And I love you."

"What did you put on your body?"

"I bathed in sour sop leaves."

"Oh, that's what smells good. Now as your mother is down the coast and Era is not in the room it makes so much difference, not that sleeping on the floor is impossible for me but it's stopping short of a penance, not having the freedom to hold you when I feel like."

He kissed her eyes and her fingertips. She closed her eyes as he kissed her mouth and soon he gently and carefully joined his body to hers in his usual way.

The dream she had was something she kept in her mind now but was not able to try something like that.

Next morning, she passed Aunt Hazel quickly, taking Era to school. Her Aunt's eyes studied her and she smiled inquisitively.

"When you come back, you going to sew at Mr Francois'? I have the cloth to give you, what Augustus wanted for the suit."

Olga dropped Era off at school and with conscious efforts, she quickened her steps. She had so much to do. Whether she would get the suit cut today was a question she asked herself. She spent no time at the house, took the cloth and carried it to Mr Francois'. She prayed that she would get this jacket cut in the shop even, as she had not gone for days now.

Mr Francois in short khaki shorts, white shirt and a bright floral tie stood at his cutting board. She had not seen his sabot before. They looked strange and he wore no socks, which he used to previously. She came into the shop as he ironed a garment. She surprised him.

"Good morning, Mr Francois, I'm back, I was not able to come but today I am hoping to do something for Augustus please."

He made a full round about turn, replaced the iron on its brick stand.

"Morning to Helen of Troy. Come and help us, your help I welcome."

Bits of thread and ends of cloth littered the floor. The big room echoed the banging of the foot pedals that went up and down. Both machines were in use, who would cut the jacket for her?

"You see, I brought the cloth with me, if you can cut his jacket for me please?"

"That's good. I must say. U-u-um! Anyway!"

He handed her a pair of trousers that needed button holes and the ends of threads to be knotted and cut. After she had settled in the room, she said,

"My *mudda* went to Bonne Terre last week, she was not too well."

She was surprised the few hours she had spent there had been in her favour, not only did Mr Francois oblige her with cutting it but he had shown her how to go about putting it together, the tacking she would have to do, the blocking, the wadding around the shoulders. She was afraid that she would spoil it but she felt that it was an opportunity to learn about tailoring, and so she hoped to make some headway the next day. She had to wash her hair in the afternoon, then pick up Era, and she left at twelve thirty and promised to stay longer the next day. It had been busy. Portly Mr Henderson was the quiet one. George laughed and talked as he worked, and how they put up with Carl, mostly standing to make a sermon when he put down a pair of pants that he had worked on. It was because they were a good-natured set of men she had to admit to herself that they put up with Carl. She left the jacket with Mr Francois. The way it looked pleased her – the way the double breast folded, the rows of tacking thread that held it flat. Mounting the collar would be a tricky bit.

Later, Augustus watched the moves she made.

"Glisse!"

He had smiled with delight in her dreams when they made love, when he had been her captive and received her administrations. His strong hand pushed her aside. She wriggled away from his body.

"Come on, Olga!"

She got up from the bed, took the blanket, unfolded it and lay it on the floor and then sat cross-legged away from him. He came to her.

"Come back."

His face was anxious in the dim light from the stub of a candle.

"The bed is more comfortable."

"I dreamt of us together, I over you, and I wanted to do so tonight! You looked very happy in my dream!"

"You dreamt that? What have these tailors been talking about in your presence?"

"The tailors? What you mean?"

"If they could not carry on decent conversations in the presence of a lady, you cannot go back."

"It's not the tailors."

"It has to be. You could not dream what you've never done. So I say do not return to the shop."

The night was ruined. Augustus could not really mean this? She had known that the Rosicrucian book he read would affect his mind. She returned to bed.

"Sorry, Olga, but as your husband, I say what we do."

"I'm sorry too, I thought…"

"I don't want to hear any more of this wayward talk. Stay sweet as you are."

The night wore on. Her disappointment lingered; her dream had given her this confidence as if she could do as she wished with him – so strong in the dream, she had felt herself stronger than she ever had been. What was he afraid of? Did he sense her new strength and wanted her always complying with his wishes?

His illusions were being smashed one by one, and in order to live as a decent couple he had to make a stand to keep her in check. Angry words passed between them, their first confrontation regarding their married behaviour. They finally kissed and slept.

She was awake with him in the early morning and again he tried to placate her.

"I love you, the way you are; you don't have to try any tricks for me. You understand?"

"Uh huh, I hear what you saying."

They could not see each other's face in the dark room. He kissed her shoulder and started to get ready for work. He felt unsettled; he could not fathom her. Then again, it could be the effect of the fire's gradual accumulative effects that was getting into her spirit as well. The idea came to him that she might be getting tired of him.

He welcomed the ride with Cyril, the easy companionship they shared, and it was soon the end of the work day.

"Let's roll down this hill, man."

Cyril wore his panama hat at an angle and removed it inside the car. He drank some sweetened water, making sure to continue what he said had helped him to overcome the vomiting; he had not gone to the doctor in the end. They spoke about football and a little about the estate. Now, children were walking up from school in town.

His eyes found Olga's face; she'd just come in with Era. Her face was close to his as he sat by her side. The wide cheeks and semi arcs of her eyes held his own full brown ones; it was a lengthy stare, assessing his mood. A chisel and hammer had made his face, with firm lines around his lips. The definitive ridge below his nose, with its long bridge above two small mounds of flesh around his nostrils, gave the nose an angular look. He returned the stare, his usual open expression. She knew where she stood with him. She still felt her love warming her in spite of the night before.

"I spoke to Cyril because he's overseer. He had heard about work at Anse Du Fort. He told me what I should do. He said I should become a Wesleyan."

"No!"

"He also said that I should write a letter to the manager down south but I need a Godfather."

"If you are sure, you can try."

CHAPTER TWENTY-FOUR

Augustus took his seat on the mail boat on Saturday morning. He hoped he would find his father without too much delay, and hastened away while the Captain collected the mail for the village. Even that had been a miracle that the postal service had been only temporarily disrupted because all the stamps had been saved.

He passed the fishing nets strung between trunks of coconut trees as usual and moved into the white light of the village. He found his brother-in-law first. Marcel told him in patois that he had been on the look out for him.

"Papa is checking the coal pits, mamma went down to customers to sell starch and garden produce."

They went to his house. His sister grated the manioc tubers and talked to him in broken English. They talked while Marcel disappeared.

The hardest thing for his sister now in her pregnancy was if it happened that she had problems in the confinement. When the time came, he told her so.

"*Pwan Gad!* Take care!" he told her in patois.

"A, A, you talk patois, *fwe?*" Then, "Papa coming, behind you, look at him."

The older man wheeled in green coconuts and he was covered in coal soot.

"So you reach, my boy?"

"How you keeping Papa?"

"I'm well; I'm strong."

"*Sa bon!*"

"I'm glad you remember how to say that." He laughed. "I have something else to give to you. You left it behind here, years ago."

Augustus walked with him and saw the new bicycle. "It's new!"

"I got it, your good luck, a man's boy growing up, who was always in trouble. He lost his foot in an accident so he was selling the bike, I got a bargain for you."

"I don't want to miss the mail boat, I must go back now."

"Before you go, take this."

The paper bag he passed to Augustus was light; he looked inside.

"Your Talisman, take it with you.

"I did not know you still had it."

His black eyebrows came an inch down to his eyelids in a frown.

"I don't need this now. I'm O.K. Papa."

Mr James took his pipe from his pocket, stuffed tobacco in the bowl and a slow smile came on his face.

"Swallowing all the English and learning can put a cloud on your mind, you know that? Take it."

"Thanks, I brought you some things, I gave to Marcel."

"Now take care my boy, you know the malicious mind some that people hide in their head." His father's time and his time met somewhere along the line. The join was not that indestructible. Augustus put the Talisman in his pocket – the thing his parents told him had got him out of a coma when he was eleven.

His father adjusted his sandal and walked with him to the jetty. He carried some flying fish Marcel shared with him from what he had for the family.

"Come next Saturday, one cow getting killed."

He made it on time. He got in to sit holding on his bike.

The short journey of seven miles in that peaceful section of the sea started. The curly shore disappeared. Fifteen minutes later the mail boat passed Duck Islet and ten minutes later, another islet. The white wake on the blue sea frothed and made a pattern on the water behind them. These parts were famous for marlin when the season came for them to be plentiful. The hot blue sky had very little cloud and they made to the town very soon.

Augustus set foot on the pier with four other passengers early in the afternoon. A sloop was at the wharf. A few wooden crates stood alongside the boat; at that moment a stevedore picked up a crate, placed it in his cart to wheel it to some lucky person in town. He stood for a moment leaning on his bicycle. Where were the shoes Mr Denbow told him were sometimes sold on the wharf? He would have to check that in the week, if he met up with Uncle Sam. Now his pockets were empty, and his best bet for shoes should the relief supplies. Later he would visit the Union shop. Even if it was only canvas shoes, they would do till he got strong weatherproof ones.

The shape of the day was round; on Market Street he rode alongside a patrol of eight police going towards an opposite direction to him, he exchanged looks with Philosophe who gave a faint smile. He was the tallest and largest of the troop.

Earlier that morning, Muriel took her seat on the Lady Joy. The boat rocked on choppy water. This part of the coast always picked up bad weather first. It was fourteen miles south of Masav. Bad weather could knock down houses near the shore in the hurricane season.

The swells in the ocean made her grip the edge of the boat where she sat. She faced the moment when she returned to town, as while she had stayed at Bonne Terre among those she had not seen for so long she had re-examined her life. What had gone on with her sister and La La, life had suddenly come riding over her without brakes. She had been seen in her fragility by her daughter and her elder cousin, Ma Boy. The broken bits of her wreck had been too much for her own eyes till she had come near to become loose tongued and angry, she had had to get right out of the way.

Going back now, the tide had come back to cover the debris on the shore, everything was once more contained and put back where they once were. She had feared that her feelings would be more and more trampled on. All these years living by straight and narrow rules, being unadorned! She pulled her thoughts back to the present. Her stomach heaved, her eyes were closed and the boat veered in position as the wind blew hard. The need to pull on her clay pipe was strong; she felt that it would settle the heaving inside. She had fallen into the habit of smoking in Ma George's company in the village. Ma George had encouraged her to find comfort there.

Now, the sultry air was oppressive. They approached Masav and the Lady Joy turned round headland, she sighed a great one of relief to see the town become clearer as the boat pushed into the harbour with its calm waters.

The other passengers collected their reed brooms, earthenware coal pots and food that they hoped to sell in the market. Muriel had her own broom, a basket of sweet potatoes, sugar apples, a straw floor mat which she had made herself with the help of her relatives. She was laden. She also managed a coal pot for which Hazel would be grateful, she knew.

She planted her feet on the concrete of the straight line of the concrete wharf and waited for these things to be handed her across the small gap between the boat and the wharf. Uncle Sam was busy in all the chatter, the demands, the complaints and also the thank yous he received.

She waited to get her land legs back.

"Muriel?"

She turned round, she saw the sloop next to the Lady Joy first, then she saw who had called her and started to walk away with her things. Her disdain was foremost in her mind.

"Muriel, where you coming from?"

He hastened after her. Her skin pricked with irritation and bitter yellow of pomegranate skin touched her lips as he touched her arm from sideways. Muriel felt bile come into her mouth. She had to place the coal pot on the wharf and press a hand to her mouth and swallow.

He peered at her closely his mouth began to form a word, but she did not wait, she swallowed hard, not wanting to be sick before him. With the coal pot in her fist, she made her neck the longest she could make it look and she moved it from side to side as she walked off. He had changed a great deal and the quick glimpse she had of him stayed before her as she moved on through the gate of the wharf, towards the market where the vendors had already settled in with their goods waiting for the town people to give them a sale.

Aunt Hazel was happy to see that Muriel's rest had made her look well again. Her back held straight, she noticed, and her face was impassive. Olga was out with Era. It was only the three older women together. Later, Muriel took out her pipe and put it in her mouth.

"But, what is that?" came from a surprised Miss Hazel.

Muriel sucked on the stem and blew out smoke.

"I did not know this pipe could give such peace of mind! I have to thank cousin Ma George for that."

Then she said in a flat voice that she had seen Harry on the wharf, but she had not spoken to him. Hazel was pleased that she could call Harry's name without looking angry. Then she gave her news of the Sampsons because Muriel had asked after them to change the subject of Harry. She managed to deceive Miss Hazel about her true sentiments after that meeting. Her heart which had banged in her chest on sight of him was still going wildly.

A little later, after she had thrown water on her body behind the kitchen and dressed again, she felt better.

Aunt Hazel held the new round mat that her sister had given her and examined it.

"So, you made it?"

She said to Muriel, "I wonder if I will go down the coast ever again?"

They spoke about things about the village and Muriel smiled broadly when Olga and Era came back. She felt joy as the child came to her, waiting for a caress that she gave to her freely. She put her arm around her and drew her to her firm body and smoothed the small hand in hers. Era felt like they had just given her a plate of red beans with pigtail bouillon. Contentment flowed through her little body. She beamed, the eyelids very close with a slither of black eye in the pale round face, her pink mouth pulled back. She looked at Muriel's face while she talked with Olga and the women.

CHAPTER TWENTY-FIVE

The Colonel, in his late forties, was regarded as a boy by Philosophe. Both were long serving officers in the force, but their different approaches to policing set them apart from each other, so much so that they did not have anything like a social type of conversation. His belief in a certain type of power – to make town people feel fear when he talked to them – was what he was after. He thought having a Police Lodge was important.

Philosophe heard a trumpet solo coming from another building in the police block from the street as he approached the station; some band boy was practicing. That was another thing the Colonel took particular interest in, that the band should have a good reputation, that they should sing the St Cecelia song at the start of a day before taking up other duties for which he had laid down the strict programmes.

That day, the police band practiced for a concert they were going to give soon, on a Sunday in the St Cecelia Gardens. Another thing, they used to visit schools in the town periodically, to play music for the good of the children and teachers, and they played in civil ceremonies, especially on St Benedict's Discovery Day bank holiday.

The day before, Philosophe saw an American jeep pull up in front of the station bringing the superintendent from the airport. He had been alerted to that event, and so the long-awaited boss arrived. Philosophe saw him and could not believe it but he was quick to stand at attention, heels together, head erect and his back straight to greet the great man.

There would be no more Lodge ideas from the Inspector now, and a good thing, he thought. Someone else was in charge. Even the administrator had come into the station the week before. This morning, they had marched around the town with the superintendent. Just now the two top men were in private, discussing things. Six policemen were on the beat. He sat at the station desk. The two policemen on the night shift made up the whole compliment of duty officers and they would have to be the same men to fight a fire in case another one happened. But the police band had sixteen men.

While the two men held their meeting, the superintendent observed, "The American-British management of the island is the way you now have it? Yes?"

"That's true. We get the involvement with both countries and pounds and dollars."

There were many serious issues to be discussed now, like the fire engines and the fire department that should be separated from the general force. Still no police allowed to emigrate would continue.

He was not told about the report Philosophe had given him about the junior police, the money stolen and their involvement as given by Electra. Philosophe was now aware that he was not alone. The meeting was over; the superintendent was now occupying the Colonel's office. He passed Philosophe on the way out. The boy, as he privately called the Inspector, smiled politely as he went. Philosophe bent his head to concentrate on the paper and notes before him.

The Colonel did not have to walk near the People's Square. He looked smart, dark trousers with red stripes down the sides, white short sleeved shirt. He always looked that way. He passed the burnt down cinema and the Singer sewing machine shop as he walked toward the western wharf where he had to meet Challo. Later he would visit Mr Popo. He passed the sweet drink factory, the one place still operating, and the library which left the clerical men and women without their livelihood. In the sweet drink factory, a low, wide concrete building, he saw the white manager walk across the doorway and disappeared inside behind the machinery.

He felt that his department had failed the people and he was not proud of it. But he felt that he was not totally to blame, because when the needs of the Windward Islands were to be considered from the same head office by the Governor for the group, some islands were doing better than St Benedict, which was why the Americans helped with school materials and finance.

Popo had told him that the bank's accounts had been short of twenty pounds that had been stolen. Popo said that the Bank messenger, O.K. Pal, had told him that policemen came into the bank while the watchman was drunk inside, so Popo had left the matter with him and now was the time – he would return the money to Popo. But Challo had wanted to hold on to the money and he planned to hold police dances to raise funds for the Lodge. He argued that Popo could not prove anything, but Challo was only a constable and he now waited for him. When he knew that the new superintendent was expected anytime, he had sent an urgent message for him to come to Masav. He had come by the Lady Joy that morning. Challo was across the road, leaning on the iron gate of the west wharf.

Colonel crossed the road sprightly. Challo straightened up. He liked the post he now held, junior police in a village with a small population, without school or church. The nearest school was at Bonne Terre and the church further on through the hills. He looked well; Colonel appraised his plump body in light shirt and light pants, he was still single – he could afford to look happy, he had to smile when he greeted him. They shook hands.

"I'm glad you saw sense and we can have a clear conscience. The plan did not work, we'll have to wait and somehow, we'll have the Police Lodge."

"Alright boss."

He handed the heavy bag, mostly sixpences. After all, the bank was called the 'penny bank' when it started; there were half crowns and some copper coins. They walked together then parted. Popo would get the money tonight.

He passed on the periphery of the town to avoid the fire refugees on his way to Popo's house in the south. He passed the market, crossing intersections till he came to the small river in the south. It disappeared behind the houses near the road where his house stood.

Popo stood on the balcony of his unpainted house on a small hill east of town. Now he took the camp chair and placed it next to the wall, sat down and leaned back, placing the soles of his shoes above the balcony rail. His eyes were on the stencil carving on the plank of the balcony – 'In God We Trust'. He had commerce on his mind because the Lafayette Company in New Orleans had written to the town Board to promise a future project which was to be the building of a store. But he had felt so much pressure at meetings of the Town Board that he expected to be voted off in December at the big town elections. If he was not leader, he hoped to stay on as a member. They could not actually kick him out. The people of the town were all invited to vote this time. He had always circulated among all sectors in the town, he was decent, but he knew how he handled the savings in the bank had upset the majority of people. There had been rancour.

The Colonel walked up the gradual slope some ten yards from the narrow road into Morne Pierre. He had had second thoughts about taking the money to Popo's house; he thought he would leave it till Monday and take it to the official Town Board. But with the intervening Sunday, he could keep the money and leave Popo to do what he felt like. He resisted the temptation. He reached the concrete step of the balcony, saw the man's comfortable position alter. He stood up to meet him. The Colonel gave him the bag of coins.

"Thanks, Inspector. I won't report this matter but I take a very dim view, you know, of this police force."

"Don't mention it. I'm a man of few words."

He walked off. Popo was thinking, 'The insufferable, think-he-somebody so and so!' If only Paine was not so docile, he should be made the senior inspector over this man.

The men's voices in her Aunt's shop drew Olga's attention as she passed on her way into the yard, and then her Aunt called to her. Mr Francois had returned her sewing machine. That meant she could work on Augustus' jacket later on.

She returned to her large basin of wet clothes and then finally hung them up on the wire lines. Her thoughts went to her mother, her first day back at work. But also she wondered about her Aunt; she had the fixed look yesterday which she had sometimes – her eyes pierced all through a person, it made her feel all worked up. She felt edgy this morning.

She had felt her mother's absence in a strange way. It had seemed unreal. She used to feel something at odd times, as though Muriel could be reached by calling to her and then she would appear, and yesterday she had spent a great deal of it in church or talking with Ma Sampson, she said. She, Olga felt, had ignored her somehow. That bothered her. She had been solemn. She had a different relationship with Aunt Hazel, even though she made her edgy, but her Aunt said things, she seemed to make assessments and judgements all the time they spoke.

"Well child!" she said in patois to Olga's comment that her mother had spent a great deal of her time the day before out of the house. "She heard something on Saturday about Harry." Aunt Hazel was oblique here. She hoped Muriel would tell Olga herself.

That evening they talked among the family. Not saying much, Olga thought. Muriel kept everything hidden. Olga sat by the sewing machine. Muriel looked her way, proud of her, with such a personality! And her father was in the island. She would have preferred it otherwise. La La and her sister making plans; she was determined to keep her dignity in that respect, not to repeat what had happened when she had stormed through her sister's house when La La had brought her son to visit, making her past hurt erupt. She now said to Olga, "Next year, please God, I should be working in Aruba."

"You must not give up hope."

Aunt Hazel said her eyes smiled but there was a set in her mouth. An almost regal smile. Olga released the cloth from the needle of the machine, snipped the thread, nodded with satisfaction, holding up the jacket away from her. Her examination complete, she took it upstairs. She would see how it looked on Augustus tonight. Muriel followed her and moved to the balcony; how would she tell her child that her father was in Masav? She thought of allowing her sister to tell her. Just speaking of him was uncomfortable. Now Augustus appeared on the street, and she knew her conversation would wait.

The fleecy clouds floated in the west, the breeze caressed her face. It had been a hard day. She had peeled dozens of green bananas and cooked food both for the priests and some of the old people on the Square, and not to mention the washing up; but, it gave her satisfaction. She thought of that instead of Harry, anything but Harry.

Next evening, Ma Boy could be seen through the haze of smoke from the fire she had lit in the kitchen. Muriel stood in the doorway of the kitchen. Olga saw her mother get some tobacco – that she had brought from Bonne Terre – and she stuffed it in the bowl of her pipe, lit it. The late afternoon sun spread its pale rays among the stones of the yard. Miss Hazel waved goodbye to them, she came down from the stairs, crossed the room and they saw her go out through the gate. She returned a short while later.

"Anything happen?"

Her steady eyes looked at her sister, and with her form of her commanding self planted in the room. Muriel looked towards her, lips with a downturn slant. Her grey cook's dress with a cotton lace high neck, which had been protected by the white apron she wore at work, was fairly clean.

Olga did not understand. Her mother's silence was expected. Olga somehow felt both interested and some apathy – things left unsaid was nothing new.

A clap of thunder came down, made everyone change modes; something real was happening in the world outside the house. They moved. A second, louder eruption shook the air and Olga put her hand to her chest. This happened in September and no warning precluded it, but its suddenness always unsettled Olga.

"I hope the rain will keep away. The town and the rain! I can see the state it would be in." She thought of debris, old ash, sludge.

"Dat's God talking, *DuDu,*" Muriel told Era, taking her hand; the child's serious expression related to the mood she sensed between her granny and her great Aunt. What was going to happen? she wondered. She stayed close while Olga went into the kitchen. The dusk had fallen but there was enough light to finish preparing supper with the old cousin. She glanced across to see Aunt Hazel up close to her mother around the table. She talked to her.

Miss Hazel only said a few words. Era did not know the patois she listened to now, but her face was avid.

The evening wore on; Muriel went upstairs after supper. A short while later, everyone went upstairs, Augustus not yet returned. Olga on the one hand wanted to wait for him and on the other wanted to talk to her mother. She sat on the balcony with Era and Aunt Hazel, thoughtful. She was going to have to ask her mother what news she had heard about Harry, and was pleased when she joined them. Muriel stood by the rail – not much to see except the street below. The feeling of space that staying on the balcony gave, reduced some of the tension of downstairs. As they were not alone, Olga wondered if she should talk honestly. If she postponed it the opportunity might not come till days later. She thought it best to try now. "Mamma, you heard news of Harry?"

She remained rigid when her mother told her.

"Yes, A! A! He is with us again."

Her body was rocked by a new invisible thunderbolt. A flash went through her mind of what he must look like.

"Tell me where he is. I'm going now to see for myself. I could curse him."

"No, Olga, not like dat."

"Tell me, Aunt Hazel, where is he? Coming now, all dis time in Panama, my fadder?"

She stood, hands on her hips, a vexed look on her face. Era hopped from one foot to the other, anxiety on her face. The women were silent as they watched her.

"First, I fot he was dead, then I hear he's alive, now he making a visit but what dis man fink? He will have me to deal wif, wi!"

She was interrupted by the bang! Boom! A new clap of thunder came.

"There will be rain later."

Aunt Hazel broke the tension. In Olga's mind the ghost of Harry, tinctured by many old thoughts, took colour and form. Aunt Hazel thinks she's just like her mother when they get vex; they could make noise. She had tried to sail her ship with all of them with hope of arriving at its berth, but the waters were choppy right now, and she would have to use her skills to navigate this new course. She said after the thunder subsided but still rumbled,

"Let's go and rest ourselves. Tomorrow we will have to make plans, Olga. What's done is done. Egal, Egal! Remember."

Olga's vexation pushed currents to destabilise the wooden panels in the house, the white floor planks and the balcony on its poles to the sidewalk downstairs, then.

"*Me'kote'* Augustus?" Aunt Hazel asked and touched Olga's arm.

"*M'a sav*, nuh!"

"Well, we have to go to sleep," Aunt Hazel said.

She wished he would hurry so she could lock up as she wanted to bolt the door downstairs. Olga thought there might be something that kept him out, was there trouble in town? But she only had thoughts of Harry as she took Era to bed.

She stood in the small room. After she had lit a candle and settled it in a saucer, she sat next to the child and studied her face, which did not resemble either hers or Augustus'. She underlined his reason for denying her what she wanted and she went along with his wishes, but for how much longer? She was not convinced about his thing that children could feel jealous of one another because customs in Masav altered how benefits fell on children like Era. Children of the same parents if they were different shades did not have equal opportunities and approval. That's what he believed. She examined her own face; her hand grasped the hairpins to loosen the two plaits on either side of her head, she loosened them. The half circle of her eyes in the face she knew looked back at her. She chupsed and returned the mirror to the grip, went out to the balcony to await Augustus. He had not taken his bicycle when he left. What was the time, she wondered.

He arrived just at the right time to prevent an overload of thoughts of things she would say to Harry when she met him. Nothing to do except to lay down after she altered Era's position across the bottom of the bed, so that she and Augustus could talk on the bed, close.

So, that's where he's been, she thought, when he said that he had spent time at Dujon's house with the Union men; earlier, he had been talking with Mr Polius. She told him about her father and felt that he over reacted in the response he made.

"I would like to meet him soon, it will be interesting to hear about Panama."

And she thought they both had separate hearts, not just in that but in other matters.

"There's good news," he said, and she waited.

"The police band will play in the Gardens on Sunday afternoon. Maybe, we could leave this house sooner than you think, because Dujon said something is going on from the Government, for us."

All the jumble of notes in her head took on a tonic accent with a more pleasant and clearer pitch.

On Thursday, Aunt Hazel waited till Augustus went out, and then alone with her sister and niece, she handed Muriel a letter Harry had given her to deliver.

Muriel stared. "From Harry?"

Her sister urged her.

"What for?"

She did not take it. She looked as if it might bite her. He has started to encroach on her carefully preserved space with this. There was a drumming in her ears. Olga saw her mother's closed look. She moved away. Olga chewed on the inside of her bottom lip and screwed her mouth in surprise at this letter for her mother.

Aunt Hazel said, "I don't know what you expect, but from what he said to me, you should read it."

She put in on the table.

"I want a Phensic," Muriel said.

She tossed and turned in the night, letter unopened. She suspected that her sister had pre-empted Harry's contact with her and was an accomplice. She thought, "I, Muriel St Juste, finish with all this man business."

A second night, she tried to lie straight next to Hazel but it was hard not to move her arms and legs about. A few times Hazel grunted, annoyed. Before it was light, she got up and dressed quickly in the dark. She heard Augustus leave his room for work. She went off to the half past five mass. Heavy grey light enfolded her on the empty streets. Mass was well attended. She was hoping all the while in the church for the answer about Harry, Olga, the best way to behave. That night she opened her letter.

Olga had given her consent to her Aunt to let Era meet Harry; she felt it was very important to let Era meet Harry to see the man whom she resembled. She dressed her carefully and the child sat on the edge of Christmas, waiting for a surprise.

The house Aunt Hazel took her to leaned sideways into the next one as though they supported each other, wooden and amber in colour with galvanise awning. The door was half open, and she encountered a toad-like old face in response to Aunt Hazel's knock. A body followed, she came out on to the doorstep. Era saw the person's eyes lost in the folds of the lids, her skin was yellow with a few brown spots on one cheek. She was old. Era observed her with awe, looking at her with wide eyes. They went in.

Then when Harry stood there to meet them, and his glinting black eyes appraised Era, she dropped her own. Aunt Hazel saw him smile, a wide smile, and he had a dark reddish colour on his forehead.

"Say good afternoon, Era."

His bright eyes, so intent on her, made her fidget.

"He is your grandfather," Aunt Hazel commanded.

She listened as he quizzed her in a playful manner after he had given her a chair to sit on. Era was shy and now the adults talked among themselves. She looked at the pink skirt with the shiny white stripes that she wore – it made her feel stiff and Sunday-ish. Her mother had forced her hair into curls all over her head. It was a style, her mother told her as she coaxed the hair with the small curls, like Shirley Temple's.

Looking back years later, she remembered that during her first visit to her grandfather they had not spoken in patois. The way his words came out she did not understand what he meant, but she remembered words he used: gold, river, mountain, fish, canal, Americans. He used gold many times.

Simultaneously as they were out on the visit, there was a small fire on the People's Square. A collection of rubbish, a candle, a careless person, but while the rubbish crackled Red Cross workers were on duty there keeping a check on the situation, and were to witness that and make a report. The people's washed clothes lay on the croton hedges close to the wire inner enclosure. Some clothes got burnt. The people ran to the fountain within the wire enclosure and managed to put the fire out.

They were without latrines. The Red Cross women knew the way it was, but how resilient they were, making do. They returned to headquarters that nestled amidst residential buildings and the Methodist Church in the east side, to make this new report in a letter to the government Executive Committee.

On the Square, Ma Sampson used the priests' toilet as she knew Muriel. This did not extend to the majority, who had used the school's, but now that the schools had reopened, they found other ways to relieve themselves. People were stuck. Now they had got big empty ex-butter containers from the grocery shops and used these in the night. In the early morning, their waste was removed.

The shadows gathered on the Square. Another night descended. The schools too had been somewhere to stay in the night for some people – now reopened, those had this no more and lay on the camp beds. The red blankets given to them kept them cosy.

The blind eagle regained its sight; it stood up after three months, opened its wings wide, and flew up towards the hill and Government House. It hovered before the bedroom window of the administrator. He had awoken but kept his eyes closed to the bright morning light. He opened them at the unexpected change; he sat up looking at the immense bird against the glass. Its eyes looked at him. He stood up after the first numbed sensation wore off. Where had this creature come from?

He whispered, "Goodness gracious! Gordon Bennet! Never have I seen such a bird around these grounds!"

The wings moved, it turned and flew away. He said to his wife at breakfast he would have to be ready to shoot it if it came back. As if to reassure herself, she looked at the picture of a hawthorn tree with its bloom of white flowers, which hung on the wall of the dining room to remind them of England.

His programme today was the usual writing of letters and minutes for his secretary to dispatch, and also there was a meeting with the Executive Council of Government in the afternoon to discuss the progress of the work going on to re-house the town people.

The business car arrived with the secretary while he studied correspondence from the Chief Medical Officer. He worried about the health of the people in the town; they needed more doctors. There was nothing from the Public Works Department.

In correspondence from the Town Board, there was something new which he focused on now; the fellow Dujon wanted to be a member on the Board, and stand in the election in December. The Union men were becoming political.

His prim-looking secretary came in; she had been picked out of the small set of clerical government workers. He saw her anxious face; her clothes were meticulous. He liked her with the white long sleeve top and grey skirt, hair brushed back, a young woman of Indian and Negro mixed race family. She normally wore stockings, but now he saw the bare legs in the black patent shoes.

Guy's sister knew much about the union's plans because of her brother. She had been one of the relief workers on the roster in the weeks after the fire, she had not been to work when the cars could not drive through the streets. She would have preferred not to be up there when she had been appointed, but now that the other offices had got destroyed in the fire and she loved being busy, she was grateful. It showed with the speed as she typed the minutes.

In the middle of the morning she handed the messenger the letters he had to take to the health centre, to the Chief Medical Officer, a file to the Director of Public Works, a file to the Superintendent of Police. That car went up and down the hill. In the afternoon, the Executive Council members would arrive. She was going to have a busy day.

She sat outside at mid-day with her lunch. The humid September air was a reminder that rain was on the way, and she gazed at the town below which was the colour of mourning. She stretched her legs for a few minutes. There were canna lilies lining the path towards the front of the house, and a policeman stood on guard some distance from the iron gate near the road. On the green lawn an old cannon pointed downwards. There was breeze from the palm trees on the slope behind the white building.

She needed this space, her nerves were somewhat ragged because of the expectation that she would be efficient. He depended on her so much. Soon her break was at an end, she returned to the house.

CHAPTER TWENTY-SIX

Olga opened the door to the yard. Morning air was sultry, slightly damp. She heard the hen's cacophonic music; the usual reminder of its presence in Aunt Hazel's shop. Olga opened that door in the corridor and the hen flew past, wings wide spread. Olga shooed at her, heard the hen screech as she jumped outside. She started pecking voraciously among the small stones. Surely the eggs had not hatched, it was too soon! She went, had a look. They were still eggs. The hen was hungry; if she had some corn she would feed her some, but not even coconut remained from what Augustus had brought from the land.

Olga dragged her thoughts to something else. It was such a relief that school had reopened; and now, for this new day.

A small shower of rain fell. She looked up – pale blue early morning sky. She went to wake Era by taking the child's arm, lifted her to a seating position on the bed.

"School!"

Now to attend to a first fire. Era followed her downstairs; they were alone for a good while before Aunt Hazel appeared. She spoke with Olga about the possibility of heavy rain – the change in the air and the thunder they had before. After her Aunt left to buy bread, while Era washed herself she made them cocoa tea. After they had the breakfast she set about to leave for the life out there, the familiar things like little children being taken to school. But the unfamiliar was Era's ears without earrings, herself without them. She thought of Ma Sampson, not leaving her jewellery to get burnt. She knew that a goldsmith, Mr Rawlins, had a small shack close by the square on some days to buy people's gold chains, bracelets or silver. People needed money for meat and fish. Those clerks with no work, the middle class reduced in their means. Another unfamiliar thing was Harry, alive, his appearance in the town. Her mother had not spoken to her any words regarding this – this incursion into their lives again. What she had felt when she had the news was now diluted from that heady potion of the day. And she had not been told who was putting him up, where was he? Poor mamma, she thought.

The house seemed empty when she got back. She sat at the machine and turned her skills that she had picked up to catch up on Augustus' jacket, and she would meet Era at twelve. She worked on it without stopping for anything. Her Aunt came downstairs dressed in a maroon and royal blue *dwiet* and matching head tie. She was going out.

"The shop is open, if somebody want to buy anything you attend to that for me please."

"Yes."

She'd hoped to have a final fitting today before completing it the next day. The soft cloth of brown check, the lining looked untidy, she thought; it would not lay flat. She struggled, adjusting, catching it with the needle and thread here and there. She had got a piece of canvas to stiffen the collar and lapels. Everything she had seen Mr Francois do, she copied. She heard her Aunt's voice talking to someone on the sidewalk a long time afterwards and then she came through into the house.

"My child, your father will have a party next Saturday."

A serious look told Olga that she, being the junior member of the family, was still subject to the well-intentioned requests that she could have thrown at her.

"You must go and be introduced, child."

She answered nothing. She raised her eyes heavenward and kept the material firmly in her hand, controlling it beneath the foot on the machine. There was something now for her information, and although unlike Augustus the thought did not thrill her, she thought that sometimes it was beneficial to take advice from relatives.

She said "Yes, alright."

Aunt Hazel meant *egal* – proper behaviour and not at any time in any way at all do things to lower themselves.

The other outfit she wanted to start would be a dress for her mother from a piece of bronze rayon cloth with small white flowers. She had encouraged her to get this from Aunt Hazel. Her mother used to wear white long sleeve dresses for church and she was only forty-three. She dressed like the spinsters on the shelf for a long time, those who kept men at a distance; although there were the others, the 'Children of Mary' who wore white long sleeve dresses with high necklines. Her mother did not belong to that confraternity, she just wanted to be a woman who showed the world her contained integrity and did not indulge in the slightest deviation from the decent type. Propriety came off her as she walked in the town, but Olga knew her quirky side – occasionally she said things from a mind that Olga knows is full of regret when the crusty short sentences made her smile. Like her mother's smoking; she had just started. Was it to shock them? She must have expected some reaction, a fuss. It was unwomanly. Maybe it was a need for calmness which was now apparent on Muriel. In this matter she did not present herself anymore as an impregnable force. She might like to wear something with an air of defiance. She'd ask her what she wanted for the style.

Olga listened to a woman's voice which came from the direction of the lane behind her Aunt's house; it was a song with love words.

Today the sky seemed lower overhead – more thunder, he expected. Cyril dropped Augustus off on Market Street, he walked with quick light steps. These days it had become a season for going into strange places. Around him were a few changes in the ground, many sword ferns grew leaning on fences or walls and beside stone steps. Men and women walked on their business on this periphery off the messy streets. He now avoided the People's Square when he walked through the town. He avoided meeting Ma Sampson.

He had told Cyril he wanted to look for shoes on sale on a certain boat in the harbour. Stevedores were placing crates on their carts with big letters bearing peoples' names and addresses. He spied someone coming down a gangway with shoes; he approached hopefully. Inside the boat, he greeted the men with boxes of shoes and as they were from Martinique they spoke to him in French. They showed him a few pairs, nice but uncomfortable. He was going to leave when they showed him another pair; they looked second-hand in brown. They fitted him and seemed a good bargain; the soles were perfect, and he offered to pay in West Indian dollars which they said they did not like – those West Indian dollars – and then accepted the money. As an afterthought, he asked to see ladies' shoes. There was a pair of black patent ones with a little heel which he bought. He returned to the house.

Olga sat by the big table concentrating on his jacket. Her arms had got round again and she looked well, and she was his wife, this lovely woman. She sensed his arrival in the room without looking up.

"See, what I got for you."

"Oh!" for the shoes he handed her.

She put them on, stood, and walked up and down.

"Just a little bit big but it's good; fanks."

She looked at him, what was he thinking, she wondered? Through his silence Era's laugh came from upstairs.

"She's with Ma Boy on the balcony wi!"

Oh yes, and he regretted that he had not thought of looking for a pair of shoes for her also. The two hundred dollars he had saved before the fire was the thing he had been thinking all that morning; what he had saved because living with his mother-in-law had made it possible. Olga said, "Stand up – let's try the jacket; last time."

He opened his arms while she put one sleeve on him, pulled across the back and put his other arm in carefully.

"I'm your prisoner."

"Move your arms, is it tight?"

It was loose fitting, she was happy to see. The double-breasted lapels were firm but the points were not as good as she would have liked. She looked at his face.

"So?"

"*Sa bon! Meci an chay!*"

And added, "*Bon toubonnman.*"

He was showing his deep appreciation. Olga's geometric eyes changed as she wrinkled her nose and grimaced in wonder. His patois words? This becoming a habit now! He had not finished, he put his arms around her.

"*U fe tje mwe kontan.*"

In this moment of closeness for her there was no one else but them for a change. This was interrupted; the hen flew past and jumped into the yard.

"By the by, I was promised a cock by Cyril, I told him I must build a coop first. So, I'll go now to search for bits of wood and start that today. It will take a few days."

Olga finished the last stitch on the jacket, snipped the thread. Tying the knots would be the next stage and she would press it to give him.

Augustus took out his Talisman – soft smooth skin. Snake – power, his mother had told him. She did not fear snakes, said that she was impervious to attacks from them, that if she stood next to a Fer de Lance it would leave her alone. Some people of her type did not get bitten, she told him. All very mysterious, he had thought, and the older generation believed what they believed; even his father did not have her kind of beliefs – he had his own mind. Augustus now remembered the incident in his childhood, the reason for having the Talisman.

He had been showing off: a boy thing, eleven at the time. They had chosen some coconut trees to climb and decided only to reach three-quarters of the way up. But he went higher, deciding to pick some nuts, he thought he could do it. He first glanced down, grinned after he had reached the agreed height, higher, higher, and grabbed a nut from its anchor among the palm fronds. He lost his grip as his legs uncurled, together with his arm as it left the support of the trunk. He held on firmly to the coconut vine, struggled to curl his legs around the trunk, but he could not break the vine and get his coconut. He flipped, did a somersault, his head swam as his feet held on to the trunk. He never knew when he reached the ground. He had remained in a comma for one month. The Talisman was given to him by an old man who had treated him with his local medicines, and afterwards told him that he should always keep this piece of snake skin scratched with his cryptic words as future protection against accidents; now he had it again. He returned it into the grip beneath the bed.

Olga kept her head down on her sewing after she saw him pass into the yard, the gate clanged as it had clanged after Ma Boy went out a little before. She waited; it had to be her who had to wait as she had done year in and year out. The thread went round her needle making a button hole, and her daughter, now at her side, watched attentively.

Augustus went into Maynard Street where he last lived. Surprisingly, the burnt spaces were almost without the wooden debris, but he managed, a lone man among metal and iron flotsam and large concrete bits worn down as a remainder of houses, to pick up wood among the broken wares. He traversed a large area and carried the awkward bundles of usable wood to their house through the early evening hour, disregarding his ill at ease feeling. He made two trips.

Muriel sat with her shoulders hunched, her arms in front of her on the big table as if she got her strength from its surface. The women by the table stopped their conversation when he came back the second time and laid the wood against the fence. He entered the room.

"That's what I could find and building this coop will take a bit of time, I'll make a start soon so Cyril's rooster can go into it and the chicks with the hen."

"Oh good! We going to have a coop, just now; coz, bring some water grass for the fowl!" Muriel looked at her sister, who spoke with her dimples showing, and she added,

"*Sa bon!*"

She nodded approval. Her son-in-law did not think himself too great to carry those old bits of wood through the streets to make something useful.

He had his own thoughts while he rearranged the pile further in the rear of the closet in a wide flat space out of their view. The town was quiet but he expected pandemonium any day now, people like himself for whom it mattered how things looked, that there had to be decency, how their psyche could be invaded by destabilisation, their loyalties shift so that people would abandon those whose love had been warming and precious, and detachment became unavoidable! The lack of money! The rumba rhythms they heard now would change to something more wild in the town. He came back inside.

"I'm off for a swim," he said.

They heard him push the bicycle out of the yard. Olga got up, moved to the door opposite the shop, faced the lane, saw him cycle by. A lady passed, nodded a greeting. Two yards down, people waited to get water from the stand pipe. They passed later with an overflowing bucket, either holding the handle or on the head, the water over flowed, plop-plop with every step on their way home. The young woman who always sang had not yet been. When she had seen her unfamiliar face, the words of the song had come to arrest Olga's senses, they had been so full of longing, so sweet: 'My dearest, my darling... it's almost tomorrow... the stars, they were shining...' The woman had not even looked at her standing in the doorway. She had had a faraway look on her face, and she was so anchored in her present – this period of her life.

The amount of new people she had seen and would remember in the future, and in the circumstances she had met them. She stood a while waiting for her to pass. Back inside, the women had been talking and did not halt when she joined them again.

She thinks of the new ways of her mother who often brought caramel boule sweets, sucking them, and Era's delight as she waited for granny to return from work to give her a sweet. Olga thought, well, that was better than Ma George's rum drinking, though she used to say that it was for belly cramps. One steady thing her mother did was to attend church services.

Ma Boy's voice, not a whisper anymore, now made her point to Aunt Hazel: they had long got over their old coldness. Olga heard her mother's old childhood name being used in this intimate moment, Apollo this and Apollo that. Muriel had to smile. When Apollo left Bonne Terre for Masav... then came Harry.

Aunt Hazel lit the lamp, now Muriel's face had a closed look. Olga knew what had put that look on her face now.

"Mamma, tomorrow I'll cut your dress, I'll make a different style ..."

Muriel's thoughts had been disturbed. She had been hearing Harry's voice, saying to her that her skin was like Ponds Sun tan powder, soft and smooth as he caressed her. She stood up.

"I doh need no stylish dress, stylish dress is for dance. My days for dance finish; long time." She moved her arms in a circular motion around her middle; her index fingers met first at her middle waistline and her hands made a circular movement as her fingers met at her back and she wiggled, a brief action that left Olga and Era bemused as she was dead serious. Olga shook her head, showing the quandary that she was feeling about all of that. What was her mother thinking? Aunt Hazel's eyes shone and Ma Boy placed a hand on her lips.

"*Wa ya yi!*"

Aunt Hazel's face cracked, her eyes were mischievous. But Muriel continued,

"Dow forget how I like my life, I'm not changing now."

"A, A, but of course, you are you."

Her sister said softly, "We are what we are."

And Olga added, "You can choose your style, that's what I meant. You fink I'd make you somefing like my own styles just because the cloth colour is not white as usual?"

They decided on the style, Muriel sat down again and Era took her position against her thigh; she immediately stroked the child's arms and smiled into her young face. The atmosphere changed, the cosy lamplight inside while the dusk became duskier, not yet night which faltered. The gentle colour of lilac and blue blended overhead in the sky, crickets of the bush waited for the first blackness to fall and start their singing.

Augustus climbed on the bike and rode off. Hunger – sometimes he ignored it; most times he ignored that there was not enough food. He took his mind off his present hunger spasms, instead he thinks, thanks to the Union boys for the inside information about plans afoot to give rooms to him and others without homes in the abandoned soldier barracks. It stood empty since the disbanding of the West Indian Regiment before the Second World War. The soldiers had been on the Island because of some unrest but he had not found it necessary to find out why.

The forbidding, trammelling waves which rose high and dashed down on the beach were magnificent. The low sun illuminated the whole sea as glinting swords which pierced the green water in the distance. It was best to sit and admire the scene for a bit, feel the breeze of the almond trees and think of his life and Olga's. The secrets they had kept from each other; he had not known that her father had gone to Panama and she did not know that he had nearly died as a boy. He thought of his Talisman, he would not tell her about it. If the sea was calmer he would have made a journey to his home to collect food for them – but it was now the hurricane season.

His feet crushed the mounds of soft sand when he stood up and turned away from the deserted beach and the drumming waves in their tireless movement, one after the other. One last look again at the sea, and suddenly a strong arch of yellow, red, violet and green spanned the sky toward the horizon. He reached his bike, stepping on the fallen heart-shaped almond tree leaves and the hole-pitted white large stones.

He started the ride back, arms straight on the handlebars. Halfway, he reached the circular paved black and white wall that held the base of a plateau before him. At his back, large balconied houses ran down a slope that ended in a gully. He rested by the wall, then turned a corner. Now, truly, Masav started. He moved forward to the apselike division of hills. He rode on the lip of the circular hill, passed it; the road went round and straightened out into Spine Road.

Before going to bed he sat on the balcony. He trained his sight on the stars; there was always something about nights, the mysteries of the sky got to him, the beauty in such stillness at the end of a day. Olga sat quietly with him, inside her own thoughts. His words came out, he was sure, before his mind had formed them.

"When I was eleven, I fell from the top of a coconut tree. I nearly died. I was unconscious for one month."

"What! I'm shocked to hear about it. *Eh be'!* Gustus? You nearly died?"

"Yes, I got better by a miracle but that did not stop me doing boy things."

She knows that Guy calls him Ham sometimes. She wonders how people like to give others nicknames; years ago, some girl used to call her 'Olga step sixteen' because of her walk, but she had not cared.

She asks him, "Why you have the joke name, Ham?"

"That was from college days, because of how I spoke."

She could understand that, he and his big words and style.

The air had started to get cooler; soon they went in to settle down. Olga woke up very early. She had not had a sound sleep next to Era. Poor Augustus on the floor had been asleep, he had not heard the voices beyond their room, coming from her mother and Aunt Hazel. She lay still, waiting till some light made a change within the room. When it showed in the gap beneath the door, she opened it slightly and moved to the balcony. The cool morning touched her body; she stretched, yawned and leaned over the balcony.

Muriel joined her. She held an envelope in her hand, and the way her mother held her head and her eyes seemed proud. Olga's eyes questioned it; had something good happened? It must be about that letter. She waited.

Muriel's reticence to make conversation was getting thin. The tides had all rushed in and covered her fragile, fire-changed self. Olga heard,

"Harry sent me a letter; he wants to come and see me here."

Olga was silent, she pressed her lips together and looked intently at her.

"I will answer the letter, and give it to Hazel to give him. I will sit downstairs and write it now." She moved away, back to the bedroom and then downstairs. Harry had been impulsive, a trait that Olga also possessed. When he had acted on the spur of the moment, and left the island to escape both La La and her, he had never thought that there may have been two choices. She began to write him, the man people used to call Silky. Silk notes from his clarinet had made him adorable – not just to her. He used to close his eyes as his lips closed round the black mouth-piece of the clarinet, his cheeks sucking and blowing air; the words that he had written with his silky hand on this paper charmed her the same way.

CHAPTER TWENTY-SEVEN

I t started to drizzle, a very soft feel in the warm air as the sun climbed higher in the sky to make its pale light scatter in the yard. Olga got busy with the lumps of coal, coaxing the new fire in the coal pot. After she had boiled the water – enough in quantity to put into the zinc tub for sharing between Era and herself – she went to wake her. Augustus was neither in the room nor in the house but she had not seen him go out. When he returned she was combing the child's hair.

"I've been along the wharf. It was quiet – only the Lady Joy was in the basin. Everything is peaceful."

His eyes rested on the three nails behind the door, clothes hanging, especially his new jacket ready for wearing.

"Thanks for my beautiful jacket, my darling, you surprised me you know? How determined you were with this. Look at it!"

He did not want to disclose that he planned to go to the town's Methodist church later.

He freshened with cold buckets of water and carbolic soap. And while Olga got herself ready for attending mass with Era, she was sure she could persuade him to go with them. He sat on the balcony not quite ready, dressed in brown pants from Mr Francois, beige shirt and he held the round tipped brown shoe as he concentrated on the patina on its front.

"You're ready to leave. It's early yet for me," he told her.

"How come?"

"I'm going to the service at the Methodist church."

She felt knocked sideways with his breezy statement as if it were nothing of a surprise, even though she knew his views on Wesleyans; still! She took note of the day, today the Twenty-Third September 1948 and he, going his own way. Definitely going out to find something, and she did not know what it was.

Augustus entered the small wooden church, sat at the back. It was so tiny compared to the eight aisles in the Catholic church. He was given a bible and everyone read Psalm ninety. He knew the pastor – a local man, and while he only paid attention to him he did not know who else was in the congregation. He followed the parts read in the gospel of James, Chapter two, '... so now my people, the poor are chosen by God to be rich in faith...' Then he preached his own words: " The rich who consider possessions should think of what kind of rich they want to be! Now, see, how many of us have been made poorer by this disaster, how do we respond? Have we reflected on our class division...?" He talked at length about the society in town, but Augustus did not feel his hackles rise as he used to feel sometimes when he'd listened to some sermons in the past.

Outside, he mingled with the crowd and felt someone tap him on the shoulder. He turned and faced Philosophe. The surprise on seeing him, he had not seen him for weeks. He was in uniform and must have been just passing as the congregation came out, or could he have been watching the church?

"Morning Sergeant!"

He walked alongside Augustus and strangely did not speak of the fire but only about the sugar estate, he had good friends up there, men from his own country. The conversation suited Augustus, and then he said,

"There are plans to re-house people in the barracks on the hill by the lighthouse, you going there?"

He was on his usual business of nosing around. Augustus walked quicker, his answer brief.

"Maybe."

Since the fire, he remembers the mess people now had to live with partly because of the fire service. He wouldn't spend time with Philosophe. He moved northwards, left him behind. He headed for Cyril's home and would check up on Harry.

He felt slightly nervous walking towards the house, a two-storey boxlike faded yellow house with galvanise awning, which was how Aunt Hazel had described it. It was the tallest and leaned into the others at the foot a low hill by St Cecelia Gardens.

Harry wore short pants, shirtless. He smoked a cigar, but when Augustus was brought in he quickly excused himself and returned dressed in long pants and presentable to meet him.

"I'm surprised to see you but it's great getting to know my son-in-law."

He welcomed him, smiling broadly.

"Likewise, sir."

They talked for a bit and Harry asked,

"So, you working in sugar?"

"I work in the laboratory now but before that I worked as a tallyman on the wharf. At the moment we don't make much sugar as nearly all our customers' shops got burnt down – it's a blow to our progress."

"That would be the case, naturally."

Harry's face was alert, Augustus noticed. He expected a man with a wasted look, somehow, and he was happy for Olga's sake. Harry looked very well, middle-aged of course. He wanted to ask him about Panama but he thought of a better idea and said,

"Before you go back, I would like you to meet my ex history teacher. He knows about everything that a person should know about in this world. I know he would like to talk about Panama with you. When could you visit him?"

Harry fixed the day and he was happy to speak some more about himself.

"I work in a hotel but my father worked on the canal, building the dykes."

He confided in Augustus that he had some business to arrange before he returned to Panama with a lawyer and he hoped he could do so during the little time he had left.

Muriel was washing up. Olga scrutinised her expression when she joined her in the kitchen, when her mother turned away from the window and the running water in the sink just outside. She was tidying up even though she required very little from the meals of the house, she had already had her Sunday lunch at work. Olga had waited till Augustus had eaten, now she said while reaching up to lay a clean saucepan on a shelf some inches from her mother,

"A, A, mamma, Gustus went to see my fadda."

Muriel turned her bottom lip downward.

"So now, bit by bit he's closer and closer."

Olga's heart thudded, Muriel added, "I gave him permission to come and visit me here." They were silent and Muriel felt that what she had said was sufficient. Olga noticed a faint smile on her mother's face when she asked her,

"I wonder what day he will come here?"

As they moved away towards the house, Muriel walked upstairs. The night before her Aunt and her mother had been talking late, she had not seen much of her Aunt. Muriel went into the bedroom and Olga moved to the balcony to join Augustus.

The house slumbered in the late afternoon. Augustus felt restless as he leaned over, taking in the length of the long road. All was quiet. They spoke in lazy gusts. Olga gave up and closed her eyes, leaning her head backwards on the partition of the balcony. Era moved from foot to foot as if counting, her lips moved, she moved to the passage. Augustus saw her move away and stared after her.

"Now we know for sure that Era was not from nowhere as we can now see your father in her."

Olga moved closer to him. Yes, it had taken her a little while to get used to their daughter. She let her mind wander about events in town, she had her eyes closed for a short while enjoying the peaceful moment with him but she surprised him changing the subject.

"It is a good idea of the police band to play in the Gardens."

She opened her eyes as her Aunt's voice came from her open door of her room, "Not long now, everyone is going to have their own families together up at Lighthouse point," in patois. Olga got up to join in, her Aunt had not been sleeping. She looked in at them, Era sat on the floor with her slate and pencil, writing. Muriel replied to her sister.

"Not me."

Hazel gave her sister one of her gazes, not giving anything away. Olga withdrew.

She stood next to Augustus, touching his shoulder. He made a joke.

"You know, Popo is like the bull with three horns to the frightened people, pick them and toss them and see them land at his feet as piles of money."

She stared uncomprehending till something went 'ping' in her mind. She laughed.

"I told Era the story of the girl turning into flour after she was picked up on the horns of the three-horned bull. So you saying that Popo will definitely make more money for us?"

"That's what he said."

"We need money now, more than we have; still, you have your job, eh? I'm going to get changed to go and hear the band in the Gardens. You coming?"

"No."

CHAPTER TWENTY-EIGHT

Olga and Era went to meet Boo. The Band Boys passed in front of the house with a quick march – really spruce-looking in khaki shorts and shirts with long khaki stockings, shiny black shoes, and white caps with a shiny black beak. Their tuba, trombones, cymbals, trumpets and everything held by their sides. Olga counted two clarinets, two trumpets, one tuba, two trombones, four round horns, one big drum, one little drum, two cymbals, amazed that they had that many instruments. Olga, Boo and her children followed them into the Garden gate passing beneath an arch of intertwined branches. Boo carried the baby on her right arm with the hand hanging down from the wrist, the baby close to her chest, the hand that was free to do some task or other if she had to with one of the other children.

The Gardens is a restful place, U-shaped, the hillocks on three sides, below is the house with its porch that the musicians enter. People gather on the grass in front of the house. Their instruments in position, they had carried their music sheet stands, these were standing on the platform in the porch. The crowd was mostly women and children. The music flowed.

Era and Boo's children giggled, amused by the cheeks of the buglers – the tuba and trombone players. Olga stood arms folded and relaxed, enjoying what was called 'Colonel Boogie'. She clapped with the others when it ended. The conductor faced the people.

"Now, we'll play for you, Beethoven's Fifth Symphony."

The men looked at their music sheets. Era and Boo's children started to run about, off to a large clump of double pink hibiscus, going round and round, catching each other.

Olga listened attentively, appreciating the grand music. It was a long piece. The baby squirmed, the notes jumped from the instruments, sharp and long and then lots of drum beats. People clapped louder still. Boo moved across a narrow pitch road, took her seat beneath a tree. Olga looked after the children till the band had played 'Goodnight Irene' and began to leave the Gardens. Then she joined Boo, sat down on the bench while the children ran on the grass close by. Olga leaned back contentedly. Across on the other side of them, over a bridge, a gardener watered red and pink roses on a long rectangular bed and the base of a hillock. Boo said, "You must not forget Lucia's christening."

Olga thought of the state of the town; Boo was keeping with tradition but Era's First Communion had been postponed till next year. She smiled.

"Uh huh, I remember, dis is one fing I think about all da time."

Those thoughts also included her longing for the baby she wants for herself.

Mornings later, it started out cloudy, the sun obscured; there was something in the air waiting to happen. Miss Hazel muttered that it was cold, they all complained that they had never felt that cold. Era curled beneath the red blanket when she returned from school.

Olga found it hard to concentrate on anything and felt relieved after Augustus returned from work. In the afternoon thunder rolled in the dry skies – deep bass.

"Hear dat!" Olga whispered to Augustus.

He put aside his book, "Let's go downstairs."

The house trembled. She was glad for the suggestion. Downstairs he took a rum bottle from his work sack.

"Get some glasses."

"Have some ginger tea," Aunt Hazel offered them.

"I'll have some rum first," he told her.

He looked up at the sky from the doorway, a hazy light from the thick blanket of grey clouds. He passed some rum to Olga, she drank it quickly and joined her Aunt in the kitchen. There was one pot in her fire hearth, steaming with the aroma of thyme.

"This is some salt pork that Mr Henry gave me yesterday, I was so glad. Without this help where would we be sometimes?"

The cold air increased, playing around their legs. Ma Boy hovered, not saying anything, stood near the table where plates were arranged for serving the meal. Olga left them.

"I'm coming back; just going for Era."

She jerked sideways, almost tripping over the bare-neck hen with new chicks in the room as they came out of the shop. Augustus picked up the chicks, the hen opened her beak, squawked with her feathers spread out around her body, Olga saw her large pupils.

"Poor little fings, dey will be cold, not a good day to hatch out!"

She tried to grab her and follow Augustus into the shop but gave up, saying "Shu!" walking behind her.

"She must be hungry, Gustus."

"Tomorrow when she gets out, she can peck around in the yard and you could throw some corn or what you can for them to eat. Four little chicks eh! Cyril has promised me a rooster. I'll have to build a coop."

"I'll check on Era. Aunt Hazel will serve the food soon."

A peal of thunder interrupted them and a vibration remained in the air.

Olga ran upstairs, came back with Era. She had woken her up.

The darkness fell early.

"We will go to bed early tonight, where's Muriel?"

Miss Hazel looked worried.

"It could be a hurricane."

They waited till Muriel came home. She had gone to church after work. They understood.

Cold air seeped beneath their bedroom door.

"I have goose flesh," Olga said.

They all huddled beneath the blanket on the small bed. They fell asleep. He awoke first and saw a golden slit on the floor from beneath the door, and thinking that someone was out in the corridor with the lamp, he opened the door. But it was moonlight.

"Olga," he called to her. He shook her.

"The moonlight is almost like sunlight, come and see."

He was thinking, *the moon goes round the earth, her wisdom guides her, she controls the sea. She protects this island. This must be a sign.* He was beguiled. Olga leaned against him, together they saw roofs of the small houses, the tall palms of St Cecelia Gardens, a palm frond flew from a tree and dropped. No rain, some wispy clouds chased the moon in the dark blue sky.

"I'm not sure dis is normal what I'm seeing tonight," Olga commented, and she thought this might portend something bad.

It was still very cold.

"There is not even a halo round the moon."

She was pensive

"You know the song 'Oranges and Lemons'? The moon and the sun have a tug of war, when children sing it? And after da words 'here comes da chopper to chop off your head', every child has to choose where dey want to go; whether to da sun or to da moon and then dey pull against sun or moon? I fink dis is da sun that's shining de tonight, dat won over the moon."

In the forested lands north of the Island, the wind started first, the coconut fronds hissed like rain. A pattern started in the winds, flute sounds, trills and whistles. Two men got their drums and small curved sticks and started to beat a rhythm: five and two and three quick beats. They understood Marie's music. A third brother joined, they drummed through the night with the wind so the hills and valleys echoed the sounds

Augustus and Olga started to hear the strange sound in the gusts of winds as they returned to bed. She was wide awake. She changed her mind that something bad was about to happen, it felt to her that what she heard was musical and not like anything she had heard before.

Aunt Hazel and Muriel listened, and Ma Boy was awake. In the early hours, heavy rain fell. Miss Hazel had heard long ago of something the older people had called Marie's music in the wind, which happened in the midst of troubled situations in the island. It meant that people could hope for a turn for the better.

When Ma Boy joined her in the morning at the open door of the drawing room, she agreed with what her cousin said: "The earth talked."

"It's a mystery."

She assented.

CHAPTER TWENTY-NINE

On the People's Square, the fire homeless crowd walked on the soft earth after a night of wakefulness. Maryse Sampson's scrunched up physical form was somehow formidable in her loud speech and waving arms, her large gold earrings bobbing around her head. She said to those near her, "How can we live like that – like pigs! I'm not staying here. No."

She gazed in disgust at the mud, and urged them to go with her to the Public Works yard and help themselves to hammers, nails, rope, a saw and anything they could collect to put up little shelters for themselves somewhere else. They understood her Cayenne French. She heard someone call her a goat and laugh with derision.

"She wants the stupid sheep to follow her," the voices rumbled around her.

There was nervousness.

"I'm not getting arrested," a man said, "the jail is full enough of people without me."

"Who want to get out from here?" She asked in English, hoping to make an impact.

On all four sides of the Square there was movement.

"Fe` vit! Vini!"

She walked quickly, leading a group on to the Public Works building on the periphery of the town four blocks away.

It was easier than they thought. Mr Lloyd, watchman, took the padlock off from the gate after he had listened to her and the urgings of others, and while he dithered the group moved into the yard and took tools. They went to a vacant stretch of land at the base of Darling Hill. The Union men split into groups early in the morning after they went to see how the people on the Square coped. They saw less people and heard how it was. Dujon felt ashamed for his people. Michael left for the Red Cross building; Gordon went to open the Union shop.

"I'll go over to the Public Works Yard and hear what is what," Dujon decided, and moved off in that direction. He was not at all disconcerted about the action that they had taken but he wanted to know what had happened to these people. There was a truck being loaded and two policemen on duty in the yard.

All was quiet. He was puzzled, returned to the Square and walked among the people. He would have an open-air meeting tonight. He waited till the Red Cross jeep arrived and they started with their hot drinks, passed them around.

Gordon had started sending articles to the Barbados newspaper about the town, and he thought of this new situation, the condition of the people on the Square. Now, on the way to open the shop with its little foodstuff and goods, he first scouted around the coastline around the hill, but it was not as quiet as he had expected. Hearing voices and banging, he moved on from an abandoned boat, upside down, where men sometimes gathered to lean on it and talk in the evenings. He saw Ma Sampson, wielding a hammer. He had found the people. There was a clump of spectators watching people with poles, old galvanise, palm tree branches. There was an open space beneath the yellow rock of the hill, not a lot of land; there would not be enough for a dozen shacks, only four at the most and all squeezed together. Gordon turned back towards the shop a few hundred yards away.

When Dujon came to the shop, all he said to Gordon was, "That's the spirit; get the ball rolling, it's time!"

The administrator got a phone call very early about the incident with the people. He had a long conversation with the director of Public Works, he finished with "... the barracks at Lighthouse point passed inspection? Jolly good, there's a good chap."

At six o'clock that evening, the Union meeting attracted many town people. Not as many as previously in the weeks after the fire, though. The weather returned to normal. They thought yesterday afternoon that there could be a hurricane but hadn't they got surprises in the night? It had been something quite different.

"The wind played music for us, did you hear the drums, boys?" Michael smiled.

"It was spiritual, something to do with Marie."

Gordon's serious face broke into a small smile. Michael walked up and down on the platform; they waited for a bigger crowd before they started. The meeting began after Mr Polius came to give them support.

Each spoke at length.

"Are you downhearted?" Dujon started.

"Yes."

To that call, in the past the answer used to be a big "NO" which was definitely a truthful answer. He reminded them that they still had some employment. There was going to be even more change after December. His voice was loud through the hand-held loudspeaker, it carried through the large centre of the town.

"I am going to contest for a seat on this town council. As you know the council members are going to be changed, and that's good for Masav. So *'let's go George!'* all the way for improvement."

On Tuesday morning at nine o'clock, the administrator alighted from his chauffeured pale grey car inside the yard of the Public Works Department, his long legs in smart white drill of his uniform suit of white, white gloves, white cork hat, black epaulettes and black shoes. Philosophe was among the guard of honour. His own thoughts were on his boss: how the Colonel had kept him out of the progress he should be making with Challo and the money they took during the fire. He looked at him escorting the administrator into the building, and heard the Band Boys playing. Other government clerks arrived and entered the only government building that had been left standing after the fire.

The Union men were going to drive up to the barracks to see how the preparation had moved forward; they got the usual bus they used so more people could go along with them. Augustus had been that way with the scout troop as a boy, making their outing on this peninsula when the Lighthouse stood.

Olga felt that they were in the wilderness, full of anxiety that they could end up living on that hill with those kinds of private brick buildings she saw on the way up, with their air of remoteness and coldness. All in all they looked unwelcoming. She was silent and the bus moved on the bumpy narrow path among trees and bush. After they alighted, she was stung by something. She stamped her feet. The grass was long and brown. She looked at Augustus' legs. Burrs clung to the cloth as he trampled the long grass. They arrived at the two-storey building. Olga looked towards its black wrought iron rails, its arches and its pillars; it was yellow. It did not look too bad. She liked the balconies. Her legs itched, she made a face and made an effort not to look unhappy at the thought of having to walk such a long distance and climb the hill at the end of it.

They had expected activity but the buildings were deserted.

"I wish I could get inside," Dujon said.

"All the work's finished and that's why no one is here, it looks like."

They walked around some more minutes in the empty place and crushed dry old leaves while the sea hissed below among the rocks. Gordon led the way back to the bus, got behind the wheel; they climbed in. Augustus looked at her face that she kept straight and looked ahead.

When he left for work she had the rest of the day to worry about it. Miss Hazel was interested in her opinion. She only had to see her face; she did not have to ask.

She said instead, "Come, you could see the cloth in the shop, pick something. You want to make something nice for your father's party?"

"No, I'll wear somefing I have already. Tanks Aunty."

She was not fussy in this situation. What was Harry? She was not quite looking forward to meeting him but she hoped that something good would come out of it for her mother.

"I'll sew on mamma's new dress; she needs it more."

"Alright, I'll sit in the shop and look at the street, see people passing, *ma Che'wi.*"

Augustus was working the two to ten shift, they would have less time to talk about the house they could live in.

CHAPTER THIRTY

Harry had seen Muriel, he watched her when she came out of the presbytery and went into the church, making sure he was well out of her view. Every time it had been hard not to call her name. He had to wait till he visited her at her sister's. He was impatient to meet his daughter; he would not see them till the following week.

Augustus passed for him the following morning to visit Mr Polius. Introductions over, they sat in his parlour and Augustus chose the morning, otherwise other men would certainly be calling on his ex-teacher. After the introduction,

"I remember when you played as a Band Boy."

Harry's round face showed a lack of recognition; their paths had not crossed. In those days, in the first decades of the present time, Mr Polius was always to be found in his home, studying, marking his students work. He had been almost a recluse, and he was not surprised that Harry did not know him.

He said to Harry, "A friend of my own father emigrated to Panama to work on the railway project."

Harry placed his Panama hat on his knees, kept his hand on it, while they had a round of conversation about first, the state of Masav.

"I was in a luckier position to my father, he was one of the four thousand West Indians that went to work on the canal, the things they suffered with landslides and the yellow fever."

"I have always been fascinated about the canal," Augustus said.

"Tell me, I believe the canal went through a mountain, that's right?" Mr Polius kept the topic going.

"The Cucaracha Mountain."

Harry grinned and his eyes became slits.

"There was gold in the land. My father did some speculating too. So, indeed, the engineers blasted the mountains for the canal and it was so difficult to make that canal because the land from the mountain kept coming in to it, blocking it up. My father worked on the locks on the canal, only one ship could go through at a time when it opened in 1913, he told me. So after I got there the canal was finished already. I like it over there."

"It must be a fast moving, high standard of living, I expect," Mr Polius said.

"I want to come back here sometime in the future to stay. This fire was such a shock for me."

"You must come again, before you go back, Harry, it's nice to see you." Augustus got up with, "I'm working later, the late shift. Good day, sir."

Augustus felt unhappy that he did not feel able to be one of the Union committee men. Dujon got his respect; he had so much fight in him to change old customs. He was pushing the colour boundary – if he got elected in December, he would definitely break the colour prejudice patterns. His own direction was focused on a house for his family. Mr Popo, poseur that he was, had his fingers in so many pies, and he was the reason why on Saturday morning Augustus returned to the vicinity of the cane estate to check on a house. He found the group of houses and it was not a good sign to bump into a work colleague coming out from some banana and mango trees. They talked. The young man held a fierce looking fighting cock under his armpit, his legs tied with string and he had some vicious spurs.

Bob said, "Follow me, I know the house you want."

No road ran through the banana trees, Augustus began to think that it was not at all suitable. Bob called out to someone. He had seen another man come running toward them calling out to Bob.

"Come on man, it's getting late."

He carried his own fowl. A bit later some small houses were visible in a clearing on sloping ground.

"These are the houses that people are getting to rent. I know one is empty."

"Thanks Bob."

The men went off. Though the area was near the cane estate, Augustus decided he would not enquire any further because Olga was not one to be comfortable among people with cock fighting for a pastime, and all the aspects of life that one with her urban style would find beyond her scope. He retraced his steps. Popo who had made him come to this place, his advice might have been some kind of having a dig at his dignity to suggest that he could live up there with his wife and child.

Down in town, Olga sat hemming the skirt in pale yellow with dull brown, a dress in Sea Island cotton that she had altered in style. She made it with little puff sleeves, and two rows of narrow white lace ran down on the centre bodice from the low round neck. It was one she had got from the fire relief.

Augustus had promised to escort Aunt Hazel and herself to her father's party in the night.

She had started sewing early; the morning light was softly shimmering outside. She was alone in the drawing room near to the back door where the sewing machine was placed. Her thoughts on the many new developments coming about, and now Augustus had gone to find out about another house. She heard a loud man's voice.

"Hello, morning!" from the gate

She put the dress down. This was a welcome distraction. In the kitchen, Ma Boy looked enquiringly at Miss Hazel.

"*Ki mun sa?*"

"It's Augustus' father. Morning papa!"

She was pleased to see him – an elderly, medium height man framed in the gateway, just holding it open a little way so that he could control his mule. He spoke to the animal after his greeting, they saw that he was not entering the yard.

"*Bonju*," Miss Hazel said.

"Morning, I brought you some food. Give me some water for the animal, please."

He placed his sacks just inside the gate.

"I will go and tie him by some breadfruit trees on this road, there's grass and shelter for him."

He returned to the house.

"How's everybody? Augustus is out?"

"He went out early on some business."

"Where did he go?" he asked Olga, while he took out the oranges, bananas, pumpkin, coconuts and limes.

She answered, "He went to look at a house close to the sugar estate, maybe we will rent it to live."

Then, "I'll go and get Era."

Olga and Era came back into the yard, she saw his broad smile, he nodded to them as he was in the middle of unwrapping cassava cakes.

"Say 'morning, Granpa,' Era."

"Morning," she said softly.

"She's growing well."

"Yes, she is."

"We are so lucky. I appreciate what you brought for us," Miss Hazel said. "Have a seat – please – rest yourself."

He entered the house and sat by the table.

Era stood at the bottom of the stairs, she swung her body in a little twirl as she held on to the stair post. Her grandfather wore three-quarter length pants, she noticed, in black, his shirt in grey, long sleeve, black felt hat, and his toes and heels peeped out from his black sandals. He looked towards her.

"How are you missy?"

He raised a brow a little, head to one side. He still could not understand why the child looked Chinese, he often wondered about

Olga's mother. As a young man he was part of the town's people before he moved to the country and he knew all about Miss Hazel, but he had not known about Olga's father. That could be the mystery of course. When his son met Olga she was a decent young woman and he was her first young man, he knew that. Augustus had told him when he had brought up the question of Era. He took off his hat and called her to sit next to him.

In the yard, the cockerel walked alongside the hen and the new chicks, pecking close to the spinach bush by the fence. As Era sat down, Olga moved to the kitchen. Mr James smiled broadly at the child, taking Era's hand. She squirmed a little.

He asked, "Do you want to hear a story?"

She nodded, Yes.

"Well, dog and crab were having a race. They ran from Anse Du Fort, coming up the coast up to Masav. When they began, they said, "one-two-three, go!" Crab grabbed his tail – he hang on to dog's tail, up to Masav. It was a long, long road. Dog was so tired, his tongue was hanging out. Almost on the ground, he gasped so much! Dog was running up to Masav, crab on his tail. When dog arrived, he stretched his tail; crab was already there, behind him. When dog saw crab he said, you have arrived already, Mr Crab?"

Era was happy that he spoke in English. Her eyes narrowed inside her wide smile, sloping down in the corners, her pink lips parted, but she was silent.

He continued: "Clever crab answered behind him, 'For a long time, I have been here, waiting for you!' Dog was covered with sweat but crab was dry. Dog said, 'Well! You won.'"

Era giggled. She loved anything about crabs; did he know that, she wondered. It was the best story she had ever heard.

She said, "Tell me again."

So Olga heard it when she brought him some soda biscuits and cocoa.

"Thank you very much."

"Aunt Hazel said you must stay for lunch. Augustus should be back by then."

"I will go and check on Eudox."

As Olga seemed surprised he told her, "The mule."

He depended on him when he went about selling his coal around the countryside, he had to get back because someone else would benefit by his absence to take over his customers.

Mr James senior had been a welcome diversion, Olga felt, and Augustus would be sorry to have missed him when he told them goodbye an hour later, eating earlier than the regular mid-day. He left about eleven and Augustus had just missed him.

Augustus lay on the bed close to Olga's dress – laid there ready for her to wear. Olga loosened the coils of her hair; she wanted to arrange it in a glamorous style. She studied him and felt sorry for him. His voice was full of despondency, which made him say a regretful 'ah!' a down scale note when he heard that his father had been. He had been sorry to miss him; Olga knew that. He told her that the house on the Morne would not suit them.

She asked him now, "You still coming with us tonight?"

"I'm dead beat, it's weeks since I've felt so tired."

"Have a nap then, there's lots of time."

She wishes that she had already spoken to her father in private and would not meet him in a place with lots of other people. What was this kind of thing she had to get herself in? Although, the idea of a party in this bleak time would enliven things a bit, just as the police band had done. She sat on the balcony; she felt a stomach cramp and felt an urgent need to visit the closet. She ran downstairs into the yard, at the back of the kitchen. She usually had well-behaved bowels, but she had been earlier as well. Aunt Hazel watched her sympathetically and acknowledged Olga's weak smile.

In the meanwhile Muriel had returned from work, and sat with Era and Ma Boy on the balcony. Olga wanted to settle her nerves and did not know what to do just then. She sat on the bed next to Augustus. She took up his shirt that hung on the nail behind the door and smoothed it out, draped it over the chair, opened the jalousies wider to let some light in. Dusk approached, they were expected around six thirty and there was not much time. Aunt Hazel was already dressed.

She called Augustus. "My dear, you should get ready."

"Alright, just another minute, I'll take a quick shower. I'm sure I'll be ready before you."

She picked up the hairbrush started to pull her hair into shape while he stood up, took the towel from the head of the bed and went downstairs. She got dressed very quickly. She just let her hair hang down in a ponytail.

"Era," she called from the doorway.

She felt it necessary to tell her that she was going to visit her other grandfather. She lit the candle and they left the room. On the balcony, Ma Boy gave one of her half smiles.

"Be a good girl for Ma Boy, granny will be here soon. Oh, I hear her voice downstairs."

Era turned and walked away, off to see Muriel. Ma Boy got up.

"I'll make supper for the child."

Muriel usually went to bed early and Olga expected her to be with Era in the bedroom. The house would be quiet by half past seven, downstairs dark and empty; Olga could see the picture. Augustus came upstairs and entered the room. She put her head round the door.

"I'll go down and wait."

Muriel waved goodbye to the three leaving for the party and stayed downstairs; she spoke quietly with Ma Boy. They shared their concerns for the town. She felt unheard words pushing each other furiously inside her head; she had to share this with her cousin.

Era looked into the small mirror on the table before her, something held her interest. Her face was very close to it and she smiled, something beguiled her.

Since Muriel had got the news of 'Bad Boy' from his wife, it had been an awful shock that Sampson was incarcerated in the asylum. She kept thinking that she should go and ask after him.

"Bad luck is one thing you do not expect, I'm telling you something about my old neighbour."

Ma Boy did not gossip, she did not know that Augustus already knew; she only wanted the information to be between the two of them. Ma Boy nodded and listened, her index finger touching her chin, her face grew more solemn as she heard the story of Sampson.

"I don't know if my legs will carry me up the hill to the asylum."

She considered it her Christian duty to visit him.

"*Sa twis!*" She said to Muriel.

Ma Boy knew Sampson, of course,; in the town, if you served in the war, it was a name talked of with respect.

"*Bondye' e'de' nou.*"

Ma Boy implored God's help and listened to Muriel's confidences. She began to talk again and told her cousin about her affairs; that, on Thursday, Olga's father would be visiting her in the house. She asked her, did she know Harry? She explained that he was in the Island on holiday from Panama. She told her that she would be seeing him. She could see the amazement on the other old woman's face.

"So, you will see him."

She stopped talking and looked over to Era, she sat near the back door on the straw mat, craning her neck over the mirror, the lamplight was dim.

"Era, go and get da dolly Ma Boy make for you."

"It's dark upstairs."

"I will light a candle and come wif you. Wait."

She took Era by the hand after she had lit it and they went upstairs and returned. She had thoughts about Aruba. Did Harry know that she wanted to go to Aruba? His visit alone would make a drain on her strength – should she make an effort to walk up the hill the next day after work, or the following Sunday on her day off? Both men weighed heavily on her mind. She sat next to the table thinking she wished that she had tobacco for her pipe. Wouldn't Harry get a surprise to see her smoking it when he came!

CHAPTER THIRTY-ONE

Aunt Hazel took them to the house; the house was in a cul-de-sac, an unpainted one-storey house, not far. Dim light from the open door welcomed them. Olga let out the breath she had not realised that she had been holding in. "Now for it," she thought. She was prepared to act nonchalantly as if this were an ordinary event and that she knew everyone present, but once inside there were only three mature women sitting together.

"Bonswe."

Aunt Hazel's voice was loud, to make sure that all within earshot heard her. A communicating door opened and a middle-aged woman came in.

"Welcome, Harry ain't come yet, we waiting on him; siddown."

Augustus took a seat and wondered how come the party was not already under way. Aunt Hazel too was amazed that Muriel's rival was not present; she started a conversation with the women. Then, voices came from the balcony, but the people made a delayed entry. Their eyes peered into the darkness through the door. Philosophe's large frame filled the entrance. When he was truly in the room La La entered, followed by her son and Harry.

Harry came straight to Aunt Hazel, Augustus and Olga. He held out a hand to his daughter. "Olga?"

A shock thrill surprised her. Frail was not the word that described him. All these years she had thought that he had died.

"Yes."

"How are you?"

"Fine."

A woman brought another chair to Harry, he indicated the space between Miss Hazel and Olga, they shifted and he settled down. He must have felt her cold shoulder. She was glad that he addressed Augustus.

"I'm happy you came."

She felt an urge to get up, go onto the balcony and put distance between herself and this man who had wasted no time to assume that she wished him to sit next to her, but a man came towards them.

Harry said, "This is my older brother."

He stood before Olga, smiling.

"I'm pleased to make your acquaintance."

Harry introduced Aunt Hazel and Augustus, and a female relative joined them. Olga wondered why these relations of Harry never visited her mother so she could have known of them. No wonder her mother had become unemotional and unsociable. The introductions over, the conversation became general. Olga looked pointedly at his brown and white two-toned shoes. He felt he concentration and looked towards her. He jumped as if struck by her slow words of scorn.

"You rogue! You left my mudda pregnant; never one word after dat?"

She felt better. She waited for a pause, her head still down. She felt Augustus' foot nudge her, on her right, and she wished there was more space between her father and herself. She waited still in the hush. He had resumed talking and so her outburst was covered over. She was released out of the sticky moment – a woman came to them with a tray of drinks. She straightened, her ponytails sat on her shoulder again, her face forward, she took a glass. She got the scent of alcohol from Augustus' drink as she turned towards him. She sipped some ginger beer, felt someone looking her way and met the eyes of her brother. He nodded acknowledgement. She settled herself more firmly on her seat, turned towards Augustus and Philosophe as they were speaking.

Another voice announced, "Ladies and gentlemen," in patois, that he was about to sing for them.

It was a fast, bouncy patois song about the morning cockerel singing and the moth disappearing. His voice made tremolos; at the end he got applause. Harry got up and spoke to his son, who came on with a love song in Creole. Harry resumed his seat. Everything changed for Olga, the small room now became a friendly place. The serving women returned with small white bowls of food. She glanced sideways at Harry as he started eating the souse, a gold ring on his finger as he picked up the small white pig's trotter. His hand went to his mouth and soon his bowl was empty. She only started to eat hers then, he had not turned to her. She thought that he dressed like a *Macaroni.* How could her mother have been his girlfriend? Plain Muriel? He was thinking thoughts about her who had scorned him, even though he did not say another word to her. He thought she was a beauty, and so unlike Era and his own son in her colouring.

Harry's brother came into the room with a fiddle. He started slowly, sitting on a chair, the pose serious as he became one with his fiddle and bow. Harry got up and together they hit the first line of "Home Sweet Home."

Olga sang silently with them. "Mid pleasures and palaces, though we may roam ... there's no place like home... a charm from the sky seems to hallow us there, home sweet home, sweet home..."

Her father became more solid as the night wore on. Everyone clapped; Aunt Hazel called "Encore!" Olga softened a little; her father may be alright after all. He did not return to his seat but went through to the back room with his brother.

There was laughter coming from the back room. La La's voice came through. Olga's thought it was really because of La La that he was in town now.

She heard Philosophe say to Augustus, "I think you would be right for the force. We want strong and respectable young men. As you know, we have so few of the local men."

Before an answer was given Harry stood in the room, holding his clarinet.

She watched her father take on a different personality as he played. His lips stretched on the mouthpiece, eyes hidden, he played something but she did not hear the tune. Standing there he reminded her of Clifford with his colouring and height, that Clifford had almost forced himself on her that day and she had threatened him. The memory changed her mood back and Harry could be any other man, not her father. Now she waited for the party to break up; the ladies from the neighbourhood left. Harry's brother came chatting to Philosophe. Aunt Hazel went through to the back room.

Augustus said, "Time to make a move."

"Goodbye," he called to Harry.

"Goodnight Harry," from Miss Hazel, and she joked about the dark streets outside.

"I'll walk with you." Philosophe moved together with them. The short walk home was done in silence.

At home Augustus took matches from his pocket, felt for a candle in the usual place, lit it. They walked upstairs.

"Bonswe," she said to her aunt and entered her bedroom.

He realised from Olga's pout that she really was in a bad mood.

"What's the matter?"

She had sat on the edge of the bed by Era, wondering whether she would sleep on it or on the floor. She ran her hand down her hair, free from the clip, smoothing it with both hands. He joined her.

"What's the matter?" he repeated.

Her rudeness she had shown Harry, as if she could not have helped herself, had surprised him, but who was he to criticise?

"You're still upset?"

The Clifford incident was not something she enjoyed remembering but it had been fresh in her mind as her father sang.

"Something about my father made me remember Clifford."

"Huh! Why?"

"One day he tried to come inside our house. I was alone. He was fresh, telling me how he liked me; trying to touch me, so I nearly attacked him with my scissors. Then, as he was leaving, he said he did not even like black women – just because I made him leave me alone. I was so mad."

"Why didn't you tell me? The sly rat. I wish I had known about it, I would have knocked him down and made him apologise."

"It was a few days before da fire and it was the oney time it happened. I made him show respect after dat."

"Let's forget him."

They undressed, dropped on to the blanket and did just that. She felt tense against him but after his kisses she melted against him and he made careful love to her. After she had moved on to the bed he lay on his back thinking.

The decision to check on Sampson was foremost on Muriel's mind. As for Olga, although her mother had not spoken to her that morning, it was nothing unusual as they went about the day's business. But her burden had lifted. Harry was no longer a phantom to Olga, and she had told her that he would be coming to the house that Thursday. At mid-day the Anglican Church bells pealed the musical chimes. Next to Olga on the table were an assortment of clothes, brassieres she had made, a shirt she had finished off for Augustus and her mother's new dress she had started. She moved them upstairs – her morning's work. In the afternoon she would work on Era's dress.

Aunt Hazel's eyes missed nothing. Things looked calm. Again she felt like the captain of this ship, at the wheel, and the goods were in good condition and it was her responsibility for their condition. She had given Muriel an account of the party.

"My daughter is hot head sometimes."

She had heard that Harry had shown his surprise, his startled body because she had watched him, anxiously; and he had made no comment.

"He must have changed," Muriel answered, "staying quiet at her words!"

Aunt Hazel had the lunch cooked and ready for them, everything really did appear to be satisfactory to her. Because Era had not gone with her mother, the child now placed herself between Aunt Hazel and Ma Boy and got in their way. She was interested in their conversation, even though in patois; she wanted to know what might be happening or might not. Life, she believed, was becoming more interesting.

"What you want now?" she asked Era.

"Nuffing."

"Go and tell mamma food ready."

Aunt Hazel faced her with a look that made her move quickly. The plates of food were already on the table for them when they sat by the big table except Muriel and Augustus. The women talked about Muriel's intention to walk up to see Sampson in the asylum.

"*Mwe` las,*" Era exclaimed, suddenly bored.

"Don't talk patois. Say I'm tired" Olga said sharply. She added, "Patois dow get people anywhere in life."

Aunt Hazel talked to Ma Boy, as Olga felt disinclined to talk. Era could feel their words pronounced with swift escape, as if it were their game to play one word against the other. But sometimes she noticed, they hung on to some word, which made her almost see the shape and taste. Now she was no longer bored. She only recognised a few of the words but it was their expressions that got her in thrall of the language. And they were not talking about Sampson.

CHAPTER THIRTY-TWO

Some people said that Sampson confessed to starting the fire – but he was mad, wasn't he? Muriel asked herself. His wife had told her that the medicine he received now controlled his abusive behaviour and stopped him being a danger to his own self.

She had not come that way for many years to see those faces staring from behind the iron grille. She had to make the sign of the cross as the building came into view. It stood isolated and she felt some pain at the thought of those inside the brown brick building. As usual, some spectators stood outside, they talked to the faces staring at them behind the grille. One inmate's arm came out through the space and took a dry piece of coconut offered, another woman grinned a wide white smile.

She stood next to women, children and men and she waited for Sampson to appear. Just as she was turning away she saw his face at the window; he did not smile but he laughed even as his eyes showed no joy, showed no recognition of her. She called his name.

"How you getting on? It's me, Miss St Juste, you remember me?"

He turned, facing the other way.

She made her way to the entrance; a breeze shook the leaves on two large trees close by and she looked up. She fixed her large straw hat to shade her eyes from the brilliant sunlight that bounced up from the sea below and pricked her face and neck, though the four o'clock direction of the sun made the heat less intense. Her dress was white, long sleeved. The breeze fanned her as she walked up to the shut-up front of the building. She rang the bell, her sturdy body tense.

A head wearing a white cotton cap looked through the narrow aperture at her. She knew her but did not ask Muriel into the building.

"How is Joe Sampson? Is he better?"

"*Non, Mantje'Muriel,*" she answered gently.

"Poor soul, I brought him some bananas and oranges."

The woman began closing the door and Muriel told her:

"You have a good heart. By the grace of God, we get by in the town."

She retraced her steps, thinking about their lives at her sister's, lives that had changed so completely and made them different people. Have mercy Jesus, she thought, and began to walk back to town. She would stop at the church and light a candle for Sampson. She huddled into herself, head down. She was disappointed knowing the extent of Sampson's condition, and his wife had not known the truth.

Walking on through the almost deserted town along market street, someone moved with dragging steps behind her, he was close, she recognised the sound of his footfalls. He was alongside her.

"Good afternoon m'am. Mary must come back..."

His usual lament since he could not find his wife. His shirt was out of his pants and he looked hungry. He left her and continued, repeating his phrase, "Mary must come back."

Ma Sampson survived in her shack of palm leaves, tree branches and galvanise. Muriel met her out in the alley, watching over a pot that stood on a pile of large stones. The size of the pot suggested that others would share in it. Betty walked by without acknowledging her, and disappeared among the other shacks. Muriel felt the abhorrence of the whole situation and wanted to flee. So after a brief conversation she did just that. All her life she had struggled against commonness. And what if all the town had been destroyed, who could say how she may have had to live at this time? People had become common not from choice, and with this sober thought she walked away, wishing it had been possible to talk to her old confidant about Harry. She missed the verve she used to display but the old manner belonged to last year.

At the house Era sat near her father, and she took in the thick hair which had not been cut for a long time, his eyes gazing down, the angle of his neck, his bare feet tucked beneath the chair and one hand up to his head, elbow bent. He was unaware of her, so engrossed he was reading his book, so she leaned backwards against the balcony to feel the warm rays of the sun. If she had been allowed, she would have been outside in the lane to play with some children and perhaps play *O'grady* games; twirling, striding, walking on tip-toes according to the order given to her by some other child. They would take turns. Now there came a voice from downstairs.

"Hot breadnuts! Come buy your breadnuts!"

Augustus raised his head, only now aware of her presence; he stood up, looked at the street.

"Kitty, go and buy some breadnuts."

He gave her money from his pocket and she hastened, skipping downstairs and out of the gate. The woman stood on the edge of the street; someone else was buying. When Era handed over her calabash for her share the woman ladled out three measures for her. She hastened back. They looked scrumptious. With a smile on her face she brought them back to Olga and her father. The bowl of hot breadnuts lay on the table. After it had been shared out, hers had been peeled, the outer black wood-like shell was too difficult and her mother had done so carefully, then she slid the inner thin skin off and handed her four white warm *chatany*. Her father had his eyes on her as she enjoyed them and was looking for more.

"I think I'll give you a spelling test. Go and get your slate."

She stared at him in surprise by this sudden request.

"I know what I can do. I can write the story about the dog and crab."

"That will be a good idea," Olga said. "I'll cut up some coconut for the fowls."

She thought of the remaining sewing and it would be done after she had given the fowls food. She held the small dish of tiny cubes of coconut in one hand and stood on the back step.

"Ki keet! Ki keet!" she called.

She saw them come out from beneath the right corner of the house; she gave the cockerel an apprehensive stare. "Shu!" He was ready to jump at her and with her eyes on him she threw the small bits on the brown earth between the stones.

While Augustus was occupied, she continued the work on Muriel's dress. The sleeves were above her elbow. She attached it to the top and then began sewing the running stitch at the waist line. The noise of the pedal and Augustus voice kept time in the minutes of the afternoon for a reasonable length of time, then Muriel returned home, glad to sit by the table and take her hat off, and she sent Era to get her water to drink.

Augustus knew that she had gone to ask after Sampson. He imagined she was distressed, but she exhibited stoicism much of the time and her words were few. It had been part of her nature to be worried about the Sampsons.

"How was Sampson?"

"I saw him but..."

She looked for the words to relate the experience that had disturbed her mind beyond words, and she stopped and opened her hands facing the ceiling.

"I hope he gets better."

"He may recover, some people do; they have different treatments, medicines."

Olga got up.

"I'll get some food for you mamma."

"I'll go and change my clothes."

Augustus felt the flush of a new emotion at the not anticipated news of a house in town that was needing tenants. Guy told him about it the night before, and Monday morning Guy came to Miss

Hazel's house so early that Olga frowned, puzzled. Augustus had gone swimming with him the day before, and as Augustus had to go to work that night she felt that she did not need Guy monopolising him again. They left the house. Guy knew those people; they were family friends. She was in the dark of the development.

They got to the house for rent; it stood on a corner. Two streets separated it from the burnt out section of town. A squat cream house, galvanise awning, gables, white window frames and jalousies.

Guy knocked at the door, a woman of tubular appearance, youngish, neat, opened it.

"My friend, Mr James needs to rent your house. My parents told me you were looking for a family to move in before you went away."

Augustus added, "Good afternoon, I have a wife and daughter, our home got burnt."

She ushered them inside. Augustus took the situation by the throat, he was not going to be backward and leave it all to fate, he wanted this house.

"I believe you have a little girl and you will not be taking her with you? This should not be a problem for us."

"Oh yes, Wanda?"

Her two sisters joined them with the girl in tow. She was about ten years old, he guessed. The sisters were in their late twenties; the tubular lady was the oldest.

"We are due to travel in a month. Our flights to Aruba are booked."

How suddenly a bit of luck can come into your life, Augustus thought. He could see no problem, two bedrooms; Olga would not turn up her nose at the appearance of the house.

"I understand that you want guardians for your daughter, it would be something I would take seriously, believe me."

"Augustus has high standards and he has a seven year-old daughter. His wife is a decent woman, I recommend them," Guy told them.

"O.K.," the oldest sister said.

They talked about rent and Augustus said he would come back next morning with Olga.

"I have to start work at two this afternoon, I'll talk about it with Olga and see what she says but personally, it looks like what we need right now."

He shook hands with the women and they left.

He told Olga. She stood up from the sewing machine and sat with him, her eyes smiled with her mouth, she clapped her hands.

"*Glisse!*"

She hoped this was really going to happen. She knew the house and who the people were.

"Oh my," she said to him.

He took hold of her hand that rested on the table next to his. Aunt Hazel came from her shop, and saw from her bridge that her boat was indeed on the right course; those on board were in good condition.

"*Zafe` a bon?*"

Her remark brought them back to the present, when he should be thinking of getting ready for work. Olga moved with speed to collect the clothes from the line. She needed to digest and relish this news, keep it to herself for a bit. She hummed 'Skylark'. Now having left the clean clothes in a basin on the balcony she returned to the sewing machine, she wanted her mother to try it on later. Augustus had not told her about Wanda.

The next morning she followed him to inspect the house. The day before, he had made a quick assessment of the child as she had sat with downcast eyes. Was she obedient, he wondered? He heard that she was a Brownie. Unfortunately, this time she was at school and Olga still would not meet her then, but it was best, he thought, if they dealt with the business side first.

Olga knew that they were Anglican women in the way how things were known about other people in town; they all had their own particular slots. She knew how they had an air of superiority because they had gone to what was the preferred primary school for the best understanding of English. They went to the Anglican Church. She knew that. Not much else.

The inside of the house was painted white. A minimum of furniture she approved of – the rattan cane sofa, the Morris chairs with brocade cushions in the parlour, the dining room was separate, even though small. Olga thought that she had died and gone to heaven.

After they had seen the two bedrooms, they sat to talk. Olga heard about Wanda. She had never seen that child at anytime she could think of. Wanda's mother was unmarried. Olga left most of the talking to Augustus and she saw their looks of approval by his words and accent. She kept her social smile in place.

When they got home Augustus could not contain Olga's exuberance. With her smiles replacing smiles, she said they should tell her aunt.

"Not yet," he said. "Let's wait till it's all settled. I won' be able to sleep tonight."

"I won't either. This afternoon, I'll return to see the child and I'll take Era so that the two children could know one another. I can't waste time."

But how would Era feel? And how could she be like a mother to this child? She worried about that.

About five o'clock she made her way back to visit the women. Era had moved with speed because she was doing something different. Olga hoped the children would take to one another, Era loved to play.

Wanda had grey eyes in her brown face. Olga was mesmerised. She could not help thinking of Clifford but the child was too old to be his – he had come from Trinidad and got the shop next door to their house on Maynard Street about two years ago. Olga spent about an hour listening to the plans they had. They were going to Aruba to work for Americans. Olga told them her mother wanted to emigrate also. The two children stood by the window looking out on people passing. They moved into the yard. In Olga's opinion the child seemed friendly and of a pleasant nature. Thank God! she thought.

When they left, Olga walked much quicker than she normally walked.

Wanda's mother Una and her sisters talked about Olga and Augustus afterwards. They agreed on one thing, that those people – they called them – were decent and that on that score they could not wish for more, but the youngest sister made her thoughts clear that Olga was nosey, trying to find out on the sly whether Clifford had been involved in their life.

Olga had been tactless, in her question to Una, while they had been talking about the fire and she had said that it was a mystery that Clifford had disappeared since then. Telling them that Wanda's eyes were so like Clifford's! Una had been right not to tell her that Clifford's brother was Wanda's father, they were all from Anse La Paix. A younger brother than Clifford, he had emigrated to America years ago. Before Una could reply to Olga's insinuation, what Olga heard came from the younger sister.

"Wanda is like a tom boy, she enjoys the Brownies."

Olga's immediate thought was that she would enrol Era in the Brownies too.

Olga could not resist telling her mother what looked like something almost miraculous awaiting her in town. Muriel took up her finished dress and assessed it again because it had a bit of *gla gla* – Olga had added a flounce in the skirt. Olga said it was suitable for a woman who was not yet old, insisting that it was not as girly as Muriel had said it was, frowning at it. She left the dress on the back of the chair and looked closely at Olga.

"So you might be having your own house without me, for the first time!"

Olga had made up her mind that they had to get the house. She told Muriel that the women said they had a lease of the house for thirty years so they could rent it for as long as they liked. Muriel nodded.

Now Olga asked, "Will you let me give you a hair style on Thursday?"

"Why? Why? I cannot comb my hair as usual?" She gave Olga an impatient wave of her hand. She picked up the dress to take it upstairs.

Miss Hazel had lit the small wick floating in oil on her dresser, she sat on her bed she said to her sister.

"I hear we have a magician in town. He came in his yacht. He's some kind of businessman too. I'm going for a walk to see that yacht."

As usual, Muriel thought, her sister had her sources for getting news.

"A magician!"

Muriel's face showed disbelief. She wrinkled her nose. What was the kind of magic, she wanted to know? Could he make people disappear or appear as needed?

"What kind of man?" she demanded, vexation in her tone.

"A white man. People don't know where from."

Miss Hazel pulled out her trunk from beneath the high bed and removed her special dress, the bright yellow one with clusters of royal blue and carmine flowers as small round buds. She heard he painted interesting people. Muriel sat on the bed in silence, watching her. The dress was ankle length, she pulled the hemline on one side and tucked it at the waist, leaving the white cotton petticoat showing a little. She went downstairs.

Muriel felt restless; the quickening pace of events, which she had not expected, turned her thoughts in all directions. The surge of the torrents washed over her, and the frailty she felt when she had gone down to Bonne Terre made her yearn to smoke her pipe. The people down in the village never knew how accustomed she had become to the taste and the sensations from it. She lay down and drifted into a short nap. She sat up not long afterwards. In the corridor outside the bedroom the light was dim. She wondered if her sister was back. Olga, Ma Boy and Era sat on the balcony. Olga stood up to let her mother sit. After a pause, she started talking about Bonne Terre and Ma George, hoping that her cousin would feel like talking with her. Olga was silent, listening to their conversation of their past; their memories were about some things that she had not known about.

It was not yet dark when Aunt Hazel came back. She looked pleased.

"A,A, let me tell you – if you see the man! He's as dry as a bone with old wrinkled red face and blue eyes."

She continued that she found out that he was moving around the Islands in his yacht, he came from Louisiana. He was painting people he saw on the wharf as they passed, and she saw a man he painted with a wheelbarrow and it was as if he knew the man's mind. Everything in his expression came on the picture. The patois words escaped like scats as she spoke, describing in detail what had happened during her outing. She observed, she said to them, that he seemed to have spiritual visions, as if he could see the way it was during the fire, that he could feel the fire they had in the town; he put red like fire in the air.

She beamed, "And he painted my face. Even around my face there was something I know about myself and he saw it. That's why they say he is a magician."

"It's not a good time for a painter to come to Masav, fings so ugly now," Muriel said.

"Tomorrow you should pass by the wharf and look at him painting, Olga," her aunt told her. At the mention of tomorrow, Muriel arose. Something to eat and go to bed, she said.

CHAPTER THIRTY-THREE

Muriel stopped abruptly on her way from work; she saw some new cosmos flowers close to a broken wall and she could not resist collecting a number of stems. They had always been her favourite – simple, single, strong, yellow petals. The urge to hold something which was rare and beautiful, made her happy.

Back at Miss Hazel's, she put them in a jar of water to make a change in the austere room. Olga observed its brightness and there was something frivolous in this display of gaiety from her mother, even as she came and sat by the table to wait for Harry and spoke in her usual Spartan style. Her eyes showed some anxiety. Olga saw her look dart to the doorway every minute and she played with the petals of a flower close by.

She smiled for a brief second at Era and again it brought her grandfather to life – the man whose face she had seen in her dreams year in and year out for decades while she became inured to the pain and abandonment he had caused. Her job had given her the right kind of safety she had found and the additional safety of having Olga and Augustus in her home. Her youthful madness was so distant! Olga began to say something, and it was then they heard a click on the side door as Harry shut the door after him. He was leaning against the door jamb, his feet crossed nonchalantly.

Muriel's eyes walked over his body from his Panama hat and down to his feet.

"Let's go upstairs, Era. Evening Harry!"

Olga moved away. He straightened and walked towards them. Muriel sat back in her chair to be steady.

She said, "After all this time, Harry?"

He sat next to her, took off his hat. They sat in silence and he broke the silence.

"I know, Muriel, that a fool can learn sense sometimes," he said lamely.

Her appraisal of him was lengthy, and he felt the mental clinch with which she held him. It was not how he had envisaged the meeting. He had hoped to make some sweet talk, woo her into agreeing to something he had to ask her. When she had satisfied herself, taking in his grey hairs at his temple which was one of the changes in his face, she said,

"You still talk patois?"

"Not so much now. People in Panama would not understand it. I learnt the local language but I have not forgotten our patois, oh no!"

"We'll talk patois now. So what have you to say?"

In spite of telling her so, he conversed in English. She had to do the same. He told her that at the moment he was working in a hotel on the canal promenade. After being unattached for a few years, he had a few girlfriends.

Her nerves were calm and she felt pleased with herself. Her eyes never left his face.

"I had married a Columbian lady, we had no children."

She sat up a bit straighter, waiting for the rest. She was not prepared for his next words.

"I've been a widower for two years."

"Eh heh!"

So he was *male'w'ez* now? Her surprise showed on her face; she put her hand up to her forehead as if a sudden pain had come on. He took the hand that rested on the table and what he saw was an old vision – Muriel at seventeen. He wanted to recapture her purity, her honesty and her wholehearted surrender he had felt then. He bowed his head.

"I know it's late but I felt something when I saw you again, I felt I wanted to marry you."

She was silent. He felt that an hour had passed. There was a sound on the stairs, quiet footsteps coming down and then retreating. This roused Muriel; she felt the warm sea's waves buffeting her, carrying her – she lay on her back looking at the blue sky, the water lapping pleasantly over her, and she closed her eyes with the happy feeling. He touched her.

She started, as if surprised to see his face. How could she indulge in such a blissful feeling when she had her own plans? She said,"*M'a sav!* I want to go to work in Aruba."

"*U pa konn'et py'esonn la.*"

His patois was meant to press home his point, telling her that she knew no one in Aruba. After he said this, she rebounded with many words, that she was a liberated woman. She knew how to work and she would be able to fend for herself.

He insisted, "I want to make things easy for you. I could get some work for you over there on the Canal. I live in Colon and there are hundreds of lights, shops, lots of people. You will like it; I'm sure..."

His voice was excited. She felt pity.

Her eyes held a far-away look. He released the hand he had been holding, and she put her elbows on the table and rested her chin on her closed fists.

"*M'a sav*, I don't know Harry, I'll think about it."

Someone was coming downstairs.

"Perhaps in January?"

He was rushing her, he knew.

"I have some money for you."

"What about La La?"

He was going to say something when Aunt Hazel came towards them saying she meant to put kerosene in the lamp, she saw the low flame and the soot in the chimney. Her eyes roamed over the couple, there were three envelopes on the table. She had heard La La's name mentioned. Harry and Muriel were silent.

"I was just going Hazel."

"Don't let me rush you, I'll just fix the lamp and go to bed. You must not go."

"Era sleeping?" he wanted to know.

"We were sitting on the balcony, Ma George just went to lie down and I think Olga will soon go to sleep. Goodnight."

She replaced the lamp on the nail on the wall and moved up the stairs. After she disappeared Harry said, "Open your envelope."

Muriel looked at the money inside and felt that the breach in her spirit was now mended. A blue bird stood on her window looking for food but it only pecked at a small morsel and flew away.

"Well Muriel, I hope you believe me. I'm going now. So, till next time, uh? I'll come to see you on Saturday evening."

He thought that her eyes looked softer as he left. From on the balcony, Olga saw him leave. She rushed downstairs to hear about this thing, what state her mother would be in, and the news that he wanted to marry her couldn't have surprised her more. Her own life now was less important as a fixation with her mother's and Harry's plans squeezed into her mind. But still more! Her disbelief grew as she opened the envelope addressed to her and saw money. She revised her opinion of her father.

On Saturday morning, Muriel returned from five thirty mass. She felt the morning gentle breeze, birds were chattering close by. She looked up; black birds stood on the edge of the presbytery balcony. One made a snappy call: four notes going up in scale. Perhaps, she thought, it was asking her a question; an urgent one like it was anxious too. She had not made up her mind what she would say to Harry.

CHAPTER THIRTY-FOUR

Muriel suggested to Harry when he came just after six that they should go up to the balcony, out of the way of the others who were downstairs. While he spent a few minutes talking with Augustus and observing Olga and Era at their sewing, she waited for him.

The two chairs rested against the partition of the balcony away from its rail, she was sitting. He sat next to her in silence. She hoped he would speak first, and she re-arranged her chair at right angles to his and gave him an inquisitive look. He began in English and that annoyed her.

"People going to Aruba was popular around the time Olga was born, you know; who's going there now? You know that island is dry, things don't grow over there, it's so different from here."

She realised he was tripping her up. She explained that it had been the one hope for a better future and independence. Yes, he thought she had mentioned that she was liberated in their last conversation. He cocked his head, almost touching her face.

"You'll be alone."

His next words tripped her some more as he turned some rope, entangling her feet.

"You have to be careful to avoid insanity when you get lonely, so lonely you don't know what to do."

She was scared of insanity. She thought of Sampson. She was quiet a long while after he stopped talking. She had always had family with her but she thought she would have been strong enough not to mind. She looked at him, he must have felt loneliness, and of course he had been married till two years ago. She leaned closer to him, surprised him by kissing his cheek. She pulled back, shocked that she should be the first to offer that kiss but she could not undo it.

"I can see now what you mean. I gave Olga a shock when I said I wanted to go to Aruba."

"So, will you come to Panama?"

"I like my work at the presbytery; it's just that I want my own house. If I come to Panama, I want a job and a place of my own first."

"I understand, *mw'e konpwann*."

His understanding of her wishes made her smile at him and he took her hand in his.

"I'll miss Olga and Era so much."

"When I return, I'll start arrangements for you. It might take a little time. I hope not too long, and I'll write you often. Promise me that you will come."

She nodded.

It did not look impossible to her that she would be together with Harry in the future, even become his wife. Her heart thudded, should she be careful? Then she told herself that during the rest of his holiday, when he would continue to prove his sincerity even to ignore La La, it would give this plan a solid place.

They were disturbed when Hazel brought them some lime squash and lingered to gauge the mood there. She looked out at the street from the balcony's edge.

"I think we will have rain tonight."

The sun had just set but the light lingered for a bit, the new quiet of the town since the fire still felt strange to her.

"Supper will be ready soon, Harry, you'll have some?"

Muriel wished Hazel would go back downstairs while she and Harry could say what was in their minds; they had so much to talk about.

Harry was in no mood to leave just yet and he agreed. Hazel walked away. Harry stood up, leaned against the balcony and studied Muriel with a smile, thinking she had the same simplicity in appearance but her looks had attracted him. She still did. He imagined her in Colon among the bright lights with him. He did not believe that she would not come out there. He heard the worry in her voice.

"Is there another woman since your wife died?"

"It will surprise you; if there was I would not be here, I would be with her. I am thinking of really settling here in the future, when this place is rebuilt and I can do some business here. I want to buy some land. This much I know and then I hope you will be with me."

Harry had supper with them and left with Muriel promising to visit his sister's house the next day, now she knew that La La was not in his plans. She stayed downstairs. Everyone was in and as she was lost in her thoughts, not listening to Augustus' words, she did not hear when he told the women that on the coming Tuesday, people who wanted to move to the barracks were to go to the Town Board to be allocated rooms.

Ma Boy said that she was not going to the barracks. The poorest people like her only had the Good Shepherd Society to give them a little money and it was a good thing that both herself and Ma George had paid their subscriptions every month, a shilling a month for many years.

Guy was the secretary of the Society, he had told Augustus of their efforts to give financial help to some older people who came to them.

So now that the move was imminent, it should have been sooner.

"Aunt Hazel, I want to rent a house in town. The people are going abroad and want tenants. Guy told me about it, so Olga and I won't be going to the barracks."

Muriel felt Olga's eyes pulling her own to look her way. Her daughter smiled, what were they talking about that caused that smile?

There were changes all around; Miss Hazel could only feel pleased for them.

CHAPTER THIRTY-FIVE

Blue moonlight touched the People's Square. Up in the hills, Augustus gazed at the blue moon and the star-studded sky. A blue moon presaged a better season for the new cane crop and for the people of Masav. He had finished his two to ten shift. The young cane shoots stretched for miles under the haunting light of the moon. Next morning, he would be joining the Union men to help the homeless people as they left the town for new homes.

The Artist, Pascal, strolled about the town, enjoying the moonlight. He passed beneath a weatherboard balcony near the Square; someone played a mouth organ. It was the only sound he heard on his way to his yacht in the wharf. A strong force came from the few people still on the Square, right now it was uncanny – he saw the glint of a knife and a man moving close to a woman. Then the vision went.

He was sure that some tragedy had happened there. It was an inspiration he would keep when he next picked up his brushes and paint – the Square in Masav.

Dujon and the Union men had opened the shop. Augustus noticed this on his way to help Maryse Sampson. He spoke to them, and though he had not agreed to be a Union Man like them, he knew that it was the right thing for him and they had not shown him any dislike.

They had more mattresses and blankets in stock and other household things from the Overseas Fire Relief goods held for that day and, over the months, they had guarded that stock. They were stacked against the walls, things that the people for the barracks would now need. Augustus said he would be back a bit later, moving on to the shacks, towards the loud talking and the thuds.

There was congestion as little pushcarts were lying around being loaded. Maryse Sampson held her waggonette with Betty's help.

"Morning, I came to help you, Ma Sampson, I'm just in time, let me do this. You have some rope?"

She was thanking him in French, explaining that she had to get her things to Uncle Sam's truck. She had paid her pound in advance. He pulled a piece of rope from the side of the shack, hoping that it was long enough, while she held on to the furniture, keeping it from sliding off from the cart. When he had succeeded, making the shack shift sideways, he secured the heavy bit of furniture. He wondered what had happened to the wares she had wrapped in the sheet when she had escaped from her burning house. Now what each carried was a soft bundle. It could be she had sold some of her China to someone who had lost all of theirs; she may have put some cups and plates among the bundles of clothes they carried. Ma Sampson hustled behind him.

As well as the truck, four American jeeps stood on the street. American G.I.s in the usual khaki shirt and pants took small items and passengers inside the jeeps. Mattresses and furniture alone for the truck they repeated. Augustus got the waggonette loaded. He went with her to collect her mattress from the Union shop, loaded it. There was another truck coming along, and also the Union's bus all lined up on the street. Now that he had helped her, he stayed to see the Square evacuated. People carried tables, chairs and bundles. Ma Sampson and Betty sat in the first jeep to be filled. Augustus waved them off. She sat erect on the floor and sighed heavily.

He saw the painter that he heard was called a magician; he was still painting from his position on the Square. He crossed the road to see what the man painted. He dipped his brush in red paint on his palate without hesitation, added yellow, and was unaware of Augustus. These were people who had run away from the flames of the town in fear and panic, and even though they were now in the bright sunlit day he tried to create the idea that the fire still raged in the air as the people came and boarded the jeeps and loaded their belongings.

Now the Square was empty, time had moved. There were no shadows, and the shadow he had walked in over the years seemed absent too.

GLOSSARY

abusack	Canvas satchel
Be'tje'	White person
Bef	Cow
Bel ti ich wi!	Pretty child, yes!
Bobdye'	God
Bodye e'de' nou	God help us
Bolonm	Supernatural character: A child with big head and cries like a cat
Bon volonte	Good will
Bon vwezinaj	Good neighbour
Bonswe'	Goodnight
Bwa Bwa	Stupid
Chaben	Very red-brown skin and brown hair
Chapit	Fortune teller
Daco	Very well
Dan-dan	Dress
deck-deck	Lifeless person
Doogla	African-Indian mixed race person
Egal	Proper
Ehb'e!	Well! And so
Frog	Mechanical structure on train tracks
fw'e	Brother
Gens mw'e	My friend
Glisse	Dance step
Ham	Sobriquet for Augustus
I pa sav	Someone does not know
Jabal	Mistress
Jain	Sash

Jamette	Loose woman
Ki mun sa?	Who is this?
Kon	Horn
Kouman pwan'y souple'	Take it please
Lizin	Evil spirit in folklore
M'a sav non	I do not know
Ma che'wi	My love
Macaroni man	Flashily dressed man
Macaroni	Plaid cloth for head-wear
Madras	Plaid material
Malewez	Down and out
Mama guy job	Tricks
Me' kote' Augustus?	But where is Augustus?
Mesi tant tant	Thank you Auntie
Mesye' Kisa	Mister, what's this mess
Mw'e konpwan	I understand
Mw'e las	I am tired
Ou pa ansent	You're not pregnant?
Pala pata	Wild talking
Pemi	Cornmeal, coconut and pumpkin dumpling
Pov peti	Poor thing
Pwan gad	Take care
Sa twis	It is sad
Sa u fe'	How are you
Sese	Sister
Shapentey, shadobene,	Bush teas
Ti madanm	Little woman
Topi Tambu	Root vegetable (Guinea arrowroot)
Tout moun	Everybody
U f'e the mwe' kontan	It makes my heart glad
U pa konnet py'esonm la	Yu do not know anyone there
u sa mange' mwe	You can eat me
Vap la pwan'y	Attack of bad mood
Vye' vache la	Old cow
Wa ya yi!	Ooh la la!
who d 'e?	Who is it?
Woy! Ma fi	Look here my girl!
Zaf'e a bon	Things are good
Zeb	Evil voodoo